PROLOGUE
END OF THE BALL

"DID you have fun?" Mercy asked as Chase negotiated the slick Sacramento streets in the dark. Their car was good—the best, actually, a Mercedes with a killer antilock brake system—but Chase concentrated hard on it anyway. He did that. He concentrated on things that he could handle when the things he couldn't handle were trying to climb his back.

"Fun?" he asked absently, turning right against a red light after checking three times to make sure there wasn't an oncoming car.

"Yeah, Chase—fun! You know that thing you have when you get all pretty and go dancing with friends? Did you have any *fun*!"

I had a blast getting fucked in the men's bathroom by the guy whose heart I'm breaking, Mercy. Next to slitting my wrists, I can't think of anything better.

"Yeah," he said with a vague smile on his face. "Of course I had fun. You know how I like to dance."

"Hm...." Mercy looked pensive, which, like pretty much any expression on her tiny oval of a face, looked enchanting. Chase sure couldn't be faulted in his taste in women, could he? His father certainly loved her—adored her, actually. Told him this was the girl who would make him a man.

"Hm?" he asked, keeping that smile on his face, his shoulders relaxed, his hands firm and able on the wheel.

"Yeah," she said thoughtfully. "I'm glad you got out. I know you were pretty sick all week, but I don't remember seeing you dance tonight."

That's because you were talking to your friend on the other side of the club when Tommy came up behind me, splayed his hands across my stomach, and cradled me in the cup of his groin and thighs.

"Must have been when you were talking to Kerry and Jeff," he said, knowing damned well that was when he'd been dancing. Tommy, who loved him, would torment him, follow him, yearn for him—but he wouldn't out Chase. Not without Chase's permission. He'd tried once. The results had haunted them both.

Mercy's hand on his thigh was intimate and suggestive. "I hope you weren't dancing with any pretty girls," she purred, kneading him like a cat. It was a skillful caress: soft, receptive to Chase's needs, kind, and hoping for a response. Chase felt like slapping her hand.

No, sweetheart. Lying to one woman about who I am and what I want is plenty.

"There's not a girl out there who would make me happier than you do." Oh God. A truth. Who knew?

They talked quietly, desultorily, on the way back to the apartment that Chase hated so badly. It looked good—Mercy was skilful at decorating on a budget, and she took pains to make the place cheerful and airy with nice furniture and eclectic decorations. Chase liked her taste—but he often thought he'd like leather furniture that matched the area rug, or the right to paint the wall behind the television hunter green to match the valances. He tried not to say these things to Mercy. She'd worked so hard, and he'd told her he'd love anything she did. Besides. They were saving all their money for a house.

They parked the car and ran through the warren of apartment buildings, hitting as many covered walkways as they could and laughing a little with the feel of the March rain on their heads. Chase loved that feeling—rain on his face, the patterns of each drop warming with his skin. He turned, laughing, toward Mercy as they hit the overhang before their set of stairs, and for a moment, she was the study buddy he'd started dating two years ago, his friend, his confidante, and the person who watched movies with him until the wee hours of the night.

She smiled gaily, like a child, and turned her laughing face up for a kiss, and that laughing moment was crushed under the steel door of all he could not say. He bent down and placed a gentle, sexless kiss on her lips, pale from the cold, and she opened her mouth and invited him in. He swept his tongue in for form and knew her arms would come around his neck as she sought desperately to capture something in him that he didn't know how to give her. He kissed her well, thoroughly, stroking her tongue with his, wrapping his hands around the small of her waist, massaging her scalp through her hair with just enough pressure.

He pulled back, feeling warm and happy from the contact, proud enough of the deception for the moment that he almost forgot it *was* one, when she murmured, "Mmm... so, ready to go inside and take up where that left off?"

No, because my lover's come is still running down the crease of my ass and leaking onto my upper thigh.

"Yeah, babe. But can I take a shower first? Someone spilled a drink on my lap and I feel sort of rank, 'kay?"

He smiled apologetically, and Mercy rolled her eyes, like she was used to his fastidiousness. "Okay," she said softly, cupping his cheek and glowing up into his face like a woman in love. "I'll go make myself comfortable."

He swallowed and smiled and kissed her forehead with all the considerable tenderness in his soul. God, she deserved so much more.

In the shower, he forgot himself.

His hand tracked the path of Tommy's hand as it rubbed his six-pack, and then up over each and every defined rib. Tommy had pinched his nipples *hard*, because he knew that made them super sensitive (it was even posted on the *Johnnies* site), and he'd whispered in Chase's ear, because their shared experience had told him that his ears and the side of his neck had a nerve sensitization express straight to his groin.

"We're going to the bathroom, okay? And I'm going to bend you over, and be inside you, and fuck you so hard you've got no room in your body for anything but my cock and my come, okay? Say no now, 'Chance'. Because once this song is over, you're mine."

He'd punctuated that with a brutal twist of Chase's nipple, and Chase had been a puddle, submissive, willing to say anything, do anything, go anywhere, if only Tommy kept touching him.

They hadn't kissed in the tiny bathroom stall, because experience had proven that they couldn't just kiss, they would suck and suckle and bite, leaving hickeys on Chase's tanned skin. Tommy's skin was pale, and Chase suckled that spot, that one right there on his neck, because Tommy had no one to hide from. Tommy gasped, ground up against Chase's leg, and then pulled back, his face a mask of hurt and anger, desire and pain.

"You don't get to do that!" he snarled. "This is for me! It's all I'm going to get, and you don't get to...." His face almost crumpled then, and Chase knew, with everything in him, how much this gamble had cost Tommy. Dex must have texted him. Chase remembered Dex asking what his plans were; he had no idea this is what Tommy had planned. Chase had left Tommy so brutally... this must have felt like his last chance. He must have just trembled in hope, anticipation, and the desire to take charge. Tommy must have—he liked to bottom, truly loved it, it was his favorite sex act, but only when Chase was on top.

So Chase turned around without comment, giving this thing, his open, spread, waxed asshole, this dirty fucking in a bathroom, because he didn't have anything better to offer.

He was lucky Tommy loved him. There was the rip of the little lube packet and then it was drizzled right in the sweet spot, before Tommy's bare cock thrust up, no prep, no stretching, no nothing. If Chase hadn't shot a scene that week with Ethan, the company's big-cocked wonder, Tommy's own big erection would have split him in two. As it was, it felt so good... so right... so wonderful.... Chase buried his face against his massive bicep and let out a sob of need.

"Shh," Tommy murmured, bending over and kissing along his back. It wasn't a company move—it was one of those things fans watched the vids for, to assure them that it wasn't all show—and it wasn't Tommy's style, not in front of the camera, anyway. Those gentle hands running along his ribs, that nuzzle of his lips and cheek along the center of Chase's back—that was all Tommy Halloran, scholarship kid

from Southie, who had freckles on his shoulders from misspent attempts to tan.

"Just move," Chase muttered, shivering with rightness and need, and trying hard not to weep with shame. "Just move, Tommy. Just fuck me and move." His shaking voice broke on the last word, because he did want Tommy to fuck him, but he didn't want Tommy to move—or at least not to move on. He wanted Tommy right here in his body, right close to him, touching skin to skin. He wanted Tommy to stay, forever, right there, poised to thrust so hard into his body that there was room for Tommy, only Tommy, and not another soul.

Not even his.

They hadn't lasted long. Chase had come into his stroking fist, and Tommy, without the condom, had blasted inside his body long and hot and hard. Tommy collapsed against his back and rubbed his wet cheek against Chase's shoulders until Chase turned around and said, "To hell with your plans, Tommy," and then held his arms open. Tommy Halloran collapsed against his chest, his shoulders shaking fruitlessly in an effort to hold back his sobs.

They hadn't stayed that way for long. Chase stood up properly and Tommy's spend gushed out of Chase's body, trickling out of the crease of his backside and down his thigh. If the bathroom hadn't smelled like piss and come and ass already, Chase's body would have done it in that moment.

"You smell like sex," Tommy murmured. "Sex and me."

"I know."

"I'm glad."

"Oh God. So am I."

Tommy looked up, his long-jawed, brooding features swollen from the cry and his lashes spiking around his brown-black eyes. "Don't... don't do this, Chase. Don't leave me."

Chase had closed his eyes and kissed Tommy's forehead, hearing his voice coming out strangled and warped, or maybe that was the men banging on the stall of the men's room, begging to come in and take a piss.

"I'll try," he muttered, sure he didn't have the courage to do any such thing.

But he hadn't promised Tommy anything, ever, before. It was as close as he'd come to a vow.

And now, Chase straightened up in the shower, fingering his stretched sphincter, reluctantly wondering if he'd erased every part of Tommy from his skin. He thought of Mercy, in the bedroom, waiting wide-eyed for him to come out and to make love, and of all the times he'd done just that, sliding his lips on her soft, perfumed skin and imagining rougher skin that smelled like sweat. He remembered the times he'd stayed awake in the dark, running his hand over her shoulders, her hips, through her hair as she slept, *willing* himself to feel his body stir. Sometimes it worked. Sometimes his breath would catch, and his cock would fill with blood, and he'd kiss her neck, her breasts, her soft belly, the slick sweetness between her thighs.

Sometimes.

Most of the time, he simply lay there, next to her, and wondered how things had gotten so fucked up that the person he loved—truly loved, because Mercy was funny and smart and gracious and all the good things a girl should be—was the person he hated, not for herself, but for what she made of him.

He thought of that time now, as he stepped out of the shower and dried off, his skin soft from all the time spent under the water, and opened the drug cabinet, his eyes dreamy and out of focus. He knew where they were. He'd bought them. They were harder to get hold of now that they made all of the really good electric shavers and disposable blade heads, but some drug stores still carried a good old-fashioned razor blade.

He'd had them in the back of the cabinet for more than a month, and she'd never noticed.

"Chase?"

"Out in a minute!"

His fingers didn't even shake as he reached for the box, and opening it felt predestined.

The metal was cool and thin in his fingers, and practically nonexistent.

So this is how she'd done it. It was easy.

His thumb and forefinger warmed the metal, and it was almost like a trickle of water against the inside of his wrist.

"Chase?"

No one by that name lives here.

"Out in a minute!"

Out… out… out….

God, how he wanted out.

JERKING OFF

One Year Earlier

THE boy in the video looked supremely uncomfortable. He had blond hair, helped along from a bottle, high and wide cheekbones, and piercing blue eyes. His voice rasped a little; not a baritone, more like a reedy tenor. But girls told him it was sexy, and his smile was half shy, half come-hither, and even though he knew his chin was a little soft with baby fat, he'd been hitting the gym and he was pretty sure he was getting more defined, even in the face. He was talking to someone off camera, and that raspy, reedy tenor squeaked with surprise.

"Take off my shirt? Now?"

"Well yeah," said the voice off camera. "You're going to have to get naked if you want to do this."

The boy blushed. "I didn't realize we were going, you know, full frontal today. No worries." With movements that were a mix of confident and clumsy, the loose-fitting baseball T-shirt was hauled over his head and he stood there, a twenty-something college-aged boy, wearing cargo shorts and flip-flops. He had an athletic build, because baseball was more his game than football, and that goofy, lopsided grin that jocks get when they're proud that they're jocks. He was outdoors, and it must have been just a little chilly, because his nipples almost immediately became pointy and puckered, like the skin on his not-quite-soft stomach.

"Do you want the whole package?" he asked, and the voice on the other side of the camera laughed kindly.

"Not necessary yet. Okay, Chance, tell us about yourself."

That self-conscious jock smile appeared, revealing two perfect dimples on the apple cheeks, next to the smile grooves at his mouth. Girls must have been falling into those dimples for years.

"Okay, well, I'm Chance." And not even a stumble at the assumed name, although anyone who knew the industry knew he had one. *"And I'm here to audition for* Johnnies, *because,"* a little bit of swagger here, *"you guys pay hella fucking good, and I'm trying to get a degree in engineering and save money for a house!"*

That kind laugh again. *"I'm glad we pay so well. So, do you have any experience in the adult film industry?"*

Blush. *"No. No. Not really."*

"What about with sex?"

"Well, me and my girlfriend, we've been getting it on. She seems to like what I got." There was a suggestive, adolescent thrust of his crotch, because, well, it seemed called for.

"So, your girlfriend. Any guys?"

Chance blushed, and then seemed to realize that this would be a selling point. *"Yeah! Yeah, actually. I had this friend who came out right after high school. He used to jerk me off."* Chance's smile relaxed, became soft and sexy. *"He was really good at it."* He shook his head. *"God, I've never come like that."*

"Mm.... Why do you think that is?"

Shrug. *"I dunno. He was a guy—I'm sure he played with his equipment a lot. Knew what to do with it."* He waggled his eyebrows. *"Brother, did he!"*

"Yeah? Want to show us if you know what to do with it?"

This time the blush was accompanied by a cocky grin. *"Guess it's time, huh? Didn't get my balls waxed for nothing!"*

His hands went to the waist of his cargo shorts, and then the voice on the other end of the camera stalled him for a second.

"You nervous about doing this on camera?"

Chance tilted his head a little, considering. *"Well, yeah, of course. You don't know what you look like when you come—for all I know, I'm hella ugly or something. But at the same time...."* He trailed off and shuddered, and his eyes got half-lidded. One hand went unconsciously to his stomach, then slid up to his nipples, which were still pointy and puckered. *"It's sort of cool. It's making my stomach all jumpy, and...." His other hand slid down under the waistband of his shorts, as he made obvious kneading motions on his groin.*

"It's turning you on?"

"Mmmm...."

"Take the shorts off, Chance, and show us."

HE STILL remembered the look on his friend Donnie's face when their friend Kevin had suggested it.

They were going out to pizza after their last baseball game of the season. They'd lost, which hurt, even for a small college team that wasn't known for its sports, and Chase was transparently grateful that Donnie was treating.

"Nice to have a rich boyfriend," he kidded—but it really was only kidding. He admired the hell out of Donnie, because the night they graduated from high school, Donnie had gone out into his parent's backyard with Chase and two purloined cans of beer. They'd leaned against the brick barbecue stand and Donnie had looked up at the sky, his blue eyes transparent in the summer dark, the slight wind ruffling hair that was so blond it was almost champagne-colored. Chase loved that color so much he'd started experimenting with hair dye, so he could have it for his very own.

Donnie had taken a swig of his beer and run his hand through that champagne-colored hair and said, "Chase, man, I'm as gay as an Easter Parade. Are you going to give me shit about it, or is this the last time we sneak a beer?"

I'm not surprised, Donnie, and I still love you.

"Yeah, man, keep your hands away from my ass, and I think we can still be friends."

He knew. He'd caught Donnie checking out his ass, his cock, his build. He'd smiled once or twice and watched Donnie's smile get all moony and sweet. He knew Donnie had a major crush on him. At least he *hoped* so, because he'd been having *the* most vivid, pornographic dreams featuring him, Donnie, and their bare cocks in each other's fists and mouths, and if Donnie wasn't the least bit gay, it would feel like sort of a violation.

So now that Donnie had a boyfriend he adored—with an independently wealthy, very distant family—Chase was happy for him. Donnie had the courage to come out, the courage to pursue what he wanted, and, to hear Donnie tell it, the idiocy to strip naked in Alejandro's bedroom while house-sitting, whack off, and fall asleep on the night Alejandro got back, two days earlier than expected, thus enticing the man of his dreams. But that didn't matter—Donnie had the courage to be himself, and if that got him free room and board while he went through college, Chase was okay with that.

So now, when Donnie heard him kidding, he knew it was kidding, and he turned a big technicolor grin on Chase, complete with slightly pointy canine teeth and lopsided twist on the left. "God, yes it is. Do you want more pizza, you itinerant hanger-on-er?"

And because he knew Donnie was paying for it using his own money from his job waiting tables, he said yes.

"So," Kevin said, his mouth unrepentantly full of Donnie's pizza, "how're you going to pay for school this year?" Kevin had sort of a round, moony face and sandy-brown hair. Although his eyes were hazel, they were frequently almost crossed, like a puzzled Siamese cat.

Chase groaned and thunked his head on the table. "I'll worry about that after I've paid for rent," he said honestly. "God, Mercy makes more than I do. Construction jobs *suck* in this economy, and I don't even want to *try* to wait tables again."

Donnie winced. "Yeah, man, I'm sorry about that. I feel like that was my fault."

Chase grunted and had another bite of pizza, wondering if his pride would unbend enough to ask Donnie if he could take home the rest of it when they were done. Mercy would probably be happy with the lettuce and cheese in the fridge to make a salad, but he was *starving.* "No worries," he said, still chewing. "That bitch had to be put *down.*"

Donnie shook his head and laughed. "Yeah, well, she hasn't been back since that night—I'm grateful!"

Kevin shook his head. "I still don't understand what happened there," he muttered.

I screamed in some bitch's face when she called Donnie a fag.

"I was rude to a customer."

Donnie made a sound that could not be interpreted, but when Chase looked up and met his eyes, they were sad. Chase could remember the first time he'd seen Donnie's eyes sad. Donnie, smiling, happy Donnie, who had made high school bearable, and there he was, his hand on Chase's cock, and Chase felt taken care of, cared for, for the first time since he was in kindergarten. Then it was over, and Chase was across the room, shouldering his way out, because touching his friend that way would make him gay. Donnie had looked at him just exactly like that.

Kevin shook his head and wiped his mouth, contemplating the last four pieces of pizza. Suddenly he jerked back and glared at Donnie, and then slid his eyes sideways to Chase. "You're always so nice," he said, as though the realization had dawned on him with Donnie's effort to feed Chase. "I've never seen you even get mad."

Chase just shrugged again, and nodded a quiet thanks when Donnie put the pizza in the takeout box and slid it in front of him. "Sometimes just takes the right trigger, I guess."

Kevin looked at him, actual reality permeating the rather thick gloss of oblivious that he usually wore. "What're you going to do, man? I mean, you could get a job at a stop'n'go or a gas station or something, or maybe a job in a grocery store, but—"

But it was either not enough money, or not enough flexibility around his school schedule. Yeah.

Suddenly Kevin cracked a smirk. "Hey—I hear *Johnnies* is recruiting."

Donnie choked on his soda.

"What in the fuck is *Johnnies?*" Chase snarled, pulling out napkins and mopping up the mess Donnie had just spit up in front of them.

Donnie recovered after Chase pounded him on the back a few times, and glared at Kevin. Kevin returned his glare with a smirk on his round face, his light brown eyes dancing the same way Donnie's did, except Kevin was a lot more likely to look confused. Chase had never dreamed about Kevin the way he had about Donnie.

"That's not funny," Donnie said with surprising ferocity. Donnie getting mad was as rare as Chase getting mad.

"What is it?" Chase asked, intrigued in spite of himself. He'd seen the booth on club day, right next to the LGBTQ booth, and was told they were "recruiting talent," but he couldn't figure out what sort of talent they were looking for.

Kevin was so full of his own joke that he was almost dancing on the little bench seat in the Mountain Mike's Pizza. "Dude! Gay for pay! You know! Straight guys boning each other! Man, I hear they pay hella fucking awesome!"

Donnie stood up with their trash and scowled. "It's not fucking funny, asshole," and his look at Chase had so much pity in it that, for a moment, Chase felt his temper stir again. He was *not* a charity case. He was living with a girl, he was going to college for his degree, he *could* support his family. He *could* be a man.

He stood up and helped Donnie with the cleanup, and then went to the fountain nearby and refilled his soda.

He came back and managed his cockiest, most fuck-it-all grin, and said, "So, Kevin. You know everything about gay porn. Can you find these guys online?"

Kevin chortled and pulled up the site on his cell phone. Chase looked at it just long enough to make note of it, feeling something thrumming in his blood, something excited, half strangled, and willing to chew its way out of Chase's stomach to be free.

Kevin left, because his folks appreciated it if he got home before midnight even on game nights, and Donnie and Chase remained, drinking as many free soda refills as Chase could stand.

A companionable silence had just fallen between them when Donnie said, "Won't your dad help?"

Chase barely looked at him. "No. He thinks college is a waste of time. He told me if I wouldn't take the training in the machine shop, he was done with me."

Donnie nodded and sucked moodily at his own straw. "I could ask 'Yandro—"

"No!" Oh Christ. Chase was *not* taking money from Donnie's rich boyfriend, and his voice was unapologetically sharp to show it. But Donnie didn't get mad. Instead, he ran his hands through his white-blond hair and scrubbed his face with his hand and groaned.

"God, Chase. You're thinking about it, aren't you?"

I want I want I want I want I want!

"Hell no!"

Donnie shook his head, that high-cheekboned, cheerful, happy face suddenly lined with worry. "Man, do you remember that hella old movie we watched with my sister once? The one with that Mary Poppins girl in it?"

Chase pulled up a corner of his mouth in thought. He and Donnie had gotten good grades in school (as opposed to Kevin, who had cheated off their homework—badly—a lot), and he tried not to be stupid.

"*Victor/Victoria*? The one where the girl pretended to be a boy who was pretending to be a girl."

Donnie nodded. "Yeah. You know. So she could sing."

"So?"

"So? Do you see any similarities here?"

Yeah. I'd be gay, pretending to be straight, pretending to be gay. Nice catch, Donnie! You should change your major to literature!

"Maybe."

"Don't give me that maybe bullshit. I'm gonna be an English major, you know that right?"

"Well, not until now!"

Donnie laughed humorlessly. "Chase—"

"Hey, that worked out pretty well for Mary Poppins, didn't it?"

"Yeah, but first it crashed around her ears and caused her a whole big bucketful of pain."

Chase swallowed, and what he said next surprised him. "Yeah, Donnie, but in the meantime? At least she got to sing."

They left shortly after that, Chase buzzing so hard from all the soda that he could hardly sit still. He got home and Mercy was sitting on the couch, her feet tucked under her bottom, her hair back in one of those bun things that girls seemed to be born knowing how to do, the kind that left the blonde tips of her dark hair splaying over the top of her head like a fan. He thought of the website in his phone, of the men, smiling like they really loved being there, sitting together, bare-chested, on the same bed, and dropped his bag of baseball stuff inside the door and bent down to take Mercy's mouth in his own.

She dropped the book and followed him into the bedroom, and he made love to her with gentle enthusiasm, for once happy and excited with the touch of her skin.

That night he filled in an application online. He took a picture of himself in the mirror while Mercy slept and made sure his cock was at half-mast so they could get a feel for what he knew was probably one of his best assets.

The next week, he was called in for an initial interview.

He reported to a rather bland-looking office building, one story only, with a small front office façade and what looked to be several larger offices branching out on the sides. From the shape of it, there seemed to be an outside courtyard, but Chase's view of that was blocked by drawn shades.

The man who greeted him and apologized for their receptionist being out also interviewed him. John—literally, John Carey—was the founder and owner of the company, and he filmed most of the opening interviews as well as quite a few of the videos.

He was slender and fit, in his mid-thirties, with brown hair that was growing neatly past his collar and a sweetly interested expression on his thin face when he listened to Chase talk. He was just old enough for Chase to feel deference toward him, like toward a boss or a professor, but not old enough to feel intimidated. This man could be an older brother you confided in, but he was definitely, under no circumstances, Chase's father.

The questions were, well, unusual to say the least, and although some of them were scripted, some of them seemed to occur to John as he went.

"So," he said, looking at the answers he'd written down so far, "no family is going to see this, right? No funny uncle is going to stumble on this when you're not looking? Your mom's not into the gay porn thing, is she? A lot of our customers are women."

My mom committed suicide when I was six, and my dad would rather I be dead than a fag.

"No one," he said with a shrug. "I'm pretty safe from being found out. Is that a problem for some guys?"

John looked at him with a faintly withdrawn expression. "Some of them, yeah. Some of them have girlfriends who know and approve; some of them have boyfriends who know and approve. We don't want to pry here, but it's good to know who we're dealing with when we pair you up."

"'Kay."

"And you're local—you drove over. I remember that, because we were all ready to get you a travel expense voucher. Is there anyone in town you're not going to want to know?"

Oh fuck. Everyone. There's one person on the planet who'd know I'm even considering this and I can't tell him….

John nodded, just watching Chase's expression. "Okay. There's a place you can park in the back. There's plenty of space, just take the spot."

Chase nodded like he understood, and John went on with the next question.

"Have you had any same-sex encounters before?"

And for a minute, Chase was going to lie, and then for another minute he was going to tell the truth, and the idea was so exciting his groin actually throbbed.

John held up a hand. "No, no—I can tell by the look on your face, that's something I want to hear on camera."

Chase nodded. "Yeah, okay. Anything else you want to know?"

John looked him in the eyes. "Yeah. Do you think you'll be able to do this, kid? Get it up, keep it up, on camera?"

I can do anything as long as I'm being touched by another man. I could probably even fly. Coming on camera is going to be no big deal.

Chase shrugged and cracked his gum. "I wanna give it a shot."

And that was it. He'd passed the interview.

The next day, he got called in to meet a stylist who played with the hair on his head, pronounced the color good, and then proceeded to rip most of his body hair out by the roots. Oh sure, they *called* it waxing, but Chase was glad the hair on his thighs and calves was sparse and blond, because she left *that* alone, and he was *stunned* at how much hair he had in the crease of his ass, because that shit *hurt* when it was yanked.

The day after that, John took him to the small courtyard behind the office building. The courtyard itself had a couple of lovely piazzas with really ritzy outdoor furniture and trees and what were they? Topiaries? Yeah. Those. Everything was designed to be soft. As they sat down and discussed the shoot, Chase realized the surface underneath the indoor/outdoor carpeting was that soft rubberized stuff they used for playgrounds. He was squishing his foot against the consistency when John looked up and smiled.

"Concrete's really hard on the knees," he explained, and it wasn't until Chase put that together in his head with what he was about to do that it hit him: this was a set piece for some of the videos. He was *on a porn set.* The thought made him partially erect even when the other members of the film crew—and two other men, standing bare-chested and casual in the thinning sun—came out to watch as he stood up in the sunshine and started answering John's questions behind the camera.

When he pulled his shorts down, and the late spring breeze brushed at his bare skin, the erection was no longer "partial."

And now, the next day, Chase watched himself masturbate on camera with complete fascination.

"God, my cock really looks *huge* without the pubic hair, doesn't it?"

John laughed a little. "Baby, you could see that cock in a pubic jungle—that's got to be one of the biggest we've got in the stable right now." He consulted his stats. "8.5—yup. Ethan is a little shorter, but he's wider, and Hunter is just about your size."

Chase grunted, still entranced by his face and body on the big-screen television in the little viewing room. Once he'd forgotten the camera was there, he'd tilted his head back, closed his eyes, and smiled. God. He looked like he was really enjoying himself.

Except for those furtive moments getting jacked off by Donnie, he couldn't remember sex ever giving him that much pleasure. But less than a day ago he'd dropped his pants in front of John and the sound guy and two other "models" and then masturbated in front of people, and he... God, he'd loved it.

Mostly—and he could admit this to himself only here, only on the set, and only in the silence of his own head—because everybody watching had been male. And they'd been appreciative. And they'd thought his body was hot, and that they wanted to touch it.

That had made all the difference.

"Oooh... wait," John said, his voice reverent. "Here it comes... here's the money shot...."

And Chase splooged all over his hand, thick and creamy and white, the camera zeroing in on it as he used it to lubricate his stroking, so he could milk the moment (and his cock) for everything it was worth.

God, his cock was hard and sore in his pants just watching it.

Chase, who had sex with his girlfriend maybe once a week, was horny again.

John was looking at him now with definite approval, and Chase tried to get his attention out of his pants for a second.

"Okay, man. Well done. I'm going to pair you up with Dex for your first time out. It'll be a double jack-off scene, no worries. You need to save your load—it makes for better camera, okay? So no coming for at least three days before the shoot. I'll call you and give you an exact time. You tell your girlfriend whatever you need to, but filming costs money, and we need the money shot, okay?"

Chase nodded, thinking about the lowest-paying option on his contract, and that it was still a damned sight better than construction.

A FEW OBSERVATIONS ABOUT PORN

THE boy in the video was in his early twenties and built like a Goliath, a Leviathan, a Greek god. He had dark hair and heavy Italian features, with a cocky, guileless smile that was charming from the first shot of him lying on the bed, casual-like, talking to the smaller blond man he was about to fuck.

But the T-shirt and shorts had come off, and suddenly both of them were naked, waxed, stomach muscles ripped, tiny nipples puckered with repeated suckling, and every corded ligature in their bodies popping in the intensity of what they were doing. The veins in Ethan's forearms stood out as he hauled the hips of the smaller, blond Cameron toward his own.

His cock was just as long but fatter than Chase's, and Cameron was screaming in a good way every time Ethan threw his hips forward.

Chase was watching the video with intensity, thinking:

That's going to be me. That's going to be ME ME ME ME ME!

Look at the angle there, the way he opens himself up to the shot. Look at the way Cameron uses the far-camera hand to stroke off, or the way Ethan smacks his dick on Cameron's stomach there to keep it hard as they're changing positions. Look at the way that close-up is filmed, can they do that with the camera or can they....

Oh God, he's going to come.

And Ethan's egging him on, grabbing his hand, hauling his ass up....

Oh God, he's going to come!

And he looks like he loves it, that big thing in his body, pure ecstasy pure bliss pure orgasm on his face as he's....

Grab your cock you moron, you're....

...going to come!

Chase shoved his hand down his jeans and squeezed hard once, twice, again, and then shot, silently, into his underwear. He sat at the computer for a few moments, shuddering, praying Mercy hadn't woken up to hear, until the final spasm rocked his body. When he'd stopped, he wiped his hand off on the inside of his jeans, cleared the video off his screen, and closed the laptop. He stood up very quietly to put his jeans in the laundry—which he made note of to do early in the morning, so Mercy didn't get to it first—and take a brief shower.

He very carefully didn't think of anything at all, not the two gods on the computer screen, not his physical reaction to them, not his effort to hide his masturbation from his girlfriend—nothing.

Not even the way his balls still ached from his orgasm.

JOHN called the next day to schedule a date in the next week for the shot. It was weird, but until Chase was told to save his load, he never really appreciated how often he and Mercy did *not* have sex. Three days? Three days was nothing. She worked overtime for two of them, and on the third, he worked out for an extra hour and was exhausted. (He'd been appalled by the amount of baby fat on his stomach and chin when he'd seen himself on camera, and determined to make that change.) Mercy was a little disappointed, but he gave her a foot rub and that seemed to be that. He went to sleep like the next day was nothing special.

His stomach had been buzzing the entire week before the shoot.

He remembered Christmases as a kid—all of that crazy anticipation, and usually, he ended up getting shit he really didn't care about. Socks, sweaters, the occasional baseball hat (which he really loved). He never got trading cards or a bike or a baseball mitt or an erector set—all the stuff had to be earned through chores, because his dad didn't believe in giving free rides, ever—and generally? The best part about Christmas had been hanging with Donnie and Kevin for the whole two weeks of vacation. Donnie's mom actually gave them *real* presents, like trading cards and action figures and stuff, and made hot chocolate and cookies and all of the things that you were supposed to get at Christmas, and Chase didn't know if he'd ever quite told Mrs. Armstrong how much those action figures and trading cards had meant to him.

But the thing was, he'd always been disappointed. Christmas was takeout food with his dad and a morning of opening shit he didn't want on the coffee table, because some years, a tree was just too much trouble. Christmas was watching his dad roll his eyes at the card he'd made at school, or the present he'd bought with his own money or even made in Dad's woodshop, because he was pretty good with tools.

Eventually, he'd stopped getting excited about Christmas, and then he didn't have to be disappointed. (Oddly enough, he'd discovered that the not getting excited made the things Donnie's mom did for him even more precious, but still, he didn't have words to tell her.)

So this stomach buzzing... this was something new. Something strange and wonderful. The last time he remembered anything like this was that set of precious minutes in Donnie's room, when he was playing video games. There had been that moment between, "God, I wonder if Donnie would touch me?" and unbuttoning his pants and pulling his erection out of his shorts that had been a caffeine/cocaine/adrenaline high of excitement, topped only by the feel of Donnie's (*Donnie's!*) skin against his, and the orgasm itself.

He could hardly keep contained in his own skin, he was so excited. It felt like his cock was *always* at half-mast, always sensitized, *always* ready to just fill up and explode. So not having sex with Mercy was easy, but in the day, when Mercy was gone and he was home (ostensibly looking for more construction work; although he was getting paid for this video and for the introductory one too, he hadn't told her that, in case this fell through), it was about all he could do not to imagine what was going to happen and then just cream in his shorts with excitement.

He didn't think men could actually *do* that, but he imagined for a moment, a hand on his body that *wasn't* his own, a male hand, one with strong bones and a sure grip, and he almost got himself off while leaning against the counter.

After that he tried to tamp down on the buzz a little. He tried valiantly to think about Christmas.

THE day before the shoot, after his workout, he got a call from a guy calling him Chance. For a second he was confused, and then he remembered: he *was* Chance. The guy on the other end of the line was Dex; it took him a minute to place the name, and then he realized it was the guy he was supposed to film with. His voice was a mid-range tenor, and he sounded a lot like the guys Chase had gone to school with as he asked if he wanted to meet for lunch at Jamba Juice.

Chase was actually relieved. It was like getting to open the package *before* Christmas, which meant the natural disappointment could begin and the terrible anticipation could stop distracting him from his goal of cleaning the apartment spotlessly, detailing Mercy's car, and cooking dinner from an actual cookbook with a salad and a dessert and everything.

And from thinking about why it was so damned imperative that he do all that shit before the shoot the next day.

Dex turned out to be… *beautiful.* Blindingly beautiful, with blond hair (his looked natural) and a long oval of a face and two slightly bucked teeth. He smiled disarmingly as Chase walked in, and offered to buy Chase anything on the menu.

Chase shrugged—he usually went for a little more protein—and that's when Dex got right to the heart of it.

"Okay, there's some shit no one wants to talk about in this business, but we've got a scene together, and I figure you'll want to know, 'kay?"

Chase nodded, his eyes big. Oh God—they were in the middle of *Jamba Juice*—was this guy gonna start talking about—

"Gas," Dex said frankly. "Avoid it. I get the banana-strawberry here with the protein supplement and a whole-wheat pretzel the day before a shoot because it settles my stomach. You're free to get what you want, and you should have some fruit and some milk in the morning for energy, but you don't want too much in the pipes, and what you do have needs to be small, near the top, and eco-friendly, do you feel me?"

No, and now I don't really want to.

"Peach," Chase said blankly, "and what you're having." Well, thank God this wasn't going to be awkward or anything.

Dex laughed a little. "Sorry, I didn't mean to scare you off. It's just that—" Dex paused for a minute and gave their orders to the cashier. He paid and they went to the back of the store. Chase realized that Dex was good at keeping his expression natural and his voice pitched not too loud. No one could hear him, but he wasn't having one of those secret conversations that made everyone *want* to hear him, either.

"It's just that," Dex said, leaning back against the glass wall, casual and self-contained, "no one really talks about what it's like to have all the pretty sex with people who are, essentially, coworkers, right? And coworkers can be awesome people—I mean, I love the guys at *Johnnies* like my brothers, you know? Kill or die for them, fuck 'em silly, whatever. But we get really close to one another, and you just need to learn that some shit is courtesy, okay?"

Okay—that's actually common sense.

"Yeah," Chase said, nodding. "I'm all ears."

At that moment, the counter-girl called Dex's name and Dex got their drinks and pretzels, and they went outside into what was promising to be a beautiful late-October day.

There was just enough wind to eddy the leaves around the parking lot, and the sky was that blue—that unforgettable cobalt blue—that always spoke of happy and sad to Chase, who was sorry to see the end of baseball season but who had always, unaccountably, loved winter.

Maybe he was still waiting for Christmas.

"Okay," Chase said, after taking a deep pull off his smoothie and savoring it. Jamba Juice was still not a favorite now, but Dex had a point: it didn't give him gas.

Dex nodded. "'kay, so the hygiene—all the time. Even if you're not sure you're going to do anal or anyone's going to do you, the enema and diet stuff just keeps your whole personal space clean and friendly. It's one of the reasons we let them rip out our sphincter hair, yanno?"

Chase grimaced. He'd had to tell Mercy that he'd won a free body wax from a school club, and that it helped with the weight lifting. She'd liked it, but he still thought his privates looked really naked without fur.

"Yeah, I hear you. So, anything else gross?"

Dex laughed. "You're going to need to kiss. I know, your resume says you're straight, and some of the straight guys, they come in thinking it's just nerve endings, right? So they plan to close their eyes, get their nerve endings fondled, and no kissing." Dex shook his head. "You've got to. We're selling intimacy here with our sex. It's why people want to see us talking to each other or watch us undress. Don't be afraid to kiss or to touch or to pat or praise. No one is going to think any worse of you on set, and it may weird you out at first, but you'll get used to it." Dex took a swig of his drink and nibbled on some pretzel. "You play baseball, right?"

Chase nodded, trying to remember that this guy had seen his profile—hell, had probably seen him jerk off on screen.

"Yeah, so think of kissing like patting other guys on the ass. It's something you do to show a coworker appreciation, and you can live with that."

Oh God yes!

"I'll try not to be too stiff," he mumbled, trying to hide the flush over his body. God, this *was* like unwrapping a Christmas present early—except finding out it was the bike you always wanted!

Dex chuckled drily. "Now don't promise *that*," he said with a wink, and Chase laughed hard enough to spit smoothie. Dex laughed some more and Chase wiped his mouth and blushed and tried to smile back like he was just some dumb jock who meant to do that.

Then Dex said, "Yeah, try not to do that either on set," and Chase was lost. He broke into giggles so bad he had to rest his face in his arms until he was laughed out.

When he looked up, Dex was grinning evilly, and Chase grimaced and threw a wadded-up napkin at him. Dex ducked and caught the napkin and threw it back.

"Thanks, asshole!" Chase said, but he was still laughing. God, it felt like he hadn't laughed in such a long time. Maybe since he'd met

Mercy in the library at school that last time, the time before their first date.

"You're welcome," Dex said smugly. "You keep laughing like that, you're going to have a good time with us, okay?"

Chase nodded, and realized he'd forgotten for a minute why he was there. Maybe that was good. Maybe that would make Dex feel like a coworker, just like he said.

"Anything else?" he asked, eating some more of his pretzel. God, this wasn't going to be enough. He'd have to have a... a... a peanut butter and jelly sandwich on whole wheat would probably be his best bet, hah?

Dex nodded. "Yeah—now I saw your profile, and you say you've got a girlfriend. Does she know what's doing?"

It would break her heart. She'd hate me, and never speak to me again, and she never did anything wrong to deserve this and God, Mercy, I just want... just want... crap, the money's good.

Chase shook his head. "She has no idea." He cringed a little, expecting Dex to blow him up for lying to his girlfriend, for hiding part of his life, for not being an out and proud straight man doing gay porn.

"Okay, then this shit is critical," Dex said, blowing Chase's anxiety out of the water, but not much else.

Chase nodded, all ears.

"You're going to have bruises—maybe not tomorrow's shoot, but any shoot where you get really physical, whether you're the top or the bottom, someone's going to be grabbing an arm or a thigh or a hip and holding on for dear life. If you're on top, you're going to get them on your hips; if you're on bottom, you're going to get them on your ass. Hickeys, whisker burn, bruises, muscle fatigue—if you've never fucked a man, you don't know, but we go at it like an Olympic fucking sport. If you're straight, it's all about nerve endings, right? Well, you've got to hit those babies hard and do it right, and that's not always butterflies and lollipops. Even if you don't like rough with your girl—or anyone— this is different. You're going to be marked. If she doesn't know, you may want to take a business trip, see the folks, something, and then do it with the lights off when you get back."

Oh God. I'm going to come in my pants.

"I can do that." Chase shrugged and drank so much smoothie he got brain freeze and had to swallow quickly and try really hard not to press the heel of his hand against his eyeball. Dex saw him do that and laughed, and reached across the table to clap him on the shoulder.

"You'll do fine," he said.

I'm gonna get sex! Sex! Sex sex sex sex sex... from a man!

"You saw the video—I've got a body made for porn." He tried a cocky grin, the kind he gave when he was at the pitcher's mound and he knew he was inside the hitter's head.

Dex rolled his eyes. "God, yes! I can't wait to fucking blow you—that's going to be a *trip!*"

Chase managed valiantly not to do anything else weird with his smoothie, but his eyes must have gotten as big as softballs, because Dex laughed some more. It was a good laugh, and his smile was charming, but Chase had a moment when he realized that Dex wasn't Donnie, and it made him almost miss what came next.

"That's another thing—"

"God, those words are starting to freak me out!" *Say them again! Say I'll be someone else on set, someone free, someone sexy, someone who can hold and touch and be held and lov—someone who is happy.*

"Well, get used to them," Dex said drolly. "See, the thing is, if there's anything you *don't* want to do, be up front. Some guys like rimming, some guys refuse. Some guys hate getting rimmed but don't mind doing it themselves. Whatever. If you've got something you just can't? Talk about it before the shoot, because sometimes, we really do just roll with it, okay? I mean, not with the huge stuff, like penetration, but tomorrow? If you're looking into it, turning me on, I may reach out and touch you. If it's weird and you don't like it, just move my hand, but don't freak out, okay? Let us know so we don't have any embarrassment on set, but if you don't let us know, sometimes the moment *does* take you, and that makes for good camera sometimes, so John likes it."

Oh yeah. I'll be doing it for someone else. And for a moment, the bike became tarnished—maybe it was used, or had a banana seat, when everyone knew they'd been out of style forever. But still… it was a bike. He'd never gotten a bike before.

"Is there anything else he likes?" John had seemed on the up and up, for a porn director, hadn't he? For a second Chase waited uncomfortably to find out that his bike was a poisonous snake.

Dex nodded so matter-of-factly that Chase didn't even have time to be afraid. "Yeah, you have to watch where you put your hands. You may want to touch someone's face or their ass or something—but watch where the camera is. They want to see our faces, our cocks, and our penetration. They *definitely* need to see us blow our wads. The guys with the cameras have the angles all figured out and shit, and they try to stay out of our way, but we've got to help them out. So if you want to touch someone's face, do it with the hand on the side away from the cameras."

Oh yay! It really is a bike, and I'm going to ride….

"Geez, I hope I remember that!" He did too.

Dex shrugged. "You'll be with a veteran for the first couple of shots. If you're good, if you get lots of downloads and some good responses, eventually you'll be the veteran, and you'll remember. No worries, okay?"

Chase nodded his head enthusiastically. "Man, I've got a lot less now!"

Dex smiled. "Any questions? I mean seriously—personal, not personal, your choice, okay? No judgments."

Chase nodded. "So, do the guys hang out, or is it business and go home?"

"Oh no. We definitely hang out. Those of us who are local go to the same gym, you know? Just to work out together—we even get a discount."

"That would be awesome. When baseball isn't in season, I've got no one to work out with. It's sort of depressing." He used to work out with Donnie, but now Donnie worked out with his boyfriend, and Kevin was unreliable at best.

"Well, there you go. We can hook you up. Anything else?"

Are there relationships on set? How many of the guys are gay? How many straight? How many bi? Is it going to matter if one of them is touching me? Blowing me? Has his cock up my ass? Will I feel it? Will I be able to tell the difference? Can I separate the need in my skin from the job I'm going to do? Can you help me do that?

"Yeah, is all porn like this?"

Dex laughed a little and shook his head. "Not as far as I know. *Johnnies* is really good about trying to keep things friendly and trying to make it seem like a family. We have our dramas, and we don't always get along, and John tries not to make us work together when that happens, and we try to keep things professional so he doesn't have to get too into our business to put sex on tape, you know?"

Chase blinked. He'd never really thought about that.

"Yeah, that would suck if you had to fuck an asshole," he said thoughtfully, and this time it was Dex who spit out his drink, and then Chase realized what he'd said and the rest of his questions got giggled into the cradle of his arms on the table.

"Oh geez," he gasped, when they could both talk again, "God, I actually had some more questions, but I can't remember them now."

Dex was busy wiping tears from his eyes and he just shook his head. "Man, you've got my number, right?"

Chase nodded—he'd put it in his cell before he left.

"Well, you give me a call if you need to. We're supposed to show up an hour before the shoot; show up three hours before and I'll show you around, let you see the other shoot going on, introduce you to some of the guys. It'll be okay. Are you nervous?"

Buzzzzzzzzzzzzzzz!!!

"Actually, I'm sort of amped," Chase said thoughtfully.

"Great, Chance. We'll have a good time." They stood and shook hands, and then it turned out they'd both parked in the same downtown garage about three blocks away, and they talked all the way to their cars.

Chase enjoyed the conversation—he honestly did. His skin still buzzed with anticipation, and the thought that Dex, with his wide smile and the cocky swagger to his hips, was going to actually sit next to him and watch his naked body. But Dex (or whatever—he must have a real name too, right?) didn't have Donnie's reckless, Labrador retriever smile. And he didn't have that suddenly thoughtful way of putting shit into perspective when Chase needed it most. It wasn't until he opened his car and had a moment to analyze that familiar post-Christmas dropping of the stomach that he managed to place his odd disappointment in the entire meeting.

Yeah, he'd finally got that new bike for Christmas. But he'd been asking for an action figure instead.

THAT didn't mean he didn't get up early the next morning, use the enema kit he'd hidden in his duffel bag, and pack an overnight bag with a few changes of clothes. He had no idea if he was going to use them, or how bad he'd look when he was done, but he figured if he had something he didn't want Mercy to spot, he'd want something to wear as he camped out at Donnie's house.

And then it hit him. If he camped out at Donnie's house, he'd have to tell Donnie.

That big buzz of excitement in his stomach cramped wickedly into dread.

He packed the clothes anyway, but he very very carefully didn't think about telling Donnie.

And then he kissed Mercy on the cheek as she lay sleeping and whispered, "It's in Tracy. I'll call you if the job goes long."

Mercy gave a sleepy "Mmmhmm...," and Chase turned around and walked out of the apartment.

On his way down the stairs and out to the car, he was suddenly there in his memory, meeting Mercy for the first time and thinking she was the best thing that had happened to him.

HIS iPod had been playing Foo Fighters, and playing them loud, but that was okay. He was alone at Sac State, because Donnie was still going to junior college while he decided what he wanted to do and saved money for State, and Chase was lonely. He was in training for the baseball season and had been working hard at his fast-food job, trying to keep his shitty apartment. He didn't want to move back home because his old man would never stop giving him shit about his useless time spent in college, and basically? If he was going to have to read *Of Mice and Men*, he was going to do it with the Foo Fighters, because they made shit better.

Suddenly an older student, in her forties maybe, was standing up and yelling. Someone tapped Chase on the shoulder, and a girl with blonde streaks in her dark hair who also had her iPod ear buds in was making eye contact. They both looked at each other and then up at the student, and Chase pulled one of his ear buds out in time to hear....

"And you two should be totally ashamed of yourself for causing such a ruckus in the library! This library is for everybody, you know!"

And about the time Chase and his new companion had figured out she was yelling at *them*, she had flounced off with her little wheeled cart and three layers of sweaters, leaving the two of them looking at each other with wide, laughing eyes.

They had both stopped their iPods then, and laughed, and then had commiserated on the English 1B reading list, and then ended up playing a giddy game of notebook-paper-football while they quoted movies. They had finally conceded that no homework was going to be finished at that point and had pooled their resources to go to the campus McDonald's for the dollar menu and endless soda. They'd talked until the place had closed down around them and made plans to meet the next day.

"Maybe we can catch a movie over the weekend!" Mercy had said animatedly. She had been animated for most of their conversation, and Chase genuinely enjoyed her smile, the way her little chipmunk cheeks had gone hard and round and shiny, and the way her brown eyes danced and she clapped her hand over her mouth when she was afraid she'd laughed too loud. But now she was blushing, and she added, "You know, if you wanted to go out again."

It hadn't been until that exact moment that he realized they were out on a date.

CHASE walked briskly to his car—a big, bruising, almost-free Ford truck in primer gray—and threw his bag in the passenger seat and slammed the door, trying to block out the memories. It didn't work. On the fifteen-minute trip to the office suite of *Johnnies*, Chase fought a mini slide show of things like their first kiss, or the first time they'd made love, or all of the times he'd orgasmed inside her while imagining Donnie's hard hand stroking him, inexpertly but willingly. That last one triggered more memories of Donnie and that one fabulous, giddy night when Donnie had stopped waiting for Chase to reciprocate and had simply laid back on his bed in his parent's house and stroked his own cock, at his own pace, until he exploded all over his hand. Chase could still remember the look—pleasure so exquisite it was past bearing—on Donnie's face, and he could remember the way his heart hurt when Donnie had innocently taken his own come-covered hand to his mouth and sucked on the webbing between his thumb and forefinger, just to see what it tasted like.

Chase had wanted to taste it too... oh God, he'd wanted it so bad. But he hadn't. He'd told Donnie he was brave, but it would never happen between them for one simple reason.

Chase wasn't gay.

And as he pulled up and around the office suite of *Johnnies* to park, he thought that maybe he would finally see the upside of being a straight man once he got behind the plain brown doors.

THE receptionist John had been missing that first day was there. She was a gum-cracking girl with a dirty-blonde ponytail, a faint sneer, and ripped jeans, and she gave Chase a friendly smile as she picked up an intercom mike and said, "Dex, your rookie is here to see you!"

Chase ducked, feeling stupid, when the words bounced around the office too, but the girl rolled her eyes self-consciously. "Goddammit," she muttered. "Seriously, why do I keep doing that?"

"Goddammit, Kelsey!" Dex snapped, coming through the door in a pair of jeans, a T-shirt, and shower shoes, much to Chase's surprise. "Why do you keep doing that?"

"I don't know!" Kelsey wailed, hitting button after button on the intercom. One of them started a feedback loop that punctured the entire compound at full volume, and the next one....

"Oh God!" screamed a disembodied male voice. "Fuck me now! Fuck me, dammit! Fucking now!"

"You like that? You like that big fat dick?" answered another disembodied voice, and the look Kelsey sent Dex was both eloquent and horrified. He grimaced, shoved her rolling-wheeled chair out of the way, and punched buttons until the assorted grunts, groans, and pants went away.

"Oh God," Kelsey groaned, burying her face in her hands. "John is going to *kill* me!"

"John is going to laugh his skinny little ass off," Dex muttered. "It's Ethan and Tango who're going to kill you."

"Oh God. It was Ethan's first bottom, wasn't it?" Kelsey smacked the heel of her hand against her forehead. "Jesus, he was so fucking nervous! Oh God...." Suddenly she stood up. "Here. Dex. You and new guy man the fort. I'll be right back."

"Where the fuck're you—"

"Oreos!" she called, grabbing a giant tapestry bag of a purse. "He loves them. I'm going to the mini-mart next door, and he's gonna have a big pack of fudge-covered Oreos and some milk when he's done with the scene if it kills me!" And with that she went trotting out the door, leaving Dex there at the counter, shaking his head, and Chase staring after her, smiling.

"God," Dex muttered. "She's a good kid, you know? I mean... Oreos for Ethan—hell, I think she brought flip-flops for you, because I forgot to tell you about them, right?"

"Uhm, yeah?" Because it was late October and who wore sandals of any sort, right?

"Yeah, so she's totally thoughtful and we all really adore her, but...." He shook his head and looked at the intercom board again. "Well, it's just a good thing John rewards people for doing their best, you know? Otherwise, she'd be fired, we'd all feel like shit, and no one would get Ethan his fucking Oreos, right?"

Chase nodded. Sure. Made total sense to him.

"So, uhm," he said when Dex had stopped clucking over the phone and intercom, "shower shoes?"

Dex looked up and shook his head. "They like pictures of our feet—and some guys really like toe sucking—"

"You?" Chase asked, and was surprised when Dex nodded his head.

"Giving and receiving," he confirmed. "So we take a pre-fuck shower, and there are wire brushes and shit to help get the feet all purty, and then there are almost always shots of our feet. Besides, flip-flops are easier to take off than tennis shoes, right? Nothing kills the mood like trying to get off a high top and a sweat sock while the other guy's got his dick out."

Chase had to giggle. "Yeah, yeah—I can see that."

Dex reached over the counter and ruffled his hair. "Just *look* at you. They're going to eat you up with a *fork!*"

I have no idea how to respond to that.

"Well, Jesus, I hope so! It would be awesome to come back!"

Dex laughed wickedly and patted his cheek. "Dude, we're men. It would be awesome just to *come!*"

Did that pun *ever* get old?

So they were still cracking up when Kelsey got back, red-faced and breathless, a cloth shopping bag hanging from her hand.

"Oh God," she panted. "Should I go back there? Do you think he's done?"

"I dunno, Kelse," Dex said dryly. "Would you like to push that button again and see where they are in the shoot?"

Kelsey let out a little wail and buried her face in her hands. Dex laughed, dropped a kiss on the top of her head, and then motioned Chase to follow him through the door and into the rest of the office complex.

"Is she going to be okay?" Chase looked behind him, half afraid he'd hear muffled sobbing or something.

Dex shrugged. "Yeah, she's fine. Once we're gone, she'll start working again and totally forget how bad she feels until Ethan goes in to work the guilt thing. Then she'll give him Oreos, he'll stop angling for sex, and the whole thing goes back to copacetic."

Chase blinked. "Ethan's straight?"

Dex rolled his eyes. "Ethan *will* fuck anything that moves," he said. "Twice if his boner won't go away. It's a good thing he's such a nice guy or we'd all hate him to pieces."

Hey! He's a nice guy! That's always good to hear!

"Yeah, well, it's good to be loved."

"Yeah, well, with Ethan, there's a lot to love. C'mon—you ready to explore the glorious world of porn?"

Chase cracked his gum. "I got nothin' better to do."

HAMSTER RIOTS

THE two boys on the bed looked relaxed and comfortable with each other as they answered the cameraman's questions.

The bed itself was nondescript: beige sheets, a beige comforter, and a worn khaki blanket on top of the comforter. It wasn't like anyone was actually getting in the bed, right? The walls were white, the furniture was cheap but sturdy, and there was a big mirror on one wall next to a dresser that looked like it could hold a man's weight.

"So," said the man behind the camera, "Chance, Dex, you guys been getting to know each other?"

The one with the cropped, dyed blond hair and slightly crooked front teeth dimpled and cracked his gum. "Yeah, Dex has been showing me the ropes, right, Dex?"

The other one with the longer, darker blond hair and the overbearing confidence shrugged. "Absolutely. Figure if we haven't scared him off yet, he's in it for the long haul."

There was a gentle chuckle. "So, see anything scary yet, Chance?"

Chance grinned. "Only Ethan's cock. He flashes that thing around a lot!"

Dex gasped unexpectedly and started to chortle into his outstretched arm, and the voice over the camera joined in. "You're right! You want to check that out sometime?"

Chance shrugged, his cheeks coloring slightly, as though he was now a little embarrassed at his brazenness. "Maybe. But first, you know, Dex has been pretty good to me. I'm thinking we should get to know each other better."

"Good idea," said the voice, and then Dex looked at Chance like they were about to have a bike race or play a game of Frisbee.

"You ready?"

There was a suddenly sober look on Chance's face, as though he was seriously considering a casual question. Then he sat up and pulled his T-shirt over his head. The thin layer of baby fat over his flexing muscles showed he'd barely entered his twenties.

"Yeah, I think so," he said, and nothing about his direct stare into the other boy's eyes or his easy movements as he sat back on the bed and started rubbing his chest showed that he had any doubts at all.

"Then do what feels good," Dex said, following suit. He tweaked his own nipple then and gasped, then moaned. Chance followed suit, and then did it again. They both shoved their other hands under the waistbands of their shorts at almost exactly the same moment, but it was Chance's toes-deep groan that electrified the action on the screen.

"MMM…," John said, looking at the final cut, "that was a good moment."

Chase swallowed, mesmerized once again by the sight of Dex, right next to him, with his cock in his hand and his knees spread wide as he stroked himself slowly and with so much pressure his circumcised, swollen head turned purple.

"Think it'll sell?" he asked, trying to sound nonchalant.

John snorted. "Kid, it's five-star hot, and there isn't even any penetration. Shh… here's the best part."

And it had been for Chase too.

DEX'S head was thrown back, his eyes closed, his fist stroking easily, when he heard Chance groan. He looked up, and some pre-come had spurted on Chance's cockhead. Slowly, he moved the hand that was on his own chest, pinching his nipples, to Chance's chest. Chance murmured, "Oh God, yes!" and Dex popped up, threw himself over the bed, and took Chance's long, thick erection into his mouth.

Chance howled, both hands scrabbling in the sheets, his chest arching up off the bed.

HE HAD hardly needed any fluffing, although those moments in the room with Dex and John and the second cameraman (another model—Grant?) had been furtive and fun, like his first remembered moments masturbating under his own bed sheets, except this time he had a friend across the room doing the same thing. There had been no moaning, no shared experience, just the simple nuts and bolts of reaching in and… oh yeah, squeezing and… rubbing… and it wasn't like he wasn't semi-hard in the first place, just from the tour of the place itself.

It turned out that the office and the viewing room were the only real professional places in the building. The rest were sets, various bedrooms or living rooms, complete with wallpaper and color schemes.

"We've got a house set with a yard not far from here," Dex said, "so we can film from the yard and into the house itself. It all depends on where John wants us, right? And of course the courtyard gets used a lot when it's warm. Not right now though—nobody wants his nuts shot when it's only fifty degrees outside."

Chase giggled. "Dude, I'm not sure why anyone would want to see my nuts anyway."

Dex looked at him and rolled his eyes. "I saw your profile, Gigantor. Straight guys would look at those nuts and think, 'God, I could get every chick on the planet with those things!' Women are going to be looking at them and thinking, 'I'd bone this guy in a hot second!'"

And gay guys? What will they think? Will they think I'm desirable? Will they fantasize about being with me? Will they hope I like men for real?

And that right there was when his erection swelled inside his pants.

Dex took him down the hall to what looked like a gym locker room, and, sure enough, there were big lockers with electronic keypads to lock. Chase had his duffel bag of clothes over his shoulder and realized this would be the place to stash it.

"The showers," Dex indicated, and as he did so, there was a commotion down the hall. "Shit!" he grimaced. "They must be done with Ethan and Tango's shoot."

Chase's eyes got *really* big. "And they're coming in *here*?" he squeaked.

Dex shrugged—he did that a lot, and it did put Chase at ease. With Dex, everything was all okay, nothing to get excited about, just two straight guys about to get naked and come, but no, nothing to see here, folks.

"Yeah, but so is the film crew. They like to film the after—sometimes fun shit happens, you know? You don't just get naked with someone, come, and stop touching in real life—you don't do that here, either. Besides, like I said, you're co-workers. You just did something difficult and challenging, and hopefully it ended successfully. You're going to want to talk about it."

Personal closure. More nakedness. And wetness. And sex!

"I hear you. Sort of like a debriefing or a report or something."

Dex nodded. "Hey—let me go ask. If Ethan doesn't mind, you can hang out in back."

Goody goody goody goody goody....

"Yeah, okay. That'll be good."

"You're pretty low-key—that's good in a way, but I got to tell you, I'm hoping you get more vocal in the sack. It's like... you know, feedback. Not only is it good for the cameras, the guy you're with, he wants to know he's not just banging an unconscious meatsack, right?"

"Yeah, I hear ya. Not a problem." Chase let his eyes get hooded and one side of his mouth pull up, which was the way he used to smile for Donnie. "I'm good at giving people what they want."

Dex gave a mock shiver in anticipation. "Awesome. Here, let me go ask Ethan."

He came back two steps in front of the camera crew and two guys in big fluffy white robes, giving Chase the thumbs up and nodding to a back corner, where they could watch unobtrusively.

The guys were followed by two cameramen, one of whom was John himself, and a girl holding a couple of towels and toiletries. The guys were breathing like they'd just come back from a workout, and one of them kept scrubbing at his face and laughing.

"Jesus, Ethan, you totally got that shit in my *eye!*"

And ohmygod! It was Ethan, the guy that Chase had been watching fuck like Apollo on his computer at night. He wasn't actually that tall—maybe 5'10"—but his shoulders. Jesus, his shoulders were *massive.* Chase looked at Dex, eyeing Ethan with an easy admiration—could have been any straight guy, thinking "Jesus, I've got to increase my workout!" and he made sure his expression was the same way. He *certainly* wasn't going to let his expression show that he'd been watching Ethan online and coming in his pants without even touching himself.

The two of them hung back in a corner of the locker room as Ethan dropped his robe on a bench, reached inside, and turned on the shower. It was then that Chase realized the showers were pretty open—only part of one of the walls was shut behind glass.

"Yeah, Tango, it's good. Hop on in, man, see if you can get some of that shit out of your eye."

For the first time, Chase's hero worship let him notice Ethan's companion.

He was taller than Ethan, but shorter than Chase. Maybe shy of six foot total, with straight dark hair and a white-pale complexion, the kind that came with freckles as a child, even though his eyes were dark brown and liquid. His face was long, with a long jaw that came to a plumb little square and a cleft in the chin, and his mouth was wide and mobile. He seemed to have a permanent grin on his face, hyper-bright, with just a touch of evil.

That evil grin flashed nuclear and the young man's dark eyebrows winged up into little pointed arches. "No worries, Ethan, man, I'll just return the favor."

Ethan laughed and they both stepped in. Without warning, Ethan manhandled Tango backward into his chest, running his hands from a taut, ripped abdomen up to his narrow chest—wide with muscles but not really built for mass—and his back. His hand dropped to Tango's groin and the surprisingly hefty erection swinging low and baggy there.

"Are you kidding? You think I'm gonna let that monster in my ass again? Man, it's hard enough to suck that thing—"

"You just like it when you get it hard," Tango taunted, that incorrigible grin amping up a notch. His breathing quickened, and everybody in the room—the two men with cameras, the girl with the bathrobes and shower bag—seemed to stop breathing as that breathless panting took over the enclosed, echoing space.

Ethan's hand closed over him and Tango closed his eyes and leaned back his head into Ethan's shoulder. "So do you," Ethan murmured. "How you doin', Tango. I'm all hard, you ready to go again?"

"Fuckin' always, you big-cocked wonder. Man, someone get this man some lube."

There was a brief rustle, and Tango stood up long enough to catch the tube from the prop girl and pass it back behind him. Ethan's motions were quick as he condomed up and greased his (oh holy God was that really swollen flesh?) cock, and Tango barely leaned forward before Ethan thrust in.

"Oh, God, you're so tight!" Ethan praised, patting Tango's muscled thigh. That flank was quivering with what looked like a little bit of fatigue, though, and Tango gritted his teeth and panted, "Tight as you were, but getting tired, man."

Ethan sighed, shivering all over. "Man, I'm still so sensitive… just hold on, I'm almost there." His arm went around Tango's stomach, and Tango adjusted his stance and then surprised the hell out of Chase and probably everybody in the room by putting his hand flat against the wall, shifting his foot up onto the soap holder, and pistoning his hips up and down against Ethan with incredible power.

His head tilted back, his teeth bared, and he started a peculiar, growling pant that told everybody in the room that just sex or not, he was *really* getting off on this.

"Oh crap, Tango, I'm gonna come!" On cue, Tango leaned over the ledge of the shower, reached between his legs, and started taking care of himself while Ethan did the same thing, ripping the condom off and giving some frantic pumps to his own member before spraying all over Tango's buttocks and back.

Tango grunted and made a keening noise, completely oblivious to the five other people in the room, closed his eyes, and lost himself in losing his wad against the shower wall.

It took a few moments for the electricity in the room to sizzle down, and in the meantime the two guys straightened and leaned drunkenly on each other while they pumped soap from the dispenser and soaped up their own hair and their own chests and groins.

"God," Ethan muttered, "*that* was a fucking surprise. Jesus, Tango, do you like live on Viagra or something?"

That evil, evil grin never diminished. "Hey, you're the one who felt like fucking."

Ethan smacked his ass playfully. "Well, you're just so damned fuckable, right?"

"Damned straight." Tango arched an eyebrow and smirked genuinely at the guy who had just drilled him into the tile. Dex bumped Chase's shoulder at that point, and Chase let out a reluctant breath. Together, the two of them edged out of the locker room, but not before their motion caught Tango's attention.

For a moment, just a moment, Chase caught the eye (one of them was still blinking closed) of the guy who had just fucked like Loki the lunatic sex god, and he was stunned to the pit of his stomach. Dex hauled him out of there, and Chase had to fight the temptation to look back over his shoulder, praying for one more look of that pale skin, with the three moles on the side of his collarbone and the wicked/evil eyes.

"C'mon, man. They'll be out of there in about ten minutes, and then John'll be gearing up to film our scene, okay?"

"Yeah, sure man."

"Here, let's go get some Gatorade. I'm *starving*, but it's going to have to hold us, you feel me?" Dex's casual grin was still in place, and it suddenly hit Chase that this guide, this mentor, was just exactly like him, except probably straight for real and not the lie Chase had put on his profile. He was young and active and starving and joyful, and for a moment, just a moment....

This thing we're doing, it's not a dirty little secret, because this isn't a bad guy.

And then he decided that maybe Gatorade was more his thing than philosophy and simply followed Dex's lead.

DEX'S mouth was skilled on Chance's cock, and Chance threw his head back against the pillows and moaned.

"Oh God!" he cried, the sound echoing loudly into the camera, and then he said it again, but this time it was forced past his throat as his hips started to buck. "Jesus, Dex, I'm gonna...."

Dex pulled back and stuck out his tongue, fisting the slick, glistening member while Chance thrashed on the bed.

"Oh God!" Chance cried again. "Oh fuck... oh fuck oh fuck oh fuck...."

His scream when he orgasmed was loud enough to be startling on the tinny sound system of the camera, but the look on his face was... was unaware. There was no camera as far as that man was concerned, splayed out, his cock spurting come over the face of the man who had just pumped it into his mouth.

"Now *that's* the best part," John grunted with satisfaction. "Kid, you come like a champion. God, that was awesome. This is going to sell like hotcakes, Chance. Let's see...." John flipped through his planner. "We'll be shooting stills tomorrow, so we need you until then. After that, when can we have you back?"

"See?" Dex said, that ever-present, casual, "It's all okay" grin just as sharp then as it had been the day before, when the scene had been shot. "I told you it was good!"

It was heaven. No gay, no straight, just a friendly hand, a climax I could be proud of, massive approval. I want to do it again.

"It was alright," Chase said, cracking his gum. He and Dex had chattered all through their shower scene, but their touches had been casual and not nearly as scorching as the one that had gone before them.

"Just all right?" John asked, honestly incredulous, and Chase rolled his neck and shook out his shoulders, like he would before a big game.

"It was invigorating," he grinned, thinking that was true. It was like the usual sex endorphins had been multiplied to the nth power by the fact that people were watching, and the fact that there he was, getting touched by another man in front of the entire world, and that it made him so straight, it was part of his job title. God, he could have gone out now and pitched a no-hitter. He could have worked a double shift on a road crew. He could have done *anything*, even and including going home and jumping his girlfriend like a Dachshund jumped a table leg.

John shook his head, his longish hair flopping in front of his pale eyes. "Right on. *That's* the kind of answer I was hoping for. So when can you do it again?"

Chase bit his lower lip and thought about it. "The problem," he said reluctantly, not wanting to share too much of his business, "is hiding the marks from the girlfriend."

He'd seen Tango and Ethan; they were covered in hickeys, and even though Chase wasn't sure if the guy he got partnered up with would want to do that, he was pretty sure with the way he came just from being sucked off that he would have something on his body to show for it if he penetrated or was penetrated by another human being.

"Mmm…." John nodded like the duplicity was completely normal and understandable. "You can stay in one of the rooms if you like, one of the ones not being used here. Guys do it all the time. What did you tell her this time?"

Chase looked away. Geez, he'd always hated lying. Donnie had always said he was really bad at it; he'd rather be a jerk and just walk away or get out of the situation than really lie.

"I said I had a construction job out of town."

John nodded again. "All right then, tell her you've got one for a week. We've got a Florida set; we'll fly you out there, shoot the stills on day one, the shot on day two, and set you up in one of the rooms in our suite for the next four days, how's that?"

Florida? *Florida?* Chase's college baseball team went up and down the state, but the truth was, he'd never really been out of California.

"Sounds decent," he said.

"We'll make it six weeks, then," John said decisively. "We'll get you in and out two weeks before Christmas, and have your check cut in time to go shopping. How's that?"

Chase actually felt a shudder of relief and excitement ripple up his spine, like scales on a muscular snake. "That's awesome. So, you said I could stay here if I needed to. Can I stay here *tonight?*"

John looked at him, an off grin on his face. "Well, yeah kid, but you don't need to. There's not a mark on you. Just come back tomorrow for the stills, okay?"

Chase flushed and masked it with a crack of his gum. He turned to Dex and winked and said, "Yeah, sometimes you think a life-changing experience is just written all over your face."

Dex smirked. "No, genius, it was written all over mine, but it washed off."

Chase cracked his gum again. "We'll see if we can keep our life-changing experiences washable then, right?"

John laughed. "Good, good—practice your banter for the shoot. People love that. Now before we ship you off to our beach house in Orlando, I've got to ask. You ready to top?"

Chase shrugged, this time truly at a loss.

God yes, but I don't want to hurt anyone.

"I'm not sure how?" He literally ended it with a question.

John nodded. "That's okay, we'll pair you with Cam. He's sort of a cock-whore—loves to bottom, he'll be fine."

Dex nodded judiciously. "Ass like a steel trap," he said fondly. "You'll love him."

Tango!

He blinked. His inner voice surprised even him.

"Sounds good," he said, swinging his shoulders a little in enthusiasm.

Tango! Tango! We want the guy with the evil smile and bright black eyes! Tango!

"Awesome," John said. "Talk to Kelsey after the stills tomorrow, and she'll make sure you get the 'Carey Industry' stamp on your check. That way your girl won't get suspicious when the money comes in."

Chase's stomach suddenly congealed, because he hadn't thought about this one detail and it could have... oh God, it could have....

Mercy! Oh, Jesus, Mercy, you're not supposed to get hurt here! Oh God, I almost hurt you!

"Thank you," he said quietly, shoving his suddenly clammy hands in his pockets. He found his pack of gum in there and pulled out another piece, spitting the piece in his mouth—mint, for fresh breath—into the wrapper very carefully, and making very very sure his fingers didn't shake with the sudden adrenaline rush of the almost. He dropped the gum in the trashcan while John said, "You're welcome," and filled out some travel vouchers for him to give to Kelsey too.

"I don't do the Florida set, but that's Dex's first week behind the camera, so it'll be him and Grant."

Chase turned around, relieved to find another emotion to put on his face. "Dude. You takin' pictures? That's awesome!"

Dex shrugged. "I'm twenty-six, dude. Can't be pretty forever."

Oh God, at twenty-six, I'll be married. I'll never... I'll never... never again.

"Make good memories, right?"

Dex held out his fist and Chase bumped it.

"Right on!"

That night he swung into the unmarked spot he usually parked his old truck in while thinking over what he was going to tell Mercy about how clean he was. Showers at the site? Hadn't happened yet, but it could. Stopped by a friend's? Why not? He knew guys on the different crews. There'd be no shame in that, right?

As it turned out, Mercy wasn't in the apartment. Like a fool, he checked the voice mail on his cell phone and heard her telling him she was going to stay the night at a friend's house, since he was going to be gone, and the wash of relief that blew through him left his knees weak and spots dancing in front of his eyes.

Oh God, he wasn't going to have to face her. Not tonight. Not when it was all so vibrant in his head and his body was still tingling from an orgasm that almost blew his eyeballs out of his head.

The thought of it made him hard again, and without thinking about it, he grabbed a towel from the bathroom and threw it on the bed with the olive-and-rose-flowered comforter before toeing off his tennis shoes and shoving his jeans down to his knees. He'd always masturbated furtively, inside his pants, under the covers in a darkened room, or in the bathroom after Mercy was asleep, but not now. Now he sprawled himself out on the bed by the light coming in from the living room and relived that final, mind-blowing moment when his cock had been in Dex's mouth and it had been warm, and wet, and... oh God... oh God....

Dark eyes, wicked black laughing eyes in a pale face, with a long jaw and an almost elfin nose, looked at hm.

His hips spasmed within moments, and his cock swelled, sensitized, and erupted in his fist. But even as his vision went white-blind in climax, even as he brought his hand, coated in spend, to his own lips to taste, he was still looking at the face of the lunatic sex god and thinking of Tango.

HE WASHED off in the silence of the apartment and decided to watch some television before he fell asleep. He found an old George Clooney movie on cable—*One Fine Day*—that his mother had watched a lot before she'd died, and he settled down to watch it, wondering if it had changed since he was six.

It had, he realized.

He saw Michelle Pfeiffer's helplessness this time, how completely overwhelmed she was, how sure she was that no help was ever coming, and her complete determination to hold on and do the best for her child without it.

Was that why his mom had watched it so often? Was she trying to find some sort of strength in that movie that she knew she didn't have?

Well, it didn't work, did it? Because she was dead, and Chase was here, in an empty apartment, feeling like a fairy (and wasn't that a godawful analogy) who had escaped from his bottle, just for a minute. Tiny, insignificant, limited creature with one power in his enormous wand, he was going to make the most of his freedom, if he could.

But that wasn't the idea that haunted him before he went to sleep that night. It wasn't the idea of freedom, or the feel of a man's mouth on the private parts of his body, or even his mother's lifeless corpse in a bloody bathtub.

It was the first time he'd ever had sex, period.

"YOU'VE done this before, right?" Mercy whispered, because she had a roommate who may or may not have been asleep.

I've gotten a hand job from the guy I'd loved since the sixth grade.

"Yeah! Of course I have!" Chase kissed the skin of her shoulder, of her neck, of her chest, steeling himself for the plump and naked breast with the extended nipple and puckered aureole.

"You're moving awfully slow," she said breathlessly, because he had just gotten to her nipple and was taking his time, trying to love the way it flickered under his tongue and the way she trembled when he touched it.

"Trying to make it last, babe," he'd murmured. And he had. The rest of that moment had been long, drawn out, slow, including his presence in her body. When he was done, she had trembled and let out a long, low cry in the dark and then clung to him, almost in tears.

"What? What'd I do?"

"God, Chase. You made me feel special. It was the first time I really got the idea of making love, you know that?"

He didn't tell her that he'd had to. He didn't tell her that it had been his way of making up for the fact that he wished he was with another person, another gender, and that this thing they were doing, this thing that he wanted to be wonderful for her, because she had made him laugh and had helped him with his history papers and had watched old movies with him and had tickled him when he'd been pissed at his coach, this sacred passage to adulthood, was a lie.

He'd hated every moment, including his orgasm, because it felt like cheating, and because Mercy deserved better.

MERCY crawled into bed with him around four in the morning, wrapping her arms around his waist.

"Mmm...," she mumbled, "you used my body wash."

"Yeah," he slurred, lying even when he was half-asleep, "I missed you."

"What was the job like?" she asked, settling her cheek against his back. "Are you going back tomorrow?"

"Hamster riots," Chase mumbled, thinking about the frantic sex he'd seen in the shower and the two cameramen moving in and out seamlessly, quiet and quietly busy. "And yeah. It pays real good. They've got a job for me before Christmas."

"Good," she mumbled softly. "Want presents."

"Yeah, babe. Want to treat you right."

She fell asleep warm and comforted, curled against his back.

EYES CLOSED IN THE SUN

THE two young men were lying outside in the sun, on big chaise lounge pads set up on a blanket. The one with the dyed blond hair was a little pale, but working on his tan. The other one, smaller, with sandy-brown hair, was already tan, and their skin, oiled and nearly hairless—at least down to the short line—glistened in the sun.

"So, Chance," said the smaller one, "how do you like Florida?"

"It's frickin' awesome," Chance breathed. His shoulders twitched luxuriously, and his smaller companion turned his head and grinned.

"We'll get a tan on you yet, Sunshine," he said with a smirk. "You want an all-over tan?"

"Okay, aren't I going to burn my wiener or something? Because that's a part of me that doesn't get a lot of sun."

The smaller guy burst into raucous laughter, his knees coming up as he rolled around the chaise lounge pad, and the camera shook as the man behind it burst into giggles.

"I CAN'T believe you're putting that in there," Chase said, red-faced, as he, Cameron, and Dex watched the rushes the next day.

Dex shook his head. "Man, it was *priceless!* There I was, getting all up to shoot some porn, and suddenly you have to talk about your burning wiener!"

Cameron snickered behind them, and Chase just shook his head. "I felt bad!" he protested. "You had to totally reset the shot!"

"HOW white could your wiener possibly be?" wheezed Cameron, who was still rolling around like a rabid monkey.

The look on Chance's face grew mutinous, and he shoved his tropical island bathing suit down with undue force, revealing that, yes, although his forearms were a little more tan than his pale upper arms and shoulders, his entire groin area, half-masted cock included, was lizard-belly white.

"I'm blind!" hooted the voice behind the camera, and Chance pulled up his shorts with a pout.

"Oh, like I'm going to fuck now!" he snapped, and the camera's perspective shifted as the cameraman sat down abruptly and hooted laughter into the fuzzy, shaking shot.

"GOD, it was hysterical," Dex said with wonder. "There we were, all serious about making a sex tape, and there you were, white as a freakin' ghost and worried about burning your johnson. And then when we finally *did* get around to having sex, it was…."

Dex trailed off, and Cameron breathed it for him. "So. Fucking. Hot."

CHANCE and Cameron were in a room now, the glistening oil from the outside shot washed off their bodies, but still wearing the swim trunks they had been in.

"So," Dex said from the other side of the camera, "Chance, this is the first time you've ever really had sex with a man, right?"

Chance winked. "Except for that time you blew me, yeah."

"That was awesome. You think this'll be as good?"

That cocky jock's grin came out, the lazy one with the hooded eyes, and Chance looked at his chosen companion for the day. "Hoping it'll be better, if Cam can show me the ropes."

Without any more preliminary, Cam rolled over in the bed and kissed him on the mouth. Chance groaned immediately, grasped Cam's biceps, and started kissing back.

THAT kiss had been... oh God. It was the first time he'd ever kissed a man, open-mouthed, with tongue, savoring the taste, wanting more. Cameron was funny and (like all of the models) beautiful, and his complete meltdown with the "wiener incident," as he called it, had certainly broken the ice. It had been fun to lie there in the sun and chat in front of the camera, and Chase had been sort of disappointed when they'd stopped shooting on account of hysterical laughter. But the camaraderie of that moment—that had more than made up for the letdown of not having sex right away.

And that's what had happened. They'd showered to get the oil off, talking in the shower like teammates—in fact, the entire thing had reminded Chase of being on the baseball team, and hanging with Donnie and Kevin.

The thought of Donnie brought him to half-mast again, and the fluffing session in the room, as they both reached inside their shorts and got themselves hard, had been unsurprisingly short.

And then, in the middle of the "pre-sex chat," as Dex called it, Cam had just rolled over and kissed him and, oh God....

"MMM...," Chance groaned into Cameron's mouth, and Cam started kissing his neck, his chest, his nipples, and Chance groaned "Oh God!" into the small room with the white walls and open shutters. Chance's body had leaned down and bulked up since the shot with Dex, and his stomach muscles rippled and his chest flexed as he palmed shaking hands up and down Cameron's arms, shoulders, and back.

"You like that?" Cam asked, moving to the other side, and Chance's body bucked against Cam's and Chance's fingers tightened in Cam's short hair, holding him there, teasing the nerve endings in the

sensitized skin until Chance groaned again and fumbled for Cam's shoulder, apparently just to hold on. Cam kept kissing, spending time on his ribs and on his stomach, and within moments, Chance was lying on his back and Cam was stripping off his shorts.

FLORIDA had been a revelation. Chase had never been on a plane before, and he'd spent half the time staring out the window, looking for marks of the alien landscape below the night-lit gray, and half the time sleeping, leaning his head against the window, wondering what things were skating below, underneath the cover of the November clouds. As the plane had descended near Orlando, he had looked beneath him and seen giant pools of water, stained brown from the tannin in the oak trees, looking mysterious and close.

The air was thick and humid, even in November, and the temperature was in the low eighties. It was sunny, with a little bit of haze and a persistent breeze that gave Chase goose bumps.

Sacramento had been forty degrees and slate-gray all over when he'd left. It was like being in a new place gave him a "Chance" to be a whole new Chase.

Dex had been the one to pick him up from the airport, with Cameron and a guy named Scott in the back, and Chase had expected to go straight to the house that doubled as a set, but they hadn't. They'd gone grocery shopping first.

It had seemed like such a pedestrian thing to do—so very, very normal—and Chase had almost giggled as Dex had sent him sprinting through the store looking for beef marinade and artichoke hearts and spices for the half-a-cart full of beef, pork, and chicken that he'd thrown in.

"What the hell is all this for?" he laughed as Chase came back with three different bottles of dressing—Italian, Ranch, and Thai.

"Dex has a bug up his ass," Cameron muttered on his way to go get potato chips.

"I wish he had my dick up his ass," Scott muttered, looking at Chase wickedly, and Chase smirked. Scott was a tall guy with dark hair, a long jaw, bold nose, and a wiry build, and Chase had watched some of his videos; he was impressively hung (and not all the guys were) and he apparently loved to be on top with a passion and intensity unrivaled on the roster. It almost went without saying that Scott wished he had his dick up *somebody's* ass, and apparently Dex was no exception.

Chase shook his head and ran back to the cart and actually asked *Dex* what it was for. Dex shrugged. "The house is full of guys, Chance. Everyone's hungry, eating out alone can suck. Let's get together and grill, right?"

Chase stopped and blinked. "Your family did this a lot, didn't they?" he said, feeling dumb. Donnie's family had backyard barbecues all the time; it was just something that happened on Sundays, and, well, it wasn't like Chase was missed at home when he went to Donnie's instead.

Dex colored. "Yeah. I'm going to Montana for Christmas, but I didn't get to go during the summer."

And Chase didn't need any more explanation than that. "What else do you want me to get? Do they have corn on the cob? Is that even in season? Because my friend's mom used to grill corn on the cob, and I *loved* that shit."

Dex's grin was cocky and insouciant as ever. "Yeah, junior. You go look for some corn on the cob."

He ruffled Chase's hair and Chase said, "Bite me!" and then he went and found some goddamned corn on the goddamned cob.

"Lots of it!" Dex hollered across the store. "There's like twelve of us!"

And of course they all worked out and fucked like lemmings, Chase thought. *More corn!*

The Cypress Point house was, well, amazing, really. It looked like a movie set, two stories with big-pane glass windows overlooking a garden that looked like something from a Jane Austen film, except sunnier.

"Fucking. Wow." Chase gazed at the house in complete amazement. "He *owns* this?"

"Leases," Dex confessed. "And honestly? I think he slept with someone's son to get the deal."

Cameron snorted from the backseat. (Cameron wasn't that tall, so he got the backseat. Chase and Scott had done rock/scissors/paper/lizard/Spock to get the front. Chase had won with Spock to crush Scott's scissors.)

"What?" Chase asked, curious. He liked John—and he enjoyed the hell out of working with him—but that didn't mean he didn't like to gossip.

"Nothing," Cameron said with an evil little smile. "I think he just gets a kick out of filming gay porn here, that's all. I'm pretty sure the neighbors don't approve, even the ones who are gay!"

Chase blinked. "Well yeah, but what porn *is* approved?" he asked rhetorically, and Scott and Cameron laughed a lot more than Chase thought the crack deserved.

"Is there a swimming pool?" he asked while they cackled like chickens in the back seat, and Dex smiled and winked as he piloted the SUV through a driveway that felt like half a mile long and parked in a carport/garage that adjoined the house.

"God, I hope so," Dex said as he killed the engine. "That's where you're going to shoot right after lunch."

"Yeah," Cam said, looking excited—and then disappointed. "But don't eat, remember?"

"He knows!" Dex reassured him, and Cameron looked woefully at the stacks of supplies they had to load into the house.

"God, Chase, I hope you can come in an hour's worth of shooting, okay? Man, I'm fucking starving!"

I could probably come within ten seconds if you wrapped that sweet mouth around my cock and begged.

"Man, I'll do my best, but I've never had sex outside before. Make sure no gators come up and eat my wang, okay?"

"Now *that* would be a crime against nature," Dex said, and Cameron chortled.

"Yeah, but at least I'd get to eat!"

Cameron was as hyper as a sugar-amped third-grader, and Chase couldn't help wonder what he'd be like in bed. Scott, on the other hand, was laconic and easygoing—but his sarcasm was a lot harder and meaner than Cameron's. Chase thought he could probably get off with either one of them—they were both good-looking, and he'd learned from touching Dex that experience counted—but he was glad Cameron was going to be his partner for the day.

But that wasn't until later. In the meantime, they spent two hours lassoing whoever was hanging around to help. Suddenly, Chase was surrounded by ten other young men his age, laughing, telling dirty jokes, singing raucously, and bumping each other in the shoulder or snapping each other with towels. Cameron was an incorrigible towel-snapper until two of the other guys each took an arm and sat on him, tickling him until he threatened to wet his pants. But while that was going on, they shucked and washed corn, peeled and cut fruit, set steaks in marinade, and dumped chips and raw vegetables in bowls that went on the front table.

"Okay," Dex said, as he and Scott were doing dishes, "that's it. Cam and Chance need to get ready for a shoot; Tango and Kenny are coming off of one in about half an hour. The rest of you freeloaders can start up the grill around six. Make sure the bug lights are on, start the fire pit if it's cold, and *don't* eat all the chips before we're done with the shoot. This is Chance's cherry top here, and he's gonna be starving!"

Chase was already starving. He'd taken Dex's advice to heart and had a smoothie before he got on the plane, and had some oatmeal when they'd gotten to the house. He could see why Cam was so worried about lunch. It was a careful balance, wasn't it? But then, as Chase put on his swimming trunks and had Cam oil his back before they went to stretch out, he figured he was probably as good at balancing as anyone else on the planet.

ON THE screen, Cameron had pulled Chance's pants down, and had his lips brushing where Chance's pubic hair used to be. Chance was arching off the bed, scrabbling and lost, when suddenly he said, "Don't I get to blow you?"

"Good instinct there," Dex murmured as they watched Cameron move his wiry little body so his cock dangled over Chase's mouth. Chase shrugged off Dex's compliment, remembering the way Cam had tasted and how swallowing his erection to the back of Chase's throat had felt imperative, like that cock was even better than food.

THE sixty-nine position could have been awkward, but Cameron was buff and a pro. He pulled his camera arm out of the way and held himself over Chance's body, doing one-armed push-ups as they both performed the requisite porn-fellatio. Chance seemed to be transported—he was making breathless sounds for pleasure when Cameron sucked him down, and greedy ones when it was his turn to swallow Cam.

Chance pulled Cam all the way to the back of his throat, and Cameron dropped his camera arm for a moment and let Chance's cock slide out of his mouth. He raised his head and grunted then, and then started to plead, and then, before Chance really seemed to know what was happening, he had scrabbled for the lube and condom waiting under the pillow on the bed and covered Chance's cock with condom first, lube second.

"Oh God!" Chance gasped, because Cam had scooted forward, seized his cock, and impaled himself in what felt like record time.

"I COULD hardly believe he did that," Chase said, watching it now. "I mean, seriously—so much for my cherry, right?"

Cameron grimaced and clapped him on the shoulder with one hand while stuffing his face with chips with the other. "Yeah, well, my cherry was gone a long time ago. You totally made me crazy there."

He looked at Dex and nodded. "Mouth like a virgin's ass," he said seriously, and Chase and Dex both closed their eyes and grimaced.

"I didn't think he could actually say anything that would gross me out," Dex muttered. "How on earth could I think he couldn't say anything that would gross me out?"

It didn't matter. They watched the rest of the video, from the change in positions (Cameron lay on his back and spread his legs to give Chase better access) to the end, the come-shots, and Chase's final kiss. Chase had collapsed forward and was nuzzling Cameron's collarbone and then kissing him on the mouth—the way they'd been told to do—when Dex suddenly said, "Cameron, aren't you ready to eat yet?"

"Yeah. Are we going to use anything from the shower?"

"You two bored the shit out of me in the shower," Dex said. "Go eat!" And Chase had to agree. Unlike that scene with Tango and Ethan, his shower scenes seemed to be a lot of him with big eyes, just agreeing to what both Dex and now Cameron said as they soaped up their privates.

"Awesome. I'm so gone!" And Cameron dodged out of the room, carrying the bowl of chips under his arm without a backward glance.

Chase was going to follow him when Dex said, "Wait a sec, Chance. C'mere for a sec, will you?"

Chase went back to where Dex had just finished rewinding the tape, and Dex said, "Look, man. I need you to watch this part here for a second, okay?"

Chase nodded, and saw the end, after they'd both come all over Cam's abs, when Chase fell forward for the kiss and the nuzzle before the fade to black.

Dex brought the camera in to where Chase was nuzzling Cam's collarbone, and Chase remembered that moment.

God, he was just so funny! And so sweet. And he felt so good. I just wanted to give him something then—was that so bad? To give him something there?

"Don't get attached," Dex said softly, and Chase's eyes jumped from the screen to Dex's suddenly sober face.

"Dude, you're the one who told me to kiss!"

"That's not what that was."

It was lovely. He was fun. We enjoyed each other.

"Man, I've got a girlfriend," Chase said, holding his hands up in the time-honored "Hey, not me, man!" gesture.

"Yeah," Dex said, nodding soberly. "You've got a girlfriend. We all know you've got a girlfriend. But so far that's twice you've fluffed in about thirty seconds. Cam can do it because he's a horn dog. He'll hump fucking anything that moves! Ethan can do it in about thirty seconds because he's a sensualist. Touch, any touch, just sends him over the moon. He's got girls wandering through his brain, but it doesn't matter when he's got someone's hands wandering over his body, right?"

Ethan's not gay? Shit.

Chase nodded. He hadn't known that about Ethan.

"Maybe I just like sex," he defended, when the long silence that followed seemed to ask something from him.

"Maybe so," Dex conceded, but he sounded doubtful. "Look. I'm just saying—Cameron's a great guy, but he's a pro. He enjoyed the hell out of today, but in two days, he's going back to his boyfriend in Las Vegas, and they're going to spend Christmas together. What are you doing when your plane leaves?"

Chase tried not to flinch. "Spending Christmas with my girlfriend, and maybe my dad."

With Donnie and his family. Please please please please... let's spend it with Donnie and his family. Mercy can come too if she wants, but Donnie's family makes us safe!

Dex nodded and ran his hand through his hair. "Okay, good. Just remember that? We're shooting stills tomorrow—they tend to be almost more intimate than this. You have to hold your poses longer, you have to look at each other and sell it. Just remember you're going home."

But I want to stay here, with all the pretty boys!

"My girlfriend's counting on it," Chase said, and waggled his eyebrows.

But Dex didn't laugh.

CHASE managed to put the conversation out of his head during the barbecue. The sun that had so worried him on his white body had gone down, and most of the guys had put a shirt on. Dex grilled and ran them around, getting food ready, and then, thank God, they got to eat.

Chase found a chaise lounge and sat down, balancing the thick paper plate on his lap, when suddenly someone shoved a little round table in front of him.

"Thanks," he said with a smile, setting his paper plate on the table, and he looked up, expecting Dex or Cam, or even Scott, but that's not who was there, setting his own plate on the little table.

"No problem," said Tango. "Okay if I eat with you?"

"God, no problem!" Chase said, smiling at him with genuine joy. They'd both had shoots, Chase had known that. Grant, the other cameraman that he'd seen that day at the office suite, had been there to film Tango and some guy named Kenny, but other than that, both of them had been busy with the shoot and then viewing the rushes—they hadn't actually said hello.

"I saw you, you know," Tango said, digging into the chicken that he'd pulled apart and scattered over his vegetables and dry baked potato. "That day back at the office site. I kept hoping they'd put us together, but they didn't."

Chase almost choked on his steak sandwich. "You mean, as in shoot a scene?"

Tango looked up. "Yeah. I mean, that's how you get to know the guys, right? You shoot scenes together?"

Chase nodded. "I didn't, well, they sent me here so I'd have a place for the hickeys and bruises and shit to go away." Dex had been right. Chase had bruises on his hipbones from thrusting into Cameron's body, and Cam had left hickeys all down his chest and stomach, and one even on his pubic area where the hair would normally be.

Tango nodded. "Girlfriend, right?" he said judiciously, and Chase nodded back.

"Don't want her to know," he explained.

Tango bounced a little more on the chaise before taking a bite. God, he was never still, was he? Cameron bounced a lot, but Tango— he damned near twitched when he wasn't on camera. Was his brain that busy? Was he still horny? Chase's usual casual pose grew even more still in response to Tango's excessive movement.

"Then why are you doing it?"

I want to be free. I want to touch who I want, even if it's just under contract. I want a reason to hang out with pretty boys and not worry about if my hand brushes their ass or if my arm lingers around their shoulder too long and not apologize for my man-pits and to not have to worry about what people think of me or wonder if they know.

"I want a house," Chase said. "My whole life, we lived in apartments. I hated them. I'm going to have my engineering degree in about three years, but until then, we live in an apartment. It's like a... a... a compartmentalized hamster cage. I hate it. I want a fucking house. And a lawn. And a cat and a dog and really beautiful pictures on the walls, with nails that say they're going to be there for a while. You can't do that as a night clerk at the 7-Eleven. You just fucking can't."

Tango nodded suddenly, and his bouncing got even more frenetic. "Yeah! The house! That's everything! My mom had this apartment, right? In South Boston? But I've been doing this gig for a couple of years—I sent her money, and she moved into a house, and it's just a small place, right? But it's everything. Suddenly she's sounding twenty years younger, and she sent me a picture last year and she's dyed her hair and she's like dating again, and I think it's all about that pride, you know? You're in a place of your own, right? It's like no one can take that away!"

Chase nodded, and on impulse reached out and grabbed Tango's hands, because on his last bounce, his knees had brushed the table, and Chase was still trying to eat.

"It's all good," he said, because he didn't have anything else. "Yeah. It's something someone can't take."

Unlike the people inside it.

Tango stopped bouncing and went back to his food. "So, you grew up with your dad, huh? I don't even know my dad. What happened to your mom?"

I hate this fucking conversation.

"She died when I was a kid." Chase kept eating. God, for the longest time, his dad had brought home squat for pay, and all it had been was peanut butter and jelly and ramen noodles. He'd never pass up good food.

Tango looked up from his plate. "Yeah? That sucks. How'd that happen?"

And this is why I hate this fucking conversation.

"I got home from school and she'd slit her wrists in the bathtub."

Tango grew very, very still. "There's so much that's fucked up about that, I don't even know where to begin."

Chase shrugged, tried to make things light. "Yeah, well, we all gotta have our fuckups, right?"

Tango shook his head. "Naw, man. Growing up with my mom alone, that wasn't a picnic, but it was alright. What's your dad like? Is he cool?"

He'd sneak into my room and kill me in my sleep if he knew what I was doing right now.

"He's pretty much the reason she killed herself," he said, and then he almost clapped his hand over his mouth. God, just like how his mom died. It was one of two things he never said—*ever.* He'd had this conversation a hundred times—he could remember every one.

DONNIE:

"What's your dad like?" Donnie asked when they were six. "You always come over here, but I never get to meet him."

"He doesn't like noise."

"We'd better stay here, then. My mom doesn't care. What happened to your mom?"

"She died."

"Yeah. Definitely stay over here."

KEVIN:

"What's your dad like? Donnie says we have to play at his house, which is fine 'cause his mom serves us cookies and doesn't care about armpit farts."

"My dad never buys cookies."

"Mine neither. My mom keeps saying they'll make me fat. Donnie's mom is so cool."

"Yeah."

"Where's your mom?"

"Dead."

"Oh."

MERCY:

"Am I ever going to meet your father, Chase?"

"Do you have all your shots and a set of earplugs?"

"Chase!"

"Honestly, Mercy, he's not all that excited about my life, okay? Can we just sort of keep it between you and me?"

AND so on.

Of course, Mercy had met Chase's dad since, a little at a time, and he seemed to not be a total fucking asshole to her in small doses. She'd even gone all out this year and insisted that Chase invite the old man for Christmas dinner and everything, because Chase had made a career, it seemed, about lying about how badly he hated his father.

Until now, when the voice in his head had veered one way, and his mouth—always so good at giving the right answer—had veered another.

Tango was looking at him avidly, those bright, black eyes hard and insistent on Chase's own, and a flush—almost the kind that Chase had seen during the shower scene, when he was having sex—blotching up his neck and his cheeks and forehead.

"Why?" he asked. "Why would you even say that?"

Chase swallowed and wrenched his eyes down to his plate, and doggedly continued to eat.

"It's nothing. I'm sorry. You got people here, and a party. I don't even know why I said that. How about another subject? Have you seen a fucking gator yet? Man, I half want to and I'm half afraid I'm gonna wet my fucking shorts, you know what I mean?"

"Yeah, I've seen a gator, Chance. But I don't know if I've ever seen someone so reluctant to talk about family drama."

Chase grimaced. "It's family drama. Everyone's got it. How big was the gator?"

Tango shook his head. "About as tall as you—but probably not hung quite so good."

That surprised a chuckle from Chase, and he thought it was all okay. Their conversation veered into comfortable grooves after that. Chase talked about baseball and how much he loved it, and how much he'd love to go pro, but "I'm not good enough. I mean, I'm good enough to pitch through college, but...." He massaged his shoulder, which had taken a workout when he'd been doing push-ups over Cameron on the bed. "I can play the next two years in college, and then it'll be rec leagues for the rest of my life." He shrugged and smiled. "As long as I get to play, you know?"

"You could always coach or something," Tango said, those black eyes wide, and Chase felt a sudden pain he hadn't expected.

"Uhm, probably not after this week."

Tango blinked. "Oh yeah. I...." His twisted mouth was eloquent. "I forget, you know? You hang out with porn stars, you fuck porn stars—it stops seeming like something the rest of the world gets all weird about, it just stays at normal."

Chase had to agree. He looked out at the pool area—it was late now, but there were bug lights and a fire pit and happy voices telling stories. Laughter. Lots of laughter. Again, Chase had to think about his baseball team—every baseball team he'd ever been on—and the matter-of-fact way they would make plays or run laps and accept the things their bodies could do. But not everybody could do those things. Donnie's mom was comfortably plump, and he remembered the way she would marvel whenever she went to his and Donnie's games.

"Some people," he said, thinking about that in sort of an oblique way, at the same time he deliberately *didn't* think about his father in that same oblique way, "some people think it's… it's almost inhuman. Either they think it's beautiful—or, you know, we wouldn't get paid— or they think it's hideous and horrible. It's like they don't see it in the middle. Regular. Like working on a road crew but a hell of a lot more fun, or taking a vacation but a hell of a lot more work, you know?"

Tango nodded, that wide, mobile mouth twisted at the corners. "Yeah, I know."

"So, how'd you get here?"

"By plane, just like you, genius."

Chase rolled his eyes. "No, I mean… you know… here? I wanted to buy a house and provide for… you know. But I'll have my degree in a couple of years. How'd you get here?"

Tango looked off into the rest of the party. The grill had been turned off, and the food was being slowly eaten to nothing. The guys— it turned out there were sixteen of them—had all broken into smaller groups. Chase looked off into the shadows, and he saw two guys—was that Dex? And Scott, it looked like—making out, softly, tenderly. Their lips were gentle, and their hands were slow. Nobody else was looking at them. In fact, most of the guys seemed to be treating it as though it was normal, even though Scott's hand was deep in the front of Dex's shorts, and back in the darkened corner of the yard, it looked like Dex was shuddering and needy. Chase looked at them and let out a subtle whine.

"Oh God," he whispered. "And they're just *doing* that?"

"Yeah," Tango said softly. "Some of the guys... it's like, when they're on set, that's the porn place. So, they, you know. They're porn guys on set, and straight guys at home. Or, they've got boyfriends at home, and are porn guys on set. It's like, if you're going to put the job in a box...."

"It's gonna be a good box," Chase said, unaware of the longing in his voice until Tango grabbed his hand.

"You wanna?" he asked, his voice husky, and Chase looked at him in the dark, those black eyes shiny and intense, and remembered the way he'd looked in the shower, with a Goliath fucking him into the tiles. Loki the lunatic sex god... here for the taking.

Yes! Yes I wanna! I wanna lick you all over and kiss you... long kisses, long, deep, slow... forever. For the entire night, until you come just from my tongue in your mouth and my hands holding you close. God, I wanna—please please please please please!

Chase opened his mouth right when a quiet washed over the crowd and Dex let loose with a groan so deep, so intense, it could only be orgasm, a real one, private, in the center of his own stomach and not on celluloid for the world to see. The whole patio looked up to see Dex, his face buried in Scott's shoulder, shuddering, while Scott rubbed his hands along Dex's arms with so much tenderness it made Chase's stomach hurt. There was a smatter of nervous laughter around the pool, and Dex looked up and grinned, his embarrassment clear. Scott stood up and offered Dex a hand up, and together the two of them disappeared into the shadows. Chase and Tango could see them as they skirted the light circle and went into the house, and Chase swallowed.

"That didn't look like porn in a box," he said quietly.

"That's not what Dex is gonna tell his girlfriend," Tango told him back.

"I'm going to have to keep my porn in a smaller box than that," Chase said apologetically, and then, with more reluctance than he knew what to do with, he added, "I wouldn't, uhm... Okay. I'd mind. But it's okay, if you want to, you know. Go talk to someone else, right?"

Tango's negative nod was all theatre. "No worries. I'm happy right here."

So they stayed up and talked. They talked until the others had gone to bed—sometimes together, many of them alone. They talked until the lights had been turned off and the guys who'd been chatting by the table cleaned up the rest of the food and put it in the fridge for leftovers the next day. At one point, Tango got up to go get them some water and came back with thick blankets, and they wrapped themselves up in the blankets and talked until the lights in the house at their back had winked out, and only the porch light was left on.

Chase learned so much. He let Tango ramble on a lot—Tango did that. Just talked and talked and segued from one thing to another. It wasn't rapid, or random, he just connected things and then ran with them.

"So yeah, there I was, going to school in Boston, thinking, 'Geez, this would be fuckin' awesome if I knew what the fuck I wanna do with my life!' when some guy just took me to dinner and then went down on me. He was a nice guy, right, but I thought the dinner was a study buddy thing—it wasn't until I was coming in his mouth that it hit me: this was better than anything I'd ever gotten from a girl, and I really loved that it was a guy doing it. I wanted to return the favor, but that wasn't his scene. Before he left, though, he told me I was hung like a fuckin' god, and I should model for *Johnnies.* I had no idea, you know? I mean, I was workin' retail, right? Fuckin' *retail*, at PetSmart—"

"Do you like animals?" Chase had to ask, because this was their second hour talking and he'd learned by now that if he didn't butt in, he wouldn't *get* in, and Tango nodded, looking embarrassed.

"My mom has this real old cat, I mean, she got it for me when I was like, eight, and it's still around, right? Because I'm only like, twenty-three, but he's getting on in years, and he was old three years ago, when I got the job because I was trying to find the change to buy poor old Buster some prime old-fart cat food, and they had a sign up, and it was better'n fast food, which is what had gotten me through two years of junior college, right? Anyway, so there I was, working at PetSmart, thinking, 'Oh hell yeah! That was one fuckin' *prime* blow job, where can I get me another one of *those*?' and this guy mentions

Johnnies. I go home, Googled that baby, and they liked me. Flew me out to Sac the first few times, flew me out here after a year, and then I decided to move to Sac, just to make it easier, you know? Mom, she doesn't know how much money I'm makin'—and I can't keep up the lie about PetSmart too long, even though I was working there when I wasn't doing shoots anyway. So, well, got a little house on F-street— it's not prime, but it's got a little yard, right? And it's okay." Tango shrugged then, and for the first time, Chase saw a crack in the "It's okay."

"What?" he asked, feeling drowsy and comfortable and strangely intimate with this guy he hardly knew. He sort of wished he could pull Tango over to his chaise. It was still chilly, thick blankets or no, and they were getting so close, so quiet. It would just feel nice, wrapping his arms around Tango's shoulders—Tango worked out and everything, but his shoulders were just built narrow, even if his muscles widened them out. He made Chase want to hold him, just because Chase could.

"I just... you go to school, right, Chance?"

Chase nodded. "Yeah. Sac State. Not too far from where you live... I forget which street... like, take one of the fifties across town, I think—hell, I think you can bike."

"Yeah, I know. It's a little town—you don't get all bent out of shape about that, do you?"

Chase shook his head. It was what it was. He'd grown up there.

"Yeah. Anyway, I just... I like this right now. I just want to have something later. I mean, I've got the money, 'cause I just send some to Mom and then the rest—I've got my little house, and I live kind of simple. John gives us kick-ass health insurance, otherwise, it would be like, you know, my biggest expense next to my frickin' car, but...."

"You want to plan for afterward?" Chase offered, and Tango's smile, the kind with the long canine teeth that looked like they could maybe have used dental work but he probably couldn't afford it when he was a kid, was brilliant.

"Yeah. Man, I want to do something with animals, right? I mean, you know. When I was a kid, I wanted to be a veterinarian, but all that fucking post-graduate work, right? So I don't know. Maybe run a shelter… shit. Something. But first I've got to… you know."

"Get a degree. Take a class. Do the grown-up thing?"

"Yeah. You know. You've got a girlfriend, a plan. You're a grown-up."

I'm faking it, Tango. Guys can't fake orgasms but they sure as shit can fake adulthood.

"You can do it, you know," Chase said sincerely. "I mean, it would be fun. My friend Don…." *Shit.*

"Don?"

Chase swallowed. "Donnie. My friend Donnie goes to Sac State. We don't have any of the same classes or anything, but we meet sometimes for lunch. Anyway, we could show you around, right?"

"Yeah," Tango said, looking excited but still sleepy. "Yeah. It would be good to have some friends there. Maybe I'll get my shit together and see if I can enroll for spring semester, or even next fall."

"That would be great!" Chase felt a sudden animation and affection for school that he hadn't really had since Mercy had dropped out. "I'd love to introduce you to the guys and to…." *To Mercy? Really?*

"The guys, yes," Tango said dryly, and Chase felt like he blushed from his toes to his nose.

"Yeah, just remember, if you meet Donnie and Kevin, they can know we work together, they just can't know—"

"Anything else." Tango rolled his eyes. "Dude, like I haven't seen a closet before."

Chase laughed, and they started telling stories about the best lies they could come up with in public that would explain the money and the friends, but Chase fell asleep in mid-sentence, so he couldn't remember any of the good ones. Shortly after that, Tango shoved his shoulder under Chase's arms and hefted him up.

"C'mon, big guy. Let's go upstairs. We've got perfectly good rooms, and they'll let us sleep in, okay?"

"Yeah," Chase grumbled, and allowed himself to be led, clutching his big fluffy blanket, as they made their way through the house to the bedrooms the guys slept in.

"I'm down the hall," Chase muttered, "in a twin bed. I think someone's got the other twin in the room."

"No worries," Tango whispered. It was dark and silent in the house—neither of them wanted to wake the other guys. "Me 'n' Scott were sharing a king—I'm pretty sure he'll be in Dex's room tonight."

Some of the rooms they slept in had doubled as sets that day. Chase had a wayward thought about that, about rooms soaked in sex, about come drenching sheets and how many times the sheets had been laundered and if the house would ever really forget. He was too tired to give voice to it, though. He just looked at Tango's wicked eyes, sober in the light-less house, and thought that, for the first time, he really wanted to give a good night kiss to someone, sincerely, and not for show, and he couldn't.

"I should give you something," he said, and Tango, who had been about to pull away and trot down the hall, his blanket clutched around his shoulders, stopped.

"Like what?" he asked skeptically. It was clear he thought Chase was just tired, but Chase shook his head. It should mean something. This conversation had meant something, and he wanted to give a thing with meaning. He smiled slightly then, and leaned forward, making sure his lips touched Tango's ear.

"My name," he murmured, "is Chase Summers." He pulled back, dreamy, pleased with himself, and totally unprepared for the stricken look on Tango's face. Oh no. Oh Jesus. He'd fucked it all up. The night had been magic. Sweet and real and full of so much that was important. He hadn't had a night like this since... since going camping with Donnie's family the summer before their senior year. God, it was the first time he'd had a conversation with someone where saying Donnie's name didn't feel like swallowing a condensed syrup of everything he regretted about his short life, and he'd fucked it up he'd....

Tango's hand on the back of his neck was strong and insistent, even though Tango was a couple of inches shorter. Chase's head was pressured, manipulated, and pulled forward, until he was so close to Tango's face that their breath mingled, and then Tango whispered, "Close your eyes."

Chase closed his eyes, and Tango's lips... so sweet. Softer than they looked. His kiss was just a whisper of tender skin on tender skin, and his tongue, sweeping lightly between Chase's lips, was simply hot and wet. Chase whimpered and opened his mouth, and Tango pressed forward, and for a moment, the world exploded and left Tango, his mouth hard on Chase, the kiss plunging, receding, plunging, receding, until Chase was leaning back against the hallway wall, panting, making little, helpless sounds of need.

Tango pulled away first, and whispered a kiss across the corner of Chase's mouth, down his cheek, until his lips were touching Chase's ear.

"Tommy," he whispered. "Tommy Halloran." And then he stood back, turned Chase around, and gave him a gentle shove toward the door at the end of the hall.

Chase barely remembered getting to bed and falling in. The only thing he remembered when the sun finally woke him up, streaming thick and merciless through the slats of the white-painted blinds, was the most important thing.

Tommy Halloran kissed me goodnight.

TIDINGS OF COMFORT

THE shorter blond boy was leaning backward, crab-style, impaled on the taller blond boy's cock, pistoning his hips up and down, his face contorted in ecstasy. With a groan, he wrapped his free hand around his own cock and started stroking, when the guy behind him said, "Dude! Want to see you do that!"

The shorter boy scrambled down, lying on his back, spreading his legs and raising his ass, and the guy behind him hurried up and positioned himself at that apex.

"Auughhh!" the smaller boy hissed happily as he was entered and invaded. "Yeah. You like it face to face?"

"Just like to know who I'm fucking, that's all."

MERCY was hell-bent on his dad coming over for Christmas Eve dinner. Her family was traveling to New Mexico to visit her grandparents this year, and Donnie's family had invited them to Christmas dinner proper, so Mercy was sort of excited about the idea, and none of Chase's half-strangled warnings did anything to dissuade her.

"It'll be nice, you know? He doesn't have anyone to spend Christmas with. Maybe it'll be, you know, like a family, right?"

Chase had looked at her helplessly as she looked up the phone number. "Babe, if that man ends up being anything but a two-hundred-pound deadweight around our neck, it's going to be because you're a really, *really* good person and for no other frickin' reason in the world."

Mercy had laughed, and raised her delicate oval of a face up for the kiss that he should give her with a compliment like that, and Chase had obliged.

I don't deserve you, Mercy Nuno.

"I don't deserve you," he said when they came up for air, and she laughed.

"Yeah, just make sure you get me a really good present, okay?"

He already had. He'd gotten her the boots she'd been hinting at for months, and a pair of jeans that the sales girl said went with them, and a zip-up jacket with a faux-fur lining that went with the jeans. The sales girl at Mercy's favorite store said she'd love it, and Chase looked at the giant packages he had to wrap and wondered why they didn't seem to be enough to make up for the way he'd earned the money to buy them.

It was partly that which motivated him to let her work on his dad.

The other thing was… well, the whole rest of the week in Florida.

Tango (*Tommy, he's Tommy now, and no one can take that away!*) had put off his plane ticket until Chase was ready to go back, and they'd been inseparable for pretty much the rest of the week. Chase watched people pair up, split up, pair up again. He watched guys hit Dex up to be on *Raw Johnnies,* the branch of *Johnnies* where the models got raw and dirty, no condoms allowed, no sweet-talk required. Dex had told him about *Raw,* and said that the guys—including Chase—all got tested every three months, but there was still risk in everything, so to think about it carefully. Chase and Tango had quietly agreed that it wasn't worth the risk, but for a moment, Chase had thought about someone's raw semen, dripping from his intimate spaces, and the thought had….

Turned him on.

But then he thought about who would be leaving his mark in Chase's body, and the answer was simple, obvious, and unattainable.

Of course. It only turned him on because he thought Tango would do it.

Much of their time had been spent talking—and Chase was surprised to find that the magic of that first night didn't fade with the dawn. They could still talk, about anything or nothing, at any given moment. It was such a wonder to find someone besides Donnie and Kevin who would sit and talk to him while they were playing cribbage or backgammon or video games and not get tired of it; someone who would lapse into the easy code of shared experiences without being self-conscious, or afraid the other guy would think he was odd because he could stare at a guy's ass or pecs or crotch the same way other guys started at a girl's chest.

Every minute he spent with Tango felt like a fucking miracle.

Even the minutes he said the shit he really hadn't planned on telling anyone, not in his whole goddamned life.

"No, seriously. You can't just drop a personal bomb on somebody like that and not expect them to check out the blast specs, Chase. What did you mean when you said that about your dad?"

Chase. Tommy Halloran had called him Chase. A Google-bomb of pictures flashed behind Chase's eyes: low-rent apartments, his dad, drunk and asleep, the ever-present cigarette burning in the full ashtray. The back of his hand, connecting with Chase's jaw when Chase was too small to know to run away. Long, drunken rants about how that bitch had left him with a worthless kid, and how the little fucker had better not be a faggot or Victor would fucking kill him.

"He's...." Chase trailed off and swallowed. They were at a tiny little sushi restaurant, on their last night in Orlando. Dex had lent Chase the SUV; both of them had put on their nicest shirt and a real pair of jeans. After spending a week living in swim trunks and flip-flops, just putting on tennis shoes felt like wearing a tux. And the button-down shirt was suddenly wrapping around his throat with merciless, nicotine-stained fingers, strangling his voice in his chest.

Tommy's hand, bony and awkward, was suddenly covering his.

"Never mind. Forget I asked."

Chase looked up into those wicked brown eyes.

"I used to dream of killing him," he said, the passionless tone of his voice almost frightening. "And now Mercy wants to stage a big reconciliation. I don't have the words to tell her that... that... you know. My mom... she cried for years. Years. And he...." *Jesus, Marnie, you dumb bitch, you can't even keep the little snotbag from climbing on the fucking couch? Stop crying! You think there's anyone out there who's going to take you in? God, just get the hell out of my way.* "He just wasn't... isn't...."

Tommy's hand tightened on his. "Yeah. It's okay, right?"

Chase nodded, his jaw so tight his ears hurt. "Yeah. No worries."

"I'll worry about you if I want."

That snapped Chase out of it. "Don't worry about me, Sunshine. I'm all golden."

"Yeah, especially now that you finally mastered sunbathing in the nude!" Tommy grinned wickedly, and Chase blushed.

"As long as it's in little, tiny increments," Chase said sincerely. Like ten minutes at a time.

"So, how you gonna hide that from your girl?"

Chase shrugged. "We never turn the lights on. And if she notices, I'll tell her I hit a tanning booth."

Tommy nodded. "I'm visiting my mom over Christmas. I'll have to remember the tanning booth thing. That's a good one."

Chase's ran a playful finger down the skin of Tommy's forearm. "It's sort of hard to sell when you're all pink and freckled," he said, and Tommy shuddered.

"Dude," he whispered, "not here." Gingerly, he'd reached down and adjusted himself, and Chase's eyes grew really wide.

"Yeah?" he asked, his voice reverent.

Tommy's gaze smacked into Chase's like a head against cement. "Yeah," he said, his voice troubled. "Yeah."

MERCY had no idea Chase blamed Victor for his mother and vice versa. She didn't even really know how Chase's mother died. Not even a little. She had no idea how bad things were—because Chase hadn't told her.

So five nights before Christmas Eve, when she was on the phone with one Mr. Victor Summers, Chase was not prepared to hear her end of the conversation.

"No, Mr. Summers, you listen to me. Chase is a great guy! We've got a home and a real nice place, and he works construction and goes to school. You're not too good to come here and eat, you hear me?"

Suddenly she gasped and turned to Chase, her face bloodless and shocked.

"What'd he say?" Chase whispered fiercely, and Mercy just stood there, with her mouth open, gaping at him. Chase grabbed the phone from her and snarled into the phone.

"What in the fuck did you just say to her?"

"I told your little spic bitch to stay the hell away from me," Chase's dad snarled back into the phone. "I don't want no fuckin' beans and rice for Christmas dinner."

Chase took a deep breath and stalked out of the living room and into the bathroom, slamming the door shut when he got there.

"Now listen here," he growled, "you worthless sack of shit—"

"You can't talk to me like that!" Victor whined, but Chase felt, deep in the seat of his balls, the horrible unfairness of it all. He could have been with Tommy. He could have been having Christmas with Tommy Halloran, with the big, dark eyes and that beautiful smile, but he wasn't, because Mercy deserved better. And instead of getting better, she was putting herself in the way of Victor and his bullshit.

"I can talk to you whatever the fuck way I want," Chase said, feeling a big pit of evil ugly open up from that anger in the seat of his balls. "I cosigned your last fucking lease, asshole, and if I pull that signature, you're out on the fucking street. Now you will clean up, sober up, get your fucking ass over to my apartment for Christmas, and treat Mercy like a fucking queen, and if you screw this up, I will plant my shoe in your face and stomp the back of your head into the fucking concrete stairs before I call the cops and charge you with being a lousy excuse for a human being, do you fucking hear me?"

There was a snarl on the other end of the line, and Chase had a sudden thought that this was a bad idea. He should just have hung up; he shouldn't have pushed this. His father was a bad man—there was just no two ways about it. There might have been something good in him once, and he might have been sort of a fucking human being when he'd met Chase's mom, but not now. Not when Chase was a little kid, living on ramen because that was the only thing Chase could cook. Not when Chase had been hysterical, rocking himself in the bathroom next to the cooling body of his mother while his father screamed, "Stop that fucking noise so I can call the goddamned cops!"

No. A good liar might have been able to find the final seeds of humanity in Victor Summers, but Chase was a jock, and he wasn't that bright, and he flat-out didn't....

"Tell her I'm sorry," Victor said on the other line, and Chase almost dropped the phone.

"What?" he asked, so completely lost from the blazing red path his thoughts had followed that, for a minute, he couldn't see past the scarlet in his vision.

"I was an asshole. Tell her I'm an asshole. Do you want me to bring anything?"

Your manners and a time machine, fuckhead.

"Rolls," he said automatically. The absurdity of asking a raging alcoholic to bring wine was not something he was willing to tackle.

"You got some fucking balls there, you know that?" And weirdly enough it sounded like a compliment.

"You fuck this up and I'm not kidding about kicking you down the stairs headfirst," Chase grunted. "Seriously. She's too good a person to put up with your bullshit, even for a minute. God knows why she's wasting her time on you."

"Yeah, well, she likes you well enough. Must be—"

"Don't finish that sentence, Victor."

"Whatever." And then the phone disconnected, and Chase was left wondering if Mercy would accept that half-assed apology.

He'd just stood up to find out when his cell phone rang, and he pulled it out of his pocket to see Tommy smiling on the front. He rang in saying, "Hey, man, what's up? Boston fucking cold enough for you?"

"Yeah," Tommy muttered. "Really fucking cold."

His voice sounded like a child's broken toy, and Chase sat down with a horrible chill. "Tommy, what's wrong?"

"My mom. Chase, she's been sick a year, and she didn't fucking tell me, okay? So I get here, and she's got hospice and shit, and the only thing she hasn't made plans for is where to put the fucking cat. So my mom's dying on Christmas, and I'm trying to figure out how to...." His voice faded out for a minute. "How to transport a fifteen-year-old cat on a plane without killing him."

Oh God. Tommy Halloran. Tango. For a week he'd made Chase feel like a god, like one whole, wonderful person and not two fractured, fucked-up pieces.

"Oh God," Chase whispered, his lips cold. "Hang on, Tommy, I'm coming."

"Naw, man. I can't do that to you—"

"It's no worries. I've got the money for the ticket, rent's covered until my next shoot. It's good. I'll leave tonight, come back Christmas Eve. It'll be no big. You'll have someone there, right?"

"For three days? Chase, that's insane!"

Yeah, but I don't think that's out of the court for me, Tango. I'm really just held together with ball stitching and glove oil, you're the only one to see it, is all.

"It'll be fine. Don't worry about it. Seriously."

And Chase came out of the bathroom with his cell phone tucked in his pocket and the regular phone in his hand.

"Babe," he said, trying to meld the two sides of his brain together with words and Oreo cookie filling, "I've got some good news and some bad news."

By the time he was done explaining, Mercy was looking as confused on the outside as Chase felt most of the time on the inside.

"Your dad's sorry, and he's coming for dinner, but you've got to go somewhere for *work*?"

Chase nodded. "A bridge went down. Don't worry. They'll get me back here by Christmas Eve. I'll probably get off the plane in time to go grocery shopping." *And you will never know where I went or why, and why it was so important, even if there's no sex involved. You'll never know that I could fuck the whole* Johnnies *stable, and it wouldn't feel as disloyal as this one goddamned act.*

Mercy shook her head. "Babe, you'd better. I can't be in here with that man by myself."

Chase nodded, promising that he would, and then went into their room to look up tickets on the computer. On his way, he made a call to John.

DEX came with him, because John had called him and apparently he and Tango were friends from way back. John also took care of the ticket, which was a load off of Chase's mind, just because he didn't want to explain the expense to Mercy. The two of them caught the red-eye to Boston out of Sacramento, and Chase barely remembered to pack his warm jacket, gloves, and scarf. Mercy had given him a deep, sad "I'll miss you" kiss as Dex had sat waiting patiently in the car he was going to leave in long-term parking, and Dex's eyebrows raised ironically as Chase got in, shivering from the concrete cold of Solstice December.

"What did you tell her?" he asked, and for a moment Chase wondered if there was judgment in his voice, and then he remembered that Dex and Scott had shared the same room—and the same bed—for a week before Dex went back to Sacramento and a girlfriend. No, no judgment there. Probably just taking notes.

"I'm working road construction and a bridge collapsed in Boston."

Dex was drinking coffee from a Starbucks mug, and he made the raspberry sound that said he'd just spit some back. "And she *bought* that?"

"What did you tell your girlfriend?"

Dex sobered. "An old friend from Montana called with a sick mother."

"Yeah, well, Mercy knows my old friends and she knows the neighborhood where I grew up and she knows where I go to school. All I got is my job, and that's a lie too. I ran with that." It was his own guilt that was making his voice sharp, they both knew it, and Dex nodded and grunted, and they didn't say anything else on the way to the airport. When they got there, it was all terse instructions and surfing on their phones as they hopped from foot to foot in the airport holiday traffic and hoped they got to their flight on time.

Finally, they were boarded, overnight bags stowed above them, and some of the tension of getting onto the flight seemed to have dissipated the tension of talking about lies they told to keep their lives from unraveling. The attendant came by with soda and nuts and blankets, and Chase was about to put his earbuds in, pull the hood of his Sac State sweatshirt up, and listen to music when Dex made a sound in his throat like he wanted to talk.

"Hmm?" Chase turned to him, all of his defensiveness apparently left on the ground in Sacramento.

"I was his first top," Dex explained bluntly, a reminiscent smile on his face. "God, he's fun in bed."

He's wonderful out of it.

"Yeah? He's a nice guy."

Dex looked at him and shook his head in confusion. "I don't know—I'd say more wicked than nice. But in a fun way. Why'd he call you?"

Chase shrugged and looked out the plane window, thinking that this was his second time in a month on a plane, when he hadn't left his home state for the entire twenty years before.

He knows my real name and I know his.

"Just needed someone, I guess."

Suddenly there was a warmth on Chase's cold hand, and Dex's long, capable fingers folded over them. Chase looked at him, startled, and Dex shrugged.

"I can fuck another guy on camera, Chance. Why can't I comfort a friend?"

Chase smiled, and when Dex smiled back, Chase could see the faint lines at the corners of his eyes that said he was getting closer to thirty than to twenty. "I'm a friend?"

"Yeah. Why not? We've barbecued together."

Chase managed a faint chuckle. "Besties forever, right?"

"You're a jock, Chase. Maybe forget 'besties'."

I'm a gay man, Dex. Maybe forget everything about myself.

"Yeah, maybe so." They were quiet for a moment, and then Chase said, "How do... how do you put this shit in boxes? You know. In your heart."

He actually heard Dex swallow. "I don't know, man. You figure it out, let me know."

"I don't even know what we're going to do for him when we get there."

"I don't think we have to do anything. I think maybe we just have to be there."

The sound Chase made then was so bitter it almost filled his mouth and choked him with bile. "Yeah. Until Christmas Eve morning, when I come back and help my girlfriend cook for the fucker who spawned me. God, I need a fucking box for that."

Dex's hand tightened on his, and Chase kept his face turned away, looking outside the plane window as the moonlit tops of the silver clouds shifted beneath the plane.

DEX was like Bruce Wayne or something. He had Tommy's mom's address from emergency contacts or something like that, and they landed, called a cab, and there they were. It wasn't a great neighborhood, but it wasn't a ghetto either: worn, working class, but with neatly trimmed lawns under the ragged layers of dirty snow. There were modest Christmas decorations on almost every house, including the one where Tommy was supposed to live, and tiny garages where the cars went to defend themselves from the cold and the salt that broke the ice on the roads.

Dex was the one who used the old-fashioned knocker on the wooden door, and Tommy looked as surprised as hell when he saw them there.

"Hey, Tango," Dex said with a forced grin. "How you holding up?"

Tommy took one look at Chase, standing there next to Dex, and threw himself into Chase's arms like a child. Dex met Chase's eyes over Tommy's head and excused himself inside, closing the door softly against the snowy cold.

Chase held him, just held him. Tommy didn't cry or say anything, just huddled in Chase's arms, a tight, shivering ball of energy, and Chase tried to shield him from the darkness and the cold and the pain.

Eventually his teeth started chattering, though—God, it was freaky cold here in Boston—and Tommy looked up, that smile flashing through the... oh God. Tommy *had* been crying, and Chase had missed it.

"Pussy," Tommy muttered thickly, trying to sound tough, and Chase felt his own chin quiver. He held up a hand to Tommy's wet cheek and then pulled the sleeve of his sweatshirt over his thumb and started wiping his face.

"Yeah. I'm a total wimp in the cold," Chase apologized, holding up the other sleeve and wiping off the other side. His gloves were still in his duffel and his hands were freezing and shaking, but Tommy was crying and it wasn't right.

Tommy nodded and wiped his face on his shoulder. "Then let's get you out of it," he muttered. "God knows what Dex is telling my mom right now. Jesus. There's a priest in there and everything, you know?"

Chase let a laugh escape. "We're not going to say we fuck each other for a living, Tango, okay?"

Tommy nodded and grinned. "That would be a helluva thing, though. I always hated this fucking priest. Mom loves him, though. Guess they grew up together or something." He sobered. "I didn't think you'd come."

"I said I would."

"Yeah, but that's easy to say. I just... I needed to tell someone who would give a shit, you know?"

"Well, you hit the right number." Chase put his hands in his pockets and tried hard not to dance in the cold, and Tommy looked at him with big eyes brimming with something that should have made Chase very uncomfortable, but didn't.

"Where you gonna stay tonight?" Tommy asked softly, and Chase shrugged.

"Tonight? Your couch. Tomorrow, we'll probably get a hotel room or something. Dex is here 'til the day after Christmas, then he's going on to Montana for his family."

Tommy nodded, some of the brightness in his eyes diminishing. "And you?"

Chase flushed. "Three days. The plane takes off like 3 a.m., Christmas Eve. Get back in time to help Mercy cook, right?"

Tommy bit his lip, so clearly wanting more, but not wanting to ask for it. His smile in the next second was as fractured as Chase's soul. "Well, you're here. You brought cavalry. I didn't even expect this much. It'll be okay."

Oh God, Tango. You deserve everything. You deserve someone here for you the whole time. You deserve to go up to bed and cry on someone's shoulder, and maybe make love to get over the pain. So much you deserve, and I'm leaving you the day before Christmas. You deserve better'n me.

"Yeah. I'll try and come back between Christmas and New Year's, okay?"

Tommy's smile healed itself, like child's magic, and Chase's heart took all the extra brokenness and it fell in pieces around his feet. "That would be great. Can you do that? Can you afford it? That would be so awesome. 'Cause that's when we're breaking down most of the house, before she goes into the hospital and everything. God, that's gonna suck. Can you really come back?"

Chase nodded his head, once again committing in a half second to do what a minute ago he would have thought was completely impossible. His teeth were suddenly chattering so hard, he could barely answer, and Tommy finally, *finally*, had mercy on him and dragged him inside the house.

There were lights in there, but it was still dim. The front room was lit by a yellow bulb under a lampshade. There was a hospital bed with a woman, thin and worn, lines of illness and pain etched around her eyes. She was sleeping, with a priest reading quietly next to her. Tommy and Dex were moving around the small adjoining kitchen, making coffee and microwaving some pizza bites. Chase knew that smell; he always had a bag in his freezer.

The priest looked up at him and smiled blandly. He was a thin, nervous man in his midfifties with longish salt 'n' pepper hair and rather protuberant eyes.

"Another friend of Tommy's," he said, with a bit of Irish in his voice, but no inflection whatsoever. "So good of you to come."

"Yeah, well," Chase muttered, unsure of what to say to a priest. He'd never been to church in all his life. "I guess it took him by surprise."

The priest actually looked at him and nodded. "Tommy was doing so well in school. She didn't want to pull him from his studies."

Oh, for the love of crap.

"Well, he takes her pride in him real serious," Chase said, and then excused himself to the kitchen.

"Pizza bites?" Dex was complaining. "If you're going to do freezer food, Tango, couldn't you at least scare up a microwave burrito?"

Tommy grinned crookedly. "Man, I'll remember that the next time two complete ass… goombahs decide to fly out across the country on… on what? Two hours' notice?" His gaze slid off of Chase's like car tires off glazed ice, and he looked at Dex and shook his head. The microwave dinged and Tommy went to get it, obviously itching for a reason to move, for something to do.

"It was more like three," Dex said, "and don't blame me. It was all Chase's idea. He asked John for a discount on the tickets."

Tommy grimaced. "Oh God—and he sent you both? That was…." Tommy swallowed. "That was nice of him. You don't expect that from a...." That wicked Loki smile appeared again. "A mogul," he finished, raising his eyebrows.

Dex shrugged. "You've been with us a while. I think he likes to know we're doing okay."

Well, it figured, right? Weepy porn stars didn't make a lot of tapes—although John was also a nice guy that way too.

"So," Chase said, hating to ask this question. "What do we tell your mom?"

Tommy shrugged. "Friends from school," he murmured, his voice really low. "Dex, you can study science; Chase, you're already almost an engineer."

Dex looked at him in surprise. "Really?"

Chase blushed. "Five more semesters," he said. "Not so almost."

"Still," Dex nodded. "That's great. You've got a place to go with this—that's awesome."

Odd how, with someone dying in the next room, their conversation was turning to how to live the rest of their lives.

"Tommy?" The voice was thin and quavery, and Tommy almost dropped the plate of pizza bites. Dex rescued them before they tipped off the little Formica table, and Chase touched his shoulder and leaned over to whisper in his ear.

"It's going to be okay. Do you want me in there with you?"

Tommy shook his head. "Maybe tomorrow. Tonight...." His look was haunted, stripped and bleeding, and Chase's stomach clenched, just taking it in. "Tonight, it'll be easier to lie when you're not in the room. But do me a favor, and don't leave, okay?"

Chase took his hand, after casting a furtive look at the priest in the other room. "Yeah, Tommy. I'll be here as long as I can, okay?"

Tommy walked into the adjoining room to talk to the priest and Chase turned to Dex.

"Dex, man," he said quietly, "is there any way I could do a shoot soon, so I can take the plane fare out of the check before John cuts it?"

Dex nodded. "You're getting a lot of hits—I don't think that's going to be a problem." He looked over Chase's shoulder as Tommy knelt by his mother's bedside. "I don't know if I'd want to leave him alone either."

Which is how Chase ended up fucking Reg two days after Christmas and getting on a plane before he could hardly walk again—but that was after the most miserable five days of his life.

THE next two days and three nights in Tommy's mother's cramped house were hard. There was a nurse and the priest, and of course Tommy to take care of her needs, and Chase felt like the world's biggest coward, because that meant he and Dex had to spend less time lying to her.

Instead, Chase spent the days helping Tommy box up stuff—some of it to give to thrift stores, some of it to send back to Tommy's little house on the opposite coast—and developing a burning, itching obsession to touch Tommy Halloran skin to skin. That first night, Dex went up to sleep in the guest bedroom, and Chase and Tommy?

They stayed up most of the night talking in the plain, white-painted kitchen, much as they had in Orlando, except with a lot less joy. Chase told the story of how his father managed to be coming to eat Christmas night at his house, and Tommy wrinkled his almost Roman nose.

"God, Chase, he sounds like a real bastard. I can't believe you got in his face like that. Don't you know when someone's going to start punching?"

Chase shook his head. "God, in his case, there was no warning," he said, and then grimaced when Tommy looked stricken. "Look, Tommy, it's no big, okay. Food, a roof, clothes—I had 'em."

Tommy scowled at him and shook his head. "Look, this place is small, right? And our apartment before it was small too, but you know? It's still got a tree. She's still got me presents under the goddamned tree, Chase. Why do you think I come back here every year? It's a good place, dammit! It may have been only us, but it was a good place." Tommy's eyes were red and he looked like he'd been up without sleep for too long. More than once Chase had seen him glance longingly at a pack of cigarettes over on the kitchen counter, and then glance guiltily at Chase, who had complained bitterly about the smell of smoke on the old man's clothes. So his voice was pitching hysterically and his hands were wobbly as they gestured in the air, but he was so passionate about what he was trying to say that he had to clutch Chase's knee or thigh or shoulder as he was talking. This *meant* something to him.

"It looks like a real good place, Tommy," Chase said soberly, and Tommy shook his head.

"You're not hearing me," Tommy whispered. "It doesn't need the house or parents or a big whole family to make it a good place. Sometimes it just needs two people who mean a damn to each other, you hear me?"

Chase had a sudden thought of him and Mercy, inviting his father, trying to visit her family, being invited to Donnie's family's house and being desperately glad of it. Two people. That's all Tommy wanted from life. Two people, under the same roof, living for each other. For Tommy, that was the most perfect thing life had to offer, and Chase was tired and muddled, and couldn't think of why someone would want more.

"I hear you," Chase said soberly. "I hear you, Tommy. I do. I'll...."

I'll move in with you. We can live in a little house with that old brown cat on your mother's couch. We can talk all night whenever we want, and I will hold your hand without thinking. We will be happy.

He trailed off, and Tommy appeared to be listening to the things he wasn't saying. When the silence had stretched on too long, he met Chase's eyes with a look that was faintly ironic.

"I wonder sometimes, Chase, at all that shit I think you're not talking about."

Chase flushed. "I think two people in a happy home is better than a whole boatload of people in an unhappy home," he muttered. "But I think I'm the last person who would know."

Tommy sighed and stood up, patting his shoulder. "I think that's a damned shame," he said quietly.

"Yeah, well, you can still have it, Tommy. You haven't made any decisions that you can't turn back from."

"I maybe made one," Tommy murmured—or at least that's what it sounded like, and Chase startled and said, "Hm?"

"Neither have you," Tommy said, his voice stronger, and Chase shrugged, wondering if he had the balls to actually talk about the tiny little woman in his room three thousand miles away.

He was saved by the Church, which was pretty fucking ironic, actually. The priest came in at that exact moment and told Tommy that his mom wanted him, and that the nurse was coming to give her a sedative and settle her down for the night. Tommy stood up and gave Chase another squeeze on the shoulder as he left. Chase patted his hand as he pulled it away, trying hard not to linger at the precious touch of skin.

"So, where did you say you know Tommy from?" the priest asked, his eyes sharp and unfriendly.

He helped himself to a cup of coffee while Chase said, "Work," feeling supremely uncomfortable.

"Oh? I thought Tommy said school?" the man said, with some suspicion, and Chase shrugged.

"Both. We work together; we know each other from school. It's a small town, we're the same age, it happens."

"And where do you work?" The man smiled like he'd cornered Chase on something, but Chase had heard Tommy when he came in, so Chase stuck with that.

"John Carey Industries," he said evenly. "I work the road crew when they have work. I don't know what Tommy does, really."

"But you're good enough friends to come all the way across the country?"

I fell in love with him in a week. I'd die for him.

"He needed someone," Chase said, and then excused himself to go to the bathroom. When he got back, the priest was in the living room, and Tommy was in the kitchen, looking like one more heavy-duty conversation would crush him into dust.

"So," Chase said, "do I get to hold the cat?"

Tommy smiled gratefully, and the next hour was spent talking about pets, with Tommy doing most of the talking. Chase held the aging tortoiseshell and listened to him purr, and wished that if nothing else, Mercy didn't have allergies so he could get a pet of his own. Letting Buster purr himself into drool on his lap was really one of the nicest moments of the visit.

Chase vaguely recalled offering to sleep on the couch that night, but Tommy led him up to a plain little room that nonetheless had some very female touches—a polished mirror and dresser set with burnished mother-of-pearl combs. A pale green coverlet with tiny, pale pink flowers dotting it at random intervals. A single woman's dress suit, pink with a cream bow at the throat, hanging in front of the closet.

"Your mom's room," he muttered, and Tommy's mouth twisted.

"I put Dex in my room, but I can't... I don't think I can sleep here... alone."

"It'll fit two," Chase slurred, thinking purely platonically. "Come in after you've had your cigarette." He pulled some sweats out of his carry-on and looked up to an embarrassed Tommy.

"I don't smoke in California," he apologized. "Something about being back in the neighborhood—"

"I get it." Chase stripped his hooded Sac State sweatshirt over his head, leaving the T-shirt on underneath. He stripped his jeans off unselfconsciously, and it wasn't until he was pulling his sweats on that he realized that Tommy was looking at him with hunger. Chase blushed, and looked sideways, anywhere but at Tommy's bright black-brown eyes.

"You can say no," Tommy whispered. "Just don't say her name."

Whose name? There's no name I want to say but yours.

"Come back up," Chase said quietly. "I'll hold you, if you want. Anything else that happens, that's between us and the walls."

AND JOY

TWO boys in jeans and sweatshirts sat on the bed, looking a little bit embarrassed and a little bit goofy because they both had Christmas bows on their head. The smaller one, the one with the faintly Latino cast to his skin, kept rubbing his chest and his nipples through his shirt. The tall, rangy one with the dyed blond hair was comfortably massaging his crotch through his jeans while the guy behind the camera talked.

"So, Chance, this is your second top. You must have liked the first one!"

Chance smirked, his grip on his crotch growing stronger and more suggestive. "It was pretty fuckin' awesome," he said, his enthusiasm making the other boy crack up.

"You can say that," the other boy said, rolling his eyes. "You're the one whose gonna stick that big thing up my ass!"

Chance looked at him and winked. "I've got experience now, Reg. I'll try to make sure you like it."

"Oh, you better!" Reg crowed, and then Chance stopped fluffing his cock and rolled over. In one smooth movement he'd pinned the other boy to the bed and was kissing him with an unhidden hunger.

"Dayum," Reg breathed. "If I'd known you were that excited—"

Chance cut off anything else he might have said with a hard kiss. Reg groaned, wrapped his legs around Chance's, and started grinding up against him. Chance pulled back and started shoving his hands up Reg's sweatshirt, muttering, "God you're hot!" before the kiss started up again and the clothes started coming off.

CHASE viewed the rushes of the after-Christmas video as he was in line for the plane. John had helped him book the tickets again, and instead of the exasperation of *goddammit, some more traveling during the frickin' holidays*, all Chase could summon was relief.

Tommy was in Boston, and Chase was going to get to see him again.

Because life in Sacramento had become completely sur-fuckin'-real from the moment Chase had gotten off the plane. Mercy had greeted him, breathless, harried, desperate for some help to get ready for the holidays, and Chase had spent the rest of the day working beside her. They started off grocery shopping together and then she'd put him on vegetable prep while she went and did the rest of the wrapping. He did what she asked, he anticipated her every need, and the whole time, while Chase was in their small, brightly lit apartment kitchen, brushing his head on the green and red spangles she'd strewn between the doorways and through the halls, he was wrenched back to a tiny house in Massachusetts where the light was a dingy yellow and the Christmas decorations were small and old, and a woman who had barely summoned four words to say to Chase was dying and breaking her son's heart.

One minute, Chase was pulling Mercy's wrapped gifts from the back of their closet, and the next minute....

TOMMY'S hard body, in sweats like Chase's, was pulled up against Chase's chest in the alien landscape of a stranger's room. Tommy's chest, ripped with muscle, was shaking hard with silent sobs against Chase's clasped hands, as he fell completely apart. Chase was kissing the shorn back of his neck, where the thick black hair was nothing but stubble, and hushing into his ear, telling him anything, anything, as long as Tommy would stop crying in Chase's arms.

CHASE thought that the schism between what he was doing (Bath & Body Works Christmas CD on the stereo? Check. Hot chocolate warming in the pan? Check. Phone call made to Donnie's harried mother to double-check they were bringing rolls to dinner the next day? Check. Onions, mushrooms, and olives chopped for turkey stuffing? Check.) and where his brain seemed to live, would self-repair when his father arrived. He couldn't have been more wrong.

TOMMY rolled over in the bed, his eyes shiny in the darkness and his face dark and flushed and crumpled from crying. Chase dotted his cheeks, his forehead, his chin with small kisses, wordless breaths, giving what comfort he could.

HIS father showed on their doorstep about a half an hour later than Mercy had asked him to be there, and for that half an hour, Chase thought that maybe he was the happiest guy on the freakin' planet. For that half an hour, he actually came out of that darkened bedroom with Tommy, where he'd spent three furtive, painful nights doing things that wouldn't look good on camera but which made their hearts feel good. For that half an hour he was Mercy's devoted boyfriend, the guy who was saving to buy a house and getting an engineering degree to build a life with his girlfriend. The straight guy who thought that his girlfriend's touch was maybe the most beautiful thing in the world. Then the doorbell rang, and Chase opened the door, and those eyes, so very like his own but bloodshot and flat, rheumy in swollen lids, stared back at him, and that part of Chase's soul that was ripping its claws on the walls in an effort to be free went hiding back in that bedroom in Boston again, taking solace from the things that hurt it.

TOMMY had brushed his teeth, so his breath didn't reek of cigarette smoke, and when his mouth found Chase's in the dark, it was open and wet, and Chase fell into it, into the feel of masculine lips under his and the faint prickle of what little stubble Tommy actually grew. Tommy gasped and breathed out into Chase's mouth, and Chase swallowed the sound. The priest was still downstairs: their every move would be as silent as they could make it.

"HIYA, Victor," Chase said, his voice sounding cocky and casual, for all the world like this was a business contact or a professor or, hell, even the name of his post-Christmas shoot-mate, but it wasn't. It was his father.

"You gonna let me in, or let me stand out here in the cold, genius?"

Chase took a deep breath and remembered that Mercy was a nice person who had done this because she thought it would make him happy. She was in the kitchen, taking over the finer points of dinner, and Chase took this opportunity to make his opinion clear.

"You say one mean thing to her about dinner, Victor, and I will throw you down the stairs facedown. I'm not fucking around. She thinks you're just misunderstood, but you and I know the truth, don't we?"

Chase's father scowled. "Yeah? What's the truth?"

"That if you could have gotten away with it, you would have drowned me at birth like an unwanted puppy. So we both know who you are, okay? But for this night? We're going to pretend you're a human being."

Victor's eyes got big, and a little shiny, and if Chase hadn't grown up with the guy, he would have said he'd hurt Victor's feelings—but he *had* grown up with him, and he knew better.

"So are you coming in or what?" he asked sharply, and Victor walked in, shoving a market bag of something at Chase as he did so. Chase took it, looked in it, and sighed. Oh, Jesus. It would be just so damned much easier if the asshole would let Chase hate him, just to keep his worldview simple.

"Thanks for the bread, Dad," he said. "You picked a real nice kind. Come sit down in the living room—*It's a Wonderful Life* is on, and Mercy needs me to help."

He stalked into the kitchen and handed Mercy the bread, and she raised her eyebrows. "That was nice of him," she said softly.

"I made note of it."

"Chase...." The warning in her voice was unmistakable. She stirred at the gravy with unnecessary force.

"What?" he asked, grateful for the resentment backing up in his chest. It kept him in the now, and for a breath, those stolen moments with Tommy simply lurked in the membrane between his skull and his gray matter, waiting for a chance to slip into his consciousness with insidious joy.

"I'm trying here to make this work," she hissed. "It's not going to work if you're going to be a spoiled child about it."

Chase blinked, and a hideous laugh threatened to burst out. "Mercy," he said, still choking on his own bile, "would it surprise you to know I have no idea what a spoiled child would actually act like?"

She stopped and wiped her delicate little wrist across her forehead, and he sighed. She was wearing a deep ruby velour blouse, with little white lacy frou-frou things puffing through the V-neck, and she'd had to shove the sleeves up to her elbows. They were threatening to fall down and get into her cooking, and for a minute everything ceased between them as he stopped tossing the salad, wiped his hands off on a bright green kitchen towel, and rolled her sleeves back evenly.

Mercy grinned gratefully. "Thanks," she said, and then, "How about you go out there and sit with him. Bring a soda. Make him feel comfortable. He looks pretty damned miserable."

Chase sighed. God. Tommy would get it. Tommy would totally understand why Chase never wanted to talk to his father again as long as he lived. But then, Chase had told Tommy more than he'd told Mercy. And whose fault was that?

"We have any ginger ale?" Chase asked, feeling a combination of resignation and dread. "He says it tastes like alcohol."

They didn't—because really, who buys that if they're not told they have to?—and Chase walked in with Dr. Pepper and glasses filled with ice. He poured his dad a glass and took his, leaning back against the corner of the couch and watching the part of the movie where Jimmy Stewart and Donna Reed answered the telephone together.

Chase could see the sexual tension, the chemistry, and even though he always rooted for George Bailey to get out of town, he saw this moment, between two people who really loved each other, and thought that there were maybe worse things than living poor and working hard, as long as you were with someone you really cared for.

"I hate this fucking movie," Chase's father said into the blue, and Chase sighed. He picked up the remote and went surfing through the cable box to find something else.

"*Shrek Christmas,*" Chase said, his voice dead.

"I mean seriously," Victor continued, like Chase hadn't done anything. "The guy offs himself and gets another chance? No one gets another chance when that happens. You should know that, Chase. That's like the fucking end-all, be-all of last chances. I fucking hate that fucking movie."

Chase blinked. "Yeah, well… maybe when they succeed, they regret it, you ever think of that? Maybe (*she*) some people regret it."

Victor's look at him was all contempt. "If she was gonna regret it, Chase, she wouldn't have gone for the second wrist."

Chase's entire body went cold and his vision went black.

"WE CAN'T make noise," Tommy whispered, when they came up from their first kiss.

"We don't need to," Chase told him seriously. They were grinding up against each other, and Chase's movements were becoming more and more frantic, more and more needy. God, they weren't naked, they weren't on top of the covers. There were no big-ticket sexual acts—no oral, no anal, no naked skin, no penetration—just their bodies, clenching together in the night, their breath mingling,

and Tommy's bright black eyes tightly screwed shut as he snuck his hands under Chase's shirt and held Chase so tight he could barely breathe.

Tommy was rubbing, hard, so hard against Chase's thigh. Chase could feel his erection through his sweats, and it was hard, and his balls were swollen, and Tommy buried his face against Chase's collarbone hard enough to leave bruises.

"Oh God!" he whispered. "God! Please... please please please please...."

Anything. Anything. Oh God, Tommy, anything. Please, just keep moving keep moving keep moving I want to feel you fall apart in my arms....

"CHASE! Dinner's ready!" Mercy's voice penetrated the fog in Chase's brain, and Chase had to jerk himself back to his living room, where his father was looking at him like he was vomiting pea soup.

"What the hell's wrong with you?" Victor asked, and Chase, caught between those stolen moments with Tommy and this degrading, depressing reality, was forced to blurt out the truth.

"Maybe she would have regretted it," he snapped, wanting Tommy's skin against his with the forcible ache of a sprained ankle or bruised flesh. "But she knew you were coming home and that killed the pain."

With that, he stood up and walked to the tiny kitchen table adjoining the apartment dining room. Mercy had set up a table with a turkey in the center, and lovely new placemats. There were candles in the centerpiece and spangled napkin holders, a tiny turkey, and Chase's stuffing, which he'd practiced before Thanksgiving and really wasn't half-bad.

Chase leaned over and kissed Mercy's flushed forehead. She looked triumphant and proud and happy, and he wouldn't kill that for the world.

"It looks really good, babe," he said, wanting her to know he was grateful. God, he was always so grateful to her. Why couldn't some of that gratitude translate to need?

Mercy looked at Chase's father, still sitting on the couch and looking shell-shocked. "Mr. Summers?" she asked curiously. "Mr. Summers? Are you going to come eat?"

Chase's father stood up and wobbled to the table, glaring at Chase like Chase had kicked his puppy. "How do you know it wasn't you?" he asked, throwing himself on the kitchen chair with enough force to make the cheap wooden frame squeak.

"What?" Chase asked. He'd almost forgotten what he'd just said.

"How do you know it wasn't you? You were a needy little bastard. She was plenty happy until you came along, and suddenly all she could do was cry. Maybe it was you."

Victor crossed his arms in front of his chest, and Chase remembered that moment when he had screamed at the woman in the restaurant and lost that job. He had felt disconnected from his body. His actual self had been floating above, watching this really hot guy screech in this woman's face that she better keep her fucking foul mouth shut, and he couldn't figure out how to make that hot guy calm the fuck down.

He could actually feel himself starting to detach from his body, floating faintly up, as he contemplated grabbing his father by the front of his rumpled, stained oxford shirt and throwing him down the stairs.

"Maybe it was," he said, clutching the chair so hard his knuckles were white. "Maybe it was, but I was fucking six, and you were the grown-up who was supposed to come home and make it all right."

"Chase?" Mercy said quietly. "Chase? What are you talking about?"

Chase shook his head and tried to clear his vision. Tommy's bright black eyes kept threatening to intrude, luring Chase into that pocket of time when they'd held each other so close they'd had no choice but to come.

"Nothing," he mumbled. "Victor, could you leave it alone? Mercy worked her ass off, okay? I wasn't even here for three days, and I've got to go away right after Christmas, could you please, at least for this one time, not make the rest of the world suffer because you're here?"

Victor sneered—but he sat down. Stiffly, Chase began to dish up food, because that was apparently his job. They didn't say grace—Mercy's family wasn't that religious, and Chase would barely admit there *might* be a God—but after a few minutes, they began to eat.

Chase felt some of the tension slip out of the air with the food. Mercy had soaked the turkey in salt water and stuffed garlic under the skin, so it was *really* good, and the mashed potatoes and gravy were food for the soul.

"It's great, Merce," he said, touching her shoulder, and she beamed at him.

"Worth coming home to?" she asked, grinning, like she knew the answer.

God help me, I'd rather be eating Chinese takeout with Tommy. I'm sorry. I'm sorry. I'm so sorry.

"Of course it is!"

"She can cook," Victor conceded, and Chase and Mercy met eyes.

"Tell her that," Chase said evenly. "She's the reason you're here."

Victor's rheumy eyes made contact with Mercy's brown ones and then skittered away. "Good food," he said gruffly. "Thanks."

They talked a little then—or at least Mercy told Chase about her day, managing a retail clothing store in the middle of the Christmas season.

"I missed you, baby," she said with a sigh of relief, "but I've got to tell you, I wasn't here much for those three days. I was so busy earning my keep so I could get today off, I didn't know which way was up. But how about you? How was that bridge thing? You don't look that busted up. I was worried you'd get hurt, you know?"

Chase shrugged. "I'm new, I'm young, I'm pretty—they put me on the back of the truck. Put the cones down, pick them up. No big deal."

Chase had actually worked on a road crew for a couple of weeks. It was terrifying, adrenaline-pumping, and dirty work. The cars seemed to hurtle by like breakneck Leviathans, and the constant whooshing of something that big, that could do that much damage, had been nerve-shearing. The money had been good, but Chase had doubted he had the spleen for it every goddamned day he'd gone in. He'd been seriously relieved when the government money had dried up for that particular job and he'd had to go find some drywalling, which he was a pretty fair hand at, even if it didn't pay as well. It almost seemed disloyal to the people who actually *did* work jobs like that to even blow it off now, but he'd left Tommy at his dying mother's bedside to lie to Mercy who had cooked for his father. Chase was officially a scumbag. A little bit of understatement was no big deal.

"You work with anyone fun?" Mercy asked. She was constantly telling him about her coworkers—they'd even had a few of them to dinner. Kerry and Pam and Emily—Chase felt like he knew these people, just like Mercy knew Donnie and Kevin. Suddenly Chase felt like he could breathe again, like he could let a little bit of the dark, secret joy that had been taking over his brain leak into the life he was living right in that moment.

"Dex and Tommy were on my crew," he said, keeping his voice absolutely casual. "Dex is sort of the leader—he's a good guy. Funny when you don't expect it, you know?"

"What about Tommy?"

He's beautiful. He has a wicked, wicked smile, and his hands on my skin feel amazing....

"He wants to be a veterinarian, you know? They're actually from around here—I think Tommy was going to try to go back to school this next semester. I might see them around."

Mercy's smile was sincere and relieved. "Good! I know you've been missing Donnie since you're in entirely different classes."

"You still hanging out with that little faggot?"

It was like his life was a film, and in one frame Chase and Mercy were smiling and enjoying themselves, and then someone took a big chunk of film out and spliced that to the place where Chase had Dad's shirt bunched up in his fist and his dad was up against the wall. Chase didn't remember the parts in between.

One fist was drawn back, and Chase was snarling, "You take that *back!*" in his father's face while Victor covered his eyes and whimpered and Mercy pulled on his shoulder with all of her 110 pounds to try to get him to calm the fuck down.

Chase came to himself then, and blinked, and looked at Mercy, who was in tears, and wished he could take the entire moment back.

He did his best—such a sorry, pathetic thing, his best—to make it better.

"Here's the deal," he said, his chest heaving. "I'm going to go outside and cool down, and you're going to sit down and finish your food, okay? And in the meantime, you're going to remember that you're kind to Mercy. Always. And that if it weren't for Donnie and his mother, I'd be dead, or I'd wish I was dead, and I'd never have gone to school and I never would have met Mercy, and I wouldn't have fuckin' eaten half the time I was growing up because you weren't ponying the fuck up, okay?"

"Yeah," Victor said, looking honestly scared. "Okay. I get it. Your house, your rules. You win, okay? I won't use that fuckin' word no more, and I'll be good. I swear. I like the turkey, I swear." He looked beseechingly at Mercy, who was all big eyes and trembling chin, and Chase nodded shortly. He pulled his hand from Victor's rumpled button-down and backed away, aware that Victor's face had lined, and his longish hair had grayed, and his teeth had yellowed since Chase had last looked at him long enough to really see him at all.

He looked at Mercy and kissed her temple, even though her whole body was stiff with adrenaline and anger. "I'm sorry," he mumbled. "This was me, not you, okay? I'm gonna go walk this off, and I'll try to be a fuckin' human being by dessert. I don't want to let you down no more. All right?"

She nodded and gave him a tremulous smile, and he took off down the hallway and to the door.

He didn't remember his coat, which was too bad, because it was fucking cold and foggy outside, so he set up a brisk march around the apartment complex, hoping by the time he was back his head would be clear, and Mercy and his father would still be okay inside.

He got halfway around when he pulled his phone out of his pocket and texted Tommy's cell.

Hey, Tango. How's is?

Sux. You?

Almost put my fist through the old man's head.
Could be better.

Sounds violent. What set you off?

Talked shit about mom.

Ouch.

I'm stupid. It was a thousand years ago.
I should just let it go.

Some shit hurts forever.

Chase?

Sorry. Lost time. You holding up okay?

Better'n mom.

How long's she got?

A week, maybe. I'm hoping she goes to sleep.
And just doesn't wake up.

Worked for my mom.

My mom doesn't want to go.

Your mom's got a reason to stay.

So did yours.

Not much. It hurt leaving you.

Hurt to watch you go.

Dex taking my spot?
Tommy?
Tommy?

> *I'm weak. I'm sorry.*
> *Chase?*
> *Chase?*
> *CHASE?*

I'll see you the night of the 26th.

> *I'm sorry, Chase. I couldn't stop crying.*
> *Please don't hate me. Please. God, I'm sorry, but*
> *You were going off to be with Mercy and....*

I don't hate you. Could never hate you.

> *Oh God. Chase. Chase I'm so sorry.*

Don't be. Merry Christmas Tommy.

> *Merry Christmas Chase.*

MERCY found him a little later, sitting on the bottom of the stairs.

"Chase? Baby, you've been out here a while."

He wiped his eyes hurriedly with the back of his hands. "It's... it's been sort of a week, you know?" His voice rang hollow, or maybe it was just the echo of the stairwell.

"Yeah," she said, coming to sit beside him. He stopped her before she could put her bottom on the concrete stair—she was wearing something new and velveteen and sparkly, and she looked lovely.

"Here. I'll go in. I'll apologize. It's my fault."

She shook her head and took his hand. "He was an asshole." He went to move up the stairs but she kept hold of his hand.

"What?"

TOMMY, moving in the dark with Dex, looking sad, sobbing on Dex's shirt as he came….

"WHY didn't you tell me?" she asked quietly. "I don't even know how she died, but why didn't you tell me you two blamed each other for it?"

Chase looked away, wishing he was imagining Tommy with Dex again, because nothing, *nothing,* could top the crystal clarity of those three hours in the bathroom when he was a kid.

"It didn't feel right to pull that bullshit back up," he said.

"Yeah, but… that's horrible, Chase. I never would have brought him here, if I knew how bad that shit was."

"It didn't feel right to talk about it," he said again, and walked back up the stairs and into the apartment, realizing he couldn't have answered her question even if he could have found any other words.

Victor left eventually, grateful for the new coat Chase had bought him, and they were left alone in the apartment. Chase turned on the TV, saw that *Die Hard* was on, and decided to watch that.

Mercy stood up and kissed him suggestively. "You want to maybe come in after a few minutes?" she said, hope in every line in her body.

He looked at her, feeling like his insides had been ripped out and the empty husk scrubbed clean. "Sure," he mumbled, knowing his eyes were half closing anyway.

She sighed and kissed his temple and left him, falling asleep in front of an old movie, half dreaming of moments in the dark he couldn't bring himself to regret. Sometime in the night she came out and took off his shoes and covered him with an old blanket, but he didn't remember when.

THE next day dawned brighter, and he gave her the carefully chosen presents, which she adored. Chase got a new shirt, very trendy—it was beautiful and he loved it—and hip-dropping jeans that she got him, "since you don't have any more hair down there, you might as well show the world!"

Holding a straight face for that was difficult, but he appreciated the gesture.

They opened gifts, fixed breakfast, and then, inevitably, made love. He closed his eyes and thought of the nameless, faceless person he would be fucking the next day, because thinking about Tommy just hurt too goddamned much.

They went to Donnie's parents' for dinner, and Mercy and Donnie's mother (She kept asking them to call her Colleen, but Chase just couldn't. He started calling her Mrs. Donnie's Mom just to make people laugh.) went into the kitchen with Donnie's sister Michelle to chatter like girls, and Chase, Donnie, Donnie's boyfriend Alejandro, and Kevin all ended up in the garage playing Ping-Pong.

Donnie and Alejandro teamed up, which was good, because 'Yandro was a *terrible* Ping-Pong player, and so was Kevin. The match resulted in Donnie and Chase facing off like they used to do during baseball practice when Chase pitched and Donnie was up at bat. The action was fierce, and for that moment, Chase lost himself in the purely physical expression of sports, crowing in triumph and pumping his fists in the air when he made the final point to Donnie's anguished "Oh *crap!*"

There was a lot of laughter then, and Chase decided to go out onto the porch to get another beer. He looked up behind him and Donnie was standing there with his hand out.

"One for 'Yandro?" Chase asked, and Donnie took his own and shrugged a no.

"'Yandro prefers wine. Preferably the pricey wine he brought in an effort to impress my parents."

"What a suck-up!" Chase teased, and Donnie laughed.

"He was so nervous. He really wants my folks to like him, you know?"

Chase thought about Donnie's mom, who had a stocking on the mantelpiece for him, and one for Kevin, and one for 'Yandro, and one for 'Chelle's best friend Alix.

"Your mom's the best, you know that, Donnie? I mean... I know you think she's just your mom, but...." Chase shuddered and tried not to think about all of the shit he'd successfully avoided thinking about all day. "Being able to come here for dinner tonight about saved my fuckin' life, man. Just know that, okay?"

Donnie must have heard something—a tremble in his voice, when he'd worked so hard to keep one out, something. He put his hand on Chase's shoulder as they stood there and looked out into the foggy Sacramento dark and drank cold beer.

"Is there something wrong?" he asked, like he was afraid of the answer.

I fell in love with a guy I met on a gay-for-pay porn set, and he cheated on me when we weren't really a couple, because I had to leave him for my girlfriend.

"Mercy had my dad over last night. It... it didn't go real fuckin' well."

Donnie looked at him. "You never talk about it."

Chase took a hard pull on his beer. "Don't want to now."

"God, Chase, please tell me you talk about it to Mercy." Donnie sounded so concerned, and Chase clapped him on the shoulder.

"Donnie, can't we just agree that Dad is a lowlife? My childhood sucked? My mom's death was... not fun? Do we have to put all these words on it? I just... I just...." Chase closed his eyes tight, remembered how badly Tommy had needed him for those three nights, how stricken he'd looked as Chase had gotten back in the cab for the airport. "God," he said, with feeling. "I just have such a hard time getting by day to day."

Donnie's arm came around his shoulders, companionable, warm—like family. For the first time in their lives, Chase didn't just stand up straight and return the gesture like a jock. For the first time, he sagged against Donnie's body, and was relieved when Donnie took the hint and wrapped his arms around Chase's shoulders in a way that was so completely and utterly relaxed that it made Chase want to cry.

"What's wrong?" Donnie asked softly, and Chase shook his head. It wasn't that he didn't want to talk about it, *all* of it… it just…. God. It wasn't fair. It wasn't fair to fuck Donnie's Christmas up the way Chase had fucked up Mercy's. It wasn't fair to any of them.

"You ever wonder how you can have the best of intentions," Chase asked, leaning his head on Donnie's chest like a child, "and still be a complete and total fuck-up?"

Donnie's hug tightened. "What'd you do?"

"Maybe someday I'll tell you." Chase took a deep breath and pulled in all the healing he could, then stood up and reclaimed his beer from the shelf by the fridge. "Maybe someday when it's more funny than bad."

Donnie looked at him there in the darkness. "Does Mercy know?"

Chase screwed his eyes shut tight. "Donnie…."

Donnie made a sound then, a faintly disapproving sound, and Chase cringed. "Chase, man, I love her. She's great. She's even good for you in some ways. She's funny and kind and smart. But you know what she's not?"

And Chase was too raw not to answer that one with the truth.

"Male," he said softly, and the word washed some of the starch out of Donnie's speech.

"Yeah, man. That's a big one to get over, you know?"

Chase closed his eyes. "I'm learning," he said. And he might have spilled it all then—*Johnnies*, Tommy, hope, sex, betrayal—but at that moment Alejandro and Kevin came out from the garage to see what was keeping the two of them. Alejandro, slightly built, beautiful, Venezuelan man-god that he was, walked right into Donnie's space and bumped noses with him, and Donnie bent down a little, grinned that gorgeous, nothin's gonna hurt me grin and kissed him. For a moment, Chase was afraid he wouldn't be able to look away, because they were so beautiful and so perfect, and then he saw Donnie's eyes close, and the entire world disappear—including Chase—and suddenly he couldn't look at them at all.

Kevin didn't have any such problems. "If you two assholes don't stop sucking face and get back into the garage, my balls are gonna freeze off before dinner."

Donnie pulled back and grinned at him. "Yeah, and since you don't have anyone who gives a shit about your balls, that would be a real fuckin' shame—ouch! 'Yandro!"

"Just because you are old enough to use that word does not mean it's necessary," Alejandro said primly, and Donnie bent his head again and silenced him with a kiss so dominant, the older man actually whimpered.

Chase shook his head, surprised that he found a genuine smile from somewhere. "Yeah, guys. I'm with Kevin—let's play some more Ping-Pong, where the balls can't actually freeze off!" He crossed his arms and shivered, wondering if the fog was going to be too thick to drive. "I prefer to spend my Christmases warm."

THE upstairs part of Tommy's mom's house had been cold in the mornings, because it was apparently controlled by some ancient dinosaur of a thermostat that Tommy needed to bang on and swear at before the heat would kick on. Their second morning after their second quiet, furtive night, making love with their clothes on using tantalizing, forbidden flashes of skin on skin, Tommy almost cried at the thought of getting up and working the damned thing. Chase had hopped out of bed in his bare feet and stumbled to the hall, hitting the wall by the thing and swearing for form, before running back.

"Jesus, Tommy, you're gonna make me freeze my balls off, and at the moment, they're the only things making me money at all!"

Tommy had draped his shorter, muscular body over Chase's, saying, "You've got a brain too, buddy. I don't see that dropping out of your ears anytime soon."

THE memory was so powerful Chase stumbled on his way into the garage, and it was a good thing Donnie's delicate, pretty sister came out to tell them all that it was time to come in and eat, or maybe Chase really would have fucked up his life and lost it, crying on all of them, spilling the entire story out to three guys who may or may not have hated his guts when they heard it.

SO ALL things considered, when Chase went in to shoot the scene with Reg, he was desperate. Desperate for escape, desperate for release, desperate for something, anything, that didn't run his insides through a cheese grater and then throw in some salt and dump them all back in with nerve endings attached.

His body, always his best emotional barometer, almost hummed when he saw Reg in the room, eyes closed, hands down his pants, probably imagining a harem of women licking his bare, bronze skin with seductive tongues. Suddenly, all of that muddle seemed to fade away, and only this moment in this faux bedroom in the office suite, the one with the plain bed and the blue plaid bedspread, mattered. That there were cameras on them only made it more real, with lines etched by an Exacto knife into his consciousness. They were a reason to focus, to move his chest out instead of in, to drop his shoulder back as he closed his eyes and allowed the flesh of Reg's rectum to grip his cock tightly and squeeze. But mostly, it was the feel of skin on skin, and how simple and wonderful it was that his entire body quivered when touched, and that orgasm would be a release so powerful even his vision would forget.

Reg cried out, shuddering, and came on the bedspread, the camera guy in front of him dipping to catch the shot, and Chase pulled out and shucked the condom, pumping his flesh so tightly the head turned purple, you could even see it on the rushes. His face was twisted into a savage snarl when he came, and *that* was the shot John included, not just the spatter of white spend coating Reg's back.

Chase looked at that moment and frowned. He texted John.

Why didn't you stay on the cum-shot?

> *Because that look on your face is the reason*
> *We watch porn.*

I'll take your word for it. It was good?

> *Yeah. You signed the direct deposit paperwork?*

Yeah.

> *Good. Your ticket should be waiting, and*
> *The check is in the bank. Tell*
> *Tango we love him, okay?*

Will do.

Chase got on the plane with every intention of making sure that the sex he'd just had, the faceless, wordless animal thrust of tension relief, was the only kind of gay sex he'd ever have again.

LOKI, THE LUNATIC SEX GOD

TWO boys sat on an anonymous bed, looking at each other with hooded, assessing eyes. One of them had blond hair that was darker at the roots and bleached almost transparent at the tips and a lazy, cocky grin as he measured the other boy.

The other young man had dark eyes, dark hair, and a goatee, and the look he gave the blond one was of a sort of cocky dominance.

"So, Chance, you're getting comfortable here at Johnnies, aren't you?"

"Yeah," Chance said, sending a cool, assessing look at the other guy on the bed. "I'm real comfortable on top."

"Yeah," said the dark-haired young man, "so am I."

"That's true," conceded the voice behind the camera. "Kane usually tops, but not this time."

Kane sent Chance a smoldering look, and Chance's cocky grin upped in wattage and intensity.

"I'll try to be gentle," Chance said wickedly, and Kane made a low, sexy "Hm...." sound in his throat.

"Try to keep up, boy, and maybe I'll break your ass in when it's your turn to bottom."

CHASE got off the plane and Dex was waiting for him, looking contrite and nervous.

"Man, don't yell at him, please," Dex said, taking Chase's bag without any preliminaries. Chase was actually surprised.

"There's nothing to yell at," he said honestly. "He needed someone. That's why we showed up in the first place."

Dex actually dropped the bag and turned around to him, right there in the airport. "No, dumbass. I showed up because he needed *someone.* You showed up because he needed *you.*"

Chase looked away, grabbed the bag, and started walking. "We had a nice week in Florida. I made more out of it than it really was, okay? I'm...." He swallowed. "I'm new to the business, right? I just didn't see it for what it was. Now I do—what in the fuck?"

There was a recessed door—probably a maintenance closet—to the right of the hallway they were passing, and suddenly Chase was being thrust into the little nook of the busy airport.

"If you tell him that what you two did was business, it will kill him, and then I'll kill you, do you hear me?"

Chase looked at Dex's hands, white-knuckled in his shirt, and wondered where all his carefully gathered composure was now. Suddenly he was shaking, his hands, his chin, the breath in his chest, and he could hardly look at Dex's eyes. Dex shook him again, and his head knocked painfully back against the wall, and he was forced to. Dex looked like he was ready to cry.

"I...." Chase swallowed. "I needed so badly to think it was real," he apologized. Dex sighed and dropped his hold, and they both slumped to opposite walls in the little door recess.

"It was," Dex told him, twisting his mouth. "I'm... I'm the one who confuses things," he said after a moment. "If you'd needed a friend, I would have blown you too."

Chase remembered his first shoot. "You're good at those," he said, and now that he'd been blown by Cameron and Reg, he had something to compare Dex to.

Dex's grin was ironic. "Not something you can really put on a resume. Now, what are you going to say to Tango?"

There was this door in Chase's chest—he'd known about it for years. On one side of the door was the guy who'd gone after Reg like a dyed-in-the-wool sexual dominator. This was the same guy who pitched a no-hitter in State Finals and threw guys out with a casual flick of the wrist. This was the guy who could ask a cashier for Mercy's favorite clothes and tell Donnie that he was doing great and hop on a plane for the second time in his life like he was a born and seasoned traveler.

On the other side of the door there was nothing but red water, darkness, and pain. The thought of another night, or another handful of nights, with Tango threatened to open the door, and it was all Chase could do to shove the door shut before that scarlet-dyed water flooded every chamber in Chase's limited soul.

"I'm going to say I'm his friend," he said, shoving that door shut with a mental shoulder. "And I'm going to ask if I can sleep on his couch."

Dex closed his eyes and blew out a breath. "God. Chase—why?"

Kick that door shut, kick it shut... kick it kick it pound on it, scream....

"Because I have a girlfriend."

A muscle jumped in Dex's long jaw. "Fuck."

"Let's go. Don't you have to be back here tonight?"

"Tomorrow."

"Yeah, good. Let's go get some takeout so he doesn't have to stress about dinner."

MEN give different hugs. There is the tender hug that they give a lover, the one with liquid bones and hands that linger, and protective shoulders, and the unselfconscious touches of skin. There is the hug that they give children and parents, which has more bones in it, somehow, as though the man is building a framework, a gentle cage in which to keep this precious person. Then there is the hug that they give a male friend—that is a different hug altogether.

If the man is not the type to clasp hands between chests and lock muscles, then it has to be a real hug, and just like the "protecting the weak" hug has more bones in it, the "platonic man hug" has more muscles. It is, in fact, *all* muscles, no skin, no bones, because skin and bones can be vulnerable, but muscles are tense and taut—steel meat on an adamantium frame. This hug usually ends with a fist thump to the back—often two of them.

That was the hug that Chase gave Tango, and the look on Tango's face was anything but resigned.

He didn't say anything there in the entryway, though. He let Chase and Dex in and took the takeout gratefully. Chase saw that the bed was gone, and with it, he assumed, Tango's mother.

Tango saw where his eyes went and nodded. "They think maybe a couple of days. We couldn't give her enough morphine here, so they took her to the hospital so they could drug her up good." A poor imitation of his usual smile peeked out. "When I was a kid, she usually dosed me to the nines whenever I was sick. The priest bitched a little about having fortitude, but I was like 'Jesus, you gotta die, you might as well go out stoned to the fucking gills, right?'"

Chase and Dex nodded and shrugged.

"I'd say that's how I'd wanna go out," Dex said reassuringly. "But you coulda told me she was going before I left, you know? I could have been there when the ambulance came."

Tom—*Tango* shrugged like it was no big thing. "I didn't do anything. Guys came, put her on the gurney, truck came and carted the bed away." A sudden shiver racked him, and that casualness shredded like rotten muslin in a stiff wind. "Of course tonight'll be weird. I mean, I'm not that used to the house anyway, but now that she's not in it…." He trailed off and turned on his heel into the kitchen, his arms full of takeout bags.

A sudden *thwack* sounded in Chase's ears right when the blow landed to the back of the head. Chase looked at him in outrage, but Dex's eyes were all for Tom—*Tango*, dammit, *Tango*—who was wandering around the kitchen singing softly to himself. The door in Chase's chest gave a groan, like it was under way too much pressure, and Chase sighed. He walked into the tiny kitchen and, just from his three days spent there before, found the silverware and some napkins and set everything out on the table.

"Wanna eat in the living room?" he asked. "There's a television, we could find something to watch."

Tomm—*Tango, goddammit, Tango!*—was standing in front of the sink while he looked out into the encroaching darkness.

"How did you spend Christmas?" he asked, his voice toneless. "I didn't even think to ask."

I spent it pretending I was a functional human being. We all have our fantasies.

"My friend Donnie's house. His mom's pretty awesome. Stockings, presents." Chase breathed out for a second, and realized his door wasn't as solid as he'd thought. "She... some Christmases, she gave me my only presents, you know? I... I'm sorry. That's stupid. Boo-hoo, right?"

Tommy (*Tango?*) turned around and looked at him. "Mom and I watched a midnight mass on television. Halloran—Irish Catholic, right?"

Chase nodded. "Traditions are nice. Did Dex watch it with you?"

Tommy (*Tango.*) nodded. "Yeah. Turns out he was just regular Catholic. He called his family, told his mother he was visiting a friend. Called his girlfriend. Told her the same thing."

Chase swallowed, and it didn't take. He tried again. "The truth," he said, but his voice cracked strangely, and Tommy came a little closer.

"And you stayed the night with your girlfriend, and was that true?"

No. No. Nothing about it was true. True was a pocketful of dark here with you, Tommy. True was your breath upon my skin.

Chase couldn't look at him. "I can't do this," he whispered. "I've got... I've got a double life already, you know? You'd be a whole other life, and I'm not that—"

Tommy put his hand on Chase's chin and forced him to meet those dark-bright eyes. "Jesus, Chase. Don't you want something that's true?"

Yes. Yes. I want something true. I want you. I want you so bad.

"But I can't know you're with someone else. I mean... doing a scene? I can handle that, maybe."

I love to watch you. You're magnificent. You're everything sex is supposed to be—glorious, uninhibited, you're the fantasy I never knew I had.

"How do you think I feel!" Tommy snapped, dropping his hand. "I've had sex plenty, Chase. I've been with the company for three years, and I've had guys and made a few runs at boyfriends. You're the first guy that I think of you with someone else and it hurts! That's why I glommed onto you like a fuckin' limpet, man. I could stand you doing a scene, but that first night in Florida, you talked about your girlfriend, and the thought just ripped me the fuck up!"

You and me both.

"Then maybe you and me need to be the kind of friends who don't do that, Tommy! Maybe you and me need to be the kind of friends who just talk into the night and don't fucking...." He couldn't finish that sentence. He couldn't. He couldn't put a label to those stolen moments, not out loud.

Who don't make love.

Suddenly Tommy was there, right there in front of him, and his hand was on Chase's cheek. He pulled it away and pulled the sleeve of his sweatshirt up over his palm and Chase felt the rough cotton against his wet skin.

"You really think we can do that?" Tommy asked, and his voice was rough and broken.

Chase groaned and suddenly wrapped his arms around Tommy's shoulders, holding him tight, so damned tight. "We gotta do something," he graveled. "We've gotta find some way. Because I've got to have you in my life, man, and we can't do that killing each other."

Tommy sighed and simply melted into him. "We'll try," he said. "You tell me you'll hold me this week while you're here, and I'll tell you I won't think about us naked, how's that?"

Naked. I want naked. I don't want another fucking guy in my bed, and I want naked with you.

"We can try that," Chase said. He closed his eyes and rubbed his lips near Tommy's ear and told himself it wasn't a kiss.

THEY did it. They slept in the same bed that night, and Chase wrapped his arms around Tommy's body, muscular, strong, sturdy, and his skin all but groaned in completion. *This* is what he'd wanted as he'd lain next to Mercy. *This* is what he'd wanted as he'd watched his cock disappear into Reg's asshole. He'd wanted nothing more than Tommy Halloran, back against his body in a pair of sweats, if that's what they had to do.

He closed his eyes for what felt like the first time in three days. When he woke up, Tommy was watching him from troubled black-bright eyes.

Chase opened his eyes and smiled a little. "I keep trying to see," he mumbled, and Tommy said, "See what?"

"See where the brown is, because they're so dark."

Tommy's puff of amused air brushed Chase's face. Tommy needed to brush his teeth, but Chase didn't really care.

"Your eyes are the color of real spring," Tommy murmured, and then his face tightened, and some of that soft morning around his eyes grew thin and transparent over his cheekbones. "Do you know you make sounds in the night?"

Chase pulled up one corner of his mouth in disbelief. "Get out of here—I do not. What kind of sounds?"

Tommy kept that black-bright gaze on him. "You cry."

Wham!!! That there is the sound of my door closing.

"You're mistaken," Chase said coldly, pulling back and rolling out of bed. "If I made sounds like that, Mercy would have told me. When do we need to have Dex to the airport?"

"We should leave in a couple of hours," Tommy said, his voice distant as he stood up on his side of the bed. "He's taking the cat with him, so we need to dose Buster in an hour. There's a bunch of boxes outside in the garage. After we shower and eat, we should schlep them up here and start packing."

Awesome. No one has to talk if we're packing stuff, right?

"'Kay. If you want the shower first, I'll go down and make coffee and start breakfast."

Suddenly Tommy's voice and eyes were no longer distant. "Did you miss making love at all, Chase?"

Chase looked over at him, and it felt like the bed was the entire space between Sacramento and Massachusetts. "For the record, you never have to ask that question. Ever. You will always know the answer. I'm gonna go start the coffee."

He padded down the stairs feeling like shit, but it was a good kind of feeling like shit. It was penance. Penance for hurting Tommy, penance for lying to Mercy. He *should* feel this bad. He was a bad person. It was only right.

And he kept that feeling of penance during his stay. He worked harder, packed stuff up harder, sorted, labeled, readied for shipping harder than he ever thought he could for a woman he didn't know. He carefully culled all of her keepsakes, her jewelry, her plain and everyday clothes, her shoes, her books, her linens, for memories of Tommy and things that he would want, before going to Tommy in another part of the house and asking him. After they dropped Dex off, on the way back from the airport, Chase bought three gallons of basic eggshell paint and supplies and repainted all of the small rooms, fixing baseboards and clogged bathroom sinks and wonky light fixtures and anything else that came his way, so the place would be ready to sell. He kept Tommy fed, disposed of toiletries, fielded calls from the funeral home where Tommy's mom had bought her insurance, and from the hospital, where Chase dropped Tommy off to spend three hours a day, watching a woman who was beyond knowing he was there.

At the end of the six days, Chase had a couple of things and he knew a couple of things.

He had a solid sense of Tommy as a mischievous kid, who'd gotten decent grades, and Chase should know because his mom had saved every report card. Chase knew that Tommy had been in baseball and soccer and even football, and had played second string—but that he'd been the most popular guy on the team. He was in the front of every picture, the boy with that unmistakable smile framed by smiling, laughing, supportive teammates who obviously adored him. Chase had a vision of a woman who had loved her son, who had come to his games when she could, who had made snacks for him and his friends, and who had been proud of him going off to live a shining, rosy future that was not at all what she had envisioned.

One part of him was bitterly jealous, because God, that could have been his own mom, if she'd been brave enough to do it on her own.

Most of him was thrilled, because he saw pictures of Tommy growing up happy, and thought that boy could be found again. He saw pictures of a reckless Tommy climbing a football goalpost to retrieve a ball caught in the net, and knew that the heart of that boy surely beat in the chest of Loki the Lunatic Sex God, who had so captured Chase from that first scene in the bathroom.

Chase also knew that holding Tommy in the middle of the night was both torture and one of the most wonderful things he'd ever done. It was better, more powerful than those furtive hand jobs he'd asked Donnie for. It was more memorable, more personal, than making love to Mercy had ever been. He knew that he would regret for the rest of his life never holding Tommy again.

And he knew that when he got back on the plane for California, that was exactly what he had to resign himself to do.

Two nights before Chase had to leave—all the better to be in the airport over New Year's Rockin' Eve—Tommy's mother died.

Chase held Tommy Matthew Halloran in his arms as he fell completely apart, and then held him up some more as they went to the tiny service with some women from the neighborhood and people from Gloria Halloran's church. He kept his arm around Tommy's waist, ignoring the speculative looks from the neighborhood, ignoring the sneering of the priest. Tommy was selling the house, giving her clothes to Goodwill, and shipping the remainder of his shit back to California. Nobody had to say anything to Chase about burning bridges and closing doors; Chase recognized all the signs.

The night after the funeral, Chase called Mercy up and told her that his flight had been delayed and traded his ticket in for one on January 3rd. Tommy heard him make the arrangements and sat in the kitchen, pulling on an unapologetic cigarette and blowing smoke out in an agitated stream.

"So that's going to make it better," he said when Chase was done. Chase swallowed and turned to him, shrugging.

"Can't make it worse," he quipped, trying a lazy smile, and Tommy ground the butt out in a rapidly filling ashtray with unnecessary force. The neighbors had brought food over to the stripped-bare little house, all of them exclaiming sadly when they saw the whole thing was packed up, right down to the doilies. Not even the pictures on the walls were left to show this tiny, rickety little house had been a home, to memories even if nothing else.

The bareness of the house had driven them away quickly, for which Chase was grateful, but he was also grateful for the leftovers in the refrigerator, because he knew that Tommy would have something to eat in three days, after Chase left and before Tommy was planning to come home.

"God, Chase," Tommy snarled. He reached for the pack on the table and Chase stopped him with a quiet hand on top of his. Tommy looked up at him, fury burning out of those black-bright eyes, and Chase held his ground.

"I'll throw the pack away if you don't stop right now," Chase told him. "I've watched my father nurse that nasty-assed habit, I'm not going to watch you fuck with it. You don't need another cigarette, Tommy. You've got something on your chest, spit it out. Be mad. You've been sad, you've been strong—now just be fucking mad, let's get it over with, and we can go back to being friends."

"Is that what we are?"

Please, Tommy, let's not have this conversation again. It's not going to get any easier.

"God, I hope so. I just painted your fucking house, Tango—tell me that gets me a spot on your Facebook page!"

Tommy stood up and took a restless step away. "Is it the faithful thing? You can't be with me if you know I'm going to be with other men—outside the office, that is?"

Jesus, Tommy, how do you think that makes me feel?

Chase grunted. "Now that would make me a complete jealous asshole, wouldn't it?"

Tommy turned around, his eyes narrowed in puzzlement. "That's it, isn't it?" he asked, like he couldn't quite put it together.

Swallow. Breathe. Shove that door shut again and ignore the cracks around the frame.

"That would hardly be fair, would it?" Chase asked a little desperately. "I'm living with a woman, right?"

"Yeah, Chase, and why is that?" Tommy's upper lip was curling in anger, and Chase flinched. "You've got 'straight' on your resume, you've got a girl at home, but the way you touch me... the way you touch *men*... why *are* you living with a woman?"

Because I'm supposed to be straight. I can't be gay, or stupid, or a failure. I can't. If I'm gay or stupid or a fuck-up, that means she left me and not him!

"I made a promise," Chase said woodenly, backing away from the table. He thought he was backing into the living room, so he could get away, but his sense of direction was off. He ended up backed against the wall next to the doorframe instead.

"Yeah? People break promises all the time!" Tommy snapped, something inside of him so jagged that his voice sounded like bloody glass. "Why can't you break this one, when it's so obvious you were wrong when you made it!"

Because I've seen what a broken promise looks like!

"It's easy for you!" Chase snapped, surprised at how sharp his voice sounded, and how raw his chest felt when he spoke. "It's easy for you! Nobody's ever broken a promise to you! Your mom promised to love you and she did—right up until her last fucking breath, and I know you're ripped up because that wasn't so long ago, but man, she fucking loved you! I just spent five days packing up her memories, and they're all about you, and they're all fucking awesome. You've been done right by promises, so you can talk. You've never seen what a broken promise looks like, but *I have!*"

He wasn't backed up against the wall anymore. His shoulders and his chest were leaning forward, and his eyes were narrow and his lips were pulled back into a snarl. That door was being forced open, but he didn't have to let it go easy.

"This isn't the same thing!" Tommy shouted, and Chase nodded his head violently.

"Yes, oh yes it is! I made a mistake and a promise and I don't give a shit if I knew damned well what I was getting into, it was *my* mistake, and it was *my* promise, and I'm not going to make her pay for it, I'm not! I can't! Don't you see how wrong that would be?" His face threatened to crumple on those last words, and his whole body shook in that terrible agony of shoving the disintegrating door shut with everything inside him.

Tommy wasn't giving him any help, either—not Tommy. Tommy was right up in his face, chest to chest, so close Chase could smell the nicotine on his breath and see the creases in the corners of his eyes where the tears tracked whenever he squeezed his eyes shut.

"Is it any more wrong than you are now? Jesus, Chase, it doesn't take a genius to figure out why you're in gay porn—you practically come when a man touches you!"

That wonderful, awful indulgence of lust with Reg slammed behind Chase's eyes like a freight train, and there wasn't enough of him to hide his next answer.

"Not *any* man, dammit! Just *you!*"

"So you gave a promise, and that's it? You're not going to leave her? You're going to graduate and get married and have two-point-four children and the whole time, you're going to know your heart's not in it? You're going to fuck guys on camera for money just so you can know what it feels like when you're touching who you want, but you're never really going to let your heart engage? Chase!!!" Tommy passed his whole hand in front of his face and shook his head, his voice graveled down to a whisper. "Jesus, Chase. That's fuckin' awful."

Chase couldn't look at him. He turned his chin away and studied a drip down the corner of the almost flawlessly painted kitchen wall.

"Not quite as fuckin' awful as that... that thing in the pit of my stomach when I found out you slept with Dex," he said, his voice raw and honest. Maybe if he slipped this bit of reality under the door, it didn't need to explode outward, did it?

"Then ask me," Tommy insisted, and now it wasn't just their chests touching. It was their hips and their groins, and Tommy was almost as tall as he was, so it was almost, almost their lips too.

"That's not fair!" Chase pulled back so his head smacked against the wall.

"Yeah, nothing about this is fair! You've got two choices here, 'Chance'. You can live without for your entire life and wonder if, or you can be the fuckin' bad guy and *know* what you're giving up. What's it going to be?"

Goddamn you, Tommy. Goddamn you. I could have just held you. I could have held you as you slept and thought that was everything love had to offer, and I would have been happy. I would have tasted it and I would have been happy. What you're asking....

"Oh God...," Chase whispered, and his hips bucked up against Tommy's, because while he could shove his shoulders and his spine against the wall, somehow that part of his body was crystal-clear on what it wanted. "Tommy, what you're asking...."

"Not me, Chase," Tommy said bitterly. "I'm not the one who's got to do the asking." Tommy shoved his groin up against Chase's, and Chase's breath caught on a sob.

"I can't do this...," Chase whispered.

"You'd better fuckin' do this," Tommy said back, and his voice caught on a hitch of desire. "You'd better fuckin' do this. I'm not gonna make it if you don't."

"I can't do this if you cheat on me, Tommy. I can't. I know that doesn't make the first amount of sense. I know we're both gonna go to work and fuck total strangers, but I don't care about that. I know that. It's fun, but it's not...."

Tommy's lips barely caught Chase's, and Chase leaned to try to catch them before he could stop himself.

Tommy leaned back. "That's not what this is."

Damned straight. This hurts a hell of a lot more than what I do at work.

"You can't," Chase muttered. "You can't. Not no more. You can't fucking do what we do with anyone else, you hear? Mercy, she doesn't exist as far as you and me. There's the office, and then there's us, you got it?" Oh God. He was the bad guy. He was. He was asking something horrible and unfair and painful and Tommy was nodding furiously.

"I swear. I fuckin' swear, Chase. You and me. There's work, and there's you and me, and nothing else in the world—"

Chase grabbed his shoulders and threw him up against the wall to his right, plowing his mouth into Tommy's like he could kiss right through his skull.

Tommy kissed back, and they were furious and ferocious, their teeth and their tongues tangling, tormenting, fighting in lovemaking like they couldn't fight in conversation. Tommy caught Chase's lower lip and bit down, hard, and Chase grunted and shoved his crotch against Tommy's abdomen hard enough for them both to gasp in discomfort, but none of it hurt as badly as the things they'd just said, as the space between them earlier, as the thought of living without. The memory of that pain made the pressure of Tommy's teeth on Chase's throat sweet, the bruises left on his arms by Tommy's bony fingers were foreplay, and the pain in Chase's balls as he ground up against Tommy's thigh was damned near tender.

"Skin!" Chase growled, mostly crazed, half desperate. Tommy's hands went to his own belt and he fumbled, while Chase kicked off his high-top tennis shoes and unbuckled himself simultaneously.

Tommy was faster—he was naked from the waist down with his hands propped up against the wall before Chase could even shove his pants down and shiver as the underheated air hit his swollen cock.

"God," Chase gasped, pressing himself along Tommy's back and kissing the rasp of his jaw and nipping his ear. "I don't have lube—really?"

Tommy was pushing a tiny prep-pack into his hand and he whined at Chase in explanation.

"I've had it in my pocket for days."

Excellent. Only one more question. "Condom?"

"No."

"No?"

"You use them with her?"

"Yes."

"No condom."

"*Tommy!*" For a moment his shock almost outweighed his need, but Tommy was bucking his ass at Chase imperiously.

"My only rule. You and me, all skin. You'd better not give me the fuckin' clap."

It had a poetic simplicity, actually, and suddenly the thought of being inside Tommy, skin to skin, almost made Chase come. He coated himself with the little packet of lubricant and then, conscientiously, used a finger around Tommy's rim to see if he was ready.

Tommy's groan rocked Chase to his bones, and he added another finger, knowing his whole hand was shaking, and Tommy slid down the wall a little, sticking his ass out further.

Chase spread his fingers and Tommy started to beg.

"Please... oh God... please... all of you. Now...."

Chase was so close. His whole life, he couldn't remember wanting something so badly, not with Donnie, not with Mercy, not with the scenes he shot. Not once in all his life had he ever *needed* with this much power, and he could no more tell Tommy no than he could tell his heart not to thunder in his ears.

He felt every millimeter. He felt his cockhead sliding past Tommy's muscle and into Tommy's body, and he felt that muscle clamp down on his shaft when he was inside. Tommy's body was soft, grainy, warm, and welcoming, and Chase slid all the way into him, shaking as Tommy's grateful howl rocked the empty little house.

"Oh God...." Tommy panted. "C'mon Chase... would you just fuck me!"

There was a sound then, from the front door, as someone did one of those "knock on the front door and turn the knob" things that people did when they felt *really* comfortable in a home, and Chase paused and looked up just as the priest entered, a rather curious expression on his face.

Tommy's face was pressed up against the wall, and he turned it toward the priest just as he yelled, "*Jesus fuck me harder!*"

For Tommy, Chase forgot the priest as he got an eyeful of the two of them and backed out of the house and fled. For Tommy, Chase pulled his hips back and slammed them forward, shivering as Tommy groaned again, from the pit of his stomach, hard enough to vibrate in Chase's balls.

Chase's hips started to rocket back and forth and Tommy kept urging him on, loud, vocally, shamelessly needing, begging, *pleading* for Chase and Chase alone to make him feel all good.

"God, Tommy, gonna—"

"Me first!" Tommy demanded, and reached down between his legs and started stroking with a hand that knew what it was doing. Chase remembered that hand, as they had touched in the dark, and on Chase's body, through his sweats, it had always been gentle. But Tommy's arm was quivering with tension as he stroked himself, and Chase thought he probably wanted it hard, rough, the way only a man could treat himself sometimes, and the thought just pushed Chase that much closer to the edge.

Chase heard Tommy's long drawn-out cry of *"Fuck!!!"* just as he heard an honest-to-God spatter on the kitchen wall, and for some reason it was that second sound that did him in. He keened once and then groaned low from his balls before spasming into Tommy and coming with enough force to drill his insides with holes.

His hands, which had been hard on Tommy's hips to hold him in place, wrapped around Tommy tightly and held him so hard Chase could hear Tommy's breath catch when Chase cut it off. Tommy gave a grunt of protest and Chase pulled back, sliding out spent and deflated. Chase didn't look at himself as his cock fell out of Tommy's body. Once it had been used up, it seemed sort of pathetic in a way it never did when they were on camera, and he didn't want to be reminded that, without it and its spectacular size, he and Tommy might never have had enough in common even to meet.

Tommy turned around in his arms then, and this kiss was very different than the one they'd started out with. This kiss was exploratory, a mild brush of lips and tongue, a tasting, a gentle act of familiarization, and Chase's relief flowed out of his chest, making his next breath feel free. He'd been so afraid they'd lose this in the heat of what they'd just done. He was almost weak with the glorious idea that the heat of passion didn't burn away the sweetness of those first moments with Tommy Matthew Halloran.

Suddenly Chase started a light laugh, not sure whether or not Tommy would think this was funny now that the sex was done.

"Crap, Tommy. It's a good thing you were leaving the neighborhood anyway."

Tommy laughed and rested his forehead against Chase's neck.

"Yeah. Well, he was a prick anyway. I'm glad he's fuckin' gone." Tommy rubbed his cheek on Chase's shoulder, a strangely vulnerable gesture that belied the tough words, and Chase backed up and kissed him on the forehead.

"All the better to spend the next three nights in a hotel," he said. Why the hell not? He'd already committed to another scene with some guy named Kane; why should he not spend some of that money on Tommy, who didn't expect anything at all from him, not even fidelity?

Tommy looked up, such a sense of grateful wonder on his expression that Chase's knees almost went weak. God—what he would not do for Tommy to earn an expression like that? It made him ashamed he hadn't thought of it earlier. Hell, they could have spent the entire week in a hotel room and saved Tommy the painful, rusty walk down memory lane.

"Can we do that?" he asked, and Chase nodded.

"Why not? The stuff is packed up—we can come in tomorrow and get it to the post office or drop it off at the thrift store, whatever. In the meantime, I pushed back my ticket because you couldn't move yours up. Why don't we... I don't know. Just spend some time...." His voice trailed off as he realized what this was, and then firmed up as he committed to it like he couldn't commit to leaving Mercy or being faithful or anything else that would make this situation easier on Tommy. "Just some time alone," he finished with conviction, and Tommy's kiss was so pure, so grateful, that Chase thought he would fuck a hundred guys for the money to earn him *that*.

The hotel was nice, but it was background. What mattered was that their first few steps into it, Chase watched Tommy relax completely, watched him go boneless on the bed. He kicked off his shoes, stretched out, and smiled like he was going to crack wise, and then those dark-bright Loki eyes closed and he fell fast asleep.

It might have been the first real sleep Tommy got since he came out here to this godforsaken icehole and found his mother was dying. (Chase knew that there were supposed to be really spifftacular American history landmarks and shit in Massachusetts, and he had a vague memory of pilgrims and Pocahontas happening here somewhere, but so far all he'd seen had been Tommy's South Boston neighborhood and snow. He wondered if he should vow to come back and see the place in a better light or something, but so far, he hadn't seen anything to make him think Sacramento wasn't just as good as any other place in the world, no matter *how* much he'd hated it as a kid.) Chase sighed and sat down on the bed next to him and thought restlessly about sleep, but he couldn't. He was just thinking about hunting out the promised gym when his phone buzzed in his pocket. He sighed and picked it up.

"Hey, Mercy," he said, smiling a little when he heard her voice. No matter who she was to him, and who she should have been, they had started out as friends, and her voice was warm and friendly when he was emotionally stripped. She sounded like home, and he needed home.

"Chase—how you doin', baby? More importantly *what* are you doing? Have you *seen* your check in the bank? It's huge. Are you fixing roads naked in the dark, or what?"

Chase laughed a little. "If I was out there naked in the dark, the light off my bare ass would scare people off, Merce. No worries. But yeah, it's a little dangerous. In fact," and here he had an inspiration of genius, since he professed not to be that great at lying, "in fact, me and some of the guys are renting a hotel instead of sleeping in the dorms, right? Figure we might as well come back some place that's gonna pamper us, yanno?"

She didn't even give him time to see if the lie was plausible or not. "Yeah, baby. You take a Jacuzzi and all that shit. If you can bring home this sort of bacon, I'd say you've earned it, you know?"

Chase had never felt such a rush of guilt and triumph at the same time. It almost opened the door, and he couldn't afford to do that right now. Not right now, when he had to be strong for Tommy and solid for Mercy and....

"Thanks," he said softly. "You going out on New Year's?"

"Yeah. Me and Kerry, her husband Jeff. She's got a whole round of clubs—you'd like it!"

Chase, in fact, did not like clubbing. He'd gone to impress Mercy at first, but then he'd discovered that bodies of all types, all shapes, all sizes were grinding up against his while he was dancing.

The torture was exquisite. Even if it was a woman behind him, the uncertainty was the turn on. It could be *anybody*. It could be someone who wanted him. It could be a man who wanted him. Every time they went, he came home ready to hump the carpeting, and Mercy had enjoyed the attention. But the guilt....

I'd rather drag my dick through carpet tacks and soak it in lemon juice than feel any worse about myself than I do at this moment.

"Sounds great, babe. You'll have to give me highlights!"

"Yeah."

"So how was return day?" She'd been working the day after Christmas when he'd left—it was always so hard on her. He'd seen the crowds, and it had always worried him, because she was so tiny and those people always seemed so angry.

He could almost hear her rolled eyes on the other end of the line. "It was a big, giant pain in the ass. My feet hurt and you weren't there to rub them. Any other questions?"

Chase laughed a little. "Not a one. Sorry I wasn't there."

"That's okay. You were off doing something for us. It's all good."

I was off fucking one guy for money and falling hopelessly in love with another guy for no other reason than that he seems to have the key to the door in my soul.

"I'm glad you're okay, though. I didn't like leaving you over the holidays."

"You were here for Christmas—that was plenty."

"Yeah, but babe... that thing with my dad...."

"Yeah, well...." Her sigh was puzzled. "Chase, I get that he wasn't father of the year. But I've never seen you hate anybody the way you hate him."

He's called me a faggot since I was two. Imagine how fun it was when I realized I was one.

"Lots of history there," he said softly, and he felt a hand on his calf. He was surprised when he saw Tommy's dark eyes open, and he grimaced and covered the phone mouthpiece. "Sorry," he whispered. "I should have taken this outside."

"You ever think it's strange that you haven't told me what all that history is?"

You don't have the key to the red door in my soul, sweetheart. I'm sorry. You never will.

"I don't want to bother you with it," he said, and thank God, his phone beeped because it was almost out of juice. Apparently the adultery gods were smiling on him, right?

"Babe, that's my phone...."

"Yeah, I know," she said. "I've got lunch with my mom anyway."

"Take care."

"Love you."

"You too."

And then they signed off, leaving Chase looking into Tommy's black eyes.

"Does she notice?" Tommy asked seriously.

"Notice what?"

"You never actually say the words?"

Crumbling door, wedge shoulder, brace feet.

"No. Not if I can help it."

Tommy's hand caressed his calf through his jeans, before he pushed himself up on the bed, scooting until his shoulders were propped up on the bed next to Chase's stomach, and it would only take a little roll to rest his chin on Chase's stomach.

"I love you, Chase Summers."

Chase's whole body went cold, and for a moment that door bulged, the weight of the pain behind it almost too huge to manage.

"I love you," he said, surprised that the words slipped through. His hand went up to Tommy's hair, which was growing out of its cut and flopping into his eyes a little. "I love you, Tommy Matthew Halloran."

Tommy nodded and put his cheek on Chase's stomach. "You got a middle name, Chase?"

"It's my dad's name. I don't like to use it."

Tommy's mouth twisted. "You got a name you like?" he asked, and Chase laughed a little, thinking about it.

"I like my porn name,' he said seriously, "but that wouldn't sound right. Chase Chance Summers? No. Doesn't work on the tongue."

Tommy pushed his sweatshirt up and started running his fingers around Chase's now-hairless navel. "Chase Andrew Summers?"

Chase shrugged. "Mmm... I always liked fancy names, you know?"

"Like what?"

Chase smiled a little and played with Tommy's hair. "Like Julian, or Sebastian, or Jude or Horace or Malachi."

Tommy laughed a little. "Okay, so, how about Julian. You can be Chase Julian Summers. And when you're with me, and we're together and alone, you'll be Chase Julian Summers, and I love you, Chase Julian Summers, like I don't know if I can love another human being ever."

Chase nodded, and suddenly the door was smooth and even in his chest, and nothing was threatening to bulge out of it or escape.

"I love you, Tommy Matthew Halloran, like I don't know if I can love another human being ever."

It wasn't a promise. Chase swore it wasn't a promise. But it sounded like a vow.

Tommy moved up to kiss him, and Chase Julian Summers kissed him back, a complete and whole person, invented on the spot so that Chase could function in this strange double life. Tommy breathed and ground against him, and Chase slid down the bed, kicking his shoes off and feeling his body start to buzz pleasantly with arousal without the least amount of guilt or remorse for this act, in spite of the lie that his life had become.

SUNLIGHT AND SHADOW

ON THE *screen, Kane's back muscles rippled with his effort to come off the bed, to throw Chance off and out of him, and to take over the scene. Chance grunted and threw his upstage hand hard onto the small of Kane's back, pinning him, even as his hips kept pistoning back and forth, keeping a steady, rocking-hard rhythm of his cock pounding away in Kane's ass. Chance's eyes half closed; he was obviously, totally, completely immersed in the sensation, and subtly, smoothly, he shifted his body so his camera-side shoulder dropped back and his chest and hips opened up a little. The camera zoomed in on where the action was, and Kane's voice sounded disembodied as he groaned. His ass stopped quivering as he stopped fighting and gave himself up to being fucked.*

"Fuck me!" he commanded, grunting and stroking his huge, uncut cock furiously. "Just fuck me, dammit!"

"I'm fucking you," Chance's voice came back, smug and breathless.

"Faster, harder, deeper!"

"I'll fuck ya like I want ya!" Chance barked, and then, using his upstage hand again so it wouldn't block the shot, he reached down and grabbed Kane's thick, dark hair. Kane's back arched and he screamed with arousal, and his fist kept up its action on his cock.

"You like that?" Chance hissed, and Kane growled, "Don't fuckin' stop!" just as he shuddered and yelped and came all over the plain blue bedspread.

IN THE viewing room John sighed, and Chase looked at him nervously over the giant cup of mocha latte Kane had greeted him with. It turned out that, off screen, Kane was as sweet as a paperboy and as eager to please as a Boston terrier puppy. Chase was both glad and humbled by the difference. Kane was a real porn actor—he knew how to make his porn person different from his real person—and Chase thought he should take a few notes.

"What's wrong?" Chase asked, fearing something irreparable. He'd already put himself on the shooting schedule for three more shots in the next few months. He'd had to schedule one scene right before spring training, which meant he was going to be a wreck during training week, but at least Mercy wouldn't need to ask about the bruises or worry why he was too tired to put out.

"Nothing," John said sincerely. He looked up at Chase and smiled. "You're great, kid. This one's going to be your first five-star video, mark my words."

"Then why the sigh?" Kane asked over his own coffee. "My man here fucks like a god!"

Chase smiled that lazy, "hit this pitch now, asshole!" grin. "Right backatcha."

John rolled his eyes. "It's just that bit, where you dropped your shoulder back. It was perfect."

"And that was bad?" Chase asked, puzzled.

"No, kid. It's just the first time I ever saw you realize this was a job."

Chase pulled the corner of his mouth up in a lopsided grin.

"Well, it may be, but I *love* my job!"

Kane cracked up, and although he was a good six inches shorter than Chase, propped his elbow on Chase's shoulder and leaned into him. It was something Kevin or Donnie would do, and Chase found he was totally comfortable with it. It wasn't the touch of a lover, in spite of what they'd just seen on screen. It was the touch of a coworker, or a friend. It was Dex's touch, or Cameron's, or Mercy's, or John's.

It wasn't the touch of Tommy Halloran.

"Yeah, but you'll love your job even more when it's my turn on top!"

Tommy needs to be my first.

For a minute Chase was going to object, even though he knew that, eventually, being on the bottom was in the cards. People expected that—you couldn't be on top all the time, and everybody liked cherry-popping scenes, *especially* from an established top.

But those three days in a hotel room in Boston were only four weeks in Chase's rearview, and although Tommy had bottomed the whole time—without even questioning or asking or even trying to reverse their position—and Chase's ass was fine and dandy, but his heart was a little bit raw.

He'd caught a cab to the airport and left Tommy at the hotel, the room paid through until Tommy left. Chase had made sure that every last scrap of business had been taken care of, and that all Tommy had to do was work out and eat and sleep. Tommy, for his part, kissed Chase with an open mouth and a pure soul. For the last three days he'd tasted like chocolate sometimes and strawberries sometimes, sometimes steak or chicken salad, and sometimes beer—but not once like cigarettes.

Chase had texted him that he got home safely, and Tommy had texted him when he was back in town. They'd texted each other regularly after that—at least a half an hour a day, and sometimes the dumbest shit too. Chase would say he was getting his classes and Tommy would tell him he had to reapply for school. Chase would tell him the hours and Tommy would ask him if he'd gotten blown recently.

No, you moron. I haven't shot any scenes!

Not your only source of blow jobs.

Yeah, but I don't let her do that.

What kind of idiot are you?

The kind who makes her come and hope she falls asleep.

God, I almost wish the sex was good!

It was good. With you.

Need to see you again.

Once my classes get settled. I swear.

And that had been a week ago. Chase had seen Tango around the shop when he'd come in to talk about his scene with Kane. They'd looked at each other and waved and smiled, but they hadn't touched, not even the way he and Kane were touching now. Chase knew Tango had shot two scenes of his own, one of them with Cam and Ethan, and other than that, it was like just another guy from work.

But that one time, from across the room, Tango's eyes had caught his, hot and dark, and Chase had blushed and turned away just as Tango disappeared down the hallway that led to the sets.

Good scene?

Ethan's hung like a fucking elephant.
Won't be able to walk for a week.

Yeah, THAT makes me want to bottom.

You've never bottomed off-camera?

Until you I'd never topped off-camera either.
I told you that.

No. You expected me to put shit together.
I'm not that bright.

Liar.

> *No, man. I just don't think that far. It's why*
> *I'm so good in porn!*

Jesus, Tommy. The only dumb thing you've ever
Done is hook up with me.

> *Need to see you. Now. I will fucking stalk you.*

Scene with Kane in two days. Day after
That, told Mercy I'd be out of town for a bit.

> *Make it a week. You can stay with me.*

God, I thought you'd never ask.

AND now, he was looking at the rushes of his scene with Kane, and Kane was leering at him, promising him a good ride.

And the only one Chase trusted to ride him was Tommy.

"Mm, I don't know," John said, thinking. "Kane, you guys were pretty hot together. We may want to milk this. We need a tag team here before we put Chase on bottom. Who would be good in the middle of a tag team?"

"Cameron?" Kane suggested, and John shrugged.

"Too passive—he takes more initiative as a solitary bottom," John mused. "Tango?"

And Chase's heart stopped.

Please God, not Tango. Please God, not Tango. Please. I don't want us to do that for money. Please God.

Then John answered his own question. "No, never mind. Tango just did a tag team. He wants to top in his next vid, anyway."

"Scott?" Kane suggested doubtfully, and John wrinkled his nose.

"No. Scott's a diva. He wants to be the prettiest, the bestest, and the most hung. We put the two of you in with Scott, he'll get his feathers ruffled."

They went back and forth for a little while without coming to much of a conclusion, and Chase felt a buzz in his pocket.

I'm outside—you parked around back?

Yeah. They're discussing a tag team.

Who with?

Me, Kane and ?

Dex.

You think?

Just broke up with his girlfriend. Needs the distraction.

How do you KNOW this?

He just came by my place asking to be distracted. I said no.

"DEX?" Chase said out loud, and John and Kane both looked at him, smiling.

"Perfect!" John said excitedly.

You have no idea.

CHASE might have walked out of there feeling smug. Chance had given him an opportunity to do what most gay guys dreamed of: bang the guy who banged your guy, right? Revenge as porn video? But it wasn't like that. It wasn't even weird. All that mattered was that Mercy thought he was going to be out of town for a week and Tango was going to be waiting out front for him.

Kane walked him out, talking excitedly about bodybuilding and asking if Chase went to his gym. Chase did, and they had just made arrangements to meet in the mornings when Kane looked up and saw Tommy.

"Tango!" he hailed, coming up to the side of Tommy's silver Acura TL. "Man, so good to see you! I haven't seen you in *months*!"

Tommy smiled genuinely. "Yeah, I know! We should get together sometime. Video games, movies, something!"

Chase had his duffel over his shoulder and he swung around to the back door around Kane's body to throw it in.

"Yeah, me and Chance here have a bargain to start working out together next week. I could use some tips from this guy, eh?" Kane gave Chase's ass a smack as he passed by. "I've got a bouncy butt, but Chance here? You could bounce a quarter off this guy's ass!"

"Tell me about it!" said Tango dryly. "Yeah, whatever his workout secret, I think he should share. I can join you guys if you like. Same gym?"

Kane nodded. "Yeah, no problem. So next week?"

Tommy glanced at Chase and Chase smiled softly back. "Yeah, Kane. Next week's good. Monday?"

"Yeah, bro. Here, give me your cell. I'll put in my digits, okay?" Chase handed his phone over to Kane, who entered his information, talking the whole time. "Yeah, see, you've got all the wrong guys in here. You've got Dex and John and Tango—seriously. Where's that going to get you?" Kane flipped the phone around and took a sleazy picture of himself so his face would pop up when his number rang. Chase and Tommy were laughing by the time he was done, so when he looked at them and said, "Where are you two going anyway? Camping or something? I don't know if anyone told you, but it's fucking

February, right? You go camping in the summer, right?" The question seemed to come out of the clear blue.

It was Tommy who answered, without even looking at Chase for permission. "Man, playing house, right?"

Kane raised an eyebrow, and with the little soul-patch goatee he was nursing, the expression made him look absolutely wicked. Tommy may have been Loki, the lunatic sex god, but Kane was definitely Puck, the mischief making hell-raiser. "Now Tango, you kept your profile cagey, but I could *swear* blondie here is straight."

Chase didn't even blush. He was chewing strawberry-mint gum; he threw another piece in his mouth and cracked it, saying, "Yeah, you know those porn profiles. People lie on that shit all the time."

Kane tossed back his head and laughed long and hard, and by the time he could stop to say good-bye, Chase was in the passenger seat and belted up.

"You two have a nice little time playing house, okay? I'll see you both next week."

Tommy was still chuckling as he pulled away from the little office suite, but he did manage to shoot Chase a sideways glance.

"That doesn't bother you?" he asked quietly, and Chase looked back at him with the same look on his face he probably wore when he was a kid and he got to spend the night at Donnie's house because Donnie's mom wanted to take them on a picnic the next day and Chase's dad didn't give a ripe shit.

"Chase Summers, Mercy's boyfriend, Victor's son? Yeah, that scared the shit out of him and pissed him off too. But I'm not that guy anymore."

Tommy looked at him, surprised. "You're not?"

"Naw. I'm Chase *Julian* Summers. I can do anything."

Tommy didn't laugh at him like Chase expected him to. He sent him an inscrutable look, and shifted the car.

"So you have to be another person to be with me?" Tommy asked, his voice troubled, and Chase swallowed and looked away. It was the beginning of February, and at the moment, the sky was the color of concrete dust, the sun barely peeking out of it like a dull pewter coin.

"I have to be a *better* person to be with you," Chase said, and Tommy sighed.

"The only person you ever have to be is yourself."

Sorry, Tommy. Most of myself is in my chest, holding shut that damned door.

"Can I be myself when we're in your house, naked?" Chase asked guilelessly, and Tommy laughed and then squinted at him.

"Aren't you sexed out? You shot a scene and some stills today, right?"

Chase nodded and was abruptly brought back to the twinges, aches, and bruises that came when you had sex for an hour some way that you would not actually ever want to have sex if you were not in front of a camera. His calves were cramping and his thighs ached and his member was raw because Kane was tighter than the o-ring on a Maserati.

"Yeah," he said, some of his enthusiasm deflating a little. "But… God, can we just be naked and not have sex? That… that would be so awesome."

Tommy looked at him as he took a right on G Street. "Yeah, Chase Julian, I can hold you."

Chase blushed. "What?" he asked, feeling foolish.

"Sometimes I think the only reason you ended up with Mercy is because she's a human being who hugged you."

No one else was going to do it.

"It's as good an explanation as any," Chase said mildly, and Tommy made a soft sound, something resigned and a little sad.

"What?" Chase asked again.

"What's the worst thing that can happen if you actually tell *me*, of all people, what you're really thinking?"

That red door in my chest would bust open and disintegrate, and all the shit that's going to barrel out will drown me, destroy the glue and fairy dust that's holding me together, and all that will be left is the

color red, and it will be so bright it will singe your hands and burn
your heart and eyes to ash.

"You'd realize what a complete douche bag I am and not want
another fucking thing to do with me."

Tommy's jaw locked, and his chest went in and out and he turned
the car into the driveway of a nice little stucco house, gray on the
outside, with a neat postage stamp lawn bordered by annuals that would
probably start blooming in a month. There were hedges in front of the
windows and bordering the fences that wrapped around the back, and
shutters, eaves, and doorframes painted construction-worker orange. He
clicked the garage door opener and pulled into a neat space with basic
man-cave requirements: basic car maintenance tools, basic home
maintenance tools, old cans of paint, and, Chase was amused to see,
brand new litter box, cat feeding station, and little cat door carved into
the door that led from the garage to the kitchen.

Chase smiled appreciatively as he got out and reached into the
back of the car to get his duffel. "Nice, Tommy! I like it! The
neighborhood association didn't give you crap about this?"

Tommy shook his head no as he got out and trotted up to unlock
the inside door. "They were thinking about it, but one of the guys on
the block is an accountant for most of the rest of the block. His
boyfriend thought it was cool, and every mommy on the block has been
trying to mother the two of them since Kit moved in anyway. They kept
it from being awkward, which was cool, because I *really* liked the
color."

Chase followed him up. "Nice," he said, and Tommy shrugged.

"Yeah, they're nice."

"So why's your nose all wrinkled like that?" Sure enough, when
Tommy wrinkled his nose and let his pointy canines show, you could
almost see him as the freckled kid from the pictures that Chase had
packed up.

Tommy shrugged. "Yanno, I think they're fans. They're too polite
to say anything, but… well… Jesse keeps looking at me and clapping
his hand over his mouth like he's trying not to giggle like a little kid."

Chase was about to laugh and give Tommy shit, but Tommy was obviously mortified. "Why's that such a bad thing, yanno?"

Again that shrug as Tommy threw his keys on a nice, plain, barely used kitchen table and threw his camouflage jacket over the chair. After Christmas and his exposure to real winter, Chase had found a pea coat in an Army/Navy store and he loved it. It was sturdy, hearty, felted wool, and Chase didn't care how it made him *look*, it made him *feel* safe. He kept it on for a minute, reluctant to give that feeling up.

"Someday," Tommy said slowly, "you're going to be an engineer, right? And that's what everyone's going to know you for. You'll probably be great at it, because... I don't know. You're just good at everything. Baseball, sex, trying to be a good person. Whatever. And that'll be you. Chase Summers—even if you've got the crappy middle name. Engineer. And you won't even have to think of porn star when you make your resume. But...." Tommy looked up at him, unhappy. "That's never what I wanted to be either, but it looks like I might be here a while."

Buster wandered out of the darkened living room behind the kitchen and Chase bent down to pet him, feeling the age in his sharp bones and loose skin. The cat didn't care, apparently, that he was like a piece of living history, because he purred under Chase's hand, insinuating himself until Chase picked him up and touched noses with him.

"Hey, Buster," he said to stall for time. He felt out of sync somehow. He'd been prepared to leave this behind. He and Mercy maybe lived three miles from this place, their apartment building by the college, graceless and inelegant off of Howe Avenue. To him, answering Tommy's call of *Need to see you. Now!* had meant that they had entered a pact of sorts, a secret world. Tommy's house would be sacrosanct, a sanctuary from all of the shit that they did and they said and they felt cornered into that they weren't proud of and couldn't look in the face twenty-four-seven.

But not to Tommy. Tommy wanted him maybe because Tommy wanted someone to hold his hand while he looked that shit in the face, and Chase felt a surge of admiration for him. Tommy Halloran was so fucking brave. Chase would never, in a million years, feel worthy.

"What do you want, Tommy?" Chase asked seriously as Buster settled into his lap to drool on his coat. Tommy looked at him and smiled, but his crazy Loki-the-lunatic-sex-god smile didn't reach his eyes. They weren't bright and gleaming anymore; they were dark and sad.

"I want you."

Chase closed his eyes. "You have me. Whatever parts of me I can give you, you have them. You have them if you work porn, you have them if you get fat, you have them if you go back to school and run an animal shelter or become a scientist or a history major or a poet. I'm a douche bag. What I'm doin' to you ain't fair. But as long as you want me, in pieces or whole, you have me."

He felt Tommy's breath on his face, and when he looked up, Tommy had moved from across the table to kneel in front of him.

"What you're doin' to me ain't half as bad as what you're doing to yourself," Tommy said quietly.

It's been done, Tommy. Don't worry about it now.

"Can we not talk about it?" Chase pleaded. "I… God. I feel… thin. Like paper. Please… I just want to hold you so I feel strong again."

Tommy's arms went around his shoulders and Chase actually trembled. The day slid away, like water down a shower drain. It didn't matter who Chase had been with or who he had touched. It didn't matter that he had spent an hour on his toes fucking Kane while Kane's foot had been propped up on a dresser and he'd been executing a three-quarter split. That wasn't a part of him anymore. All that made up Chase Julian Summers was Tommy Halloran's arms around his shoulders.

One of Tommy's long, bony hands slid beneath the heavy blue wool on Chase's shoulders, and Chase shuddered. With the other hand, Tommy scooped Buster off his lap and put the poor old man gently on his feet, scratching him on the top of the head before giving him a gentle shove toward the living room. Tommy stood up again and positioned himself in front of Chase, looking down at his upturned face in a way that made Chase feel pinned to his seat by the weight and the heat, and the longing.

"Take your coat off," Tommy whispered. "Stay a while."

Tommy slid the coat down his arms, and before Chase could do much more than shudder, Tommy had cupped his hands around Chase's face and captured his mouth in a kiss.

Porn kisses were quick and hard. It was like every touch of lips to skin was a power exercise in finding an erogenous zone and lighting it up like a pinball machine. Tommy's kisses weren't like that at all. This started out with a brush of lips, a whisper. Tommy whispered against Chase's skin once, twice, again, and enough for Chase's lips to practically tingle, and then Tommy opened his mouth, pulling Chase's open with it, and Chase gave a whimper and melted.

Chase's mouth was open and wide and Tommy was plundering him with his tongue, and Chase's skin felt like it was jumping off his body.

Chase's breathing started to quicken, and his groin gave a tortured throb and the sound that was strangled in the back of his throat was hungry and pathetic at once. Tommy pulled back and rubbed Chase's lips with his thumb.

"No worries, okay? Here. I know what you need—it's what I always need after a scene, okay? It's Tommy Halloran's treatment for being oversexed all day and needing to give your dick a break, okay?"

Chase laughed a little and closed his eyes, enjoying Tommy's hands framing his face. "That sounds amazing," he said, and two hours later he felt the same way, only squared.

It turned out that in addition to painting the house gray with neon-orange trim, Tommy had also added a Jacuzzi bathtub in his bathroom, big enough to sit two.

Chase spent an hour in that bathtub, just stretching in the quiet with Tommy at the other end. Tommy had put some music on the stereo—Coldplay, a band Chase loved—and they talked softly, desultorily, covering everything from Chase's classes to Tommy's unfortunate ennui.

"Man, it's gotta be something," Tommy said with a sigh. "I mean, I love working out, but I can't do it more than two hours a day, it makes me fucking crazy. But... it's like none of the stuff I want to do makes any sense, you know?"

Chase slid down to his neck in the water and gingerly moved his feet around Tommy's hips so he didn't accidentally kick him in the balls.

"You know that guy—whats'isname—Adam Somethin-or-other? Used to do *The Man Show*, now he does some sort of thing about cars?"

"Adam Corolla?"

"Yeah! That's the guy. My friend Kevin is crazy about him, mostly because Kevin's crazy about things with tits, and me, not so much, right?"

"No kidding," Tommy said dryly, and Chase splashed some water at him, too relaxed to do much more in the way of "fuck you."

"Anyway, so this guy wrote a book, and it's a best seller, and the thing is, one of his favorite things to say is, do something you love *not* for money, just do it to do it. Do it to get better at it, do it to enjoy it. Do it because you love it, and eventually, you'll find a way to make a living doing it. And it worked for him, you know? He started off working at a radio station for free, and he just kept... I don't know, going there and learning his trade, right? That's what you've got to do."

Tommy blinked. "Work in a radio station?"

"Volunteer with animals, dumbass! Go into a shelter or a vet's office and volunteer, and see what sort of jobs are out there and what you need to do to get them. Then you'll know what to train for, right? And in the meantime, after you work out, you've got something on your roster that makes you happy!"

Tommy reached down and ran a hand along Chase's calf. Maybe, on another day, Chase would have gotten hard from that touch alone, but after the shoot with Kane, the touch just made him want to be touched all over—but not sexually.

"We've been here a while," Tommy said. "Here. Let's get out, and you dry off and put on some sweats or something. I'm going to go get us some food and meet you in there, okay?"

Chase shuddered. "It's real nice of you, taking care of me, you know?"

"Shut up and get out of the tub."

Chase did, and he was sitting on Tommy's bed with a shitload of books spread out in front of him, looking curiously at the big painted plates of what even Chase knew were classic painters. Tommy must have had a thing with color, Chase thought happily. The bedspread was rust with indigo highlights, and there was an indigo area rug on the hardwood floor. The kitchen had been white and yellow and china blue, and although he hadn't gotten a good look at the living room, Chase imagined that it would be something pretty and coordinated and rich too. He loved it—it was like his whole life he never thought of how happy that much color could make him, and he was content to wait for a little while and just indulge in all of it. Still, he was starving and relieved when Tommy came in with what looked to be delivered Thai food in two bags and a towel to put over the bedspread so they could just sit on the bed and eat. Chase realized that he'd barely had half a grapefruit that morning for breakfast and almost swooned with the smell of some real fucking food.

"God, I love you," he swore, and then carefully closed up a volume full of Vincent Van Gogh paintings and stacked it on top of one with Renoir and Degas, then very respectfully put them back on the bookshelf behind Tommy's bed. Tommy spread out the boxes with the food and gave Chase a ceramic bowl—pretty, in a deep indigo color—and sat down with his own, and for a minute they were occupied with dishing the takeout. Tommy had specific preferences—but only two—and it was easy to see when he took almost all of the Thai noodles and did the same with a neutral steamed vegetable dish, leaving Chase just enough to taste.

That was fine with Chase. He loved to try new stuff, and Thai wasn't one of his and Mercy's usual go-to places, so he put a little bit of everything on his plate and tasted carefully. He looked up and caught Tommy smiling at him when he had a mouth full of noodles and semi-spicy curry, and he had to take a quick drink from the glass of milk that he'd set on the end table.

"Wha'?" he asked, still trying to swallow down his food.

Tommy shook his head. "You're just cute, that's all. You eat at a buffet like a little kid. You'll try anything, but you look at it with deep suspicion before it leaves the plate and graces your lips, you know?"

Chase blinked. "Graces my lips? Have you been reading our press releases or something? That's sort of corny."

Tommy giggled and gestured with his chopsticks. "Eat your food, Chase, your eyes are drooping, and I want to give you a body rub while you're still appreciative."

Chase looked out Tommy's windows and realized that the late late afternoon when he and Kane had left the suite had turned into night. He gave a half laugh.

"You'll lie down next to me, right? God, that's what I've missed. It's like with you, I'm not all alone."

Tommy sighed and reached over and took his almost empty plate from him.

"Lie down and let me clean up, okay?"

Chase wanted to object, but it was easy, so easy, to let Tommy take care of him. He longed to return the favor, of course, but this time, he thought it might be okay if Tommy got to do the honors.

Cleanup took minimal time, and Tommy came back shaking his head and saying, "I hope the damned cat sticks to the stuff I put in his bowl. Anything else is going to just rip up his stomach, you know?"

"You didn't eat a lot," Chase mumbled, his head pillowed on his hands. "Why didn't you eat that much?"

Tommy stood up and started stripping off clothes until he was in his sleep shorts and a plain T-shirt, just like Chase.

"Because the less I eat is the less I have to throw back up, baby," Tommy said, his voice so casual that Chase practically hit him in the face with a hurriedly thrust up shoulder.

"You do *what*?" Chase asked, sure he had misheard.

Chase saw Tommy's shrug and felt his food congealing in the pit of his stomach. He knew that shrug. He *made* that shrug.

"I can work out all I want, but that doesn't mean food doesn't go straight to my ass. If I don't watch my calories like a madman, sometimes that's the price you pay, you know?"

"Tommy, that's horrible."

Tommy bent down and kissed his temple, then put his hands firmly on Chase's shoulders and pushed inexorably down.

"It's life, Chase. I'm pretty sure you've figured out by now that it's not always pretty. Now relax. I'm so hungry to touch you, I'll probably get off just rubbing your back."

He didn't use oils or anything, just touch. He rubbed Chase's skin, mostly, although he put enough counter-pressure on Chase's muscles to make Chase's body relax even more, and Chase lay there with his face pillowed on his hands and tried not to cry, it felt so good.

Above him, as Tommy was rubbing, he started to make "mm-mm" yummy porn-sex noises, and if Chase hadn't been so relaxed—and so sexed out—he would have gotten hard just from those sounds alone. As it was, Tommy's hands grew slower and dreamier on his skin, and when Tommy went to straddle Chase's hips to work on him better, Chase felt his hard-on through both layers of sleep shorts, riding the crease of his ass.

He actually felt some stirring in his groin, and his hips moved sinuously to prove it.

Tommy rewarded him with a flick to the flank. "Stop that," he ordered. "You keep doing shit like that and I'm going to forget all the shit I need to remember."

"Like what?" Chase asked lazily. He wasn't going to disobey that order; he just liked Tommy talking about something besides hurting himself to stay pretty.

"Like the fact that you really don't want sex right now and that you've never bottomed."

"Mmm...," Chase mumbled. "They're gonna ask me soon. Nervous."

The pleasant sensation of Tommy's hands on his shoulders was interrupted by a string of gentle kisses down his spine, and his groin started to throb quietly, reminding him that he may have had sex all day, but it hadn't felt like this.

"Don't be nervous, baby. I'll show you how, if you want. It'll be good."

A buzzwire of tension that Chase hadn't known he'd been carrying just flattened and eased, making him that much more relaxed—and, unfortunately, less turned on. The same could not be said for Tommy, however, who was grunting in frustration behind him. Chase pulled himself out of his torpor long enough to take pity on his savior.

"Tommy, where's your lube?" he asked, and Tommy made a little whine and bucked his hips, not even asking why Chase would ask.

"That drawer that your milk's on top of."

Chase was close enough to reach over and open it, and then hand it back to Tommy. "Use me," he mumbled. "Whatever you want. I want to hear you make yourself happy."

"Oh God," Tommy moaned, kissing his back some more, "you *do* love me."

"Never doubt it." It was the last thing he said for a bit, because Tommy had straightened up and scuttled out of his shorts, and Chase turned sideways to see him standing by the side of the bed, oiling his cock with lube.

"Mmm...." Chase thought he looked beautiful, his chest and stomach muscles so taut and defined Chase could count them, and his long, bony fingers wrapped solidly around his cock. "You're sooooo pretty," he said with dreamy wonder, and Tommy slid his fist down to his base and then forward, twisting his fist when he got to the end.

"Pull on my balls, wouldja?" Tommy begged, and it was such an easy thing to do, just reach out and fondle him, tugging a little as Tommy groaned.

"God, yeah. Keep doing that." Chase did, and scooted closer to the edge of the bed so he could turn over and take Tommy's testicles (which were large and heavy and hairless, *thank you, stylist*) into his mouth and suckle on them delicately, applying just enough pressure to hear Tommy moan.

"God...."

Chase kept doing that, and then, since the angle was right, he snuck a finger backward, using spit as lube to just barely tease Tommy's rim. It was hard—Tommy's body was trembling and his hand was moving violently and fast—but Chase didn't want him to do this alone.

Tommy gave another groan, and then hollered, "Oh *yes!*" and then erupted, the come spattering across Chase's chest. Chase pulled his hand from between Tommy's legs and gave his balls a chaste kiss before scooting back a little so he could prop himself up on his elbows.

"Stay right there," Tommy told him, bending down to kiss him quickly on the lips. "I'll be right back."

There were sounds from the bathroom, and then he came back with a warm washcloth. He used it on Chase's chest first and then on himself to get the last of the lube, and then he pulled on his shorts and told Chase to get under the covers.

"It's not bedtime," Chase grumbled, although it was nearly ten o'clock by now, and he was so relaxed, sleep seemed the only option. It just didn't seem fair: the first night of this week, this precious week, in Tommy's arms, and it was almost over. He'd had to lie for this week— hell, he'd had to *fuck* for this week. He'd had to hide his car and tell Donnie and Kevin he'd miss video night (when Donnie had barely forgiven him for missing football on New Year's Day) and shop for groceries for Mercy and clean the apartment, right down to the windows, until he felt like he was even capable of leaving. He'd bought Mercy a floral arrangement that cost at least two tanks of gas and left it on the table before he'd gone. He couldn't remember when he'd felt more like slime.

But not now. Not when Tommy was sliding in next to him and his flesh was so warm and so pliant, and his muscles were so taut underneath his hands. Their full bodies, together and under the covers, legs tangling, skin soft and clean rubbing together. This was that moment, that feeling he had wanted so badly in the car on the trip over.

He felt foolish for forgetting that moments like this had to be worked for.

Tommy grabbed a remote off his end table, clicked on the television that was mounted on the opposite wall, and started going into his menu of taped shows. "*Hawaii 5-0*," he said happily, pressing start. "Alex O'Laughlin—now there's a guy I'd do a shoot with."

Chase laughed a little and rested his head on Tommy's chest. "Yeah?"

"Yeah. How 'bout you?"

"Mmm...." Chase thought about it. "That Jinx guy from *Warehouse 13*. He's sort of beautiful."

Tommy laughed softly and the hand not draped over Chase's shoulder came up to rumple Chase's hair. "So're you," he said.

The show started then, and Chase settled into it, enjoying the normalcy of it all. He and Mercy would probably be doing this same thing—even this same show—if he was home this night, but for some reason, it just *felt* better with Tommy. It felt real, in a way that didn't feel real when he was sitting on the couch and Mercy was leaning on him.

But still, his attention was wandering and his eyes were half closed by the time the first commercial came on. Later he blamed it on the relaxation, on the endorphins from the sex and the Jacuzzi and the massage, but as he drowsed on Tommy, the door opened for a moment. He opened his mouth to ask if Tommy had something sweet, remembered that Tommy would probably throw that right back up, and in the space between pain and honesty, some truth slipped out.

"Your mom loved you," he said, too tired to tell if Tommy tensed up when he said it or not.

"Hope so," Tommy said softly. There was a soft puff of air at Chase's brow, and Chase wished he wasn't just weighted down, because he'd stop talking and kiss Tommy instead.

"Mmm. Did she know you were gay?"

"No." The word was a whisper.

"It doesn't matter," Chase said. "She didn't want to leave you anyway. My mom didn't even know and she left."

"Chase...."

"Maybe if someone knows all of me, that's just too much fucked up to stand."

"Chase...."

"Show's on, Tommy."

Tommy's arms were tight around his shoulders and Tommy was dropping kisses in his hair, but Chase was too close to sleep to tell him it would be all right, the door was all the way closed now and Chase wouldn't let anything more slip out.

IT WASN'T a honeymoon, really. Chase still had school—he just had to look really carefully to make sure Donnie didn't spot him on the few days when they had overlapping classes. They both still had to work out in the morning and they both went running in the afternoons. Chase still had homework and Tommy still had to clean the catbox. But they were playing house. They were together. It made even stupid shit like cleaning the catbox or stopping to get milk on the way home a hell of a lot better than real life. Chase had the shoot with Kane on Monday. On Wednesday, they reroofed the garage (because Tommy said it had been leaking and he wanted to fix it while the gray, constipated weather held), and the next day they went down to the outlets in Vacaville to go shopping.

The shopping thing happened by accident. They'd finished the roof and Chase threw his clothes into the washer and fished out another pair of faded jeans and a Henley shirt. Tommy looked at him and winced.

"What?"

"You can actually afford real clothes now, you know," he said.

Chase looked down at himself and shrugged. "Why would I want clothes? I'm not working in an office yet. And even if I was, I gotta tell you, we took a tour of Intel with my electronics class last year, and those guys do *not* dress up."

Tommy looked at him and shook his head. "Chase, do you dress up to go dancing?"

"Yeah."

"Dress up for the holidays?"

"Yeah."

"And that's enough for you?"

Chase sort of boggled at him. "Isn't it enough for everybody?"

Tommy shook his head. "Why do you dye your hair?"

That was easy. "So I can look like Donnie."

Tommy blinked then, hard, his eyes big and dark. "And that's important to you?"

"Donnie...." Chase looked away. "See, his mom was my best person. His house was... it was like everything I wanted to have. It was messy and there were toys and there was always food. And Donnie was beautiful, you know? And open—his heart is as open as a puppy's. Did I tell you how he got together with his boyfriend? He's house-sitting for Alejandro, right? And he goes in there right after his shower, looks around, finds the visual porn collection, and jerks off. I mean... you know, because he's there, and it feels good, and why not? So he falls asleep, buck naked on the guy's bed, and Alejandro gets home early. And you know? It turns out, 'Yandro had a thing for him all along. He was just waiting for Donnie to get a little older, right?"

Tommy laughed a little, because the story was funny, and then just kept looking at him, searchingly.

"So Donnie comes out, right? And my old man—" *SLAM! The red door wasn't going to open on that one.* "Anyway. Donnie comes out. And I don't. Donnie comes out, and he's honest with me, and I think he was scared to death, and I tell him it's all good, right? I mean, because he's *Donnie*, and even if I didn't already know I was... the way I am, it would have to be okay because he's *Donnie*. So he comes out, and... and nothing. Nothing happens. He gives me a couple of hand jobs when I ask, and then I stop asking because I'm being a douche bag and not giving them back, and I... I love him a little, you know? But not enough. Not enough to admit I want to do more than let him touch my dick. So I love him a little, but not enough, and he says straight up he's always loved 'Yandro, and even if I loved him enough, it's not like it would be worth it, right?"

Chase was babbling. He was babbling and not making any sense, and he tried to remember where this came from and then he remembered that it all started about why he bleached his hair.

"So I figure I don't have anything he's got. I don't have the boyfriend or the family or the balls... but... but damn, he's cute. His hair is just naturally this blond color. It's gonna go silver when he's forty, and he's going to be beautiful. So." He stopped and swallowed and looked away, feeling like an idiot. Jeans and T-shirts or Henleys. Good enough for school, good enough for everyday, good enough for life, right? Didn't mean anything was wrong. Just meant you'd never thought you'd be the kind of person who would dress up and have people pay attention to you, or even if they did, they wouldn't want to be the people *you* wanted to pay attention to you.

"You just wanted to be him," Tommy said softly, and Chase smiled weakly.

"Yeah. Because, that's real fucking mature, right?"

Tommy nodded, and then smiled, and Chase prayed there wouldn't be a hug or tears or pity or anything, because the week had been going pretty damned awesome, and he didn't want to come apart in the middle of it. Tommy was putting up with enough from Chase, thank you, and watching that red door crash down—that wasn't what he'd signed on for.

"So, you wanna go shopping and see if you can find a look that's you? You've got the cash now, right? I mean, I know you're saving some of it, but you don't need to save *all* of it, right?"

Chase smiled. Christmas had been exactly as awful as he'd expected it to be, exactly as painful and disappointing. But this... this felt like a hidden Christmas, a surprise bike under the tree that not even Santa or his dad had known about. It was a Christmas do-over, in the first week of February.

It was grand.

CHASE had seen Tommy on the set, and in his mom's home, where he was wearing jeans and sweaters. He'd seen that he had a fleece-lined leather coat in Boston, and that it looked pretty cool, and he'd seen his hair was almost always cut short, and it always looked good. Their first three days together, when Chase wasn't at school, they worked out and worked on the roof—or stayed naked.

Chase had never really seen Tommy dressed up, but before they left for Vacaville on Thursday, he actually got to open the closet in the guest room, and he was amazed.

"Ohmygod—I thought this place would be fuckin' empty!" he breathed.

Tommy leaned over his shoulder and rested his pointed chin on Chase's shoulder, because he knew it hurt and he was waiting for Chase to say "Bug off, dammit!" but Chase was too impressed.

"Jesus, Tommy. I need to see you around town some more."

Tommy made a "hmm" sound. "Sacramento has a club scene," he said, "but mostly I wear this shit when I'm going to The City."

Like everyone else who had grown up in Sac, Chase had grown up thinking of "The City" as a mystical place—a *real* city, where there were lots of music clubs and world-class food and science and art and a real business district with a skyline that people knew around the world. It was a place with history and an ocean—a place where Chase could walk hand in hand with Tommy and no one would spit on them for just being.

"God," Chase breathed, thinking dreamily about being in a club where dancing and grinding was something wonderful—where being on the club floor and dancing with all those bodies surrounding you and one you really loved touching you was nothing to be feared. "Do you think we could go to the city after we go shopping?"

Tommy wrapped his arms around Chase's bare chest and rubbed his cheek on the back of his shoulder. "How long do I have you?" he asked quietly.

"I told her I'd be back Sunday evening," Chase responded, and both of their bodies had gone still, like maybe if they didn't breathe, this moment of talking about Mercy didn't count.

"You don't have school this morning?"

"I sort of do," Chase said, "but I've got a friend taking notes." It had galled, having to leave him when they got so little time, so he'd made arrangements so as not to worry about it.

My fault. My fault you don't have any time. If I was braver. If I could just let this door open, we could have all the time in the world.

"Tomorrow morning too?"

Chase turned away from the rows of tight pants, acid wash jeans, suits with slacks that went below the navel and jackets cut to show off a belly button, and into Tommy's arms. Every night but the first one, they'd made love. A couple of times in the afternoon too. Once, in the Jacuzzi, Chase had bent Tommy over the edge of the tub and given it to him so hard he'd had bruises on his hips. Chase had tried to apologize—Tommy wouldn't let him.

"You love me," he'd gasped when they were done. "You love me. You want me so bad."

It was irrefutable.

Chase would have flunked out of school if Tommy had let him, just to spend more time like this, in each other's company, in each other's arms.

"You've totally got dibs on me," he said now, smiling, anticipation shining out of his eyes.

A bike! A bike! Finally, dammit, a bike for Christmas it's really a fuckin' bike! And it's exactly what I wanted, I knew it!

"Let's go, then, baby. Let's have some fun!"

It was almost too beautiful for words.

FLYING

CHANCE, *long, lean, tan, and blond, was on his knees, pumping his hips into Dex. Dex was on his hands and knees, his mouth in front of Kane's cock—but Dex was having trouble focusing. Kane was doing his bit—held his cock in his fist and slapped Dex's cheeks with it gently—but Dex—Dex was losing his mind.*

"Oh fuck," he moaned. "Fuck... oh Jesus. Chance, Jesus, fuck... fuck... oh shit... just fuck me with that thing... oh God!"

It was completely spontaneous and hot as holy hell, and Kane cocked his head for a moment, like he was listening to something, then nodded and smiled.

"Pull him up, brother," he said in a way that was totally practical and didn't sound at all like a guy in the middle of a sex act with two other men.

Chance nodded and bent down, clasping his hands around Dex's chest and pulling him up flush, back to front with Chance, while Chance remained buried in his body.

Dex groaned and whimpered, clearly wanting more penetration, more of everything, but Chance kissed his shoulder, kissed his ear, and whispered something there with a smile. It looked like "Don't worry, we've gotcha," but the words themselves didn't matter. What mattered was that Kane was lying down on his back under Dex and mouthing his balls and fisting his cock. Dex groaned and shuddered in Chance's arms and Chance lowered him gently, gently, down onto Kane, and then continued his job, thrusting inside Dex's body, while Kane's mouth drove him completely insane.

"GOD, that's hot," Tommy breathed while looking over Chase's shoulder. They were looking at the rushes from Tommy's house, which was where Chase retreated after every shoot now, whether he needed to or not. One week a month he went "to work"—and then ended up here.

"You think so?" Chase asked shyly, grateful for Tommy's arms around his chest. There wasn't room for shame when he did that, and Chase was grateful.

"Yeah—that thing you did where you whisper in his ear and then kiss his back? Totally works."

Chase blushed. "Well, I learn from the best."

Tommy chuckled softly and nuzzled his ear, and for a moment, neither of them was there in Tommy's kitchen, watching porn on Chase's laptop. For a moment they were in a crowded club, in a piss-stinking back alley, in a darkened hotel room reflected dimly with mirrors. For a moment, the air smelled like ocean and industry, and it clung to their skin, and they were in San Francisco.

THE trip to Vacaville to shop had been something of a revelation, mostly because Chase had never realized what a slob he was. He'd always thought of dressing up as wearing club clothes or suits: it had never occurred to him that simply wearing a T-shirt and a pair of jeans could be a revelation in feeling good about himself.

"You can wear those tighter," Tommy said critically, and Chase wrinkled his nose as he stood in the dressing room at Hugo Boss, looking with skepticism at a pair of jeans that were ripped systematically into horizontal ribbons, held together by the occasional fine chain.

"Not unless people want to know if I'm circumcised." He turned around in the mirror and grimaced. "Not so much metal, I think," he said, and Tommy let out a whine. "What?"

"It looks so good!"

Chase blushed. He knew his body was beautiful, especially now that he'd worked so hard to lose his baby fat, but he hadn't ever really *felt* beautiful until he'd seen Tommy's eyes on him. Suddenly he would do anything, *wear* anything, to make Tommy proud to be with him.

"It...." He blushed again, feeling gauche. "How am I going to wash it?"

Tommy shrugged. "Dry cleaning, I guess. I mean, you've got the money...."

Chase shook his head then. "No—I'll do the fancy clothes, baby, but nothing that's going to make more work for...." His voice trailed off, and he looked back at the jeans, carefully not looking at Tommy's face. Fuck. "Never mind. I'll buy them." He'd do the damned dry cleaning himself. And seriously? What were a couple of nice outfits in the big scheme of things? Mercy had a shitload of dry-clean-only, because she had to look like a goddess and she worked that. He'd just throw his stuff in.

Suddenly Tommy was there, in his face. "Go ahead and say it," he hissed, and Chase flushed.

"Mercy," he said evenly. "Remember? I told you about her when we met."

I hate her. I even hate her name for taking this moment and making it hurt.

"If you can't even say her name in front me," Tommy paused, his breathing harsh, "maybe you shouldn't go back to her after this."

Chase closed his eyes and leaned his face forward, grateful when Tommy was still there, and their foreheads touched and their breath mingled. "I'll buy the pants, Tommy. I'll buy the jacket. I'll pierce my ears and wear your jewelry. I'll wear your clothes. You can look at me on any day and know who I really belong to."

Is that okay? Will that do? Will that make up for the deceit? The hurting? For leaving you alone and vulnerable when we like to pretend you're not?

"Me," Tommy muttered. "Me. You're mine." This kiss was voracious, and ended up with Chase pinned up against the back of the wall while Tommy ground against him, biting his neck—*hard.* Chase grunted softly, to keep from screaming, shuddered, and came a little at the pressure of Tommy's teeth alone, the come soaking through the new underwear he'd just bought at the Armani store and staining the jeans a little on the inside. Tommy reached inside the jeans and grabbed him through the underwear, squeezing enough to make him come some more, and Chase hissed sharply in his ear.

"Yours," he rasped, shuddering in Tommy's arms. "Yours. I swear."

Tommy held up his hand and shoved it into Chase's mouth. Chase suckled on the webbing between his thumb and forefinger, then licked his palm, then took each finger into his mouth and pulled.

Tommy's face was flushed, and his eyes were hard and bright. He pulled his hand away and pulled back, leaving Chase's body cold and shaking as he stalked to the pile of clothes that Chase had tried on, most of which he'd discarded because they'd been too high maintenance.

"I'll buy these," he said, glaring at Chase and daring him to protest. He strode quickly over and grabbed the tag dangling from the belt loop, jerking hard until it came off. "Put your shoes on and come by the register so they can take off the dye pack. You can wear those out."

Chase did, flushing as the perky blonde salesgirl reached inside the back of the skintight jeans to take the back of the little dye pack tack. She'd smiled at first, looking excited to touch him, but when she was standing that close, he flushed, and the smell of come on his skin was so strong that he could see her eyes widen and her cheeks turn pink. Her fingers fumbled with the whole extraction kit, and Chase kept his eyes locked on Tommy, standing at the end of the counter, chewing a stick of Chase's gum. His cheeks were still blotchy, and his freckles stood out in high relief on the pale parts of his cheeks, while his throat was still flushed and pink with anger.

The dye pack was finally gone and Tommy turned quickly on his heel, expecting Chase to follow without comment.

Chase did.

The ride to the city should have been horrible after that, but it wasn't. Tommy was driving, and as soon as he started the car, his fingers found his iPod in the stereo jack. In a few minutes Linkin Park's "Bleed it Out" was shrieking on the stereo, followed by "Faint" and "Nothing Else Matters." When that was done, The Foo Fighters were there, and sometime between "Statues" and "Let it Die!", both of them had started to sing at the top of their lungs, screeching the lyrics like a steel door on a concrete floor.

Chase closed his eyes and screamed "Did you ever think of me? You're so considerate!" and he and Tommy hit the chorus "Why'd you have to go and let it die?" at the top of their lungs just as they hit the Bay Bridge.

The city at twilight was beautiful. Looking across the skyline from the Bay Bridge at the industrial, concrete-and-glass Christmas tree that made up the city at night was always such a rush. Chase only had muddled memories of Mercy navigating while he tried to drive to the baseball stadium (whatever name it was going by at the moment) or Fisherman's Wharf on a turn-by-turn basis. This time, though, Tommy drove like he knew what he was doing, taking a few deep turns into the heart of the city, right to Castro, where even in the midst of the lurid lights and the promise of XXX up the ass and out the ass, the rhythm of a brightly lit club titled Wilde's eclipsed the action on the streets.

Tommy found the parking garage without hunting for it or taking the wrong turn or pissing people off, and his self-sufficiency rattled the breath in Chase's chest. He'd looked out on the street as they'd parked, and he'd seen men, dressed a lot like him and Tommy, in jeans that couldn't be machine washed and leather jackets. When Tommy reached out and grabbed his hand and hauled him down the stairs because the elevator was taking too long, Chase practically skipped into the street like a little kid.

It was a bike. He had to be careful, so careful how he rode it, but it was a bike, and they were going to go zooming downhill and through this world with the neon throbbing on the black of the February night like a hallucinogenic *trompe l'oeil*. Chase was barely cognizant of the other bodies they passed. Tommy led, he followed, their hands locked together so tightly his hand felt bruised. To Chase's surprise, they didn't go to the back of the velvet-rope line for even a second when they got to the club. Instead, Tommy walked right up to the bouncer— six feet three inches of dark-skinned testosterone and steroids—who grinned at him and dropped his hand for the low-five.

"Heya, Tango. Howyadoin'?" His voice was almost too deep to hear beyond the throb of the music and the gull-chattering of the crowd.

"Heya, Lester," Tommy grinned. "Doin' great. This's my man—"

"Chance!" Lester burst out, and held up his hand for a high-five. Chase gave him five, riddled in bemusement, and Lester started to gush. "Ohmygod! You're the new boy! We've been watching you, yanno? We haven't seen anything like you since... God. Since Tango topped Ethan, yanno? You're like... I dunno. Porn-fuckin'-gold right now!"

Chase pulled one side of his mouth up slightly and narrowed his eyes, cocking his hip and tilting his head, making like the sophisticated city mouse when he'd been real fucking excited about being the clueless little country mouse.

"Glad you liked," he drawled, and Lester shook his bald black head admiringly, then stepped back and let the two of them in. The line of excited people—both guys and girls, although none of the guys were straight and none of the girls were dressed for anything *but* dancing—gave a collective, shrill groan, and then someone from the back shrieked "Tango? Chance! Ohmygod!" and the chant of "Tango" and "Chance" followed them in.

Tommy kept his fingers tightly wound with Chase's, hauling him past the coat check and past the bar, straight to a dance floor that was just a pulse of pounding bodies. Without ceremony, Tommy pulled Chase so close they could feel each other's cocks through their insanely tight jeans and reached around Chase's ass, pushing his hips forward and grinding them up together. The music, the crowd—it was loud, insanely loud, but Tommy thrust against Chase so hard it hurt, and Chase tilted his head back and groaned.

Tommy was suddenly leaning forward, shouting, "Hurts?" in his ear, and Chase nodded his head and grunted because he could barely talk.

"So good!" he shouted back truthfully. Tommy grabbed both of Chase's hands then to the music and thrust them up, shaking them hard so Chase was there, reaching for the sky and rotating his hips while Tommy slid hard hands slowly down his wrists, his elbows, his biceps, practically rippling through the leather. Chase let him, and when Tommy's hands squeezed at Chase's tight, v-cut waist, Chase dropped his hands to Tommy's shoulders and ground up against Tommy some more.

Tommy groaned, nipped at Chase's jaw, and turned around, offering his ass, and Chase took him up on it, pulling it flush with his groin, feeling the vibrations of Tommy's groan right in the pit of his balls. Suddenly there was another body right behind him, big hands on his shoulders, the hiss of breath in his ear, and Chase was rocked back into a set of hard thighs even as he clenched Tommy tighter. A stranger's crotch was thrust against his ass, and even as it made him harder he resented it, resented anyone who threatened to come between him and Tommy Halloran. He closed his eyes though, for a second, and danced, and then whirled Tommy around to face him, stepping away from the massive stranger behind him.

Tommy came into his arms and started kissing him, hard, possessive kisses, almost dancing kisses, in time to the pulse of music that controlled the crowd. Chase kissed him back, keeping their rocking to the music hard and relentless.

Chase's cock was still covered in spend from Tommy's aggression in the changing room, but suddenly that didn't matter anymore. It was aching and the skin seemed to feel overstretched, as though the blood inside had filled it too full, leaving it sensitized and vulnerable and swollen. Tommy ground against him and Chase grunted into his mouth, almost in pain.

"Hurts?" Tommy snarled in his ear again, and Chase said, "Not as much as going without you!" He belted it out too, loud enough to be heard over the crash and thunder of the club.

Tommy kissed him again, pulling back and biting his lower lip enough to leave a mark. Then he pulled back and grabbed Chase's hand again, pulling him through the crowd. Their time on the dance floor had been hot, and people must have been watching them because the hands, random male hands, random hip thrusts and groin thrusts at them both slowed them down and caressed them, sometimes with strength and sometimes with tenderness, but always, always arousing, enflaming, teasing.

By the time Tommy found a tiny, black-curtained back room that stank of semen, sweat, and used beer, Chase was almost weeping with the pain of heightened excitement. Tommy dragged Chase inside and all but threw him against the back wall and then sank to a crouch on the floor (because no one wanted to actually touch it) and fumbled with the buttons of those gorgeous, impractical, skin-tight jeans.

The noise Chase made when his cock flopped out of his boxers and into Tommy's mouth defied description. Tommy took him in, straight to the back of his throat, and Chase's hands scrabbled in Tommy's short hair, trying to find purchase.

"Oh God!"

Tommy pulled back and gripped him tight, glaring up at him with those bright black eyes. "I'm gonna make ya come," he snarled. "I'm gonna make ya come, and I'm gonna swallow it down, and I'm gonna take you back to the hotel and I'm gonna fuck ya!"

Chase had professed to be afraid of that, but God, his cock hurt in Tommy's hand, and he needed... oh God, he needed so bad. "Yes," he panted. "God, yes...."

Tommy pulled Chase's cock back into his throat again and swallowed; the pressure on Chase's crown exquisite and hard at the same time. Tommy pulled back again and then forward and back, sticking two fingers into his mouth that he slid over the head of Chase's cock at the same time he was getting them good and wet. He slid his fingers backward between Chase's legs, tickling his perineum, and then, without warning, thrust them inside.

Chase howled. His hands flew backward, like a startled infant's, hitting the wall on either side of him, and his vision exploded into scarlet, trimmed in black. He came, dumping come into Tommy's mouth, and Tommy swallowed, his throat bobbing once, and Chase's hands clenched and released, shaking in front of his chest as he lost control of damned near everything and shook, wracked with the force of the orgasm.

He couldn't get it back, couldn't, and he must have whimpered because Tommy suddenly stood up and pulled his head against that hard, muscular chest, whispering soothing things into his ears.

"Gonna take ya back, 'kay? Gonna be in a room, and I'm gonna fuck ya, and you can lose it then, okay? It'll be just me and you, and you can fuckin' lose it then, I'll catch ya, right?"

"Right," he panted, his shoulders jerking. He was close, so close, ah gods so close, to crying, to ripping that red door off its hinges and blacking out under the force of it, but Tommy just whispered in his ear.

"It'll be all good, Chase, I swear. I'm gonna take such good care of you."

Tommy's hands were tender as he pulled Chase's jeans up and fastened them in a jingle of those dead-sexy chains, and then Chase was guided gently down the end of the darkened hallway. The fire exit had been propped open, and they emerged into a foggy, drizzly night, the overhanging clouds lit by the city's excess and creating an ambient, muted light. The alley smelled like ass and come and piss, like wet metal and trash from the dumpster that blocked it partially from view. Carefully they walked, ignoring the other bodies in the darkness of the alley, doing the same things they had just done, or worse. There was a boy, probably younger than Chase, taking it from behind while he bent over and took another man, older than Chase's father, into his mouth. Chase couldn't look at his expression, refused to, because if the kid was lost in passion, that would be too raw, too much what Chase had just been, and if he was hopeless and trapped, that would hurt too.

Instead, he and Tommy wobbled, walked, finally ran, first to the car for their duffels, then to the hotel room, and Tommy had reservations so it only took a minute to go get his keys. It wasn't until they got into the elevator that Chase actually turned to look at him, turned to say anything, and it was only then that he saw the drying white streak on the corner of Tommy's mouth.

He licked his thumb automatically and stuck it out, wiping at it, using his fingernail. Tommy caught his wrist then, his hand hard, and keeping his dark Loki eyes locked on Chase's, sucked Chase's thumb into his mouth deliberately, getting it wet, and then letting it go so Chase could resume cleanup.

Chase rubbed at the drying come futilely, his breath coming faster as Tommy kept up that fierce eye contact. Finally, he wet his tongue inside his mouth and stuck it out, leaning forward to lick it off. He licked once, twice, three times, tasting himself on Tommy's skin, and then Tommy caught his chin and whispered fiercely.

"Leave it. There will be more."

Chase's cock, sated and sleepy in his stained jeans, woke up abruptly, pulse pounding in its base.

Tommy grabbed his hand and hauled him, willingly, from the elevator to the room. There was no kissing at the door, no giggling, just grim purpose as Tommy inserted the key card and shoved in.

"Naked," Tommy ordered, swallowing hard enough to make his Adam's apple bob. "Naked. Lie on your back. You're going to see everything."

Chase peeled off his new jeans and kicked the nice leather high-tops he'd worn off with them. His leather jacket went next, and then the brightly colored silk shirt, and then he pulled the comforter off the bed and laid back with his knees spread, his eyes looking soberly up at the angry, wanting man who had been his first lover, no matter what his film roster said.

Tommy was naked very quickly too, and he rifled through his duffel bag for the ever-present, super-humongous tube of lube that he kept. He came up to the bed between Chase's knees and suddenly the grim, flat line that his mouth had become softened and relaxed, showing the full lower lip and the wide mobility of it. His long, square jaw loosened, and although his erection was as rampant and as brutal as it had been, the rest of him was suddenly unbearably happy.

"What?" Chase asked, relieved a little to see gentle Tommy, nice Tommy, come to their bed.

"Your socks," Tommy said softly. "You left them on."

Chase flushed delicately and went to sit up, but Tommy's warm hand on his calf stopped him. "I'll get it. Here. Just lay back and let me look at you, okay?"

"I'm... uh...." Chase trailed off and closed his eyes. Tommy shucked off one sock and then the other and then began rubbing hands down the surprisingly sensitive skin of the backs of his knees, the inside of his thighs. Chase gave a little moan and a shudder and his thighs fell open, spreading his body out for Tommy's pleasure, as relaxed and as needy as a spoiled cat. Tommy palmed his thighs, and Chase shuddered when the soft skin was stroked. He closed his eyes and saw red again, and the color scared him, terrified him, but not enough to tell Tommy to stop.

"Open your eyes," Tommy said, his voice still gentle. There was a mirror on the bathroom door, and Tommy had shoved it open while Chase was getting undressed. With strong, capable hands, Tommy lifted Chase's hips and dragged him on the bed until the apex of Chase's body was exposed to the mirror. "Grab that pillow," Tommy muttered. "Put it under your head. Now put that other one under your hips. There. Can you see? You can see?"

Chase closed his eyes against his body, his balls, saggy and bald, his cock, erect and terrifyingly huge. He closed his eyes against his crease and his opening, spread for the world to see. He recognized the parts: this was Chance's body, and Chance fucked men for money. But Chase's heart was in Chance's body right now, and Chase was afraid.

"Open your eyes," Tommy ordered gruffly, obviously unaware that doing so would sand the membrane that kept Chase intact to a raw, bloody veil. "It's beautiful, Chase. If it wasn't, people wouldn't pay to watch." Tommy's fingers, lubed and hot, crept between Chase's ass cheeks, and Chase's eyes flew open in pure surprise.

He watched as Tommy's first finger penetrated him, and he gasped. It burned, it stretched it... oh God... what was he... he could feel it, that same thing he felt under his cock when the other guys had begged for it. It was small and round and spongy, and Tommy was rubbing on it, slowly, while that delicious burn traveled his body, making him shudder with need.

"Tommy?" he asked, scrabbling on the covers, trying hard to find something to ground him.

"Watch," Tommy murmured, and Chase did, watching himself be penetrated and stretched while his insides threatened to shatter through his skin.

"Why?" Chase begged. His eyes fought to close and Tommy scissored his fingers, and they flew open again. "Oh God... why?"

"Because this is real," Tommy told him, stretching him some more. "You're here, now, and this is real, and you can't pretend I don't exist...."

"Tommy!" Oh God. His whole body was shaking, and he couldn't keep his eyes open, he couldn't, but he still knew he was here, his legs spread, his cock weeping pre-come, needing more of Tommy's touch, more of his body. "You're real," he cried. "You're real... Tommy...." He needed... he needed... behind his eyes, that door was buckling on its hinges, and he couldn't keep it together, couldn't keep the door shut, couldn't do anything, he was so lost, so terrified. His hands flung out at his sides again, then contracted against his chest, shaking in a terrible clench. He keened, beyond words, and suddenly Tommy was there, lunging up over the bed and penetrating Chase's stretched, open body.

Oh God... oh God... he needed. Tommy was inside him, invading him, yes, and that was important, because that was pleasure and pain and intensity and all of the things his body craved, but it was more than that, because Tommy was also giving him something to cling to, and Chase's hands came up, unclenching long enough for him to dig his fingers into Tommy's ripply, ripped shoulders and howl.

"Oh God... oh God... fuck... fuck me... fuck me... fuck... fuck... oh shit... shit... God faster... Tommy... Tommy... *ohmy godfuckin'now!*"

It didn't take long. Tommy was desperate for him, crazy, frantic with needing to bury his flesh into Chase and mark, claim, possess, and Chase was sick with wanting. Tommy plunged into him, the fullness overwhelming, painful in its intensity, and Chase lost himself, fragmenting, too many Chases to keep track of, scattering into the searing white light that, for a moment, ripped the door off its hinges and left Chase crouching, naked and shivering, in the light pouring in from that place in his soul.

He came to in the shower, his head cradled helplessly against Tommy's wide chest while Tommy ran a soapy washcloth up over his come-spattered stomach and down between his legs, to his balls and his still stretched, dripping asshole. He was saying Chase's name in sort of a frantic litany, like he was trying to get his attention.

"Chase? Chase, man, c'mon. Chase, you there? C'mon, Chase. Tell me you're there. Chase? Chase, would you say something, buddy? Please? You in there?"

"Yeah, Tommy," Chase muttered hoarsely. "Yeah. What do ya need, baby? I'll do what I can."

Suddenly he was engulfed in Tommy's wet, soapy arms to the point where he almost lost his balance, and Tommy was laughing helplessly above his head.

"Oh, Jesus, Chase. Jesus. What in the fuck happened there? You... man, you were coming and then you just wouldn't stop shaking! You wouldn't. You just kept talking to yourself and shaking and... God." Tommy stepped back in the confines of the shower and shook his shoulders. "Jesus, Chase. You scared the holy fuck out of me!"

Chase felt a semblance of his usual grin come back, even though he still had black spots swimming vaguely in front of his eyes. "You think you're that good, hah, Tommy? Getting fucked by you is a religious experience?" He giggled a little over that, even though it probably wasn't funny, and Tommy swore again and gave him one of those terrific, engulfing hugs, and even though the water and the hug made it hard to breathe, Chase still didn't want to leave that hug because he couldn't remember ever feeling that safe.

"Fuck you, Summers," Tommy muttered. "Jesus, I'm serious. Where in the fuck did you go on me?"

"Mmm...," Chase said, feeling like he was going to fall asleep right there. "That little room in your head you go to, right? When you're scared. Mine is full of red water."

He almost stumbled then, because he couldn't keep to his feet, but Tommy pulled him out of the shower and then sat him on the toilet to dry him off. Chase was too spent to even shiver in the cold air, and Tommy put him to bed naked and then turned off the light and crawled in bed after him.

Chase was there, halfway between asleep and awake, when Tommy asked a question in the dark, and Chase's inside was as naked as his outside. He answered without pain or fear or any of the things that would cause him to startle awake, sweat staining the sheets, breath shredding his throat, terrified, the next morning.

"Chase, why's there red water in your little room?"

"Cause Mommy got blood in it when she was in the bathtub."

"Oh God."

"Mmm... don't leave me, okay?"

"Backatcha, big guy."

"I'm so afraid of falling."

There was a gentle kiss on his shoulder blade. "Don't worry. I gotcha."

But nobody really has me, Tommy. I'm still all alone in that room.

AFTER he'd woken up in the dark of the morning, drenched in sweat and breathing in bare, tortured gasps, Tommy had soothed him and settled him and calmed him back down into a quiet sleep. They'd gotten up the next morning like nothing had happened—no scary fugue during sex, no night terror, no deep, dark confession—but Chase should have known Tommy wouldn't let it go.

They'd decided to stay checked into the hotel room—it was Friday and Chase had until Sunday, after all—and went to the Exploratorium in Golden Gate Park instead.

It was a clear, sunny day in the city, and there was a fierce wind in from the ocean, bringing with it the smell of salt water and diesel, of freedom and terrible, earthbound necessity. After they sat in the planetarium and allowed the three-dimensional projections of the universe to make them look small, and then traveled the natural history part of the Exploratorium just to feel evolved, they went outside to the square in front and simply held hands and walked the paths of the park, not saying much but appreciating the gentle tang of the eucalyptus trees and the chilly shade they wandered in.

They were wearing jeans—expensive jeans, yes, but simply jeans—and hooded sweatshirts with an expensive name across them, and Chase was wearing leather high-tops, but it felt like Tommy had gone out of his way to make sure Chase felt like himself as they wandered this exceptionally innocent part of the city, and Chase was grateful. He figured that they would simply forget about the events of the night before, and he'd be grateful for that too, except he'd forgotten that Tommy was only gentle sometimes, and most times he was a little wicked and a lot persistent, and that he was not good at letting things go.

They sat down on a hillside across the street from the museum, using an old blanket Tommy kept in the trunk of his car to keep the wet lawn from seeping through their jeans. The quiet between them was peaceful, and Chase was suddenly so fucking grateful that he didn't feel compelled to fill it with noise like he did with Mercy that he felt a burning behind his eyes.

"Tell me about when your mother died," Tommy said out of the blue, and Chase's breath stopped so quickly his vision almost went black. Tommy's reassuring hand on his back was the only thing that let him pull in air, and he let out the breath shakily, without any sort of guarantee he'd have the wherewithal to repeat the action, no matter how necessary.

"Not much to—"

"Don't bullshit me, Chase. Please. Man... I'm fighting ghosts here, okay? You won't tell me anything and sometimes... last night was scary as fuck. You are *always* so careful about what you say, what comes out of your mouth. Last night it was like that wall just disintegrated—I swear to God, baby, you were speaking in tongues for a minute. And then... then when you finally spoke English, the things you said... how can I love you like this and not know these things?"

"Not important," Chase mumbled, thinking about his father, yelling to break the door down. Thinking about the paramedics rushing in, checking on him, shining lights in his eyes, then wrapping him in a blanket and trying to take him out of the apartment to treat him for shock. *Leave him the fuck here! Little faggot's gonna have to toughen the fuck up if he wants to make it without his fucking mother!*

Tommy's hands were not soft. He lifted weights and did housework and garden work; he put a roof on his home and repaired window frames and dry rot. They were strong and bony and uncomfortable. So was their grip on Chase's hand.

"Do not fucking bullshit me here, asshole. You pony up now or we go back to Sac and I drop you off and the next time we see each other is on the set, *maybe*."

Chase looked at him, hurt beyond words. "*Tommy!*"

Tommy shook his head and pulled Chase's hand to his lips. "I love you like I have not loved another human being ever, and if something is hurting you this bad, I need to fucking know the shape of it, do you hear me?"

"I...." Chase looked at him helplessly.

Go ahead. Take me back to Sac. Desert me. You should desert me. I'm a douche bag. This shit that I'm doing, making you be faithful, cheating on Mercy, deserting you—I'm a bad person. You deserve more.

Tommy leaned forward and feathered a touch across his forehead—a gentle touch from a man who didn't specialize in those. It proved to be Chase's undoing, because suddenly he craved that touch, that softness from this tense, taut-wire man.

"You gonna tell me?" Tommy asked quietly, and Chase nodded to buy time.

"I, uhm, found her," he said after a minute. "She'd only partially closed the bathroom door. It was locked on the inside, and I saw the water running under the door and opened it and went in and closed it behind me." He paused for a minute, wondering at why a six-year-old kid would close that door. Did he think she still needed privacy? "I don't know why I did that," he mumbled to himself. "It was a stupid thing to do."

Again, that whisper across his forehead. "Chase, baby—how long were you there?"

Chase shrugged. "I dunno. I just sat in the water. The red water. I sang to her, because she was asleep and she always sang to me when I was asleep and I didn't want to leave her alone." He felt so detached, really, from the whole event. Like it didn't mean anything to him when every spare synapse in his psyche was scrambling, trying to shore up the door that led to that spare white bathroom covered in blood and slam it shut.

Tommy's arm came around his shoulders again, and they just sat there in the thin February sun.

"Who found you?" Tommy asked, and Chase shrugged.

"Victor had to come home eventually. I guess he had to call the fire department to bust down the door. He was pissed because he had to pay the landlord for it, and to replace the fucking carpet." *"Jesus, couldn't she have offed herself and not wrecked the fucking carpet? And you, you little bastard, was there any way you could have turned off the goddamned faucet? You were in there for fucking hours!"*

"Fucker."

Suddenly Chase found himself in the unlikely position of defending his father. "I think," he said thoughtfully, "that a lot of his bitching was trying to hide... I don't know. His pain. His disappointment. He... he didn't know how to say it. But I remember...." And he did. Oh God, he did. "He used to bring her flowers sometimes. He'd smile at her when he came home. He...." Was it true? Was it a story he was making up so the truth would be better? There'd been hurt on his father's face when Chase had yelled at him over Christmas—Chase hadn't expected that. It made everything that followed that much more likely.

"Maybe sometimes he wasn't such a bad fuckin' guy," Chase said after a minute, shocked as hell.

Tommy grunted, clearly not believing it, and kept his arm around Chase's shoulders. There were no tears then, no grand epiphanies; they simply sat quietly and listened to the sounds of families running around the park. Eventually they left and Tommy took him to a tiny bistro with thick slices of roast beef and the tangiest gravy that Chase had ever tasted. That night Tommy kissed him and eased his way into Chase's body so gently that when Chase came, his vision washed in white, not red, and it did for him what sex with Tommy always did for him: set him free and let him fly.

DRIVING home on Saturday was fun: they tested each other on movie trivia and recited song lines to see if the other one knew his shit. They stopped at the outlet stores again, and Tommy made Chase pierce both his ears and bought solid, square diamond studs for them. Chase looked and thought they looked good—male and not girlie at all.

Saturday night they made painful, aching, good-bye sort of love, and Chase woke up the next morning with Tommy's cheek sliding on the back of his neck, stinging and wet with tears Tommy wouldn't cop to, wouldn't even let him see. Chase groaned, and Tommy thrust against him, naked and erect, and Chase was still open from the night before. Tommy slid inside him with enough friction to make Chase lose his mind, and Chase lifted his leg, threw it backward over Tommy's hips, as Tommy thrust into him in a frenzy. They both came, and Chase was a mess—his own come was sprayed across his stomach and Tommy's was sliding down between his cheeks. They showered together, quietly, the strain between them telling, and Tommy wouldn't give Chase the washcloth. He washed Chase's stomach, his neck, his back, even his balls, but he wouldn't wash Chase's backside.

"Tommy...." Chase complained, because it was petty and Tommy knew it, but Tommy didn't care and Chase wouldn't hold it against him. Tommy had to drop him off and watch him go sleep in someone else's bed for a couple of weeks. Tommy got all the pettiness he could manage.

"You wash it off yourself," Tommy snapped, "but not here. When you're here, you're mine."

And Chase let it be. He knew Tommy was looking at the big hickey on his neck and thinking, *She'll see that. She'll see that and it will be over. The earrings he can explain, but not that big fucking love bite. It's over. He's mine.* He didn't tell Tommy that he had a plan for that, because he'd gotten really fucking good at being a two-faced douche bag when he hadn't been paying attention.

Johnnies was closed on Sundays—apparently people only *watched* porn on the Lord's day, they didn't make it. Chase kissed Tommy through the window of the car with so much mastery, so much dominance, that Tommy's eyes were dazed and he had trouble putting the car into reverse before he backed out of the driveway and went back to his snug, wonderful little home with the aging cat and the desperate need for company.

Chase took his duffel to the back parking lot and spotted the pile of rocks and gravel in the corner, left over, he thought, from when John had probably landscaped the interior courtyard. There were some sizeable chunks of gravel under a tree in the parking lot, the kind with the rough edges because the top had been finished to make it durable and shiny. Chase found one of those pieces, and stripped off his sweatshirt and the shirt underneath it. Looking into the side mirror of his car, he scraped at the spot on his neck just enough to make it sting. Then he stood up so he had better leverage, and dug that fucker into his skin, scraping it down his neck, his shoulder, his arm, with enough force to leave a vicious wound. He stared at it in his side mirror for a moment, watching incuriously as the blood welled up to replace the space left by the missing skin. It hurt—God, doing that to himself hurt, but it was okay. He deserved it. He deserved it for cheating on Mercy, he deserved it for leaving Tommy when Tommy needed him so badly—he deserved the pain, he knew he did.

He deserved it so much that he spent some time slamming his fists into the tree to bust up his knuckles so no one could say he hadn't been doing construction. He stopped at a drug store to buy gauze and taped up the wounds himself, feeling a curious mixture of disgust and pride.

God, he really was a fucker sometimes, wasn't he?

MERCY had fawned all over him like he was some sort of hero, and Chase had refused to take a painkiller because the pain had been so damned affirming of everything he knew about himself. He deserved to be alone. He deserved the pain. It was perfect. The scrapes had been all but healed by the time he'd done the shoot with Dex—Tommy didn't notice them in the shot itself, but he sure as shit had noticed them after he took Chase to his house and got them naked. He didn't say anything, but his jaw tightened and he spent a wordless moment kissing the still-tender skin.

"I'm sorry," he whispered, looking at Chase miserably. "I thought... I mean I hoped...."

Chase kissed him, so he wouldn't have to say it. Chase had hoped too, in a way, but apparently Chase's cowardice was too overwhelming even for Loki's deviousness, and that alone made Chase a little sad. No one could save Chase from his own deceit but Chase, and he was well aware he just wasn't that fucking strong.

But right now, it didn't matter. Right now, they were watching the rushes, and Tommy was telling Chase that he'd done good, and Chase was remembering that moment, that beautiful, terrible, frightening moment, when he had lost himself for good and Tommy had found him.

Find me again, Tommy. Find me again. It'll be better than a bike, better than Christmas, if you'll find me again and I never have to be lost in that room again for as long as we both shall live.

TURBULENCE

"SO, CHANCE, how long have you been with us?"

The young man on the bed had cut off the dyed part of his hair— the blond color underneath had hints of red in it. His eyes were still open and blue, though, and his cheekbones were still high. His mouth was still wide and mobile with full, fuckable lips, and he still held his jaw like he was used to a piece of gum there, ready to crack when he felt like it.

"Around seven months," he said, obviously doing the counting in his head and coming up surprised.

Another young man—this one smaller, with dark hair, an irrepressible grin, and no clothes whatsoever—leapt onto the bed and bounced there, as eager as a child. The voice behind the camera laughed a little.

"So how is it you've never bottomed?" it said.

"He hadn't met me yet!" said the naked young man, and Chance grinned at him, clearly delighted.

"Yeah," Chance said, winking at him. "Guess I'd just never met Digger."

Digger rolled over onto his back and started to stroke his erect penis. It was decent-sized, but not huge, although he clearly enjoyed having it touched. "Well, get naked, buddy, and I'll treat you to the whole 'Digger experience'."

Chance, who had been reclining, rolled over onto his stomach spontaneously and took the head in his mouth. Digger kept his eyes closed, although the rest of him shuddered deliciously all over.

"Now that's not playing by the rules!" he protested—but not hard.

In response, Chance lowered his head and took Digger's cock all the way to the back of his throat.

"That was a class act," Tommy said approvingly when giving Chase his backrub after the shot.

"I don't know what got into me," Chase mumbled. This was the fourth time Tommy had cared for him after filming a scene, and Chase didn't know how he would have done it without him. He'd tried, the second time, to think about Mercy rubbing his back, kissing his shoulders, whispering sweet things in his ears, and he'd started shivering so bad that Tommy had gotten out a heating pad and given him Ibuprofen for a fever. He couldn't help it: his entire body recoiled at the thought of Mercy touching him like this when he was raw and vulnerable and sensitized in the extreme.

It was hard enough when they were roommates who shared a bed.

He never mentioned Mercy when Tommy could hear the name. It was like they had *finally* agreed that his week a month at Tommy's was magic—a period of time out of time, it didn't exist to Mercy and Mercy didn't exist here in Tommy's little house. And the thing was, not mentioning Mercy to Tommy was almost as hard as not mentioning Tommy to Mercy.

He *loved* Mercy. He had once watched her curse out a stray mouse in the corner of their apartment for over a half an hour. He had run out and down the block to buy a mousetrap, just to spare her the pain, but when she had seen that it was the kind that actually *killed* the mouse, she had burst into tears. He had to capture the damned thing in a jar and let it out on the lawn. He hadn't pointed out that the poor thing was probably doomed anyway; the fact that she'd watched, anxiously, as the disease-carrying vermin went scampering off to its doom had made him love her even more.

He just didn't want to sleep with her.

He bought her a car instead. It was stupid and transparent and he wondered that she didn't just turn to him and say, "Chase, you asshole, stop dicking with me. If you're cheating, just own up." She didn't though. She teared up and hugged him and cried some more on his neck.

"I hated you driving around in that deathtrap," he'd told her truthfully, because her little Toyota had a tendency to stall whenever it went over sixty miles an hour. Fortunately she'd been using all of the surface roads, but still. When he saw what the returns were on his threesome with Dex and Kane, he traded her car in without batting an eye.

"You take such good care of me, baby."

I'm a guilty douche bag, Mercy. I don't deserve to kiss the dirt under your feet.

After that moment, after the next shoot, on the third day at Tommy's house, when they were eating roast beef and au jus that he'd prepared just to get Tommy to promise not to throw it up, he hesitantly mentioned that he couldn't go shopping again for a while.

"Why? What'd you spend your money on?"

Chase sat there, opening and shutting his mouth like a stunned salmon until Tommy muttered, "Fuck," and walked away. He left the bathroom door open, so Chase could hear him toss his cookies. Chase couldn't listen. He tore out of the house without a jacket, when the sky was pissing down March rain.

Tommy caught up with him in the car, and when Chase refused to get in, he screeched to the curb in front of some random family's house and got out.

"Get in the car," he snapped, and Chase shook his head. His eyes stung so badly he could barely see, and his shirt was soaked through. He couldn't seem to feel that, though. He was sitting cross-legged, like a pretzel on a pancake, looking at that door in his chest, wondering if opening it would hurt when the red water overwhelmed him, cut off his breathing, went over his head.

"We shouldn't do this anymore."

Tommy's face, pale in the rain, went bloodless: his lips even turned blue. "What in the fuck…?"

"I'm not good for you, Tommy. There's so much shit... I'm still in the fucking closet. I've got a fucking girlfriend, for Christ sake. I'm hurting you. I'm making you hurt yours—"

He couldn't finish because Tommy strode forward and grabbed Chase's shoulders so hard he left bruises. "*Nobody* makes me hurt myself," he hissed. "*I* make me hurt myself, and I'll do it whenever I goddamned well please. You don't get to call this quits on count of my hang-ups, you bastard!"

"I don't want to hurt you anymore!" Chase told him, his teeth chattering almost too hard to get the words out. "Look at me! I'm fucking ripping you to pieces, Tommy! You will *never* find someone better than me if I keep leaning on you!"

"Look at you?" Tommy yelled. "*Look* at you? I *am* looking at you! You think I'm the one getting ripped to pieces, you aren't paying enough goddamned attention! You come to my house and you sleep like you ain't slept in a *month*, and you know why? You know why—c'mon, Chase, let's hear us some fuckin' truth. You fuckin' tell me why!"

Because I can't sleep when you're not next to me.

"That's no reason for you to let me do this," Chase said desperately.

I'm trying, Tommy. You're the best person I've ever known. I'm trying to do right by you, I swear.

"Let you? Is that what you think?" Tommy laughed, the sound so bitter Chase was surprised the rain didn't steam up around him, hissing like acid. "*Let* you do this to me? I'm fucking *begging* you to do this to me. How fucked up is that? That here you are, saying 'Let me go! I'm hurting you!' and I'm saying 'Hurt me some more, you fucker, do anything... fucking do anything to me, just don't get lost like I know you're gonna!' I *see* you, Chase. You think I don't see you? You think I don't *know* that Chance the sexy bastard on the screen isn't some scary person you made up? That the real person you are isn't the poor fucker trapped behind your eyes, screaming the shit you won't say? You think I don't know that? I know that! I know that and dammit...." Tommy trailed off a little, and his hands relaxed their bony-fingered death grip on Chase's shoulders. "I can't let you lose that guy, Chase. He's the guy who comes apart when I hold you."

Chase squeezed his eyes shut, praying for Tommy to hold him at the same time Chance, the brave one, hoped that Tommy would leave and find someone who would make him eat and help him quit porn and live in his house and pet his cat. Then Tommy wrapped arms around him, strong arms, and Chase slouched and lowered his head to Tommy's shoulder and tried to ease the stinging in his eyes. Tommy's arms tightened to the point of pain and Chase let him, because he was shaking so hard it felt like that clasp might be the only thing to keep him from falling the fuck apart.

They made it into the house eventually, and stripped down and dried off and climbed into bed, and they might have made love but neither of them got hard. They just held each other, not speaking, until the shivering stopped, and then they watched television and fell asleep, their legs twined tightly together.

So Chase had given in a little, ceded to the double life, and it sucked a little because on his fourth "business trip," the one in April right before spring training that was held in a little kid's camping facility up in Pollock Pines, he only had a couple of days with Tommy, and he felt the missing time like a rent in his skin.

He had Tommy drop him off at Donnie's boyfriend's house and was unprepared for Donnie to come outside as they were pulling up. He was *really* unprepared for Tommy to take one look at Donnie and narrow his eyes.

"That's him, right?" Tommy asked, his voice flat and his South Boston more pronounced than Chase had ever heard it. "That's the blond guy you wanted to be, right?"

Chase cleared his throat and looked out to where Donnie was glaring at him like he was pissed, which Chase couldn't figure out since he'd said a friend from work was dropping him off and Tommy hadn't done anything yet to *not* be a friend from work. "Yeah. That's him."

Tommy put the car in park then and turned to Chase and grabbed his chin, plowing into him with a hard, carnal, possessive, angry kiss. Chase gasped, surprised, but that only gave Tommy better purchase, and by the time he was done Chase was liquid, sweating, and embarrassed, backed up against the car door.

"You can't have another life, Chase," Tommy said, his shiny-dark eyes unforgiving. "You've got plenty going as it is."

"He's a friend," Chase whispered, and Tommy nodded.

"If you're lucky, he's still a friend."

Chase nodded, and then stood and retrieved his duffel from the back, but kept his hand on the front seat before Tommy could pull away. Tommy looked at him from under dark, plucked eyebrows, and Chase said, "C'mere."

Tommy leaned forward then, reluctantly, hurt in every line of his body. "Yeah?"

"I didn't love him like I love you. Be mad at me, Tommy. Not Donnie. Donnie didn't make me the fuck-up, okay?"

Tommy's anger, his attitude, slipped then, and this time Chase kissed him, his lips soft, his breath feathering Tommy's temple as he pulled away. "I do love you, Tommy Matthew Halloran. Don't let my love hurt, okay?"

"Too late. Enjoy your baseball warrior ritual, ya dumb jock."

Chase winked and pecked him on the cheek. "Will do."

Then he pulled out of the car to face a curiously unsurprised Donnie. Tommy pulled away and Chase forced himself to meet his best friend's eyes.

"So, you missed my birthday last month." His tone was conversational, and Chase eyed him warily. His car—a little Toyota a lot like Mercy's old one, only green—was open, and Chase went to throw his duffel bag in the back.

"I sent you a card and a raincheck for a River Cats game!" Chase protested, because he wouldn't have forgotten Donnie's birthday for anything. "Is Kevin coming?" Kevin usually drove with them, but his duffel wasn't back with Donnie's and Chase's.

"Kevin'll be here in a little bit. I wanted to talk to you. Did I mention my birthday?"

"You're twenty-one, you can drink now." Of course, both of them drank beer at Donnie's house frequently. "What, you gonna lord it over us 'cause you can buy? 'Cause I've got like, what? Two weeks until I'm twenty-one too? Gloat away!" Chase was joking—or trying to, because Donnie's pretty blue eyes were narrow and dangerous, and his usually full mouth was flat and compressed.

"Yeah. Well, I needed a drink, lemme tell you. Cause you know what Alejandro got me for my birthday, as sort of a joke, mind you, because he wanted me to see what I was missing out on since he turned twenty-six this year?"

Oh shit. Chase went with a cheesy smile and a waggle of his eyebrows. "A stripper?"

"You wish," Donnie told him sourly, stalking over to his car just to kick the damned tire. "He got me a porn subscription, you asshole. Wanna guess which provider?"

Chase couldn't dissemble anymore, not to Donnie. "*Johnnies*," he said weakly. "You got a subscription to *Johnnies*."

Donnie sighed and whumped back against his car, all of the piss and vinegar leaking out of him like his spine was a sieve. "And guess who's there on the front of the website, their new boy, the next big thing?"

Chase sighed. He didn't know for certain, but he could guess. He didn't visit the website after the first week. He'd liked seeing the comments at first, but there were like a thousand of them, praising the size of his cock and his stamina and his body—but not anything about *him*, even his smile. He'd had to stop looking; he was doing this for himself, not for anyone else, and that was just how he had to treat it.

"Some homely asshole named Chance," he mumbled, leaning back against the car next to his dearest and oldest friend.

Who promptly whapped him on the back of the head. "You're a god, you know it, now shut the fuck up. What in the fuck do you think you're doing?"

"I thought I was supposed to shut—ouch!" This time Donnie meant it when he smacked Chase's head.

"Don't play with me, Chase," Donnie snapped, and Chase was suddenly confused and relieved when Donnie—the same Donnie who had draped his arm over Chase's shoulders after nearly every game they'd ever had, from the second grade on—draped a sexless, kind, comforting arm over his shoulder. Chase leaned his head on Donnie's shoulder, feeling a tight string break in his stomach. The guy was pissed. There was no doubt in his mind that Donnie was pissed. But apparently being pissed didn't mean that he wasn't a friend, and Chase wanted to cry, he was so relieved.

"Not even baseball?"

And now Donnie's chest relaxed under Chase's head. "Yeah, you stupid fucker. We can play baseball. What in the hell were you thinking, Chase?"

Chase closed his eyes, and for one of the few times outside of Tommy's bed or even his home or his car, allowed himself to feel like Chance did. Chance was cocky and sure of himself. Chance was adventurous and sensual. Chance didn't let anything get in the way of his pleasure and was damned proud of the fact that he could pleasure another person.

Chance didn't have any pesky morals or worries about hurting another human soul interfere with fucking or being fucked in the most outrageous, loudest, prettiest, sell-it-to-the-cheap-seats way possible.

I was thinking I'd rather be Chance than Chase any day of the week.

"I needed the money."

"There's better ways to get it," Donnie sighed, his voice unyielding. The guy was going out of his way to be human to Chase, after Chase had blatantly lied to him. Chance the porn star did *not* belong in Donnie's sweet little fairy-tale world—but Donnie hadn't kicked him out of it. No, Chase's best friend since the second grade had draped his arm around Chase's shoulders and invited him to talk, really talk. Chase needed to do better.

"No, there's not," he whispered, and because Donnie knew him, Donnie looked at his face, and Chase wasn't sure what his expression really was, but it made Donnie close his eyes in pain.

Donnie looked away, toward the house, and for a panicked moment, Chase wondered if Alejandro was coming out, because if he was going to talk, Tommy would have been first on the list, Donnie second, and Alejandro somewhere behind Kevin and before Mercy. He liked the guy, but he wasn't going to pour his heart out to him.

"Chase, man, I love her. You know that, right? She's great. She's fun and she's not stupid and she's a nice, nice girl. But you know what she's not?"

"You think I don't know that?"

"Say it. Just once, I need to hear you say it. You've obviously admitted it to yourself, because otherwise you wouldn't be... f... fuck!"

Donnie couldn't say it. Oh shit. Donnie couldn't say it, and Chase *had* to say it.

I'm gay. I've always been gay. I've always known. You've known it too. I'm sorry I've lied, I'm sorry I hurt you with my lie, but mostly I'm sorry I'm gay.

His voice was liquid and floating in his ears when he said, "I fuck other guys for money." The red door bulged at the hinges, bowed out, oozing liquid at the seams, and Chase's breathing quickened as he shoved up against it, putting his shoulders into it, forcing it flat and seamless, reinforcing the caulking at the gaps.

"Yeah," Donnie whispered, tightening his arm. "Look at you. You're sweating and your face is practically gray. God, Chase. What the fuck are you doing?"

Chase took a few deep breaths and straightened up, shaking off Donnie's comforting arm. "When I'm on the set," he said roughly, "I'm flying."

Donnie closed his eyes. "You know, if you could just tell her the truth, you could fly someplace *not* on camera. You know that, right?"

Chase could still taste Tommy—he'd snuck a cigarette in the back yard before he'd come in for coffee, and the bitter smoke of it had been on his tongue. Chase didn't care. He wanted Tommy there, wanted to clench his hand so tight it hurt. Tommy would make this moment with Chase's best friend easier; Chase just knew he would.

"I made promises to her," he said weakly, because the thinness of those promises, with everything he was doing behind her back, was almost as transparent and bitter as the smoke.

"Those promises include that guy who dropped you off?" Donnie asked quietly, and Chase took a step away.

"We can't talk about Tommy," he said, knowing it was childish. He crossed his arms in front of his chest, like he could keep Tommy right there and nobody could know and nobody could comment and nobody could ever take Tommy away.

"Yeah, why's that?" Donnie had never been hurt. He wasn't afraid of anything. He took two steps toward Chase and put his hands on Chase's shoulders and Chase felt his spine collapse in on itself. He kept his arms crossed, but now he was protecting his own heart as much as he was holding Tommy to it.

Tommy's perfect. Tommy's not part of my bullshit.

"Tommy…," Chase mumbled, maybe just to cling to his name. "He's special."

Donnie nodded. "I recognize him from the site, but you haven't done a scene with him."

Tommy's not a scene. Tommy's real. Tommy's mine.

"Tommy's special."

Donnie pulled Chase back in under that comforting arm again. "Chase, man, what's the worst that could happen if you tell Mercy you're gay and that you're going to live with Tommy and do something that doesn't make you break into a cold sweat and turn the color of Kevin's underwear?"

Every bad thing my father ever said about me would be right.

"That's just being mean."

"Answer the question, jerk-off!"

I'd be the reason my mother… my mother… I'd be the thing behind the red door, Donnie. I'd be that thing. I'd be the worst thing I could imagine. I can be a cheater and a porn star and a douche bag but don't make me the thing behind the red door.

"I'm sorry," he mumbled, because he couldn't answer the question, and God bless Donnie, and all men who had grown up loved and knew how.

Donnie's arms wrapped around his shoulders and tightened. "You love him?"

"Yeah."

"Try to do right by him."

Too late.

"I'm a douche bag."

Donnie's voice broke a little. "That's a fucking lie. You take that back!"

"I'm… the things I'm doing—"

"You're fucked up, man. I'm not denying it. But there's not a mean bone in your body. Hell, I've watched you fuck on camera for *hours*—you fuck like a god, you know that?"

Chase pulled back, absurdly pleased. "You think so?" and Donnie started to laugh, but the laugh was wrong. It sounded more like tears. "What's wrong?"

Donnie shook his head and wiped his eyes. "It's your voice, Chase. Just now. It's that same voice you used when you first pitched a game. We were like, seven, and you were so good, and I'd never seen you look happy, and you did." Donnie shook his head again. "Man, Kevin's gonna be here any minute. I forgive you, okay? Just—just be careful." Donnie put his hand on Chase's chest for a minute, splayed it out, big fingers, wide palm and all, and Chase looked at it dumbly, not sure why it was there.

"You got something wrecked in you, Chase. If you ever want to fix it, let me know."

Chase nodded, and they heard the distinctive backfire of a Ford Escort that had been made before any of them had been born. Kevin had arrived.

"Aw fuck," Donnie said, backing away and wiping his eyes. "That asshole's gonna park that thing in 'Yandro's driveway for a week. I gotta go get some newspaper or it's gonna stain the fuckin' pavement."

By the time Kevin pulled up, Chase felt like maybe, maybe, the next breath wasn't pulling his lungs over a daisy field full of razor blades.

SPRING training was awesome. Chase had forgotten the simple joy of physical exertion, one that didn't involve contact with another human being and that simply demanded he did his best. His body was an amazing machine. On the conditioning field he enjoyed toning it and tweaking it and basically preparing it for top performance. There was no soul-searching on the conditioning field or in the baseball diamond. The rest of his life could have been acres of carnage from a bloody emotional war, but when he was on the field he was perfect, golden, and happy.

Donnie didn't mention his job, Kevin didn't know about it, and all the other guys cared about was whether he could send that ball from the pitcher's mound at over eighty miles an hour, and he could, and every time he let it sail through the air and knew it rang true, it was like his whole life, his whole body, became that little point of perfection in the strike zone.

Even the coach—a taciturn man in his late fifties who didn't do a lot of happy-happy/joy-joy encouragement—told him he was going to have the season of his life. He started thinking about ways to get Tommy and his other friends from work to come see him play. He wanted to share this with them. He wanted Tommy to be proud of him, in this area, even if Chase could find nowhere else in his life that Tommy could praise with a full heart.

I'm beautiful here, Tommy. Come see me be beautiful.

He texted Mercy every night before she fell asleep, and Tommy every morning when he woke up. Then Tommy again, right before Chase went to sleep, so he could pretend Tommy was the one he'd give a kiss good night to if he was home.

I'm beautiful on the field, Tommy. I'm a douchey fucker in real life, but come see me be beautiful here.

DEX, Tommy, Scott, Cameron, and Kane came to see his third home game. Mercy was there too, with her girlfriends, and Chase waved at all of them when he came out on the field. *Friends from work, meet girlfriend. Girlfriend, meet friends from work. I gotta go pitch my heart out now; it's gonna be somethin' special.*

And it was. All of the extra time in the gym making his body pretty had paid off in unexpected ways. His fastball was faster than it had *ever* been, and his throwing speed was phenomenal. He fielded three pop-up flies in one inning, just because he could dance so fast, he could beat the catcher to the midline. When the game wrapped up—Hornets eight, Gators ten—and he retired from the field, he got an ovation, and when Donnie, who played first base, ran toward the dugout, he gave Chase a shove and told him to bow like a good trained monkey. Chase took off his cap, and people—not just his people, either—stood up and applauded—and he thought he'd ride that applause for maybe the rest of his life.

Mercy knew he was going out with friends afterwards, so she ran down to the bottom rail and kissed him in the spring sunshine. He smiled at her, gave her a kiss, and waved to her girlfriends, who all smiled at him like he was some kind of hero, and then waved to the guys from *Johnnies* who had all come down too.

"We still going out?" Dex asked, and Chase nodded, trying hard not to see Tommy's fierce and miserable expression next to him.

"Was planning on it!" Chase said enthusiastically. Normally he would have gone out with Donnie and Kevin and the other guys from the team, but it was one of those nights where everyone seemed to have something going on. Donnie had his sister's birthday, Kevin actually had a date, and half the team was flunking history and was having a study weekend starting that night. Chase had texted Dex and offered free tickets to anyone who wanted them, and the rest had evolved from there.

Tommy caught his eyes and nodded quietly, and Chase turned to Mercy. "I'm gonna stay over at someone's house tonight, 'kay babe? I'm pretty wired."

"'Kay—I gotta be at work early tomorrow, Chase, that's fine." She gave him a good-bye peck on the cheek, and Chase turned to the guys saying, "Meet by the locker room!" before he trotted after his team.

He was happy—blissfully happy—before a painful slug to the arm almost knocked him off his feet.

"Holy fuck... Donnie?"

They were in jog mode, and Chase caught up to him

"Jesus, Chase—you're really aiming for that douche bag thing, aren't you? God, after that, I think I'll fucking make you a nametag and stick it on your front door!"

Chase just looked at him, puzzled, and Donnie smacked his own head repeatedly with his palm. "God! Chase—you are the most clueless bastard I have ever fucking *seen!* How bad do you think that little display with Mercy just hurt the guy you say you love?"

Chase stumbled, all pretense of jogging forgotten. Suddenly the brilliant game, the spring night scented with lilac, the excitement of seeing his friends from work someplace where they could keep their clothes on... it all drained away, and he hardly felt like he had the energy to walk to the locker room.

"Oh God," he muttered, his lips going cold. "I didn't mean... I mean, I wasn't thinking about it that way... I mean... Oh Jesus, Donnie!" His lower lip was trembling and he felt like he'd been slugged in the stomach and not just the arm.

Donnie turned around and looked at him and stopped his own jog, dropping his head and pinching the bridge of his nose.

"Jesus," he muttered. "Didn't even hit you, did it?"

Chase shook his head, feeling like he had when he'd been in fourth grade and his dad had told him that if he ever brought a kitten home again, Victor would run it over with the car. Chase had shown up on Donnie's doorstep that night with the kitten, and Donnie's mom had kept it for him for the next eight years, when the poor thing had died of some sort of cat disease.

"I... I just wanted them to see me play. I didn't know Mercy could make the game too." She'd originally had to work, but she'd traded shifts for the next day so she could see him play.

Donnie sighed and came back, throwing that arm around his shoulder and steering him for the locker room in the back of the college gym. "Chase?"

"Yeah?"

"Has it occurred to you yet that you're not really cut out for the double life thing?"

"I tried to break up with Tommy once."

"Why?"

"Because I'm not good for him. He needs someone better."

Donnie's laugh was humorless. "Now see, if you're going to break up with someone, the least you could do is tell them the truth."

"That is the truth."

"It's a big fucking lie, baby. That's why it didn't work. If just once you could tell the truth to everyone involved, you might actually survive to be happy."

You don't know what you're asking.

"I'll try to keep that in mind."

And he did too. They went out that night to a gay bar, because even Scott, who claimed to have a girlfriend, knew that dancing in a gay bar could be a lot more fun—and less strings attached—than dancing in a straight bar. Besides, his girlfriend knew what he did for a living, and apparently the fucking of other people didn't bother her, as long as the other person was male.

But Chase saw Scott and Dex dancing to a slower song, Scott's hands framing Dex's hips, and Dex staring at Scott like the world was in the guy's eyes, and something in his chest twisted hard enough to hurt.

"What're you looking at?" Tommy asked. In spite of Donnie's words, Tommy had been ebullient all night, cracking jokes, hyper as hell, cackling with glee. They had danced—not like they had in San Francisco, but in a way, the lack of intensity was refreshing. They actually heard the music, felt each other's bodies, moved in sync. The other guys jumped on the floor with them, and it was like the game— total immersion into physical activity, muscles, sinews, heartbeat, blood and bone, all of it throbbing to the music. Dancing with Tommy was better than beer, and Chase was old enough to drink legally now.

But still, as the slower song took over the floor and Dex and Scott writhed together, sex without skin, intercourse without penetration, orgasm without climax. Chase couldn't help but watch them and wonder at the desolation on Dex's face whenever Scott wasn't looking at him.

"I'm feeling bad," Chase said, wrenching his face away. The guys had called him "Chance" all night, in spite of the fact that they'd seen his real name on the lineup flyer and heard it over the intercom. To them he was "Chance," but not to "Tango." He wondered if he'd slipped up and called Tommy by his real name that night. They'd all heard Scott call Dex "David," and no one had even blinked.

"About what?" Tommy put his hand on the back of Chase's neck, and in spite of the boniness and the big knuckles, it was comforting. Chase closed his eyes and leaned back into the touch, feeling the slow music in his bones.

"I shouldn't have made you see us together," he said softly, standing up and taking Tommy into his arms and pulling him out onto the floor while Staind's "It's Been A While" eddied around them like a black whirlpool. "I didn't mean to be a clueless dick."

He felt rather than saw Tommy's smile. "You *are* a clueless dick. Don't let it shake you."

Chase let out a breath and pulled Tommy closer. If Tommy cocked his head just so, he could nestle it against Chase's shoulder, and Chase liked that so much.

"For you, tonight, I won't," he said.

Kane and Cameron came bounding by, restless with the slow music. "You guys ready to blow this place?" Kane asked, playfully dragging Cameron by the hips so his crotch ground up against Cam's ass. "I'm *bored!*"

"Go the fuck away," Tommy said dreamily and without rancor. "I'm dancing."

"Oh God! Boring!"

"Don't worry," Chase told them, winking at Kane, who had the attention span of a drunken monkey. "It'll pick up in a minute."

Sure enough, it did on the next song, and the throbbing, joyous dance mob resumed. But later that night, after they closed the place down while singing with The Ramones and "What I Like About You" at the top of their lungs, Chase got into Tommy's car and that other song, the slow, pensive one, seemed to gather around them like a cloak, like they'd been pulled under by it and never come clean.

Tommy went with it and pulled it up on his iPod, and they were so close to his little house that he'd only played it twice before they pulled into the garage. It was enough. Chase heard it in his head as they moved without hurry through the darkened house and undressed, the sweat and bitter alcohol from the club still on their skin.

Tommy shucked off his T-shirt, his silhouette dark against the glow from the sodium light outside the window, and while his hands were in the air, Chase captured them above his head. Slowly, so slowly, because he wanted this to last, he kissed down Tommy's jaw, enjoying his stubble as it rasped against Chase's lips. He scraped his teeth along the join of neck and shoulder, then scraped them along Tommy's collarbone, loving the feel of the smooth skin, the tang of his sweat, the prominent ridge of his bone. There was a lump directly between Tommy's shoulder and his chest, from when he'd broken the bone in the sixth grade, and Chase loved knowing where that was, loved knowing why it was there. He'd seen the picture of Tommy in the hospital bed, looking surly and embarrassed, and had felt Tommy's mother's worry, whether she knew who Chase was or not.

But he couldn't spend forever there, and he deliberately kissed his way down the center of Tommy's chest, moving to the side to suckle a rose-colored nipple (colorless in the dark) into his mouth, and Tommy grunted and scrabbled in Chase's short-cut hair for purchase, wanting to hold him there at the same time he wanted Chase to move. Chase didn't want to move, though, wanted it slow, and when Tommy finally pushed him off, he only moved to Tommy's other side. Tommy grunted.

"Jesus, Chase!"

"Want it to last!" Chase's erection was tight in his new jeans, and he wanted to feel Tommy's bare chest against his, but he didn't want to let go of Tommy's taste.

"Make it last while you're fucking me!" Tommy ordered, pulling back and grabbing Chase's jeans, dragging them down to his ankles. Chase was going commando—it had made being on the dance floor almost excruciating sometimes—and his cock flopped out and almost directly into Tommy's mouth. Wet... wet, hot, smooth, with pressure around the crown and... oh God!

"Tommy!" he breathed. "You think I'm gonna last long enough to fuck you?"

Tommy pulled back and said, "You'd better!" while he shucked off his pants and toed off his shoes and socks with movements so smooth they were almost preternatural. Chase scrambled to catch up, shucking his pants and shoes off and then bending to get rid of his socks. He left his shirt on, mostly because Tommy was bent over the bed, rifling through the end table with his ass in the air, and it was begging and needy and Chase needed it right back. Chase was behind him, grinding up against Tommy's crease before Tommy could find the lubricant, and Tommy's next breath sounded like a sob.

"You got it?" Chase asked, and Tommy said, "No, dammit! Where the fuck is—oh you *bastard!*"

Chase was tonguing him, and he was salty and musky, because he hadn't just come out of the shower, but Chase didn't care. It was Tommy, concentrated Tommy, and Chase licked him with a flat tongue again and again until Tommy screamed "*Arggh!*" into the pillow and almost clocked Chase on the head with the lubricant.

Chase pulled back and dumped lube on his cock, shivering because it was cold, and then drizzled a little on Tommy's asshole while Tommy howled into the pillow again. Chase couldn't wait anymore. He wanted to, he wanted to make it *forever*, but he couldn't. He positioned himself and pushed, and Tommy was so soft inside, grainy like satin, locked tight around his shaft like a fist.

"Oh God!" Tommy groaned and Chase couldn't ease his way in anymore, he had to snap his hips forward with as much thrust as he had. "*Yes!*" Tommy reached back and stroked himself and Chase pulled back and thrust again, almost angry but mostly passionate, mostly wanting to claim Tommy, possess him, make him never ever doubt that no matter who else Chase fucked, no matter who else he kissed, it was Tommy, Tommy alone, who could make Chase this crazy, make Chase need this much.

He was needy and on the edge, and he pounded into Tommy like fucking him through the mattress would save both their lives. He heard Tommy shout, felt Tommy's sphincter lock so tight around his cock that Chase wasn't sure he *could* come. Tommy sobbed and released, and Chase angled his hips and nailed Tommy's prostate to milk that orgasm for as much as they could get. Tommy groaned again, and Chase continued, fucking until sweat rolled down his face and his breath came in pants and he was seeing black behind his eyes in the effort not to come.

"Please, Chase!" Tommy sobbed. "Please… God, please, baby, let me feel you come!"

"*Geeeaaaaawwwwwwwwwdddddd!*" He poured into Tommy, spasming, coming, pulsing, his vision going blank and his bones going liquid as he collapsed on top of Tommy, bearing them both to the mattress.

He caught his breath and went to roll off, but Tommy made a sound of protest.

"I'm crushing you," he said apologetically.

"Crush me," Tommy murmured. "Crush me. Just don't leave me. Just don't leave me."

I'd die first. "Love you." *I can't promise anything.* "I'll love you forever." *Except that.* He wasn't sure if Tommy noticed that just like he never said, "I love you" to Mercy, he never promised tomorrow in Tommy's arms.

But Tommy noticed. Later, in the bathtub, he laid back in Chase's arms, both of them drowsing in water scented with something sharp and male and bubbly.

"Couldn't you lie to me," he said, sadness saturating his tone like that sexy, male smell saturated the air. "At least once? Couldn't you lie to me about forever?"

"No," Chase said, wrapping his arms around Tommy's shoulders a little tighter. "Because I keep hoping I'll have the balls to mean it someday, and I want you to know it's real."

"God, I hate you."

Chase sighed, wishing it was true. "You hate that you can't hate me," he said resignedly. "Sometimes I do too."

But the bitter mood sweetened as they crawled into bed together. Chase nuzzled the back of Tommy's neck and Tommy all but purred.

"Mercy was your first sex, right?" he said, his voice soft with sleep. Chase was too tired to even startle.

"Yeah."

"And your first guy was Dex, but that was on set, right?"

"You know that."

"Then I'm really your first lover, aren't I? I'm the first person you've ever loved that you've had sex with, aren't I?"

Chase smiled against Tommy's skin. "You're my only lover, Tommy. Don't doubt that, okay?"

"You too."

"Love you."

"Love you back."

They had to sleep then, and for a few hours, their lives were perfect.

CRASHING

THE tall blond boy was on all fours, in a sixty-nine with an uncircumcised boy with a soul patch on his chin. A big, burly, brown-haired giant of a boy fucked the blond guy from behind. The sounds coming from the blond boy's throat were not quite human. The dark-haired one with his cock in the blond guy's mouth gave a shout from below, and the camera zoomed in on blondie's face as he let come slip from his lips while he tried to swallow, and got creamed across the cheeks from his sixty-nine partner's final blast. He groaned again, his noises so raw and real the other guys echoed them. Sixty-nine buddy was out of his mind, gibbering, "Please, please, please, please...."

The blond guy was just gibbering. Half words were coming out, but every time the man behind him plunged harder and deeper into his asshole, they stopped, and what was left was a keening sound, almost eerie in how much it yearned. Sixty-nine-buddy groaned and rolled, getting out of the way, and the blond boy was still quivering, his movements so out of control it was obvious he didn't even realize his buddy was gone. Blond guy let out a howl, his hand jerking his cock in painful bursts, and shot cream all over his hand, his wrist, the bedspread. The guy behind him said, "Oh fuck!" before pulling out, ripping off the condom and pumping himself to a quick, almost painful spatter on the blond guy's back.

The blond guy was still howling, still keening. He pumped himself some more, lubricated by honest-to-god come, the thick, white kind, and his entire body jerked and spasmed as he came again.

"God, Kane, he's still coming!" said the guy in back, and Kane had gotten up on the bed by now and was supporting the blond boy's head against his own dropped shoulder.

"Chance, buddy, you still with me?"

Chance kept pumping, and his body kept quivering, and his hands came out from under him and he lay there, his face buried in Kane's chest as he twitched involuntarily on the bed.

"God, Ethan, he's still coming!"

And he was. Kane rolled him to his side a little and Ethan grabbed the still-erect cock almost gently. The camera zoomed in on Chance's cock and it gave one last jerk and spit a final wad on Ethan's hand.

Kane's voice was still softly crooning, "Chance? Chance, man? You with me?" as the scene went black.

CHASE came to in the shower, feeling sick to his stomach and out of it, while Tommy held him tight against his chest and murmured shit that didn't make any sense in his ear.

"Tommy?" Tommy shouldn't be there. God, Chase had pulled out his total bastard to make sure Tommy didn't have to waste himself on Chase's worthless ass anymore.

"God, Chase—you're so fucking scary when you do that."

Helpless tears started leaking out of the creases of Chase's eyes. "I'm so sorry. So sorry. I didn't want you to be hurt anymore. I wanted you to...."

If I say 'move on', I'll throw up.

"You can't even say it," Tommy snapped. "You're no more convincing now than you were a month ago."

Chase started to cry softly, clutching Tommy around the waist, weak with confusion and aftermath, emotional in a way he never let himself be.

"I can handle anything," he choked. "I can let her touch me, I can live without you, I just need to know you're okay. I wasn't there when you weren't okay. I wasn't there. I wasn't there. I wasn't...."

Tommy sank to his knees in the shower and Chase went with him, sobbing softly on Tommy's shoulder, completely unable to pull himself back together.

MERCY managed to drag Victor to two of Chase's home games that season—Chase was never sure how. They had awkward conversations over pizza afterwards, where Victor would praise him extravagantly for being a jock and say things like, "It's too bad you gotta take all those classes to play the game." Chase managed to be on his best behavior for most of that. He made conversation, talked about the game, avoided talking about Donnie or Kevin or any of the shit that would make Victor go off. They'd take Victor home and Mercy would look up at Chase luminously, telling him how proud she was.

Making love to her on those nights was sort of a penance, like a reward for lying about not hating the old man anymore, punishment for letting the world think his heart was anywhere near at peace.

So Mercy saw two more home games, and that made Chase happy.

Tommy saw every one of the other twelve, with or without the other guys. Most of the time it was with—Dex, in particular, came out with him a lot, since Dex was newly single.

Chase never asked, but he suspected that Dex was to Tommy as Donnie was to Chase, except Tommy and Dex probably had fewer secrets. He thought about being jealous, but he couldn't. Tommy had promised. Dex had apologized. And Dex looked so damned lonely without Scott. Who was Chase to keep the two of them from being friends? Didn't he have enough neuroses without adding insane jealousy into the mix?

Besides. Tommy wouldn't do that again. Not to him. Chase sometimes thought it would be easier on them both if he would.

In the summer, when Mercy still worked but Chase didn't have school, they often ended up spending days together before Mercy got home. They worked out with the other guys from *Johnnies*, and if Chase didn't have anything going with Donnie (which he did at least once or twice a week) then it was the two of them, Chase and Tommy, playing video games, volunteering at the local pet shelter, working on Tommy's house, driving to Folsom Lake or the Sacramento River to swim. Sometimes the guys would come with them, and once or twice they even went with Donnie and Kevin and Alejandro. But, more often than not, it was the two of them, having a plan, even if it was just sitting around the house and watching television, twining their lives together without escape.

Tommy had been in the *Johnnies* stable for three years and his toys were infinitely superior to Chase's, but as Chase continued to make a film or a set of still shots about every four weeks, he had enough money to upgrade. Mercy didn't really notice—and when she did, she didn't care. They were comfortable, they were happy—she worked her job, Chase went away for a week a month—to her, it was a fair trade-off.

So when Tommy took him to go buy the newest, best, most amazing video game system, Chase talked about it unabashedly, and Kane and Dex ended up going with them to pick it out after two hours at the gym.

"So this one, right?" Kane insisted, hopping on one of the models. It was his third in as many minutes, and Chase and Tommy grimaced.

"Not that one," Chase said seriously. "Don't you read consumer reports? Man, that one's games are the lamest in the industry. No, if we're getting one, we're getting the wireless remote and the—what?"

Kane was tilting his head back and pretending to sleep, tongue extended, eyes rolled in his head. Dex took advantage of his pose and reached under his arms to tickle him, and Kane yelped loudly and doubled up, protecting his vulnerable pits.

"Serves you right!" Tommy crowed. "Man, you buy a new setup like twice a year, because you don't look shit up! You've finally got a guy who does the research because he thinks it's cool, and you're gonna blow him off?"

Kane blinked and straightened up warily, casting a dark look at an unrepentant (and laughing his ass off) Dex. "Yeah, yeah. I forget the guy's got a brain, so frickin' sue me." He came up behind Chase and smacked his ass, getting a big, lascivious handful. "What can I say? I'm checking out his other ass-ets, right?"

Chase rolled his eyes and pulled up a corner of his mouth. "That's harassment," he said, and Kane started laughing again, forgetting Tommy's little lecture and bounding away to the next big thing. Dex watched him and pinched the bridge of his nose theatrically.

"Needs. A. Keeper."

Chase and Tommy bust out laughing and Tommy said, "You volunteering?"

Dex grimaced. "Naw, man. I'm still on a string."

Tommy and Chase met eyes, because Chase had opened his mouth to say he needed to cut that string, and Tommy knew it. They hadn't had another fight since the one in the rain, but Chase had said, on more than one occasion, that he did *not* want to be the anchor weighing Tommy down.

Tommy said that he'd be the buoy keeping Chase above water, and as, more and more, these days with Tommy seemed to mean as much as the nights, Chase had to agree. But he hated himself more every day for leaning on Tommy when he had no right, for keeping Tommy from seeing someone who had the balls to be out and proud and love Tommy forever and ever. Maybe not as much as Chase did, but better, because it was unafraid.

So Chase bit his tongue about watching Dex break his heart, and Tommy's expression grew dark and grim. Dex looked at them both and sighed, then went to stop Kane, who was juggling with the DVD cases to the complete dismay of the overworked clerk who could be heard saying, "Please sir… could you not do that?" while Kane shined him on.

"They're talking about coming to my place when we're done," Chase said hopefully, and Tommy closed his eyes.

"It's logical," he said, his voice completely neutral. "They're all invested now—they want to know if that's the one *they* should get."

It was true. Chase couldn't believe he was the only male his age who had ever heard of consumer reports. He'd read the damned publication like the frickin' Bible before he bought Mercy her car.

"I was thinking some beer—'

"Since you're of age," Tommy interrupted dryly, and Chase blushed. Tommy would be turning twenty-four in November. It wasn't a huge age difference, but Chase wondered if Tommy thought all of his fucked-up bullshit was because he was younger. Chase hadn't ever felt young in his entire life.

"Yeah, and some pizza and snacks and shit. You, uhm... I'll ask you now, so you can say no—"

"No," Tommy said softly, meeting Chase's eyes with a sort of angry misery. "No, I do not want to come and see the apartment where you lie to your girlfriend about who you are and what you need and what sort of monsters are buried in your brain. I can't think of a single more painful thing on the planet right now than going to your apartment and playing videos."

And with that Tommy stalked off to go buy one of the games that Chase was going to get, so they could hook up their systems over the net and play each other that way. It was stupid—a totally juvenile—trivial pastime, but the thought that they couldn't sit next to each other on the couch and play did something serious and irrevocable to Chase's heart.

You'd better do right by him.

Chase wasn't sure if it was Donnie's voice or his own echoing in his head, but it was getting increasingly angry.

Dex and Kane had driven to the gym together, so Chase piled into Dex's car (a black Acura—leather seats, very sweet), so Tommy could go home. They had their little video party, and Chase called Donnie, and Kevin showed up with him. ('Yandro begged off, and Donnie rolled his eyes. Apparently he didn't really get video games, which was heresy in Chase's world.) Donnie's eyes widened slightly when he saw the two guys from *Johnnies*, but he didn't contradict Chase when he told Kevin they worked construction and road jobs with him. Dex raised an ironic eyebrow, but Kane didn't have an ironic *anything*. He just nodded earnestly like there wasn't a way in hell that could possibly be a lie, and by the time Mercy got there, their first real college party had hit its stride.

Mercy walked in and waved to the guys, getting some catcalls and whistles as she came in. She laughed gaily, grabbed a piece of pizza and some beer out of the refrigerator, and then called next for the video game. It was official. She was one of the guys.

But Chase was playing when she called next, and in spite of how happy she was—and how sweet the guys were to her, making room for her, getting a coaster (!) for her beer—he still made an effort to zag instead of zig in the next game, losing when he should have won.

"Aw, baby, I wanted to play with you!" she protested, and he got up and gave her the controls, kissing her on the cheek when she was aiming for his lips. She didn't seem to notice, and her little oval of a face lit up at the greeting.

God, Mercy—I just wish you were jealous, that's all. I just wish you weren't so patient, and then this would be over, and I could disappear in the room with the red door and have nothing to anchor me to the here and now.

"That's okay, Merce. I've got to go to the head."

He pulled out his phone when he was done taking a leak and hit text.

God, Tommy. My house is full of people and I have never In my life felt so lonely.

> *Serves you right, you dumb bastard. Did You enjoy your hello kiss?*

Fuck. It was like he had a secret camera in Chase's living room.

No. I wish I could have.

> *Yeah, it would actually be easier on me if You had the possibility of loving her even a little bit.*

I love you, Tommy. I'm sorry it's all I've got.

I love you too. I'm sorry that's not enough for you.

It should be. It's my stupid fuckery, you know that, right?

Don't do this to yourself. Please.
I'll talk to you tomorrow.

EXCEPT when Chase woke up the next morning, Tommy wasn't there. He texted him around nine after cleaning up the beer cans and the pizza mess and the ice cream bowls, because Kane's hyperactivity couldn't *possibly* have been fueled by anything but sugar, and he'd found a kindred soul in Kevin and they'd gone on an ice cream run at around nine o'clock at night. Usually Chase and Tommy met at the gym around ten; the text was a formality.

Chase worried when Tommy didn't return it.

Tommy usually picked him up. Chase didn't even bother with his workout bag. He texted Tommy again and backed his car out of the carport, driving without thinking to the little gray house with the Day-Glo orange trim.

He had a key. He wasn't sure when it had wormed its way onto his ring, but it had. It was plain silver—Mercy hadn't even remarked upon it—and Chase barged into Tommy's house without preamble. The kitchen was a hot mess—what was left of a half gallon of ice cream was melting, and a big, greasy pizza box, the kind that advertised the stuffed crust, was sitting in the middle of the table. Buster was up there, chewing forlornly on a piece of pepperoni because his bowl was empty, and Chase passed all that shit up and bolted for the bedroom. If Tommy was getting gangbanged in the bedroom, well then good for him, but Chase had this terrible gnawing, this empty thing going on in his chest, and sure enough, Tommy barely lifted his head as Chase crashed through the door.

His room smelled like raw sewage, but Chase ignored the smell and came to crouch down by the bed.

"Jesus, Tommy!" he mumbled. "What the hell's wrong? You got the flu?"

Tommy's mouth lifted humorlessly. "Yeah. Got the flu. Couldja get me some water or somethin', baby? Gatorade? Somethin'...." His eyes closed and Chase came back with the Gatorade and tried to wake him up. The third time he screamed *"Tommy!"* right next to his ear, he found his phone in his hand and he was dialing 9-1-1.

He rode in the ambulance and tried to answer questions about the "stool" that they'd found all over Tommy's bedsheets. Was it always so dark?

Chase actually narrowed his eyes then. "How in the hell should I know—he usually flushes like a fuckin' human being!"

The paramedic sighed as he was putting a needle of clear liquid into Tommy's arm. "Is your friend bulimic, Mr. Summers?"

Chase blanched. "Yeah, he barfs sometimes when he's trying to keep off weight," he said quietly, thinking about the major-proportioned pity party he'd seen going on Tommy's table. Jesus. It wasn't drugs. It wasn't alcohol. It was just a little obsession about weight. Tommy was perfect—it didn't make a lot of sense really—but he'd been doing that before Chase even walked into his life. Chase accepted it. He did. Just like Tommy accepted Mercy. He didn't like it. It scared the hell out of him. Oh Jesus... it did. It scared the hell out of him, and here, right fucking here, was the reason why.

"What happened?" he asked, feeling his vision swim.

"He got dehydrated. Took a shitload of laxatives and flushed the potassium and everything else out of his system that keeps his brain firing on all cylinders. We'll admit him, pump him full of fluids, but you really want to help your friend here, man, get him to seek some treatment, okay?"

Chase nodded, his skin broken out in wet heat from pure anxiety. It was good advice. It was, in fact, how Chase met Doc Stevenson.

They admitted Tommy, and Chase produced Tommy's insurance card. In fact, he'd brought Tommy's whole wallet and a change of clothes to the hospital, and when he produced the card to the admitting nurse, he asked if mental health services came with it.

He was promptly introduced to the resident shrink on call at Mercy San Juan, who shook Chase's hand and said he'd seen him on campus.

Chase tried to fit one more oddly shaped puzzle piece into the shattered picture his day had become. "Campus?" he asked dumbly.

"Yes. I work pro bono at the student health services center three times a month. You've probably seen me puttering around campus at the college."

Chase blinked, thought about Tommy lying pale and still sleeping in the big hospital bed, and shook his head. "I'm probably too self-absorbed to notice you," he said baldly, without apology. "My... my friend is here because he... he's bulimic and he crapped his load out and he did a binge purge because he's seeing a real douche fucker who won't leave his girlfriend. He's got the health card. Can you see him? Can you talk to him? He... he needed someone to talk to last night, and... and...."

His head was aching. His head was aching and the big red door was crumbling behind it and Tommy had looked so small and *he* had done this, *Chase* had done this, he'd known Tommy had been vulnerable, he'd wanted to take care of him, but he hadn't had the strength to leave Mercy and do it. He hadn't ponied up. He hadn't, and Tommy had needed him, and Chase hadn't been there.

Chase had thought that he hadn't made any promises, but he saw it so clearly now. Texting to Tommy while he was hiding from his own girlfriend in the bathroom—that had been a promise, and the pain of that.... God, had Tommy been eating, stuffing himself so full he felt like stuffed crap while they'd been on the phone? Or had he been downing the laxatives, hoping that when he got it all out of his system, everything would be the fuck all right? It was late August, and around a hundred and three outside, and the air conditioner in the hospital was fighting that heat with everything it had. But Chase didn't feel it. His skin was clammy, and his face was flushed, and for a minute he thought he wouldn't be able to fucking breathe.

Doc Stevenson was an older man, with a bald head and a white fringe around the outside, a white beard and a white mustache, and a T-shirt that said "Hugs not drugs" in pink letters on a navy blue background. He had jeans that bagged in the ass, Birkenstocks, and a man-purse at his hip that was leaking different colored pieces of yarn. But when he put his hand on Chase's shoulder and very gently told him to breathe, it was okay, his friend would be okay, Chase actually, for the first time in his life, thought that maybe a grown-up knew what he was talking about.

But that didn't mean Chase didn't have to clarify some important parts.

"You're gonna help him, right?" he asked, feeling a little bit desperate. The nice hippy headshrink nodded his head.

"Yes, Mr. Summers. As soon as he's conscious, we'll sit down and discuss treatment for bulimia. Your friend looks to be in good shape—his muscle mass hasn't degraded, this is mostly an emotional thing for him. We get to the root of that emotion—"

"No worries," Chase said seriously. "We'll dig that root right out. That asshole ain't ever gonna get a chance to hurt Tommy again."

He visited Tommy before he left the hospital. He'd called Dex to come get him, and the guys had set up a visiting rotation, with Chase on the first watch. Considering they all knew that Tommy didn't have any family but Chase and *Johnnies*, Chase thought it was really fucking human of them and that he worked with a first-class bunch of people.

He wondered how they saw anything in him.

But he had learned how to play perfect for too long to fall apart now. He sat in Tommy's room and held Tommy's hand when no one could see him. He'd already texted Mercy and told her he had a sick friend from work. He could say that now. He didn't have to lie about a job; he could tell her honestly that he had a sick friend from work, and she was okay with that. So he sat there, and cried on Tommy's hand, until Tommy woke up toward late afternoon.

"Jesus," he mumbled, "I'm so fuckin' embarrassed."

"Don't be," Chase said quietly. "I'll go back and clean the place up, okay? No one'll ever know. They'll think you got laid low by the bug or something—food poisoning. That's what we'll tell 'em. Food poisoning. No one has to know that I treated you like shit and you broke your fuckin' heart over me, okay?"

Tommy squinted at him. "My problems, asswipe. This had nothin' to do with—"

"Don't lie to me, Tommy!" Chase's voice rose and cracked. "Don't fuckin' lie to me," he mumbled. "I've done some pretty shitty things, but I never lied."

"Not to me," Tommy muttered, his voice bitter. "Only to yourself."

"Yeah," Chase felt his pocket buzz and pulled the phone out. Dex was downstairs and Kane was coming up. Fair enough. He'd do it now.

He stood up and leaned over, kissing Tommy full on the mouth, fetid breath and all. Tommy made a sound of protest when he pulled away, and Chase leaned his forehead against Tommy's, crying and not able to stop it.

"I love you forever, Tommy Matthew Halloran. But I'm too fucked up for you to fuck yourself up over. I'm gonna leave you here, and you're gonna get better, and you won't ever have to see me, okay? I'll just not be a part of your life, and you can find someone who will be there when you need him, because I ain't good enough to even clean up your puke."

"God, Chase!" Tommy's hand came up to his cheek and Chase pulled away, wiping his own cheeks off with his palms.

"I really do love you, you know." Chase shook his head, because that was self-indulgent and he didn't really get to do that, not anymore. "There's a headshrink coming in to see you. He's gonna help you not throw shit up. Listen to him, okay? Remember that I'll love you if you get fat. I don't give a shit. And the better person, the person who's probably... aw fuck, I can't fucking say it—anyway. Anyone who deserves you doesn't give a shit if you get love handles or a bubble butt or what the fuck ever. So listen to this guy for me—"

"I'm not doin' *shit* for you!" Tommy snarled. He had a hospital sheet to use on his cheeks and for a second, Chase wanted to just bury his head on Tommy's middle and use the same thing and sob out all this horrible, horrible razored redness pressing against his chest. But he didn't deserve that either.

"Then listen to him for you. Cause you're a good person, and I'm a douchefucker, and I don't want you hanging around no douchefuckers no more."

And Chase spun around and pushed blindly past Kane, who was standing in the doorway of the ICU cubicle, for once in his life still.

He almost didn't make it out of the elevator, and when he did, Dex had to honk his horn loud before Chase turned from his blind stumble into the parking lot and found Dex's car.

"You gotta take me to Tommy's," he said through the thickness in his throat, in his nose, and in his head. "I gotta clean up. When he comes home, he's gotta know that the place is clean, and there's not a fucking trace of me or what I've done to him fucking anywhere, okay?"

"I'll help," Dex said reassuringly, and Chase shook his head.

"He doesn't want you to see."

"Yeah, Chase, but neither do you, and I've got a front-row seat."

Chase caught his breath and let it out on a sob.

"What?" Dex asked, pulling up to a red light and looking at him in concern.

You called me Chase.

But he couldn't say it, because he'd finally given in and wrapped his arms around his knees and started sobs that didn't feel like they'd ever stop.

THE cleanup was ghastly. Chase threw all the food away first—after feeding Buster, of course—and Dex came in from a run to the trash cans to find Chase hugging the reluctant brown cat and gazing sightlessly into space.

"He loves this cat," Chase said by way of explanation. "He's sort of old. We should get him old-cat cat food. He's going to be all Tommy has for a while."

"We can do that when we're done," Dex said, and Chase nodded, smoothing the whiskers back against old Buster's cheeks. Buster purred into his hand and Chase rubbed his own nose against the whiskers, because the old cat liked that best. Tommy said it was because he was marking his people, and Chase would miss being one of his people. Yeah. The cat. That's what he'd miss.

Dex was so patient, too. He stood in the kitchen, the smell from the bedroom enough to gag a maggot, and didn't say a word until Chase reluctantly put the cat down and went to grab a Hefty bag.

"We'll take the comforter to the dry cleaners'," he said, talking to himself. "They've got one of those super-big washing machines, right? They'll get the stains out. I'll put the sheets in the washer to soak, and we can use some carpet cleaner on the mattress top and then leave it out to air."

"Yeah," Dex said, as Chase made himself at home in a way that he never felt like he could do at his own apartment. "Whatever."

Chase looked up. "What?"

"You're just going to a lot of trouble to clean up for a guy you just dumped in a hospital room."

"Yeah, well, you love your way, I'll love mine."

Dex grimaced, and Chase wondered if he was thinking about all of those stolen times with Scott, times that Scott had apparently decided were part of his porn life and not his real life.

"He shoots, he scores!" Dex said ironically. "There any rubber gloves in there? Man, the smell alone is bad enough, I don't want anything gross on my hands."

Chase tried to block the next part out. It wasn't that he had a weak stomach; his stomach was pretty cast iron, actually. Feces didn't bother him, and Mercy had been sick with food poisoning once and he'd had to clean her up, both exits, no waiting. He'd been scrubbing the walls of the bathroom—and doing laundry—for a week.

This was different.

The thought of Tommy lying here in his own excrement made him want to howl. Not Tommy. Chase—Chase deserved seven kinds of hells for being a coward, for keeping Mercy in the dark and Tommy on a short leash, for hurting people around him for fear of the big hurt inside him—but not Tommy.

Chase scrubbed the mattress until it looked factory fresh. He gave Dex his credit card and had him go out and buy a wet and dry vac and made the beige carpet pristine. He scrubbed the bathroom, and threw his toothbrush away in the outside trashcan where Tommy would never see it, and vacuumed and dusted the weight room, taking his extra clothes from the closet and putting them in trash bags to take home. He was sorting through the CDs when Dex came back in from the dry cleaner's and took the few he'd gathered out of his hands.

"Leave them," he said quietly, and Chase looked up, red-eyed, and shook his head.

"He doesn't need any reminders," he said brokenly, and Dex put the CDs back in the rack.

"Yeah, he does. They're going to comfort him, okay? Just trust me on this one, Chase. You don't strike me as a cruel guy."

Chase's jaw tightened. "You have no idea," he grated, and Dex turned around and snapped, "Bullshit!"

Chase recoiled and gaped at him, and Dex scrubbed his own face with his hands.

"Bullshit, Chase. I get why you're doing this—it doesn't take a genius, you know? I sat in your apartment last night and ate your pizza and played *Halo* with your girlfriend, and she's great. She's awesome. She's fun and cute, and you know the only thing that keeps me from sleeping with her and putting you out of your misery so you can run here and make Tommy happy?"

Chase blinked. "She's a girl?"

Dex nodded and put an ironic finger on his nose. "Bingo, asshole! She's not my type. And you know what really sucks? She's not yours either."

I've even stopped wishing she was.

"Your profile says 'straight'."

"So does yours. Most of the guys are. When they close their eyes and dream of ponies, their ponies have tits. I thought mine did too.

Hell, last year, when I met up with you, had a smoothie, and thought you were a decent kid for a dumb jock, I'd mostly convinced myself I was in this gig for the money." Dex sighed and flopped down on the floor next to Chase and wrapped a solid arm around his shoulders.

"How come you're even talking to me?" Chase asked him, shamelessly leaning on him even as he said it.

"Because I know it's complicated," Dex said quietly. "I'm living complicated. Sometimes I think, 'Jesus, if he would just fly away and get married, I could live my life again.' But he won't. And he won't let me go. And it's killing me. And even though I hate you for breaking Tommy's heart, and ripping your own to shreds, I'm thinking, 'Jesus. At least he's trying. He's trying to do the right thing.' And I admire the hell out of you for it, because I think it just might kill you, and you're trying anyway."

"I'm a coward," Chase whispered, shaking against his friend's arm. "I'm such a fucking coward."

"Aren't we all, baby. Every fucking one of us."

"Tommy's not."

"You made Tommy strong."

"You'll check in on him, right? Keep him company?"

"I'm not gonna sleep with him."

It was more than Chase deserved. "I'm fucking grateful."

"I know you are, baby. I know you are."

They finished late into the night, and Chase gave one more reluctant good-bye to Buster. Dex got a text that said Kane had turned "Tommy-watch" over to Cameron, and Chase was grateful. Dex said he had to stop at the all-night Walgreens on the way to Chase's apartment to get some more scented soap and laundry detergent for himself because, in his words, "I'm gonna be smelling shit for weeks if I don't wash everything I own twice after that."

Chase wandered in with him and gazed sightlessly at toiletries, since that was the row the scented soaps were in.

That's when he saw the razor blades.

He bought them, with some masculine-scented hand cream and Reese's Pieces, and stashed them in his medicine cabinet behind the shaving cream. He came into his apartment late, tiptoeing quietly in, and jumped into the shower to get rid of the last of the smell. He ran the water until it was cold and didn't look his red eyes in the mirror while he brushed his teeth. He wasn't really sure if he'd focused his vision once since the drugstore, and curiously enough, it felt like he'd managed to keep that same detachment, that same sense of seeing but not seeing, for the next few weeks.

It was surprisingly easy.

"Can you fill up the car, baby?" Mercy would ask, and Chase nodded and said "Sure." Then he'd wait until the *Johnnies* guys were done with their workouts (because Dex texted him, that's how he knew) and then go to the gym, work out on automatic, and then drive home.

"Baby," she'd say the next day, "you said you'd fill the car, but it's empty!"

"Sorry," he'd say, turning his face in the direction of her voice but not really seeing her. "I'm sorry. Did you run out of gas?"

"No, but seriously, Chase, where is your head?"

In a hospital room with Tommy.

"I don't know."

Suddenly Mercy was there, on top of him as he sat on the couch, kissing him, and he gazed sightlessly into her eyes.

"Chase, is everything okay?" she asked, and Chase smiled vacantly.

"Yeah. It's fine."

She pressed her lips to his, and he opened his mouth and responded. His body could do that, respond when his heart wasn't engaged. That's what he did. They made their way to the bedroom, and Mercy grabbed a condom from the drawer and gave it to him.

"Different brand?" The strangest small things caught his attention these days.

"Yeah. Just got them."

But he wasn't really listening for her answer. Most of his soul was still in that damned hospital room.

Tommy wasn't *in* the hospital room, of course. He came home on the third day, with strict instructions to eat well, and Chase and Dex texted furiously to make sure it was nothing but healthy, vitamin-rich fruits, vegetables, and lean meat. Dex told him sourly one night at the gym (because Dex surprised him there and said it wasn't a fucking divorce) that *Dex* had lost five pounds in the last couple of weeks because now *he* was eating healthy.

"Thanks a lot, you rat bastard," Dex grunted as Chase spotted him for a bench press. "I was sort of enjoying my pizza/cookie dough days. I was gonna eat that shit until I turned thirty and absolutely had to stop."

Chase's mouth quirked upward on both ends and he grunted, setting the bar in the slots. It seemed to be the expected response.

Dex stopped and sat up, looking at him closely. "Chase, is anyone home up there?"

"I dunno," Chase said, forcing a smile. "Was there ever anybody there?"

Dex looked at him and shivered. "You don't look right, man. Tommy, he's looking healthy—sad, but, you know. Like he's going to do okay. You—I'm not sure about you."

Chase's smile got a little more real. "He's going to be okay?"

Tommy.

"Yeah," Dex said, walking to their next set. It's a good thing he'd opted to go after Chase on the bench presses, because Chase wouldn't have remembered where to go next. They were working on upper body today. They did the same routine every other day.

It's all I need to know.

"I'm so glad," Chase said, and then watched what Dex was doing carefully because he couldn't quite focus on this next exercise and he didn't want to strain anything.

THE Hornets lost their last game, the one that would have gotten them into the play-offs. When the game was over and they were trotting dispiritedly to the dugout, Chase had a sudden sense of dislocation, a giant twitch, as though he had stepped off a step when he'd thought he was on flat ground. His shoulders jerked and his ankle turned and he went down on one knee, and Donnie turned to him in alarm.

"What's wrong?"

"I'm the reason we lost," Chase muttered, but for a minute, he couldn't remember if that was true or not.

"Were not!" Donnie muttered, looking with irritation over his shoulder. "Kevin dropped that fucking fly ball in the sixth inning. But don't tell him that. He'll feel bad enough as it is."

"It was me," Chase said, and then, he seemed to remember that he'd pitched a nearly flawless game. Three hits? In the third game of a series? He'd been awesome. He seemed to pitch from the same place he did math or attended class. It was so strange, this last month, how this entire portion of his brain had seemed to be engaged without him. "It was me?" he asked, and Donnie came back and draped an arm over his shoulders.

"No, buddy. It's just the way things are. One more year of ball, right?"

One more year without Tommy.

"Yeah," Chase said, his voice flat, and Donnie stopped him on their jog to the locker rooms.

"I haven't seen your guy out here in the last couple weeks."

"I wasn't doing right by him," Chase said, proud of how his voice didn't quaver.

Donnie shook his head and sighed. "God, Chase. All the best intentions, all the wrong fucking moves. I don't even know how to respond to that."

Chase looked around, surprised. "Where did everybody go?" The field was still lit, but the rest of the team was gone, probably in the locker rooms. Even most of the fans had disappeared, trickling into cars and disappearing, in spite of the almost balmy late-September air.

Donnie's arm tightened on his shoulders, and for a minute, just a bare fucking minute, Chase felt like he was himself and he could breathe again. Contact. Uncomplicated, unconditional human contact. He shook his head and laughed a little.

"We should get inside before Kevin thinks we hate him. He's going to need some beer and some ice cream tonight."

Donnie grunted.

"He's not going to need some beer and ice cream tonight?"

"Chase, how long's it been since you've slept?"

I can't sleep. I just lie there awake and listen to Mercy's breathing and wonder if she'd hear it if mine stopped.

"You know school, Donnie. I'm not that bright. The homework takes a while."

"Yeah. You ever think about maybe talking to the school shrink? Maybe he could help you sleep."

"I've met him. He's a nice guy, but I'm fine."

Donnie looked away. "Chase, when we were kids, I wanted you and Kevin to be my brothers. I mean, 'Chelle was fine, but I wanted brothers like you can't believe. Now Kevin is the goofy one, and I love him, but I don't worry about him. But you... you, I worry about. Even when we were kids, I knew there was something to worry about. But you—right now? I swear, I want to call my dad and have him just take you home and lock you in my old room until you don't make my stomach quite so weird. It's... I don't know. Remember when we were kids, and my parents took us to Disneyland? We got home, and you were waiting on our porch, and you were wrapped up in a blanket and there were granola bar wrappers everywhere. How long had you been there?"

You were gone for a week. I slept there for three days.

"Couple of hours."

Donnie hawked and spat. "That's a fucking lie. I've never seen anyone look so lost in my life."

"Your mom made the best meat loaf," Chase said with a game smile, and Donnie stopped right there in the middle of the parking lot and hugged him. Chase sagged into him and then straightened. It was dangerous, falling into that human touch. It was one thing with Mercy—he got to be all he-man and protective. He could hold a distance while he was pretending to shield her from his mighty muscles. But not Donnie. Donnie could hold him up, so he couldn't come even close to falling down on him.

"Chase," Donnie whispered in his ear, "if you ever want to leave her, or even just want to talk in real words, call me. Don't worry about the time of day or what I'll be doing or what you think you'll be interrupting, just call me. I'm not going to be sleeping real well until I hear your voice anyway."

"'Kay," Chase said, trying a reassuring smile. It must not have worked, because Donnie shook his shoulders hard.

"Promise. You don't ever fucking promise anything. Promise you'll fucking call me!"

I can't keep promises!

"Donnie!"

"Promise!"

And for a moment, Chase was in the *here* and the *now* and he was startled enough by the *here* and the *now* to say something rash.

"Fine. I promise."

And that seemed to appease Donnie, which was good, because it meant Chase could drift away from the *here* and the *now* and go back to that place where some other part of his brain took his classes and talked to his girlfriend, and the part that was really Chase simply drifted, in an endless sea of numb and gray, thrilled that it didn't have to care.

That all went away the minute the scene with Ethan and Kane started.

The second Kane bore him to the mattress with one of those punishing, hard kisses that he specialized in, and Ethan engulfed his cock in tight, wet, heat, he screamed into Kane's mouth. The intensity he'd always felt on the set, the freedom, the absolute joy in feeling, surged to his skin, but it was like when you'd slept on your arm for too long, making it dead to the world.

The surge of emotion, even joy, was so intense, it hurt.

Kane had taken his scream for pleasure, and it had been, but it had also been the moment when Chase, who had existed in such a comfortable, gray, detached fugue state for the last month, completely checked out of his own head.

It wasn't until he was kneeling on the floor of the shower, sobbing into Tommy's shoulder, that he realized that the whole time his emotions had been asleep, his heart had been flayed and bleeding. The pain... God, it was excoriating and unbearable, and it ruled him as he howled into Tommy's body and bled his sorrow all over the bathroom floor.

He eventually had to stop. He had to. The pain was still there, but his body just ceased to sob, and he found himself clean and dry, huddled in one of the gargantuan, plush white robes they handed the models when they got out of the shower. His head was in Tommy's lap, and Tommy was just running his fingers through Chase's lengthening, natural-colored hair.

"You with me?" Tommy asked softly, and Chase made a sound, because that was about all he could manage.

"I talked to that doctor you set me up with," Tommy said, and Chase relaxed a little more. "He's a good guy. You're right. He's got me looking at that food thing in a whole new way."

"No more barfing?" Chase asked, pleased that he had words now.

"No. I'm tempted sometimes, and I've had to work out like a motherfucker because sometimes I binge when I shouldn't, but no barfing."

"I'm glad."

"Of course, when I realized I was just hanging around the gym waiting for you, you big stupid bastard, I stopped eating ice cream at night."

"I didn't want things to be awkward."

"Fucking coward." But Tommy's voice lacked venom.

"You knew that all along." Oh God, it felt so good to talk to him. Chase started to feel like he could sit up and look around, but he put it off a little longer. As soon as he could sit up and collect his thoughts and pretend to be a person again, he was going to have to bail. If this part hurt, this one little part with Tommy, what would it feel like to have a whole conversation again?

"I just wish I knew what you were afraid of," Tommy whispered. "I don't think it's of people thinking you're gay, because there's a whole other closet for that. I think I know what it is, and what it has to do with, but you won't say it, and it's just like Doc Stevenson says, if you won't say it, we can't fix it. So won't you tell me what you're afraid of, Chase? It would be awesome if we didn't have to dance on nails anymore."

"Is that what we've been doing?"

"Isn't that what it feels like?"

"You forgot the rubbing alcohol and full body contact with the razorblades."

Tommy laughed a little, and Chase closed his eyes. "Can I get a bottle of water, Tommy?"

"Yeah, sure. You're not going to run away while I'm out?"

Chase grunted. He was lucky, because Tommy apparently considered it a "No."

It was, in fact, a "You bet your sweet ass I'm going to run away while you go get me a water, because otherwise I'll promise you the world."

Not a soul in the building, not even Kelsey the receptionist, who kept the guys supplied with gum, bathrobes, and an endless supply of sarcasm, saw him sneak out on wobbly legs and drive away.

He'd been going to check into a hotel, but he found that he barely had enough strength of will to get to his apartment. He walked up the steps and into the apartment and kicked off his shoes and shucked his jeans, turning the ringer off his phone while he did so.

He crawled into bed and didn't get out for the rest of the day.

EVENTUALLY he had to get up. He told Mercy he was sick, but the horrible truth was, he couldn't even sleep. He just lay there with his eyes closed, listening to the angry buzzing of his cell phone on vibrate until the battery ran down. His bladder drove him out of bed at one point, and he sighed and plugged his phone into the charger, skipping over Tommy's increasingly desperate texts and settling on a reply to John's request for an opinion on the rushes. He okayed them without looking and closed his eyes again, and apparently that was enough activity to send him to sleep, because sleep he did.

For eighteen hours.

Mercy checked his head every four hours, and grew increasingly suspicious when he didn't spike a fever.

"Are you just trying to get out of Saturday night?" she asked, trying to mask her suspicion with the faux-joke. "I thought you *liked* dancing."

Unless Tommy's there it makes me queasy.

"I love dancing." *With Tommy.*

"Then you kick this thing, okay? We haven't been out in a dog's age, Chase! I need something to look forward to!"

Chase managed a smile.

I'm glad one of us can have something to look forward to. I certainly don't.

"I'll be up and around, I promise," he said.

And he was. He even made it to the gym two days in a row, and to his classes one of those days. He picked up his extra work and came home and did it, and was feeling pretty damned good about himself by the time their dance date arrived.

He could function pretty well for a dead man.

WHICH was why it was no surprise to find himself standing there, in front of the mirror, holding the razorblade to his wrist. A thin line of scarlet-colored beads had gathered where the blade was touching the skin, running vertically in the direction of his vein, and he pushed down curiously, to see when exactly they would become fat enough to break, join each other, and run crimson down the sink.

His skin was so soft the blade almost whispered through it, and as Mercy pounded on the door, he wondered how hard he'd have to push to feel pain.

He gave it a try, finding that finally, after these weeks of missing Tommy, he had something to look forward to.

THE BOY WITH THE DETACHABLE SOUL

THE boy in the bathroom was staring at the mirror, the trick of the steam on the glass making his eyes look vacant and soulless, which was fitting. His skin was pale, his hair was colorless with wet, and the towel was white. Even the bathroom walls were basic apartment white. The only color on the set was the steadily increasing line of crimson draining into the sink. Oops... must have hit a vein there, because it spurted, badly, spattering the mirror, the sink, the white towel, and suddenly the boy gasped, blinking his eyes like a waking sleeper.

OH *SHIT!* Chase was *bleeding!* And all he could think of was "Someone's going to have to clean this up!" He'd *done* cleanup on Tommy's apartment, he'd *seen* the mess a cracked soul left behind. Hell, he'd practically *waded* in it.

He couldn't leave that mess for Mercy to clean up.

A small arterial spurt hit him in the face right when the irony did, and he pulled a hand towel off the towel rack and wrapped it tight around his wrist.

Tommy's mess to clean up would be worse.

"Chase, are you okay?" Mercy was sounding truly panicked now, and Chase's vision was swimming with little black dots.

"Mercy." His voice sounded thin to his own ears. He shored it up. He was going to need to be strong here. "Mercy, sweetheart, I'm going to need you to do a couple of things for me, okay?"

"Yeah, sure. Do you want me to come in?"

"No!" No. No. He had a plan—an entire plan, in his dumb jock brain. Whodathunkit?

"What do you want me to do?"

"Okay, darlin', I'm going to open the door a little, and I want you to throw me some clean clothes and my cell phone, okay?"

He heard the rustling around the apartment as he twined the towel around his wrist again, tighter, concerned at the way it just saturated so quickly without stopping. He was leaning back against the toilet, holding his hand over his head, when Mercy shoved his jeans, some boxers, a T-shirt and a hooded sweatshirt on the floor. His cell phone was on top. Excellent. No questions so far. Batting a thousand.

"Thanks, baby," he said, thinking that might be the last time he got to call her that. "Now, I'm going to call Donnie, and I need you to do one last thing for me, okay?"

"Chase, why are you going to call Donnie?" The door started to inch forward and Chase slammed it shut with his foot.

"Darlin', I need you to hold your questions for a bit, okay? Now, I'm going to ask you a huge favor, and try not to hold it against me." He had Donnie's number pinned to the front of his smart phone, or he might not have been able to dial it. "I want you to gather all of my clothes together and shove them in a garbage bag or two, okay?"

"You want me to do *what?*"

"Donnie?"

"Chase? It's 2 a.m.!"

He felt a sudden shaft of hurt. "You promised!" he said plaintively, and then Donnie's voice woke up a little.

"What's wrong?"

Mercy started pounding on the door. "Chase? Chase Victor Summers, if you don't get out here and explain...."

"Mercy, please, just do it. You're going to want the head start, okay? You're not going to want my shit here, and I'm going to need to wear something when I get out of the hospital, so just do it!"

"Hospital?"

"Hospital?" Donnie's voice was actually a lot more panicked and a lot less puzzled than Mercy's.

"Donnie, could you do me a favor and come get me? I'm going to need a ride. I can't see too good, and I hate ambulances. I rode in an ambulance with Tommy, and I'd rather bleed out, okay? I just would. I don't know why, but I swear, it was worse than the damned hospital." There was a silence, and then Chase heard some thumps and a muffled curse word over the phone. In the background he heard Alejandro's voice, sleepy and protesting, and Donnie saying "Please, 'Yandro—God, I think he really needs me!" 'Yandro mumbled something else, and when Donnie spoke next, it was into the phone.

"I'm fucking coming, Chase. Remember, I'm like ten minutes away. I'll be there in two."

"Good," Chase mumbled, and then he made a pad out of a clean washrag and shoved it under the saturated towel. He found the last hand towel and swore. Dammit, he was going to need Mercy's help for this.

"Mercy? Mercy, have you thrown all my shit in a garbage bag yet?"

"No!" Oh fuck, she was crying. Well, he was sure she'd be pretty crying too, but he didn't want her to be sad. He'd been sad all his life. Sucked.

"Mercy, don't cry, okay? You're gonna be pissed at me—go with that. Be pissed. I've seen you clean the apartment when you're pissed. Be pissed. But first, I need your help, okay?"

He opened the door then, and she gasped, literally gasped, and started to cry harder into her hand.

"You can't do that, baby. You can't. I need you to tie the new towel around the pad, or this isn't going to be a failed attempt, okay?"

"Chase? Oh my God… let me call an ambulance—"

"*No!*" Because when he got in the ambulance, Mercy would be his girlfriend, but if Donnie took him, he'd have a say. He didn't have to be anybody. He could just be an admittee in the psych ward, and he'd be good with that. "No ambulances, Donnie's on his way. I want to be dressed when he gets here, though, so could you help me out?"

Her hands shook, but she was brave, so brave. She tied the towel and he grimaced in pain and then had her tie it tighter. His hand was already cold and his fingers were stiff, so the pain was probably worth it.

"Good. Awesome. Now I need you to do that garbage bag thing, okay?"

Her little hand came up to his cheek. "Chase, baby, why are you throwing away all your clothes?"

"I'm not," he said, smiling dreamily into her pretty brown eyes. Now *her* eyes were a warm brown. He liked that. But not as much as the black-brown, with the wicked Loki glitter. "You are. Now go do it, so I can get dressed."

She walked away uncertainly, drying her hands on the big bath towel that was left on the rack. He thought he'd grab that on his way out. His pad was already pink. He stayed sitting on the toilet mostly, but managed to struggle into his clothes by the time Donnie got there. He was pretty sure his sweatshirt was going to be stained, but she'd grabbed an old one, so that was okay.

He heard Mercy let Donnie in, still crying, uncertain, and he thought that if it had been Tommy, Tommy would have shouted in his face and called the paramedics already. But then, if he'd been living with Tommy, he wouldn't be bleeding right now, so he could probably forgive her.

"Donnie?" he called plaintively, needing to see his friend's face. His vision was getting incrementally darker, but he still recognized Donnie's wide happy features, his expressive, full mouth, and his shock of blond hair. Donnie just *was* Donnie. It's what made Donnie so much awesome!

"Chase, man—you don't even have any shoes on!"

For some reason *that* seemed funny. "Get my flip-flops, 'kay? They're the leather ones in the closet," Chase mumbled, trying to remember if they let you wear those in the hospital. Donnie helped him into his flip-flops, and he unselfconsciously leaned on his best friend. He remembered to put his cell phone into the pocket of his hooded sweater, because he was going to want to make another call when he got into the car. He looked around vaguely at the three garbage bags of clothes in the living room and felt some satisfaction.

"Mercy, you need to throw them over the stairwell, okay? So Donnie can put them in his car."

Mercy squinted at him and Donnie's eyes widened as though he understood something *truly* shocking. Without asking, Donnie shoved Chase against the door frame and started popping garbage bags full of clothes over Chase's head and over the landing—they must have been pretty securely tied, because Chase didn't see anything burst on the ground.

"Chase?" Oh God. She sounded so lost, and so hurt. There was no good way to do this. None. There was only the worst way, and he'd been going to do that, but he figured he could spare her that.

He looked at her in her prettiest nightgown with her makeup running from the tears.

"You were such a good friend," he said seriously. "I loved you so much as a friend. I wanted to make you happy. None of this is your fault, Mercy. None of this. But if I'd died in the bathroom, you wouldn't have been able to hate me, and you've earned that. You had so much invested in our future—you *earned* the right. So here you go. This is gonna set us both free." He paused for a minute and almost slid down the wall, then felt Donnie's hand under his arm, shoring him up.

"I'm not your future, Mercy. I'm so sorry. I'm *so* gay. Gay. Gay gay gay gay gay." He giggled a little. "Gay!"

Mercy gaped at him, her mouth opening and closing, the hurt spreading across her delicate, lovely face, every bit as awful as he'd imagined. Good. He was glad he was conscious. He'd earned this.

"Chase?"

"I'm gonna miss being your friend, Mercy," he said mournfully. "I really love you, just not like that. The apartment is paid up for the end of the year; you can keep the car. I'd appreciate it if you didn't burn anything, but I get it if you do." Oh fuck. "Jesus, Donnie, you need to get my wallet, man. It's in the slacks by the hamper."

Donnie grunted. "Thanks a lot, asshole. You couldn't have remembered that before the good-bye speech?" He shoved Chase against the wall then and trotted inside the bedroom, leaving Chase woozy and dripping single, thick drops of blood onto the carpet.

"You're gay?" Mercy repeated, her voice wandering, and then she seemed to focus on the big towel and blood, and her eyes widened as though the truth had finally dawned on her.

"You'd rather *kill* yourself than be with me?"

Chase shook his head adamantly and almost lost his balance. "No, sweetheart. You can't think that. I'd rather kill myself than live without Tommy. I broke up with Tommy 'cause I hated cheating on you. That was the right thing to do." He shook his head gravely and thought that he really didn't have a whole lot more consciousness to go. "Donnie, man, I'd hate to die on my porch. Can we go?"

Donnie came out with Chase's wallet in one hand and a boxful of Chase's old trophies under the other arm. Chase nodded approvingly.

"Thanks. I would have missed those."

"Tommy?" Mercy was looking confused and lost and out of it, and Chase was just not going to be able to hang around for the rest of this part. He felt bad, like he was cheating her of something important, but it couldn't be helped. "The guy you work with? From the road crew?"

"Porn set," Chase mumbled. "But we never shot a scene together," at which point Donnie said, "That's my cue!" and tucked the wallet in his pocket so he could wrap his arm around Chase's shoulders and help him totter his way down the stairs.

By the time they got to Donnie's little Toyota, Chase's vision was black and he thought he was going to puke. Donnie belted him in and grabbed the big white towel Chase had clutched on his way out, folded it, and wrapped it over Chase's wrist, swearing up a storm.

"God, you were going to fucking go through with it, you stupid prick." He started the car and screeched backward, ignoring all traffic laws and picking up his cell phone and dialing as he jammed the car into gear and tore out of the complex parking lot. "Kevin? Do I give a fuck what time it is? I need you to do me a favor and come over to Chase's apartment. There's a bunch of garbage bags on the ground under his landing with his shit in them; I need you to pick those up for me, okay? Why can't I go? Because Chase changed his mind about killing himself tonight and I've got to take him to the hospital. Yeah, fuckin' genius, it's better than the fuckin' morgue! Now get your ass in gear and hurry! She may decide to have a bonfire on the lawn if we leave her enough fuel, okay?" Suddenly Donnie was quiet and Kevin's bright, spacey voice pattered over the line. "How'd you know? Seriously? You knew? Yeah, he finally came out. Jesus, Kevin, you think you know a guy. No, not him, you! Thanks, okay? Yeah, I'll tell him. Bye."

Donnie disconnected and Chase looked up in time to see his friend giving him a quick once-over. Chase opened his eyes, feeling a little better now that he'd been sitting, and tried to smile.

"That was Kevin," Donnie said, all of the anger leached out of his voice. "He wants me to congratulate you on coming out and tell you he'll come meet us in the hospital after he gets your stuff."

Chase frowned. "How'd he know?"

Donnie shrugged. "He said he knew in high school when you had the big crush on me. He said it was okay, we never made him feel left out."

Chase felt the sudden urge to cry. "God, you think you know a guy."

"Yeah. Kevin's good people. And you're fucked up. How're you doing?"

Chase wanted to sleep. He did. But dammit, he had a plan. "Gotta make a call," he said drunkenly. He rooted his phone out with his good hand and typed in the passcode, then Tommy's number. He was expecting to leave a message, so he was startled when Tommy picked it up on the first ring.

"Chase?" His voice was as lost as Chase felt, and Chase's eyes stung.

"Sorry to wake you, baby," Chase said, suddenly feeling better. "Just wanted to call and beg you to wait for me. Won't be much longer. Moved out. Just gotta stay in the hospital a while. It'll be good. Wait for me."

"Chase?"

Chase started a slow giggle. God, he felt good. Who knew? Who knew that watching your life slip through your fingers would make it so much less awful?

"You'll wait for me," he mumbled. "I promise. I'm promising you, I am. I'm free, and I promise you, how's that?"

His arm was too tired to hold the phone up, and he could hear Tommy shouting on the other end but couldn't say anything. His eyes were closed but it was darker behind them than it should have been. Dark. So dark.

Tommy? Tommy can you hear me? I love you, Tommy. We'll be together. I'll make it up to you, I swear. You won't ever be alone again. I promise, Tommy.

"Chase?" Donnie sounded panicked and Chase tried to tell him that it was all good now. Finally, finally, all good, but he was too tired, so tired, maybe when he woke up from his nap.

HE WOKE up with a splitting headache, a mouth that tasted like cotton and acetate, and a pain in his leg *and* in his wrist.

Tommy was asleep in the middle of the bed, his head buried against Chase's thigh, and Chase went to stroke his hair, which had grown out a little in the last month, but there was something around his wrist, the one that didn't hurt.

"What the hell?" he muttered and then tried to swallow. Donnie was suddenly there with a little bucket of water and a straw.

"It's a restraint, genius," Donnie muttered. "In case you change your mind and go after the other wrist."

Chase sucked in what felt like half the bucket in one slurp. "I called for help. Doesn't that count for something?"

"Yeah," Donnie muttered, taking the bucket when Chase had finished. "Yeah, it counts for you can have friends in when normally they'd isolate you during suicide watch." He looked up and glared, and Chase followed the glare to an orderly, sitting inside the room, reading a magazine. Oh. Suicide watch in action.

"Aw, fuck," Chase closed his eyes against the various pains in his head, arm, and legs. "I feel too shitty to kill myself. A real friend would do it for me."

"NOT. Fucking. Funny."

Chase's eyes were closed, but he had the feeling Donnie's eyes would be narrowed and he was scowling.

"It was a little funny," he said in protest, because his shoulder felt about a million pounds lighter. Why did he feel like a helium balloon? "Why am I so loopy?"

Donnie hissed out a breath. "You know, in a million years, I didn't expect you to have health insurance. What are you doing, twenty-one years old, and you've got this kick-ass fucking health insurance? I mean, the whole rest of the world would be sentenced to group therapy, but you get one on one. What in the fuck is that? I get mine from my parents."

"I actually get it through *Johnnies*," Chase mumbled. It was something John did even for graduates. "Can't fuck if you feel like shit. Why are we talking about this?"

"Because if your health insurance had been less fucking stellar, I think they would have let you die. They had to go… what's the word… resection your femoral artery so they could put a vein in your wrist. What in the fuck were you thinking?"

"It didn't hurt," Chase said thoughtfully. "I was thinking that I'd stop when it hurt."

"What made you stop?" Tommy asked, sitting up next to the bed. Chase's restrained hand twitched and Tommy reached out to hold it. Oh God. Tommy. Chase's hand tightened over those bony, uncomfortable fingers. *I didn't think I'd ever touch you again.*

"I was thinking…." *I didn't want anyone to clean up my mess. I was too afraid to face the red water. Maybe I would make my own red water and I could disappear in it.*

Tommy's hand tightened to the point of pain and Chase jerked against it, then winced because he couldn't go anywhere, because of the restraint.

"Answer me," Tommy muttered.

"I was trying to think of the answer."

"Bullshit!" Tommy stood up so quickly the chair he was sitting on shot backward, and Donnie barely dodged it as it clattered to the ground. "Bullshit!" he shouted again. He was furious: his lips were curled up in a snarl, the veins in his neck were popping out, and his shoulders were thrust forward like he would wrestle the world.

"Bullshit?" God, he was gorgeous. Chase's fingers twitched because he just wanted to touch that little triangle of flat moles on Tommy's neck. He always expected to feel a difference on his skin, but he never could.

"You say that, you fucking *dare* to say that to me? *Look* at you, Chase! You're in a fucking hospital bed! I... I just can't even believe you! A year... a year, I listen to the fucking silences in your head, wondering what you're really saying, and *this* is it? That little voice in your head said you had to fucking bleed out? What in the *fuck*!"

"I don't know what you want me to say!" Chase shot back, suddenly feeling the weight of not being able to stand and be taller. Usually he'd have some leverage in an argument like this. Usually he'd be able to touch Tommy and make it okay.

"Just fucking tell the truth! Just once! What is it going to hurt? Who's going to hear? All we want to know is why you chose to live, and you can't even tell us that? It's the one thing on the planet guaranteed not to piss us off!"

That's what you think!

"Don't I get some sort of space here?" Chase asked desperately. "Don't I have to feel better or some—"

"Oh bullshit, you get your space!" Tommy snapped. "Last time I gave you space you snuck out on me. You could barely fucking walk and you snuck out on me! Do you know I followed you back to your apartment to make sure you got home okay?"

Chase closed his eyes. "I'm sorr—"

"Fuck sorry! Just tell me why you lived!"

Chase didn't hear what he shouted back, but he stopped and blinked because it must have been something. Tommy's whole body went tight and then loose, and Donnie cringed like something hurt.

"What?" he asked, feeling suddenly tired. "What'd I say?"

"You said you didn't want me to hate you," Tommy said, his knees giving out. He was lucky Donnie was right behind him with the chair, or he would have ended up ass-flat on the floor.

"Well, yeah," Chase mumbled. "Okay. Didn't want that."

The fight bled out of Tommy, and he rested his cheek next to Chase's thigh again.

"Why would you think I'd hate you?" Tommy asked, his voice soft and broken.

Chase was tired. The whole scene had just done him in. His eyes were closed and he barely knew he was moving his own lips, but that didn't mean he didn't hear what he said.

"Because of how much I hate her."

"Who's her?" Donnie asked softly, and Chase was tired, too tired to answer him, but Tommy did it, sounding absent, like he was thinking about something else.

"His mother."

"Why does he hate his mother?" Donnie sounded so much like Kevin it made Chase want to smile.

"Because she killed herself, what, are you stupid?" Tommy's prickly nature showing. God, Chase wished he was awake so he could smooth the way between them. Donnie could get along with almost anyone, but Tommy, not so much.

"Oh fuck." There was a thump, like a head hitting a wall. "Fuck. Jesus, Chase."

Tommy's voice went soft as he asked, "Why? How did you think she died?"

Donnie shook his head. "He never told us. When he started school in the second grade, he was just... just this quiet kid, you know? So Kevin, he could talk to anyone, and my mom always told me to make friends, and there we were. And... we just never asked. That was just Chase."

Tommy's sound was broken, and Chase felt those bony fingers stroking the back of his hand with surprising gentleness.

"God. No wonder it was so easy. He's been bleeding since he was a baby. He just never told anyone. How do you even know it hurts after all that time?"

Because you loved me, and I knew what it meant to feel.

Sleep.

WHEN he came to again, Donnie was gone and Tommy was on a little couch, cuddled up with his knees almost to his chest. His head was pillowed on Donnie's bright yellow Sac State hooded sweatshirt, and he had a hospital blanket draped around his shoulders. He'd changed from the last time Chase had been awake. Chase could see that he'd gone from a black hooded sweatshirt to something brighter, sportier. Vaguely, he recognized it as one of the mock-baseball T-shirts that Chase had bought the last time they'd gone shopping. Apparently Chase's clothes had made it to Tommy's house, and a little tense part of Chase relaxed.

"He hasn't gone home in three days," said a pleasant, mildly familiar voice, and Chase looked up and squinted.

"Aren't you Tommy's shrink?"

"And Tommy was only the tip of the crazy iceberg, young man, because now I'm yours."

Chase groaned. Oh God. He knew this would happen. A shrink.

"I stopped," Chase complained. "I stopped. I changed my mind. Doesn't that get me a free pass out of a headshrinker?"

"On the contrary!" Doc said. He had wooden needles and a lovely, lush purple yarn in his hand, and apparently he was really big into appearing serene because he simply sat there and knit, keeping that tranquility around him like a handmade sweater.

"No?"

"No, my boy. It just makes you a hell of a lot more interesting and less surprised than my usual suicide watch. It doesn't mean I'm going to assume that my job here with you is all done."

"Why I gotta talk to you?" Chase wanted to know. "Why couldn't I talk to Tommy? He's the only one I ever talked to anyway."

"Yeah, I know. Donnie and Kevin were most unhappy to hear how much you didn't talk to them. Kevin said it felt like he wasn't a real friend after all."

Aw, fuck. "That's not fair! Those guys are my *brothers*. I just, you know, didn't want to tell them dumb shit."

Doc Stevenson grunted and then peered at his knitting for a minute. "Dammit, kid, you made me drop a stitch. 'Dumb shit'? Really? That's what this falls under? Because that's a new one. I could publish your case and be famous, if I did that sort of thing. You're like... like a combination of textbooks with a monkey wrench thrown in. And you're afraid of burdening your friends with 'dumb shit'. I'm boggled."

Chase's head didn't feel any better than it had the first time he'd woken up. "Oh, God. Don't I get a pass? I mean... shit. I'm still hooked up to—what is this shit?"

"Blood and fluids," the Doc said without looking at the two lines hooked up to the inside of his restrained arm. "About twenty strapping, beautiful young men trooped in here to try to donate blood in your name. Some of it even matched, but you may want to think about writing a thank you note to your, uhm, company."

Chase groaned. "You know what Tommy does, you know what I do," he said, trying really fucking hard not to be defensive. "Yes. My fellow porn models came out and donated. Does that make their blood not as good?"

"No," the Doc said, his voice growing gentle. "But it means that maybe you've got more people who care about you than you think. Maybe you want to try giving some of them a straight answer before we have to restrain your other wrist."

"But I *told* him the truth," Chase said plaintively, and he knew he sounded like a busted third-grader. *But I* told *the teacher I was mad. But I* told *the girl not to bug me.*

"Well, how about tell me the truth, and I'll count this really frustrating ten minutes toward your forty-five hours of counseling before I send you home."

"Forty-five *hours*?" Now *Chase* was boggled.

"One hour a day, or until I sign your release papers. Whichever comes first. Given your prickly nature, you're lucky your health insurance is the expensive, private-jet kind."

"Why is that?"

"Because otherwise, you'd be in group therapy for the month and a half. As it is, you're just here."

"Is that standard operating procedure?" Really? He was stuck in the psych ward for a month and a half? God. Just knowing that alone might have kept the razorblade out of his hand.

Or put it in the other one.

"Only because I know you, Chase. Not personally, mind you, but through Tommy here. You're his primary topic of conversation. If you weren't so fucked up, my boy, I'd be bored with you by now, but I'm not. I'm worried. Is there any possible way we could come to an agreement about this?"

"About what?"

"About you voluntarily commit yourself, you get the nice room, the freedom to visit the store for the cigarettes—"

"Gross!"

"Or gum of your choice, and are allowed as many visitors as can stand you, as long as you don't go too far when you talk."

"And what do you get?" Chase asked warily.

"I get as many hours as I think you need. You knew how to cut, you knew when to cut, you were in a prime position to finish the job. You didn't. That makes me think that you *really* want to live. If that's the truth, let's get to the real reason you're here, and then you won't have to be here anymore."

Chase grunted. "What day is it?"

"October fifth."

"Can I maybe be out by Thanksgiving? Tommy's mother died last year. I don't want him to spend the holiday alone."

There was a masculine and very paternal sigh. "You know, these things don't always happen on a timetable, Chase. And from everything I've seen, you're one incredibly stubborn young man. You want to get out of here, you're going to have to do the hard stuff. You think you can manage that?"

Tommy rolled over and looked at him. You'd think he'd look all frowzy with sleep, but not Tommy. His eyes were a little red, but still bright, and still sharp, and they seemed to bore into Chase's soul. Without a word, Tommy stood up and made it to the other chair next to Doc, the one he'd been sitting in when Chase had first woken up. He reached up and squeezed Chase's fingers and Chase closed his eyes. Tommy would know if Chase promised. He'd know if Chase went back on his word.

"Fuck," Chase sighed. "Yeah. But maybe we can wait to do more of this until the needles get pulled out of my arms? I'd really like the part of the hospital visit where everyone gets all dewy-eyed and tells me they're glad I'm okay."

Tommy's shoulders shook for a minute, and when Chase looked at him, those Loki black eyes were focused on his face.

"I'm so glad you're okay," Tommy said softly. "I can't be okay if you're not. Can you listen to the Doc, maybe, and make sure you stay that way?"

"Yeah, Tommy. But God," Chase closed his eyes. "I planned this so bad. I was going to go to the hospital and get all cured and shit, and then go home and be all good and strong for you. I wanted to be that guy, the one you need. And I'm not him yet. I wish you got to see me as that guy."

Tommy's laugh was soft and bitter. "Chase, do you really think I would have followed you this far if I didn't think you were that guy?"

"Hell, Tommy, I don't know why you stuck with me. I just wanted to be worth it, that's all."

Tommy yawned and stretched and smiled a little. "Chase, are you falling asleep?"

"God, yeah."

"I'm gonna go home and cop a shower, okay? A real one. Don't panic if I'm not here when you wake up. I'm coming, can you remember that?"

Chase had a random inappropriate thought, and it must have shown in his smirk.

"Jesus," Tommy said, shaking his head. "You can take the asshole out of the porn vid, but—"

"You can't take the porn vid out of the asshole?" Chase finished, giggling a little, and the last thing he saw when he closed his eyes was Tommy, giving an honest-to-God smile. Who knew? Maybe he'd be out early?

As he was fading out, he heard that paternal, masculine sigh again, and realized he'd never really answered Doc's question. Maybe not.

FRAGILE FUCKING FLOWER

THE young man on the couch looked tired. He was wearing loose jeans and a hooded purple sweatshirt, and he had his knees drawn up to his chest. He was resting his cheek on his knees and closing his eyes tightly, like he could block out the world—

"CHASE, you need to open your eyes and answer the question. Wait. Here's a new question, maybe not so hard. Where are you when you do that?"

Chase grunted. Compared to some of the questions in the last five days, this was a new one. "I'm trying to see myself from the outside," he said, and Doc Stevenson grunted.

"Really? Why?"

"To make sure I don't look too off."

There was a digestive silence. Chase opened his eyes and cast a glance at the Doc, who was knitting meditatively.

"Have you always done this?"

Chase thought a minute. "Well, not when I was filming." He smiled. "That was actually pretty awesome, you know? I could see it on film, people told me it was good. I knew that I was doing okay." *Almost as good as the flying part, when people touched me.*

"Finish that last thought," Doc commanded, and Chase grunted again. He hated this. It was creepy—Doc, Tommy, and lately Donnie and Dex and even Kevin kept making him finish the thought.

What happened to having peace in my own he—

"Now, Chase!"

"What happened to having peace in my own head?" he snapped, and perversely, Doc smiled.

"Your peace isn't peace, buddy. It's a festering well of emotional pus. Now finish that first thought, the one about being on film."

"Man, you've got a wife. Do you really want to talk about gay porn?"

Doc sent him a droll look. "Chase, you are more than a private person. Your entire psyche is locked behind a steel vault that's buried in a well that's covered in sixty thousand pounds of radioactive concrete. You're a human Chernobyl. The fact that you, out of the blue, decided not just to have an affair, or start going down on guys in stairwells, but actually *star in pornographic videos* is probably the only reason you're still alive. Until you met Tommy, it's probably the only emotionally authentic thing you've done in your life—"

"That's not true," Chase defended.

"No?"

"No. Donnie's house. I went to Donnie's house. His mom was nice to me. I liked it there."

"But you didn't bare your soul at Donnie's house, Chase. Hell, you didn't even bare your ass—and from what Donnie told me, you had an invitation—"

"Donnie *told* you that?"

"So did Tommy. They thought it would help."

Chase covered his face with his hands. "God. God. Porn was *so* less invasive than this is. There's a picture on the net of Ethan spitting in my asshole to lube me up, and I'd *so* rather put up a fucking billboard of that than have complete strangers know all this shit about me that I didn't tell them."

"They're not strangers, Chase! They're your lover and your friend and—"

"And you!" Chase accused, and Doc winced.

"Is it just the me that bothers you?"

"No! It's the *anybody*!"

Doc paused for a minute to let that sink in, and Chase looked away.

"So, Chase. Why *is* there a picture of some guy spitting in your asshole posted on the net? What could you possibly have to gain from that, besides the money—but things weren't that desperate, so don't feed me that crap."

Chase glared at him. "Okay, I saw *Good Will Hunting*, but from what I understand, shrinks really aren't allowed to talk to us like that. That was a movie. What makes you so special?"

Doc smiled, the expression rife with weariness. "I'm old, Chase. I'm old, I'm close to retirement, and I give a shit. No one's going to fire me at this stage of the game. I've seen so many young men and women like you—maybe not quite so spectacular, but I've had my share. I had one young man who was scarred in a fire when he was younger. As soon as he got old enough, he tattooed over all those scars—must have hurt like a son of a bitch too, but he never complained. And I asked him why, and he said, 'This way people look at what *I* want them to see.' Is that why the porn, Chase? If you were going to expose yourself to the world, was it going to be on your terms?"

Chase thought about it carefully. "A little," he said slowly, feeling the answer out as he said it. "I liked the idea of a pretty picture, so yeah. That was part of it. If I was going to be gay, I wanted it to be pretty, and hot. I wanted it to look perfect."

"Part but not all?"

Chase was lost in the idea now. Talking was easier, because that part of his brain—the part that had done homework and pitched games after the breakup with Tommy—that was what was working. It seemed to be completely detachable from the part of him that hurt.

"It was free," he said after a moment. "I felt free. No worries, no judgment. People—men—touched me, and it felt good, and I was rewarded for that, I guess. I was rewarded for feeling good. It was like flying."

The little room, with the dark paneling and the battered couch and the stained beige carpet and the creaky leather chair for the Doc, was quiet for a moment, and then a sound broke it up, something alien and unexpected.

It wasn't until the Doc passed him a box of tissues that Chase realized he was crying.

THE best part of the unzip your innards and count your intestines on the table exercise that the Doc called "counseling" was that afterward, Chase got visitors. Tommy was there every day, but he came in the evening for a couple of hours. In the meantime, he had Donnie or Dex or Kevin or Kane or any of the other guys from the set. There was a modest little exercise room with a set of weights and a couple of treadmills and elliptical machines. Chase had felt like crap warmed over for the first couple of days—going out for a walk was about all he could manage. But today his muscles were cramped and his body was protesting the lack of the workout, so Chase asked Dex if they could do that.

"I'm sorry the facility is crap," Chase apologized. "You could probably get a better workout at the gym."

Dex looked at him sorrowfully. "Does it occur to you that I like you, Chase? That I consider you a friend?"

Chase swallowed. "Yeah," he said, blushing. "I'm just sort of a lot of trouble, you know?"

"Yeah, you are," Dex said, no apology in his voice at all. For all of a second Chase was hurt, and then he looked at Dex's smirk.

"Bite me!" he muttered, and now Dex looked positively evil.

"I did that already. Now I think that's Tommy's job!"

Chase was laughing when Kevin and Donnie came into the weight room, looking for them.

"See, here he is, laughing like a mental patient!" Kevin grinned and sat on an unoccupied weight bench, cracking his gum. Chase was in the middle of doing bicep curls with his undamaged arm and a *substantially* reduced weight load, and he looked up and grinned.

"If you wanted a porn star instead, I think I'm retired—but Dex is still shooting!"

"Oooh!" Dex hooted, pretending he'd taken one in the gut, and there was a burst of raucous laughter. Chase looked at Kevin to make sure he was joining in, because he still felt bad about not trusting Kevin in the first place, and that's when he had a sudden flashback. It was him and Kevin in the fourth grade, and Kevin was teaching him all about gum.

"Yeah, here, like this. You gotta chew it loud, with your mouth open, to get the most air in it—that's what makes it crack. Be careful though, or you'll bite your tongue." Kevin's face, pleasant and roundish in adulthood, had been very very round in childhood, and when he was glum, the effect was heartbreaking, even to another child. "It hurts when you do that," Kevin confided quietly, "and afterwards, you can't eat potato chips because it hurts."

"Chase?" Donnie asked, his voice all concern. Chase looked down and realized that Donnie had moved forward and taken the weight out of his hands, because he'd stopped doing bicep curls and was just standing there, looking at Kevin, and, oh shit, really?

"Oh God!" he groaned, tilting his head back in complete mortification. "Am I fucking crying ag*ain*?"

"Where'd you go?" Donnie asked, and he pulled a box of Kleenex from the sill of the industrial yellow wall. The gymnasium had an orderly reading a newspaper in the corner of the room, a guy who looked like a really stressed-out stockbroker running the treadmill, and them, Chase and his friends, and it was almost as private as Chase got these days.

For once, Chase didn't think about making a glib answer. He couldn't. He was just so surprised by the memory, by the sadness—he didn't even have a lie prepared.

"I was just remembering Kevin," he said, smiling a little at his friend before everything just spilled out, unstoppable, babbling like he couldn't ever remember babbling before. "We were kids, right, and Kevin, God, you were so fuckin' cute. Not coming on to you cute—you were just this adorable little kid, right? And you were talking about biting your tongue when you cracked your gum and it just... it never occurred to me, that it was a secret. You told me a secret, and we were friends and I should have maybe, I dunno... trusted you guys. I should have trusted you guys, and you were just so young. I was just so glad you let me hang out with you, and I didn't even know until just this minute that you might have wanted me in the club too."

"Aw, man!" Kevin wore his emotions on his sleeve, which wasn't very macho of him, but it had always been very Kevin. Now he was crying too. "Of course we wanted you in the club. You were so cool—you never said anything."

Chase's laughter was suddenly cracked and jagged. "That's because everything inside was just so fuckin' awful!" he said, his shoulders shaking with a sort of hysterical laughter. He didn't get a chance to laugh, though, because suddenly Donnie had wrapped his arms around his shoulders, and Kevin was there in the hug too, and Donnie reached out and grabbed Dex by the shirt front and dragged him in, and suddenly Chase was surrounded by the press of bodies, a press of touch, and it wasn't Tommy, and it didn't have anything to do with sex, and the words in his chest couldn't stop spilling out.

"I'm sorry," he sobbed again and again, "I'm sorry. Man, I should have trusted you... I'm sorry."

He must have been really lost in the tears, because he didn't even feel when one of the guys—Kevin—moved out of the way and the orderly was there. He startled at the smooth, cool pain of the needle in his arm, and then groaned.

"Aw, fuck. A sedative?" he sniffled. "Is this trip really necessary?"

"A group hug in the weight room?" The orderly was a squat black man with a sweet face and a sharp tongue. "Man, that is the *meaning* of the word necessary. Now c'mon, Dr. Phil, let's take a nice wheelchair to your room and you can sleep it off, okay?"

Dex and Donnie helped him into the chair, and he felt his head loll back a little. "Bye, guys!" he said, feeling loopy. "I'll see you when I'm feeling less emotionally available!"

Donnie was suddenly right there next to him, squatting by the chair. "You just keep on being like this," he said softly. "Because that's how I know you're gonna be okay."

Chase nodded, then remembered something and felt miserable. "God, please let Tommy visit, okay? Even if I'm passed out. I may not be awake for it, but I wanna know he's there."

Donnie patted Chase's arm solidly. "Yeah, man, I'll see what I can do."

HE BARELY remembered Tommy's visit that night. Mostly he remembered that Tommy crawled in bed next to him, tucked his cheek in against the back of Chase's neck, and stroked his stomach as Chase struggled to wake up for a moment, any moment, just to spend some time with him.

When Chase woke up in the morning, headachy and queasy from the sedative, Tommy was gone and Chase was pissed.

"This is bullshit!" he raged at the Doc, pacing from one end of the dark paneled room to the other. "I'm supposed to be getting better, and it's like I'm crying at pictures of little girls and kittens!"

"Or charming friends who taught you how to crack your gum," Doc said gently, and Chase remembered to open his fist at the last moment when he stopped at the wall and pounded it with the flat of his hand.

"But *why*? I'm supposed to be getting better!" Doc made a suspicious sound, and Chase glared at him and then continued to rage. "I'm crying all the fucking time—I don't even know it's fucking coming and then, there it is, just fucking waterworks! It's like... I don't know, I'm a girl on her period or... some sort of emo guy who's—"

"Suicidally depressed?" Doc inserted dryly when Chase was floundering for words.

"*I fucking stopped!*" Chase roared, and he turned around to glower and found Doc regarding him with such terrible serenity that he couldn't manage to maintain his momentum. He turned around and sighed and flopped into the couch, which creaked because he was tall and still had the mass of a bodybuilding jock.

"I did!" he complained to Doc's raised eyebrows. "Doesn't that mean I'm not suicidal anymore?"

"Hardly," Doc said quietly. "It just means you stopped."

"But shouldn't I be over this part?" Chase asked, tearing up a little and feeling just totally pathetic.

"Did you cry before you slit your wrist?" Doc asked, and Chase looked at him in disgust.

"Twice," he said when Doc didn't look like he was giving an inch. "Once when I left Tommy, and once when... my last porn shoot. Tommy was there."

"Tommy told me about that. Trust me. We'll get there. So, no other time?" Doc asked, prodding.

"No." Chase sighed. "Christ. Isn't that plenty?"

"Not even close."

"So, what's that mean?"

"Well, I'm pretty sure it means you need to think of this as paying your dues. Tears are a natural part of depression, Chase. So is acting out sexually. So is destroying your possessions—"

"I didn't want them destroyed—I just didn't want *her* to destroy them."

The Doc stopped then. "Why would your girlfriend destroy them?"

"Because if I was going to live, I was going to have to come out, break up with her, tell her our lives were a lie. Wouldn't you want to break something after that?"

Doc stopped knitting for a minute. "You planned all of that from the bathroom when you were bleeding out?"

Chase blushed. "I'm not normally that much of a planner."

"The hell you're not!" The old man's hands had actually stilled in their usual rhythmic movement. "You bought the razorblades ahead of time, are you aware of that? You told me that yourself! You told me you were saving for a house! You're barely twenty-one—even if you weren't suicidal, that's still pretty damned impressive. Donnie told me about how you had the entire exit planned. Chase, to say you're not much of a planner is like saying Frank Lloyd Wright wasn't much of a designer: it's like criminal understatement."

Chase looked away. "Okay," he muttered, "so I like things pretty."

"And why is that, exactly?"

Red door, red water, little boy, cross-legged, watching the door bow in—

"Chase, dammit, I'm going to start adding five minutes to your counseling requirement every time you do that!"

"But I don't have words for this!" Chase complained, running his fingers through his hair. It was getting long enough to do that now. "It's just a picture in my head! I can't help it if I'm lookin' at it!"

Doc blew out a breath and looked at the clock. "Chase, we're running out of time today, but tomorrow? I want to take you into a state of hypnosis—"

"Awesome. Are you going to pull a rabbit out of a hat too?"

"It's not magic, dammit—it's just getting you really relaxed so you don't—God, I can't even think of the *word* for this thing you do when you don't answer a straight question."

"Is there a word?" Chase asked, suddenly curious.

"Yes, yes there is a word. I'm just so irritated with you right now that I can't think of it."

Chase looked at him, smiling a little in spite of himself. "But you're still knitting."

Doc's intense scowl cracked a little, turned itself inside out, and dimpled inward at the sides.

"Crazier people than you have tried to stop me," he said mildly, and Chase grinned. Then the old man had to go and ruin it all. "So tomorrow, you come in, we relax you, because *that's* going to be a neat trick, and in the meantime, I'm going to throw you a softball."

Chase grinned slightly. "Pitch."

"What's your father like?"

He's six foot something of nicotine-stained dick, except I like dicks, and I hate him so bad I want to think of a word to call him that doesn't have anything to do with sex, like turd, or cockroach vomit or pig shit or—

"Really? Tell me how you really feel."

Chase had a sudden sense of dislocation. "Oh God, did I say all that out loud?"

"Say all what?"

"Turd or cockroach vomit or—oh, Jesus, you *tricked* me!"

Doc looked inordinately pleased with himself. "Not intentionally, no—but now that I know that works, I'm going to try it more often! Now *why* do you feel this way about your father?"

Red door, bulging in the center, water like scarlet pudding, easing under the gap in the door, a male voice shouting, "C'mon, ya little fucker, open the door!"

Doc sighed, and Chase looked at him uncertainly. "He's not a nice man," Chase said, feeling odd. "He's... he calls people names, and he yells, and he hits you if you're not quick enough with his cigarettes and he—" *He yelled at my mother until she killed herself, and then yelled at me until I wanted to join her.* "Oh fuck, Doc?" Chase grabbed more fucking Kleenex from the fucking box. "I don't want to do this anymore? Can I stop doing this? I hate this. I'm sick of crying, I'm sick of the shit in my head, I'm sick of trying to talk to the world when all this shit... it's just sitting there, just big as a fucking movie screen, and I don't want to talk about it because you can't make it pretty, and you can't fix it, you just can't, so why do I have to talk about it...." He was sobbing again, and Doc actually put his knitting down and got up.

"Please don't drug me again," he pleaded, gasping for breath. "Please. Please just make it stop."

"No drugs," Doc promised, and Chase felt an arm over his shoulder, just like Donnie's arm, sexless and comforting and human. "No drugs, just a hug. Is that okay? Can you do a hug?"

Chase nodded miserably, his cheeks on the knees of his jeans, and wondered when this part of the healing process got better.

KANE came by to visit that day and dragged Chase outside for a walk whether he wanted one or not.

"It's shitty outside!" Kane said with the same enthusiasm someone else might have used for, "It's *gorgeous* outside!" "Let's go see what sort of shit is hiding under the leaf mold in the little walk around the pond, okay?"

Chase looked at him, not really objecting, just wondering why that was a good thing.

Kane blushed. "Didn't you ever study bugs as a kid, man? We used to talk about the ones with exoskeletons, the arachnids, all that shit. I *loved* that shit! I was so totally into the whole science thing, yanno?"

Chase stood up, still smiling in bemusement, and grabbed the tennis shoes from the corner, along with the jacket to go over his hooded sweatshirt. He followed Kane outside of the little in-patient dormitory to the foggy, gray facility yard, waiting until they were far away from any listeners before asking, "Why did you stop?"

Kane looked at him in surprise, and then shrugged. "I was sort of a wimpy little kid, right? And sort of goofy—I couldn't keep my attention focused on anything. So, I got like, picked on, all the fuckin' time. And I hit middle school and thought, 'Enough of that shit!' I started working out like a mad dog, and suddenly girls were just fuckin' hitting on me, right? And I did them if they asked, and I loved it. I mean, girls, right? They're like—" Kane held his hands out to indicate breasts, and Chase nodded.

"I do recall," he said dryly.

"Yeah, but you didn't really appreciate," Kane said, and Chase had to concede that no, he didn't really appreciate.

"But you did?"

"I did...." Kane's voice sort of trailed off. "And I spent most of my high school fucking around. Man, you name a place you could get laid and there I was, banging away, right?"

"So you ended up at *Johnnies* because…."

Kane looked at him with admiration. "Listen to you, sounding all headshrinky and shit. You should be one of those psych guys—you're hella good at it."

"And…." Chase actually enjoyed this—he was genuinely curious, but at the same time, he knew what Kane felt, how reluctant he was to talk about personal things. For the first time, Chase knew why people looked at him like they were going to either strangle him or hug him when they tried to ask him this shit. For the first time, he sort of got Doc and Tommy.

"And those girls I was banging? They were using me. So I was pretty good at sex, right, and I didn't have no education, but I wanted one. I was like 'Porn, motherfuckers!' and then…." Kane shrugged. "Then I just wanted it to be all about sex. I wasn't going to meet my dream girl on a porn set, and I was sort of sick of that whole 'Oh, Kane, you're hot I want to do you!' thing. I figured I'd do boys for money, and then I'd do girls for—" Kane stopped himself and blushed. "Corny, isn't it?"

"For love?" Chase shook his head. "No. I think being careful who you do for love is really fucking important, Kane. I think you're miles ahead on the subject."

Kane sighed, looked away, looked sad. "Now that I've been doing boys so much, I'm starting to wonder why I couldn't…" He trailed off, so pensive that Chase was actually concerned. Suddenly he brightened. "Look! A praying mantis! This late in October—you don't usually see them! It's sort of warm here, 'cause the generators for the hospital are right there." Kane pointed to two beige-painted outbuildings that hummed. "Hey, guy, how you doin'?" Kane got close to it, like a little kid, as excited and reverent as Chase had ever seen a boy about a bug. For a moment, he'd been going to ask Kane what Kane intended to say to the girl of his dreams while he was explaining how he'd earned his college tuition, but at the last moment he decided not to. Chase *had* to answer all of those fucking invasive questions; Kane did not. Kane had been a good friend these past months, and Chase figured he'd earned a pass.

Kane left, and Chase got to eat sort of a glum, average dinner of institutional pizza and then go back to his room. He told himself he was going to watch television, but the truth was, he was going to brood until Tommy got there.

"What's wrong?" First words out of his mouth. Chase was actually so relieved to see him that he grinned at the bluntness.

"Careful with me," he said, trying and failing to keep his voice light. "I'm sort of a fragile fucking flower today. You raise your voice too loud, I might break."

He was sitting on his bed, dangling one foot to the ground and clutching his other knee to his chest, and suddenly Tommy was there, where Chase had needed him all day, with an arm wrapped around his shoulders and a kiss to Chase's temple. Chase drank in his touch like water, pure, clear water, and almost shivered at the analogy.

"You're a fragile flower all right, but neither of us is fucking."

Chase looked at him sadly. "You could always shoot a scene," he said helpfully, and Tommy's look grew dark.

"I think we both know that's not going to happen again."

"I sort of miss it. It was something to look forward to."

Tommy shrugged. It was undeniable. There was a rush before a scene, an anticipation, just like a relationship with a new person in real life. What was this adventure going to be? And, well, you *knew* you were going to come, right? How awesome was that?

"Look forward to being with me instead," Tommy told him, and Chase had to smile.

"I do," he said sincerely. "I just… I hate being this… this breakable *thing*. I hate all this crying. I'd say it's driving me crazy, but I'm obviously already there!"

"You know," Tommy said, his voice so gentle Chase wondered what sort of fresh pain he'd put in the blender *today*, "when you broke up with me, I cried for three days."

Oh yeah. That helped. "I'm sorry," Chase mumbled into his knees, knowing his chest was growing tight with tears and with the loosening of them too.

"I didn't tell you that to make you sorry, although you should be, because you were an asshole. The *second* time you left me, and I had to follow you home to make sure you didn't drive into a tree, ya big fuckhead, I went home and broke a kitchen chair."

"Oh shit, which one?"

"Does it fuckin' matter?"

Chase blushed. "No."

"The old creaky one that we let Buster sit in. Buster still hasn't forgiven me, but that's another story."

And the point of this one would be?

"Don't say that, whatever it is going on in your head. See, the thing is, I cried, I broke shit, I raged. I called Dex over and we went to the gym and had a sparring match and he kicked my ass because I'd been out of the hospital for like, a week, and all the time, I was doing that, what were you doing?"

Cleaning your excrement out of your carpet and buying razorblades.

"Yeah," Tommy said, without making Chase answer again. "You were cleaning my own shit out of my house and buying fucking razorblades. Dex remembered that, you know. He thought it was weird, and then after Donnie called me and I called him, he almost crapped his pants—"

"That's not funny!"

"Neither of us was fucking laughing, ya fuckin' fuckhead. But are you hearing me now?"

"Sort of," Chase mumbled.

"Speak up, Chase, I can't fucking hear you. What were you doing while I was bawling my heart out and breaking shit?"

Chase sighed, so safe in Tommy's arms it felt like he could say this and be okay. "Keeping it all locked in my head," he said quietly, and Tommy's arm tightened around his shoulders.

"You're smart, Chase, but your noggin's only so big. You didn't let it out, and now it's busting out, and it's not always safe. It's like a dam or something, right? The water's threatening to knock the whole thing over, and you can either let it out those waterways where it's supposed to go, or it's going to be like in the movies where big chunks of rock are shooting everywhere and the first place to give is right above the family and the second place to go is heading for the power plant that's going to destroy the city. And it doesn't have to be that way, man. All you gotta do is let it out at the right places, the right times, and it'll go, and when it's done, you'll feel lighter, because all that water was putting pressure on shit, and now it's gone. Right?"

Chase nodded, suddenly exhausted by his day even though it was only eight o'clock at night. "Tommy?" he said plaintively, "can you tell me something not serious? Can you tell me something happy?"

Tommy looked at him carefully, trying to see if it was some sort of ruse, or evasion, Chase was sure. Chase wasn't sure what Tommy saw in his eyes, but he was relieved when Tommy started scooting down on the bed and nestling against Chase, until Chase's face was pressed up against Tommy's chest and Tommy's lower leg was thrown over Chase's hips, and they were as twined as two people could be with their clothes on.

"I got a kitten today," Tommy said, and Chase pulled back to grin at him.

"Yeah?"

"Yeah. And a turtle too."

"A turtle?"

"Yeah, he's in a terrarium. The pet store had them on sale all month, and he was the last guy in the tank. He was sort of puny, you know? Not really spectacular, like the other turtles, so I took him home. They were nice—they gave me a terrarium for free, because I volunteer with the rescue cats on the weekend. You've helped me, right?"

"Yeah. I like doing that." The rescue cats needed their litter changed and their nails trimmed and their cages cleaned while they waited for someone to adopt them. Tommy went once a week, because some of the same people worked with the rescue cats at the ASPCA who did the pet store adoptions, and Chase had helped him on more than one occasion. They both liked the idea of perfectly nice animals given a second chance to have a home.

"So anyway, they gave me the terrarium and I took it home and set it up in the living room, on that shelf by the TV—"

"What'd you do with the models you painted?" Cars—Tommy liked them in small form, but he said all he wanted from the big ones was for them to get him somewhere when he stepped on the gas.

"Just moved them to the side. Anyway, so it looks sort of peaceful there, and the turtle—"

"What'd you name him?"

"Am I supposed to name him?"

"Well yeah. You can't just let him hang out without a name. Then he's not a real person."

Tommy kissed the top of his head, mostly, Chase figured, for something to do. Chase may have gone all delicate fragile flower on him, but this sitting still shit still didn't work well for Tommy, and Chase could feel his muscles jumping even as they lay there. That was okay though. He did the same thing at night, when he was lying down to sleep, right up until his eyes closed and his body went limp. Chase knew because he'd stayed up on more than one occasion just to feel that moment.

"I think I love you just 'cause you'd say that. What do you want to name him?"

"I don't know. I haven't met him. Don't you have to know them before you name them?"

"People name babies all the time without knowing them. They just hope that kid's gonna be like the name when it pops out of the oven."

Chase laughed. "I think sometimes kids just sort of turn into who they are because of the way they're named, but I don't know."

"Why not?"

"Because I've never met a person on the planet who's more Tommy Halloran than you. I don't know what the hell you were dreaming of when you came up with 'Tango'."

Tommy laughed. "I was thinking I wanted to dance with all the hot guys, that's what I was thinkin'. Now about this turtle. Oliver. I think I'm gonna name it Oliver."

"Why's that?"

"Because he's leaving little turtle poop 'Oliver' his terrarium."

Chase laughed at the horrible pun and suddenly felt better. Tommy was warm and muscular and wonderful, wrapped around him this way, but Chase had a thought.

"Tommy, why aren't we horny?"

"Who says we're not?" For form, Tommy thrust his hips forward, and he had a semi, but that was sort of standard for Tommy—he was like, at perpetual half-mast.

"You know what I mean."

Tommy sighed. "You're not horny because your body's still sad. Your brain, your heart, your body—they're all still grieving for the shit that fucked you up in the first place. I'm not horny because...." Tommy trailed off and swallowed, and his arms tightened around Chase's shoulders convulsively.

"You're still pissed at me," Chase mumbled, because he deserved it.

"A little, yeah," Tommy confessed, "but mostly I'm so scared."

Chase looked up. "Scared?"

"Yeah. You're crying all the time, and in a way that's good, Chase. I mean, it's better than that whole 'disappear in your head' crap you were doing. But you're also sort of... I dunno. Helpless when you're like this. And I think that dam is gonna burst anyway, and I have to keep going home. Who's gonna help put you back together?"

"You'll be here," Chase mumbled, suddenly completely terrified himself. Oh God. He was going to feel *worse* than this? The prospect was just... just *horrible*. If this was how he felt the whole time he was locked in his own head, telling himself he'd be fine as long as he kept the girlfriend and the apartment and the picture-book life, how was he going to deal with feeling *worse* than this? All of a sudden, like a monstrous, light-sucking black wall, he was hit with the actual depth of his desolation, and how fucking miserable he would have had to be to do what he did. His arms tightened around Tommy's middle, and for a minute they just stayed there, clinging to each other.

"The Doc's gonna do something new tomorrow," he said quietly. "Hypnotherapy, which sounds sort of hokey and *Lifetime* television, you know, but he just wants me to relax enough to talk about shit."

Tommy made a suspicious noise, and when he spoke his voice was really gruff. Chase didn't want to look to see if he was crying. Chase had had enough of tears to last him forever and ever and ever.

"I think that's a real good idea," Tommy said after a minute. "I think that's gonna help you, but you're gonna have to be brave, Chase. Brave ain't your strong suit, you know?"

"I know," Chase whispered, because it was the truth. He swallowed. Tommy would have to leave soon, and Chase didn't want him to leave when they were like this. He wanted Tommy to leave happy, and optimistic, and ready to come back the next day and tell Chase about what he did.

"So," he said when he could talk with a steady voice. "What're you going to name the kitten?"

Tommy went to kiss the top of Chase's head again, but Chase tilted his head back and Tommy got his lips instead. The kiss was salty, but sweet.

When Tommy pulled back, his full lips curved up into a smile. "Paulie," he said happily. "He's sort of a little scrapper, like Buster, but he reminds me of this guy from my neighborhood. Guy grew up to be a doctor, you know? I figure this guy's got a future, he gets to be Paulie."

"How's Buster like him?"

"Buster thinks he's a punk, which is okay. Buster's gonna school him, teach him some manners, and then lick his ears when Paulie needs a little TLC. They're good."

Chase nodded and settled in to Tommy's comforting body again.

"We good?" Tommy asked him, and Chase found himself mumbling the truth, spontaneously, with no prompting.

"Tommy, I'm so scared about tomorrow."

"Me too. When a dam breaks, it leaves a hell of a puddle."

"Bring your mop," Chase joked feebly, and Tommy didn't say anything to that for a minute.

"I'm going to talk about the kitten some more," he said apologetically, but that was fine with Chase.

"Yeah. Yeah, do that. It makes me happy."

"Good."

RED WALL, RED WATER

THE boy was lying down, staring at the ceiling in a darkened room. The doctor's voice was sonorous, soothing, and patient, and the boy's eyes fluttered closed—

"CHASE, are you doing it again? Seeing yourself like in a movie?"

"Yeah, Doc. Sorry."

"Don't be. I want you to go with that, okay? This time, I want you to see yourself, like in a movie. You've got the wide shot, and there's this good-looking kid lying on a couch in his shrink's office, and then I'm going to count backwards from ten. With every count, that camera's going to get closer and closer, okay?"

"Can I stop before it goes up my ass?"

"This is a shrink's office, not a porn set, kid. That ain't where the camera is going and you know it."

Chase sighed. "It would be a lot more fun if it was going up my ass."

"For you, maybe. By the time I get to one, I want that camera in your head, where all the action is that you're not telling the rest of us about, okay?"

"Worst. Porn vid. Ever."

"And action!" The Doc's voice slowed down then, soft and slow and mellow. "Ten. Okay, Chase, close your eyes and see yourself, just like I told you. You're stretched out on the couch, your hands are crossed on your chest, and your breathing is regular... in and out... repeat. Good, and your body is relaxed. You're limp, melting into the couch... completely at peace. Now, at the next count, the camera is going to zoom a little closer, and your breathing is going to get a little deeper, okay?" The Doc took a deep breath himself. "Nine. Good, can you see the expression on your face? Right now it's all tense. I want you to relax your expression. We need to make it a good shot, right?"

"Right." Chase concentrated on easing the muscles in his face, making them relaxed, making them peaceful. The camera in his head saw that, and his breathing evened out a little more, and his bones seemed to melt, just like the Doc said, until by the count of four, he was just this big, peaceful blob on the couch, so serene he was almost unconscious.

Three. And now the camera was inside his head, taking a look around.

"What do you see?" And Doc's voice wasn't intrusive—it was like he belonged there, in Chase's head. He had an invitation with the film crew to come inside and check shit out, and Chase's job was to give him the guided tour.

"There's a red door," Chase said, and for the moment, his heartbeat was pretty still.

"Yeah? What's it look like?"

The description was so easy. He'd been looking at this door all his life.

"It's square, not like a rectangle, and it's, you can see light all around it, at the seams. There's water coming underneath it." His breathing sped up a little, but he forced himself to calm down. He'd invited the film crew in, right? "Red water."

"Where are you, Chase? In relation to the door, I mean."

He looked up at the door, holding onto his knees and getting ready to pull them to his chest. "I'm sitting in front of the door, looking up at it."

"How are you sitting?"

"Like a little kid, with my legs crossed and my arms wrapped around my knees."

"That's a protective position, Chase."

Beat. Beat. Chase took a deep breath and swallowed. "The red door is scary."

"I know it is. Let's not look inside it right now. Is there anything around you?"

"No, it's dark around me. All the light is behind the door."

"Okay then, how about smells?"

"The toilet ain't been cleaned for a while."

"Toilet?" Doc sounded puzzled for a minute, and Chase felt he had to clarify.

"It's behind the door."

"Oh. Okay. I understand. How about sounds?"

"Water dripping." Chase squeezed his eyes shut, and let the other sound permeate. "And him."

"Him?"

"He's yelling."

"Who's yelling?"

"Victor. My father."

"What's he doing?"

"He's pounding on the door, screaming shit. Usual shit. 'Get out, you little faggot! Just fucking open the fucking door! Stop that fucking noise! Stop crying, you little pussy, and open the fucking door!'"

"And you're not?"

"No."

"Why not?"

Had anyone ever asked him that question? Ever? "Because it's safer," he whispered. "It's safer, in here with her, than it is out there with him."

There was a breath, and Doc's voice was incredibly firm when he spoke again. "You said 'in here with her'. Where are you now?"

"I'm inside the bathroom."

"Are you alone?"

Chase looked over to his left, and saw what he always saw. The closed eyes, the waxen, blue lips, the red-blonde hair swirling in a cloud in the scarlet water.

"No, my mother's with me."

"What's she doing?"

"Lying in the bathtub. Her eyes are closed, and she's not moving."

There was a pause then, like Doc had to pull himself together, but that was sort of funny, because he was always together, right?

"What color's the water, Chase?"

"It's red."

"How'd you get into the bathroom?"

"Well the faucet was running when I got home, and the water was coming under the door, so I opened it."

"Were you afraid?"

"Naw. It was just water, right? I wasn't afraid at all when I opened it, I just ran in."

"Were you afraid then?"

"The… the water was all red, and she was naked, and you're not supposed to be naked around kids, right?"

"No. Was she taking a bath?"

"Not anymore. She was just lyin' there, with her eyes closed, and not moving, so I turned off the water and started talking to her."

"Did she answer?" The voice was gentle, like Doc knew how this ended.

"No. She didn't answer. But he was coming home, and he was coming home and that was always scary."

"Scary how?"

Scary was such an amorphous feeling. Chase actually had to think hard to come up with the details that made Victor so scary to his mother.

"Well, she'd clean the house faster when he came home or turn off the television and make me go do my homework in my room, and she hated it when he was coming home." And suddenly, what hadn't made sense when he was talking to Tommy made sense now. "So I couldn't let him see her like this, with all the water on the floor, but she wasn't moving, so I closed the door, right?"

"Right."

"I closed it and I locked it, because I didn't want him to come in. Because things just got worse when he came in. They got worse and horrible, and he'd call me names and she'd cry and I hated it when he came in. So he couldn't come in. He'd yell at her if he came in. So I locked the door."

There was a digestive silence, and Chase was trapped in that moment, inside the bathroom, waiting for Victor to come home. It was a forever moment, one that didn't have any breath.

"What happened when he got home?"

"Like I thought. He started pounding at the door and yelling, and I hated the yelling. I really fucking did. He started screaming at me, that I was a faggot and a pussy and all that shit, and that if there was anything wrong with her, I probably did it. And there was something wrong with her, right? She wasn't moving. She wasn't trying to get up. She was just lyin' there, and even if her eyes were closed, it felt like she was looking at me like I needed to do something, and he was yelling at me like it was all my fault. I was a faggot and a pussy and a nasty little shit and an obnoxious little fucker and it was all my fault."

The red door was bulging, the mass of the water behind it forcing it open, and Chase couldn't make himself stand up to brace it closed. He couldn't be two places at once. He couldn't *be* sitting in that bathroom and talking to Doc and standing up to that door with the red water. It needed someone to hold it shut, and he couldn't. He *wasn't* standing up to it, forcing it closed. He *wasn't* shoving or banging at it to keep it from bursting on him. No, there was nothing he could do to protect himself from that fucking red door, because he was on the floor, his ass in the water, holding onto his knees and rocking back and forth, rocking back and forth and sobbing, sobbing, with the effort to keep himself there, like he'd told Doc, sobbing because the red door was going to open and he was afraid, so fucking afraid, what was behind it was so awful, so fucking terrifying, it was going to rip him up and shred him into pieces and he'd never take a breath without his lungs being filled with filthy, bloody water and little bits of him.

"How was it your fault?"

"Oh God...." He didn't want to say this.

"Chase, she'd filled that bathtub when you were at school. You weren't even there. How could it be your fault?"

"Because I was... I *was* a little faggot, I *was*, and I kissed a little boy and she got called into the office and she was all in tears saying I couldn't be, I couldn't because he'd never leave me alone, he'd never leave me alone and I *was* the reason he hated me he hated us because I *was I am I am I am*—"

The red door bent, bowed impossibly, the water roaring at the seams, and Chase wrapped his arms over his head to protect himself. In his head he heard the giant fracture as the boards cracked, the hinges ripped free, and the door burst open. The red water crashed over his head, shocking, painful, freezing cold, and the force of it slammed into his body and stopped his breath, covering him, wrapping him in red, until it filled his vision and filled his mouth and trammeled his chest, and even then, even under water, he could hear his own screams.

HE WASN'T sure how long he was sedated and he really wasn't sure how long he had just lain there, being nothing, after the sedative wore off.

He was vaguely aware of people—Donnie? Doc? Tommy?—shaking him and trying to get him to eat.

"Later," he mumbled. "Later. I'll eat later."

Then Tommy didn't just shake him, Tommy hauled him up by the shirtfront and shoved him against the wall.

"Fuck later, asshole! Get up and fucking eat *now!*"

"Tommy?" Chase squinted. Hadn't Tommy just been there, telling him it was okay, he could sleep this once? "I thought you told me I could sleep?"

"That was *last night*, Chase! I was here all night, I tried to get you up this morning, and now I'm pissed. Now get the fuck up. I went and got you some Thai food because it's your favorite, and the clerk was fucking pissy about making Thai noodles without any spices and you'd better fucking eat it."

"Thai?" Chase was intrigued in spite of himself. "I haven't had Thai in forever. You're the only one I know who eats Thai food."

Tommy let out a shaky breath and let him settle back down into the bed. "Yeah, well, maybe you need to get better and stop this catatonic shit so you can come home and we can eat some. Hell, I'll learn to cook it if you want. I'd love to fucking sit home and cook you Thai food for the rest of our lives if you'd just get up and eat *now*."

Chase nodded, feeling a little teary, but not, thank God, like he was going to fucking lose it. "Can I brush my teeth? My mouth tastes like...." He smacked his tongue on his palate. "There's not a word for it, but it's not good."

"Yeah, knock yourself out." Tommy sat back on the bed—he'd been on his knees as he'd shoved Chase against the wall—and Chase went to stand up. And almost fell on his ass.

"Jesus," he said, feeling woozy. "What the fuck's wrong with my legs?"

"Twenty-four hours, Chase. You've been in fuckin' la-la land for twenty-four hours. They were talking about feeding you intravenously until I told them to hold on a fuckin' minute, I'd be back with Thai food. I don't know what they feed you in this place, but it can't be good."

Chase grimaced. "It's not Thai food."

"Need my help to the bathroom?"

Embarrassingly enough, yes, but once Chase got to the cubicle and could lean on the walls, he could pretty much take care of things from there. Tommy helped him back to the little bedside table with two chairs and sat him down, straightening the napkin extravagantly and tying it up around Chase's neck.

"Ha-ha. Are you going to put this shit on platters and present it to me, or can we just eat?"

"Hey, forgive me if I'm trying to make a thing out of it, Chase. You're eating without a needle in your arm—it's cause for celebration, you know?"

Chase looked at him for a minute, *really* looked at him. His eyes were bloodshot, and he had luggage you could ship to China. His bounciness—that constant, vital movement Chase had loved from the very beginning—wasn't there. Tommy was exhausted—with worry, with being there, with everything.

"I'm sorry," Chase said softly. "I'll try to give you more to celebrate."

Tommy looked him in the eyes and grimaced. "No worries. We ain't cleaned up the champagne yet from when you left your girlfriend."

"You think Doc'll let me come home for Thanksgiving?" Chase asked optimistically, and Tommy looked up and smiled. It was tired, but there was no forced cheerfulness in it, and Chase felt a little bit of optimism himself.

"God, I hope so. That woman—you know, Donnie's mom? She keeps coming over and bringing me food and plants and shit, and cleaning the house, like she's getting it ready for you. She wants us over to her house really bad."

Chase looked at him funny. "Really? She hasn't come to visit."

Tommy nodded, looking sad. "Yeah. She says she'd just cry all over you, and she didn't think that's what you needed right now. I guess you and Kevin were like her kids or something—she said you came over almost every day. Man, that woman really fuckin' loves you."

Chase looked away, saying, "God. I was sort of afraid, you know? I brought Mercy over there for two years. I thought she'd be mad, you know?"

Tommy shook his head. "Naw—I think it's like when your kid goes through a divorce. Anyone else, they get to pick sides, but not the parents. They stick with their kid. You're her kid."

Chase smiled a little. "That's nice," he said, and Tommy nodded. Their eyes met, shiny and wordless. "I never thought about it, but it's good to be somebody's kid."

"It's good to be somebody's *everything*," Tommy said seriously.

"You're my everything. I could have lived my whole life locked in my head, but you forced me out."

Tommy looked down at his hands, where he was dishing up Thai noodles onto a little paper plate.

"You can be grateful for that *now*?" he asked in a whisper. "'Cause coming out of your head ain't been a picnic."

"That depends," Chase said, taking the noodles from him and grabbing a plastic fork. "Are we going to eat—what meal is this, anyway?"

"Lunch."

"Yeah. If we're going to eat lunch it's totally worth it. I'm suddenly starving."

Tommy's smile was huge, the kind of smile that showed the long canines and made his eyes bright and shiny like obsidian, and for a moment, Chase saw Loki the lunatic sex god sitting right there at the little institutional table, eating Thai food.

His hands were shaking, and he still felt a little queasy, and Tommy was right—he was still a big puddle. But he was pretty sure he could be cleaned up.

DOC let him go after the forty-five days. They were not easy days. Some of them were just fucking horrible. Some of them were days when Tommy came to visit and Chase just huddled in a corner and cried, Tommy's hand in the middle of his back, his head tilted back against the wall, like he was conserving his strength for another battle on another day.

Some days he came out of counseling with Doc almost frighteningly euphoric, dancing with lightness, like he'd lived his entire life wearing a three-ton weight on his shoulder. Those days were hard;

he saw Tommy, and his entire soul ached with an unbearable *need* to be touched. One night he pulled Tommy by the hand into the dark, foggy little wooded area behind the facility and kissed him, kissed him so hard and so urgently, with so much terrible desire that his skin almost hurt.

Tommy groaned, and growled, and their bodies heaved against each other, needing bare skin but not wanting to bare it in the chill, gray air. The kiss never ended, never faltered, never stopped, and when Tommy's hands slid under his sweatshirt to glide on his bare skin, Chase almost wept. Those cold fingers on his sensitive nipples were perfect, and he leaned back against a tree because his knees almost buckled. Then one of those chilly hands slid lower, down over his stomach, under the loose waistband of his jeans, and the clasp around his aching erection made him groan. One stroke, two strokes, and while Chase was still fumbling for Tommy through his pants, he felt it, everything from his testicles to his asshole clenched, and he shuddered so hard with orgasm it felt like his skin exploded. One second he was trying to give Tommy some reciprocation, the next he was sobbing into Tommy's neck, so overwhelmed by it, by the joy of it, by the lack of shame, by the glory, that he couldn't even stand.

Tommy helped him slide down to sit down and then sat down next to him. Chase leaned on his shoulder without reservation and panted through the tears.

"Thank you," he said when he could speak. "God, I'm so sorry—I shot early."

Tommy looked at him, a wry smile on his face. "Don't worry. I'm sure I'm beating off a lot more than you. I'll get my turn."

Chase chuckled. "God yes. You will. I swear, by the time we visit Donnie's mom on Thanksgiving, you'll be raw. Giving, receiving, oral, anal, manual, clutch and stick—it's gonna be fuckapalooza at Tommy's house, that's for fucking sure."

"Our house," Tommy said softly. "Our house. You're coming to live with me, right? Please?" He looked away, although he kept the comforting hand on Chase's knee.

"Yeah," Chase said, clasping his hand. "Yeah. I want to live with you. I want to live with you forever. I want to go live with you and Paulie the kitten and Buster the grandpa cat and Oliver the turtle. I want to get my degree and be an engineer and figure out what you want to be—besides a pet shop owner, but maybe we can do that too. I want a future. A real future. Not a movie set one. I want an us."

Tommy's shoulders shook, and Chase looked up in time to see him wipe his cheek with the palm of his hand.

"Aw, Jesus, Tommy. Aren't I the one who's supposed to cry?"

Tommy shook his head. "Oh God, Chase. I never thought you'd say it. This whole time, I never thought you'd say it. I wanted it so bad, for so long, I never thought you'd say it, and now you have, and...."

He leaned over sideways into Chase's lap, and this time he cried, and Chase picked up the pieces, and he was shocked as hell to realize that he could.

They couldn't stay that long—the ground was damp, and Chase's jeans were wet, and eventually they had to make their way back to the hospital, where they checked in under the censorious eyes of the admitting nurse, who gave them a strong speech about hours and admitting times and reiterated that, if it happened again, Chase's checkout might be delayed.

They both took the advice very soberly and then smiled shy and secret smiles as Tommy walked Chase to his room.

"Why?" Tommy asked abruptly as they turned on the light and went in. Donnie's mom had sent Chase a quilt that she'd sewn just for him. The squares were all baseball-themed: catcher's mitts, bats, players sliding into first. She'd backed it with something soft and cushy—fleece, probably—and Chase loved it because this was *his* room, until he took that homey, tacky quilt to Tommy's house, and then that would be his too, without the smell of ammonia and piss, which had only recently begun to bother the hell out of him as he tried to sleep at night.

"Why what?" Chase asked, taking his customary position on the bed with one knee pulled up against his chest. He'd lost weight, no two ways about it. He'd lost muscle mass and any fat at all that he'd had, and it made holding his knees to his chest feel like that was the only defensive position that would work.

"Why so hot and horny?" Tommy grinned again, and if Chase hadn't been in love—deliriously, perfectly in love—that grin right there would have done it. "Not that I mind in the least."

Chase smiled and blushed. "'Cause my father's a tool, and I may be a faggot, but that's not a bad thing. I like my body. I like sex. I like sex with you better than any sex on the fucking planet. And that's nothing to be ashamed about."

Tommy stood up then and took Chase's face between his palms, stroking Chase's cheeks with gentle thumbs. His throat worked, and Chase could tell he was moved, because those Loki-bright eyes were intent on Chase's face.

"So that's therapy?" he asked after a minute.

Chase smiled shyly, blushing under that intense scrutiny, trying his best to keep looking at Tommy like he was proud and unashamed. "I'm sayin'."

"I like it."

"Yeah?"

"Yeah." Tommy's lips were as gentle as they ever had been. When he broke off the kiss, he whispered, "Keep your eyes closed and think of me," and then he backed away. Chase did just what he asked, and when the light turned off and Tommy was gone, Chase was still sitting in the dark with his eyes closed, thinking for the first time of their future together.

There were very few things in the vision that frightened him, and he thought maybe the shit that was scary could be overcome.

"So I can go home?" Chase asked Doc Stevenson for what must have felt like the hundredth time. "Seriously—three days, you promised, right? You said as long as I come back a couple of times a week, I'm good."

"And take your medication."

"I promise," Chase said with the fervency of a child. It didn't matter. He felt like a child, a kid let out of school early, or that kid at Christmas—he knew how that kid felt now, the kid who got the bike. Tommy had given him plenty of Christmas bikes, and there weren't any strings attached anymore. They were beautiful and shiny and bright and they could take him *anywhere*, and he was thrilled to have gotten them. This felt like a Christmas bike. He wanted it. He wanted to go home with Tommy so badly. He wanted to start that future of the two of them. He'd talked with the Doc about it; he knew there would be tough times. He knew he'd get sad again, and that the Prozac and Cymbalta might be for life. He was aware that there was some shit that might set him off.

And he knew that his biggest test was waiting in the lobby of the facility even as he finished up his session.

Doc knew it too. "Well, Chase, I think it all hinges on how well the next half hour goes, don't you think?" His voice was gentle, and Chase sighed.

"You're not going anywhere, are you?"

"No. I'll be here in my office, doing paperwork if you need me when she's gone. And Tommy knows about the visit, you said that. He'll be here early today, so you've got your support staff, Chase. But—"

"I know, I know." Chase nodded and swallowed. "This part I've got to face myself."

Doc smiled at him and cocked his head. "Have I told you that I think you're brave?"

Chase looked at him with a fair amount of shock. "I fuckin' doubt it!"

"You are. Not everything you've done has been noble, but until the very last part there, you had some sort of vision for a happy future. It may have been with the wrong person for the wrong reasons, but you kept hoping that the future would be a good one. Maybe now that you've found the right person and the reasons that you can live with, you can maybe forgive yourself for this. I know it's trite, Chase, but

I've been with you for a month, and the one thing I can tell you that's true is that you truly never meant to hurt her."

"Yeah. But that doesn't mean that I didn't."

"That's true too. And that's why this. You ready?"

"Fuck no." Chase stood up from his habitual position on the couch, one knee tucked in front of his chest. "But I'll do it anyway."

"That's the spirit." Doc stood and, to Chase's surprise, walked him through the echoing tile corridors to the lobby. The lobby was not actually too bad—for one thing, the walls were a nice sky blue, and the furniture was beige with little matching highlights. It was peaceful and pretty, and there was green carpet, and in general, it looked like the lobby of an old folks home, the kind that had Easter egg hunts for the grandkids, and nothing at all like a loony bin.

Chase was grateful for Mercy's sake, even if he didn't have any illusions as to where he'd been the past month and a half.

She was sitting nervously in one of the chairs and she startled when she saw him, frowning automatically in concern. The Doc smoothed things over, of course, offering her some water and a small sitting room with some privacy. The walk behind Doc, as he led them to the room, as Chase and Mercy stood together, almost as a couple, was one of the most awkward moments of Chase's life.

But eventually they were in the little room, which had a couple of recliners and a love seat and a little lamp between them. Chase was just as glad his visitors had come to the weight room or his room or gone for walks with him outside. This felt like an edict from the mental institution to behave as a family, and he wasn't sure he didn't resent the hell out of it.

Mercy did too. "Great," she muttered. "God, I feel like Martha Stewart's ugly stepchild in here. Could there be someplace like that movie? With the bars on the windows and the people screaming in the background and shit?"

"Most of us are here voluntarily, Merce. No bars on the windows, no people screaming. Just a lot of fuckin' Kleenex."

She turned around and looked at him, and her face was a little rounder than he was used to, but there were bags under her red-rimmed eyes that said the extra weight wasn't due to good health.

"You shed any tears over me, Chase?"

He kept his gaze steady. "You wouldn't believe me if I told you how many."

She shook her head then. "You look like hell."

"Awesome. I'll put that on my list of happy things."

"Fuck you. I… I just pictured this moment, and I could tell you that I hated you, and how bad you hurt me, and I got to be a raging bitch, but I can't."

Chase swallowed. "You earned the right, hon, but it's not really you."

She whirled, her face twisted. "And you lost the right to call me things like 'hon', asshole. And don't think I don't have some ugly in me, Chase. Because I totally do." She deflated a little. "But not right now. I think it would have been one thing if you'd been all buff and shit, looking like a model like you have this last year, living with your boyfriend and being all happy, but you look like hell. I mean, I really thought I could hate you, but you look like shit, and this hasn't been any easier on you than it has on me, has it?"

A corner of Chase's mouth turned up. "I'm probably going to be on antidepressants for the rest of my life. Is that what you wanted to hear? I left you and woke up in the hospital in restraints, so I didn't finish the job. They had to take a section of the artery in my thigh and use it in my wrist so I didn't bleed out." He held up his wrist, where the scars were still pink and raw from the stitches they'd taken out the week before. "Mercy, whatever you may think of me, however you hate me, you gotta believe this hasn't been anything like easy."

She hit the table with the flat of her hand and looked him in the eyes, her own eyes wet and red. "But *why?*" she demanded. "*Why?* I think back to when you and I started, and we were *friends.* You were my buddy, you know? And you didn't judge me when I had to drop out of school and you made me laugh. And yeah, I hoped for more, but if you'd just once said 'Mercy, sorry, don't swing that way!' I would have been okay!"

Chase's laugh held no humor whatsoever. "Mercy, I had to slit my fucking wrist to be able to say it *myself*, don't you get that?"

"Why? What's so bad about being gay that you had to do all this other shit—you had to lie to me, and to yourself and... fuck, even to the guy you had on a string—"

"I never lied to him," Chase said softly. "Me, you—yeah. I never lied to him."

"And that's supposed to make me feel better?"

Chase swallowed. "It's supposed to explain why I had to pick him over you."

"I almost don't care about that now. I just really want to know about the lie!"

Chase cringed. "Mercy, that shit, the reason I had to lie, it was private—"

"We were gonna get *married*! Don't you think I get a guest pass?"

Chase winced and thought randomly of that picture of Ethan spitting in his asshole on the Internet. Yeah. So much less intrusive than conversations like this.

"My mom killed herself—did I ever tell you that?"

Mercy's face went white, and she used one arm on the little end table to lower herself to the love seat. "No."

It hurt. It hurt to say. *Almost* but not quite as much as he'd imagined. In his head, he was back, the little kid in front of the red door, just like when he'd been with Doc. But Doc had made him open the door, and made him face what was inside. Tommy knew what was inside, and now he had to tell Mercy, he *had* to, because she deserved the truth.

"She killed herself," Chase whispered, and it hurt his throat. "She slit her wrists, and bled out into the tub, and I found her, and I spent hours locked in the bathroom with her while Victor, the guy you invited to Christmas dinner, screamed at me that if I wasn't such a little faggot pussy, she would be okay." He felt queasy, saying that to someone. He felt queasy talking about it to Doc or Tommy, and saying it to *Mercy*? It violated everything in him. He thought maybe Mercy would be the last person he'd tell, and then remembered Donnie and Kevin and Dex and Kane and all the people who had visited him when he'd been in the loony bin, and that maybe he owed it to them not to draw lines like that anymore. Wonderful. He never knew he'd have to be this strong.

"That's horrible," she whispered, and he nodded and struggled for words to put that moment, that terrible, distant moment, into context for where they were right now.

"You see, I had this idea. The perfect wife, the perfect future, the perfect me—and if I could make that future true, it wouldn't be my fault."

Mercy frowned at him, puzzled. "What wouldn't be your fault?"

"That she killed herself. It wouldn't be my fault if I could have the perfect, you know?"

"It wasn't your fault," she said, sitting back and rubbing her face like it was cold. "Chase, how could you think—"

"But you see, I *did*. I *did*. And it sort of all boiled down to this one word. If I wasn't this one word, then it wouldn't be my fault. It wouldn't be my fault, and it sounded so grown-up. And you and me living together was a lot better than the shitty apartment I had after high school. But mostly it was just grown-up. I wanted grown-up and pretty, and...." He grimaced, not sure if she could hear this yet. "You were so pretty. You were. And you were nice. And I loved you so much. I still do. If anyone on the planet could have made that picture come true for me, Mercy, it would have been you. But...." He trailed off and took a breath, meaning to finish the sentence because he was trying not to be a coward anymore, but Mercy finished for him. Maybe Mercy needed to finish for him, for her own good.

"But I'm not the one you needed."

"No."

"Tommy is."

Chase nodded. "Yeah."

"Besides the boy thing," and she laughed, like realizing this was stupid, "is there anything else about him?"

He doesn't take my shit. He's not always nice. He's wounded and he needs me.

"No." Some truths really were best unspoken. He'd tell Doc, he might even tell Tommy. But he wouldn't say that shit to her. Dex was right—cruelty wasn't his style.

She looked up at him, her face ravaged and pale. "I'm pregnant, Chase."

His vision honest-to-fuck went black.

His knees went out, and he found himself sitting down on the floor, wondering if that red door in his head was going to fill up with water again and how he was going to manage to keep breathing if it did.

"I... I was going to have an abortion. I walked in here absolutely sure I hated you that much, that I couldn't carry your baby in my body. I actually *willed* it to die, this last month, I was so mad. Do you hate me for that?"

"How could I?" His lips were bloodless. "How could I?"

"I don't hate you that much anymore. I don't."

"I don't see why," he muttered, his mind going blank at the absolute levels of pain this could bring.

"'Cause you were hurt," she whispered. "You were hurt and I didn't see it. You were talking about a pretty future, and you wanted it because it would make you something. I did the same thing. And... and I must have felt you slipping away, Chase. I must have. Because I fucked with your condoms—isn't that awful?"

Chase felt his lips twist. He could remember that night, the change in the brand. And he'd already been so far away.

"Yeah," he said in wonder. "It's awful. But that's okay." For a moment he was giddy, absolutely giddy with relief. Doc, Tommy, they'd been telling him he'd done some shitty things but that didn't make him a shitty person. But Mercy had done a shitty thing, too, and he still thought she was an okay person. Maybe life really was doing your best and hoping that weighed in.

"So I made this baby, but I can't get rid of it—"

"We made this baby," he said through a dry throat. "We."

Mercy passed her hand over her eyes. "But… but Chase—"

"I let you hope, Mercy. I told you that future was for us. If I hadn't done that, you wouldn't have done this. We made it. We made this baby."

Mercy started to cry harder. "Well, we may have made it, but I can't raise it."

Chase closed his eyes. He'd seen this coming. He had. "You can't…?"

"I can't kill it, Chase, but I can't raise it, either. I'd look at it, and every day I'd see that future you dreamed. It was so pretty. I loved that future so much. And it was a lie, and I'm still so mad at you for that lie. I can't raise that lie, have it eat at my table, have it love me and only me, you understand? Even if I helped make that lie, I can't do it."

"God."

"I looked into some adoption agencies, and they don't have to know for a couple of months. But…." She swallowed, and then stood and walked over to him, bending down to put her soft little hands on his face.

"You wanted a pretty future, Chase. I get that. I wanted it too." She was sitting in a chair about a foot from him, and then she knelt on the floor suddenly, grabbed his hand, the one lying cold across his thigh, and shoved it, palm first, against her stomach. "Here's a pretty future too. You're not an evil fucker; it took me a little while to remember that, but you're not. Do you want this future, or do we give it to someone else?"

Chase was crying again, but he couldn't even be mad at himself for it. "Of course I want it!" he snapped bitterly, his hand convulsing against Mercy's smooth skin, the warm, slight rounding in her ordinarily flat belly. "But Mercy…." He pulled the hand away and showed her the inside of his left wrist. "The scars aren't even healed."

She rubbed her thumb against the scar softly. "Yeah. I hear that. But you got yourself a man, a place to stay. You sure as shit are not your old man. You got a future. You've got money—lots of it. I sold the fucking car, moved into my folks'; I haven't touched a penny. I don't want the money, Chase. You gave too fucking much of your soul for that money. It'll get you through school, it'll last you 'til you find a job, especially if you've got someone to help with the bills. It'll help you raise your child. You ready to do that? Can you own this, or do we give it away?"

Chase met her eyes and swallowed. He thought of someone helpless, depending on him, and a part of him panicked and a part of him screamed, and a part of him yearned. "I want it," he confessed. "Of course I want it. But I'm afraid, Mercy. I always was a coward—you know that now. And I just stopped the screaming in my own head, and I'm not sure if that's gonna come back and drown out a baby, because that wouldn't be fair. So can I talk to some people?"

"Your man?" she asked, half-angry, and he nodded.

"Yeah. But my shrink, and Donnie's mom." He half laughed. "Because you *know* who I'm going to be running to for help."

Mercy nodded. "Yeah, I know. Okay, Chase. You talk. You get better. You think. But not too long. I need to go start making plans by March, because I'm due in May. So you let me know before then."

She reached into her purse and pulled out a piece of paper. "I got the same cell phone, but here's my parents' phone. They're under strict orders not to hang up on you if you call."

Chase sighed, having to ask the question. Her parents were pretty traditional, third-generation Mexican immigrants. "Your folks okay with you?"

She shrugged. "They hate *your* gay ass, but they don't blame me so much. They don't get about the baby, though. They think I'll just keep it, but—"

"You've got a whole different future," he said softly. "You deserve a whole different future. I... I love you, Mercy. For no other reason than you're even letting me think about this. Because you forgave me just enough to let me know, even if I don't take it."

She nodded and wiped her cheek with her hand. "I'm glad you're okay," she said, her voice shaking. "I am. You scared me so bad. But I don't think I can see you much until the baby is born, okay? It just hurts too much to know you're not mine."

She bent and dropped a kiss on his forehead and then determinedly stalked out, grabbing her purse and striding through the door to the little "family room" with the single vision of getting the fuck out of there.

Chase briefly thought about going after her, of stopping to comfort her, because he knew she was going to cry and he hated that she would cry alone. Then he realized, truly realized, that holding her when she cried was not something he was allowed to do anymore.

So he sat in the room for another few minutes and did his crying alone, too.

BICYCLE

THE boy in the living room was not really a boy. He was a man in his early twenties, with dark hair, long canines, and a fierce grin. He was holding an infant against his chest and dancing gently while an acoustic version of Foo Fighters' "Statues" played in the background. The baby wasn't screaming, just fussing a little, and the blond boy, the tall one with the rangy baseball player's body, was in the kitchen, frantically mixing formula into a bottle before the fussing got louder.

"Daddy Chase!" called the dark-haired young man. "Hurry up! Baby's not waiting!"

"I'm doing my best, Tommy!" Chase said, laughing a little. He looked happy. Tired and a little bit frantic, but happy. Tommy, holding the baby and singing softly, looked luminous.

CHASE told Tommy first.

It was hard, because Doc came in to make sure he was okay, and he wasn't, but he was tired of just spilling his insides out for no other purpose than to make them shiny and clean. He wanted to talk to Tommy. As much as he'd shared with Doc, as much as the guy had come to mean to him, this news was for Tommy. Doc would go home to his wife, but Tommy would have to live with what Chase had done, and it was only fair.

So Tommy walked through the door and Chase was sitting on the bed with both knees drawn up to his chest, feeling like he needed to invest in one of those big padded armor suits like they wore in *The Hurt Locker* for defusing bombs.

"What'd we talk about in therapy today?" Tommy tried to joke. "Have you gotten to the point where you reenact the porn, because I've been looking forward to that!"

Chase was proud of himself. He actually managed a half smile.

"Sit down," he said softly. "I've got news, and it's sort of something we haven't talked about and... God. It's like a cosmic fucking joke, actually."

Tommy didn't sit on the chair anymore. He sat up on the bed across from Chase, one leg folded and the other dangling down to the floor.

"Hit me with it," he said pragmatically, nodding his head. "In fact, tell it like a joke—it'll make it easier. Like, 'Didja hear about the porn star who....'"

Chase cracked a half smile. God love Tommy. That picture in his head suddenly felt so real. "Okay," Chase said, "this one's fuckin' hysterical. You're gonna laugh yourself to San Francisco while you find another guy without so much fuckin' baggage—prepare yourself."

Tommy reached out and grabbed his hand. "Hit me."

"Didja hear about the porn star who knocked up his girlfriend before he tried to kill himself?" Tommy's mouth fell open in surprise and Chase kept going. "She's so deluded she actually thinks he's a better bet to raise the kid, and if he doesn't, she's giving it up for adoption."

Tommy's hand, bony and uncomfortable, tightened on Chase's, and Chase could hardly look at his face, but he could hardly look away either. That smile—that manic Loki smile—dawned slowly, so slowly that for a horrible heartbeat Chase didn't know which way it was going.

"We're gonna be *daddies?*"

Chase laughed helplessly. "I haven't decided yet."

Tommy nodded like that last part didn't mean shit. "We're gonna be daddies."

"Tommy, I'm still in a *mental institution.*" Because he felt like that needed emphasizing.

Tommy shrugged. What, didn't *all* daddies go to the fucking funny farm before they became stellar goddamned parents? "We're going to be daddies!" he said happily, and Chase tried to inflict some reality on the situation.

"Tommy, I'm not even sure I can do this! I'm a mess. I've got maybe one good role model in my life, and all I really know about her is that she gave me cookies when I was a kid. What makes you think I can say yes?"

Tommy's expression grew suddenly fierce and stubborn. "Fuck that!" he snapped, and when Chase recoiled a little, Tommy stood up and started pacing, because he did his best thinking when he was moving.

"I'm serious, Chase. Fuck that. Fuck the 'I'm crazy' bullshit, fuck the 'I don't know how to do this' bullshit. Fuck the whole thing about the world scaring you shitless. I get it, and now I don't give a shit." He stopped for a second, as though remembering he really *was* talking to a mental patient, and revised. "Okay, I *do* give a shit, but you need to stop that crap right now. You're not letting that get in the way. You're *not* letting the shit you're afraid of fuck this up for us."

"Us?"

Tommy whirled, his Loki-bright eyes suddenly so hopeful it hurt. "What, Chase—you think you're the only one with pretty pictures of a future in your head? For the last year, my pretty pictures have been you and me, and, yes, sometime in the future, a kid. And then you reminded me, almost when we met, that we'd made choices that made that maybe not so easy, you know? Because who's going to give a kid to a couple of gay porn stars, right? Well, now someone is *dying* to give us a child." Tommy's eyes grew brighter, and he unashamedly wiped his hand across his cheek. "And not just any baby. A baby who's going to look like *you*."

Tommy suddenly stopped pacing and walked up to Chase then, his hands out beseechingly. "Don't you know how beautiful you are? The pretty, yeah, you know that or you wouldn't have gotten paid, right? But... but *you*. This baby is going to look like you." Tommy wiped his cheek again and got close enough to pull Chase's head against his lower chest. "Please, Chase... God, please. Please tell me we can keep this fucking gift from heaven that's going to look like you."

Chase nodded, tucked in against Tommy's body. "I'll try," he murmured. "I'll try."

Neither of them mentioned the fact that it was the same vow he'd uttered before he'd slit his wrist. Maybe that's what do-overs were for.

"SO, ARE you going to take the baby?" Doc asked, his voice neutral, and Chase shot him an annoyed look.

"I'm in a mental institution."

"Well yes, but only for two more days. Tommy's right: this baby is an opportunity for you, one that gay men don't always get."

Chase glared at him, knitting so serenely in his little chair, looking so smug like he knew Chase was going to be all okay. Was Chase the only one who had doubts about that?

"You've been listening to me for a month and a half, you know how fucked up I am!"

Doc put down his knitting, and that was always a bad sign.

"I've been listening to you get healthy for a month and a half, Chase. You continue to point out that you stopped. Midway through a *very* well-thought-out suicide attempt, you stopped what you were doing and revised your plan, very thoroughly and considering every angle. Well I'm letting you go home, and I am not immediately worried about any more attempts on your life. I don't see you as a threat to yourself or anyone else. And you have a relationship waiting for you that, as far as I can see, saved your life. If Tommy wants this baby, I don't see why you shouldn't."

"But... but... but I'm fucked up!" Jesus! Was he the only sane person in the fucking loony bin?

"So is the rest of the planet, Chase. I could understand if you didn't want this baby. I could understand if you didn't have a way to support it. I could understand if you hadn't worked so hard to be healthy. But you want this child—anybody can see it. Why would you give up this opportunity to somebody else?"

"I'm... I'm just not good enough to be a parent," Chase mumbled, feeling naked again. "I'm a porn star, right? Isn't there a law there? I mean... God. My resume sucks for shit. And I'm what—twenty-one years old? If you had to apply for a license here, the league of respectable citizens would totally reject me, you know that, right?"

Doc nodded, like he was seriously considering it. "Yes, I know that. But they'd be wrong."

Chase swallowed. "Don't make me beg, here, Doc. Why would they be wrong?"

Doc smiled a little. "You keep your promises, Chase, or you try to. You work really hard to treat people decent, in spite of not having a lot of examples for how to do that. You broke up with the love of your life when you weren't healthy enough to be with him. You accepted the consequences of your actions with Mercy, even though that obviously hurt. And you stopped. You've pointed it out a thousand times, and this is where it counts. You could not hurt the people in your life that much, no matter how much pain you were in. That says volumes about what kind of person you can be, if only you let yourself have some happiness. I know you're thinking Tommy is more than you deserve. But why don't you deserve it all?"

"Like getting the bicycle and the action figure for Christmas, and the baseball glove and the tickets to the game too?"

Doc smiled a little. "Sure, Chase. Why not?"

"Because all I ever got was sweaters and underwear, which I needed, because by that time of year, I didn't have either."

Doc nodded. "Well maybe it's time Christmas hit your house, you think, Chase?"

Chase shrugged. "Maybe I should wait until after Christmas to decide," he said quietly. "Maybe by then, I'll know, really know, that I'm gonna be okay to do this. You think?"

Doc smiled. "I think that's the planner we all know and love. And I think Tommy's going to be begging you to open that present early."

Chase smiled a little then. "Yeah," he said thoughtfully. "If I say yes, I think it could be the only present he really wants."

CHASE was not expecting the crowded living room or the "Welcome Home" banner across the kitchen. He wasn't expecting his friends from *Johnnies* to be there, or Donnie's parents or Kevin, or even some guys from his baseball team who had apparently heard the whole story.

He was not expecting Tommy's house to be full, or to see the little black kitten terrorizing everybody and their mother, while Buster sat quietly in Tommy's bedroom, curled up in a little ball of "Can this fucking end now?"

He didn't expect Tommy's hand to clench his so tightly, or Tommy's voice in his ear. "It's okay, right? I wanted you to know you were loved."

Chase turned to him and blinked hard. "Oh, Jesus, Tommy. Don't you know you don't surprise a mental patient if you don't want them to fucking cry on you?"

Tommy grinned and wrinkled his nose, then grabbed a box of tissue—the good aloe kind—and shoved it in his hand. "Cry away, you pussy bastard. I stocked up."

There was cake and pizza—and Tommy ate both. Why not? They'd both lost weight in the past month and a half—they could afford it.

Chase got hugs from all the guys, who were apparently his friends whether he was in the company or not. He got some smirks from the guys on his baseball team, but some hugs too, and that was nice. He had a couple of good conversations, one of them with John.

"So, I had this idea," John said, and Chase looked down, feeling bad. He'd been slated for two shoots in the time he'd been away, and he wondered who had covered.

"I'm sort of not doing that anymore," he said, embarrassed, and John's friendly hand on his shoulder eased that a little.

"See, the thing is," John said, "people get attached to you guys. Your stuff is gonna sell for a while, and that's good. But I think an exit interview—you and Tango, no sex if you don't want to—that might help it sell better. You don't have to if you don't want to, but...." John shrugged. "Like I said, it's just a thought. I know you're both going to school—if you're not doing shoots anymore, this might help the money stretch, okay?"

Chase blinked and smiled. "Yeah, John. I'll talk to Tommy. Either way, it's really nice of you to offer."

John shrugged and looked embarrassed. "There's a lot of drama behind the scenes in this business, right? But people show up, they shoot, it's all good. But when they suddenly don't show up, you realize they were friends and you sort of miss them. It would be nice if I could do something for some friends."

Chase nodded, and promised to ask Tommy again, and then he spotted Donnie's mom across the room and shook John's hand (and got a hug instead) and then excused himself to go talk to Donnie's mom.

And he realized that he didn't know what to say to her.

It didn't matter. She greeted him with a hug, and then a faintly disapproving expression as she eyed the people in Tommy's little house.

"Porn?" she asked, her voice dry, and for the first time Chase realized he didn't know much about her. "Porn. I mean...." She shook her head and then rethought what she was going to say. "I'm sorry. I mean, I can't approve, Chase, but I guess it's clear you had so much more going on than just the porn. I'm glad you quit before I knew you were doing it."

Chase blushed in shame and held his hands behind him like a little kid. "I'm sorry, Mrs. Armstrong. I didn't mean to let you down."

"Ouch, Donnie!" Colleen Armstrong looked at her son, and Chase realized that he'd actually given her a solid whap on the back of the head.

"Donnie!" he protested, and Donnie shook his head.

"You can't make him feel bad, Mom. It's the rule. It's the one thing I said when you were coming over here, remember? I said he needed our support, not our bullshit, remember? 'Yandro got it, Kevin got it—but I didn't bring you guys here to make him feel bad."

Chase looked at his oldest friend and smiled. "It's okay, Donnie. I'm not that fragile. I can take some disapproval—it's not gonna kill me. I just...." He sighed. "I'll talk to you later," he said apologetically to Donnie's mom. "I will. I'm just glad you came."

Donnie wouldn't let him walk away, though. He had turned to go into the bedroom and pet Buster, but Donnie followed and Chase didn't argue as they both sat on the bed. Buster started licking Chase's fingers, so Chase figured he was forgiven for being gone so long, and Donnie said, "What's up?"

He didn't even think about lying.

"Mercy's pregnant."

"Oh fuck! And you were going to tell my *mom*?"

Chase blushed, realizing how idealized that relationship had been, how he had blown Donnie's mom up to be the be-all and end-all of mom-hood. Well, shit. Something else to talk to the Doc about the day after Thanksgiving.

"I don't know any other mothers," he said apologetically, and Donnie sighed.

"Yeah, well, I guess there's that. And you're right, she's not a bad one. But she's not going to get this situation, Chase. She's not. She gets that I'm gay, but it's all okay because she thinks Alejandro is a nice boy. She doesn't understand that there's a whole different way of looking at sex and at pictures and porn. She doesn't get that it's guys, sometimes, and that we just get raw and blatant when a girl—even a really uninhibited girl—would still need to be treated like a lady."

Chase smiled a little. It was true. Mercy was pretty forward, but the way he and Tommy manhandled each other was still very different than the way he'd touched her in bed.

"Yeah. Tough explaining gay porn to your mom, but it's okay, Donnie. In fact...." Chase frowned and tried to put it into words. It was a new experience for him, putting things into words. He was used to disappearing into his own head, staring at the red door, coming up with words in his head that would never be uttered, but he couldn't do that anymore. The thought of doing that to a little kid who just wanted to know why the sky was blue made him shudder.

Donnie waited. He sat with simple patience, and Chase wanted to just hug him, because Donnie knew.

"See," Chase said slowly, "I was afraid. I was afraid I couldn't be a good parent, because I couldn't be perfect. Like your mom—"

"My mom's *not* perfect!"

"I know that. I mean, she's great—I've always thought she was great. But until just right now, I always thought she was perfect. But she's wrong, I think, about the disapproval thing. Not because that's what you want your kids involved in, but because... I don't know. Because the guys who came here are pretty fucking awesome, and I don't know if she gets that. But it's okay. It's okay if she's wrong. I mean, I hope she still lets me in the house, but in the meantime...."

"If she can be wrong, you can do this?" Donnie supplied, and Chase managed a smile.

"Yeah. I mean... I dunno. I've been home for five minutes, and I haven't even had my little mental patient nap," he yawned, because all the people had been exhausting, "but it's something to think about. You can make a mistake or two, and you still won't be as heinous as...."

"As everyone who let you down."

"She must have been so desperate," Chase whispered. That was another thing he still needed to talk about. God, so much work to do. For a moment, it was overwhelming how much he still needed to hammer out. But still... Mrs. Donnie's Mom had been wrong... she'd made Chase feel bad, and not on purpose. It was something to think about.

Donnie stood up and came around to hug him. "I'll go tell everyone you're resting," he said quietly. "Don't worry—no one will get their feelings hurt. You said hi to everyone, you don't look like you're going to self-destruct anytime soon—you've done your job."

Chase yawned again, and stretched out on the bed, his head resting on one arm while he continued to stroke a luxuriating Buster with the other hand. "Thanks, Donnie. Text me tomorrow?"

"Never miss it."

"Send me some good porn, 'kay? It's like I was in the hospital and everyone lost their sense of humor about that."

Donnie laughed. "Yeah, you big 'mo. I'll send you some raunchy shit so you can feel all grown-up and better."

"Donnie?"

"Yeah?"

"If I say I love you, 'Yandro won't get jealous, will he?"

"Naw, Chase. Love you too."

And with that, Donnie was gone and Chase was left stroking Buster and listening to the comforting sound of his purr.

Tommy woke him up an hour later because it was time for his medication and because everyone was gone. Chase had some cold pizza (which tasted *so* good after hospital food for a month and a half) and then sat with his head on Tommy's chest as they watched television.

They got ready for bed just like they used to when Chase had stayed over, and the comfort of it was unbelievable. It was like warm slippers when his feet had been so cold he couldn't feel his toes. When they crawled into bed and turned out the lights, the beauty of Tommy's body in the dark was absolutely sublime. Chase started tasting him, his stubbly chin, the strong column of his neck, the hardness of his chest, the sharp little points of his nipples. Tommy sucked in a breath and then stopped and muttered, "Why is your face wet?"

Chase shook his head, rubbing his wet cheeks on Tommy's chest and then suckling on the nipple again, tasting tears.

Tommy gasped again, and pulled at Chase's head, pulling him up so he was on Tommy's shoulder. "What's wrong?" he asked, like he was afraid to.

"You're mine," Chase whispered, turning his head to a collarbone. "You're mine. You're all mine. No... no other things. No other people. You. Are. Mine."

"Oh God," Tommy groaned. "Keep saying it. I think you're gonna make me come."

"You come before I suck you off, I'll kill ya!"

Tommy laughed and Chase kept kissing him, down his chest, the wonder of his stomach, and.... "God, Tommy. You're so thin. You shouldn't be this thin. You should eat."

Tommy breathed deliberately. "You make it a point to hang around, Chase, I'll make it a point to eat, okay?"

Chase sank his teeth gently into Tommy's soft stomach just to hear him gasp, and then made his way to the jutting hipbones, while Tommy tried not to giggle with frustration.

"You're teasing me!" he accused, and Chase gave a fluttery little lick across Tommy's balls.

"Yup," he said. "Because I can."

He moved down then and pushed at Tommy's thighs, so Tommy's whole body was spread out, and he started at Tommy's taint and licked a line up. He paused for a minute and giggled a little himself.

"What?"

"You've got hair on your balls!"

Tommy started to giggle too. "God, I do!" His hand came down in wonder and he started to walk his fingers across his skin with an unconscious sensuality that made Chase squirm in the dark.

"How did that not itch like a motherfucker?"

In a half a second, Tommy had rolled over and rolled him over, until Chase was on his back and his boxers were down around one ankle. Tommy was ruffling the blond hair on Chase's balls, his taint, even the stubble between his ass cheeks, and Chase was trying and failing not to laugh his ass off.

"God! Tommy! Stop! Oh fuck!" And Tommy stopped tickling the hair on his balls and moved up to his stomach and then to his ribs and then to his armpits, and when he got that far, Chase started to retaliate by tickling the same places. It was an explosion of laughter, of wrestling, of touching, and when it finally wound down, they were naked, their full bodies touching, their chests heaving from a tickle fight.

"Isn't it funny," Chase panted. "You know, the stuff that happens when you're not looking."

Tommy was suddenly serious. "Getting better is going to be like that," he said softly. "I know you worry about all the shit you haven't wrapped up in your brain, but... but I haven't thrown up in three months. I haven't. No laxatives, no puking, no binging on bad shit. I just... like you said. Life happened, and I was still trying to stay healthy and life happened, and eventually I was better. It'll be hard—you came home during the holidays, and you don't have school, and you'll feel a little lost. But then life will happen, and you'll keep seeing Doc, and you'll get better, and the awkward itchiness won't happen quite so much. Right?"

Chase laughed a little and nuzzled Tommy's neck. "The itchiness of a healed psyche?" he said, and Tommy giggled, and then before they could start that up again, he turned his head and caught Chase's mouth in a kiss, hard and deep, and this one didn't stop.

The kiss went on and on until Chase was hard and aching and Tommy was grinding up against his thigh, and they both reached down and grabbed the other, thrusting into each other's hands with little grunts and hard sobs, until Tommy groaned, "*Fuck!*" and came in Chase's hand, hot, sticky, and wonderful. Chase didn't say anything; he just bit Tommy's shoulder, hard, and then spilled himself, both of them panting into the darkness. Tommy reached over his shoulder and came back with a clean towel that he'd apparently put there for this exact use, wiping them both off before pitching it back into the hamper. Then they both clambered into their boxers before pulling up the covers.

Chase laughed softly when all of the busywork and cleanup of making love was done. "It's a lot easier on the porn set, isn't it?" he asked, chuckling and settling into Tommy's arms. Tommy was being the big spoon tonight, and Chase didn't mind. He needed the security, this first night away from the hospital. He'd grown used to night sounds, people walking the halls, the bright light beyond his darkened doorway. It was almost frighteningly quiet here inside Tommy's four walls.

"It should be harder in real life," Tommy said quietly. "There's no tomorrows on the porn set, Chase. Tomorrow's something you've got to work for."

Chase snuggled in a little deeper. "Here's to tomorrow," he said in all sincerity, and he appreciated Tommy's kiss on the back of his neck. There was a movement, and Buster jumped creakily up onto the comforter, followed by the kitten. The two of them curled up together so Buster could groom his little friend, and they started a purring that practically vibrated the bed.

It was a night noise, and it was comforting, and Chase fell asleep to that and Tommy's breathing in his ear.

HOME MOVIES

THE two boys on the couch were fully dressed, and nicely so. They wore button-up shirts, slacks that went all the way to their belly buttons, and nice loafers with socks. They were fit, but not really buff— the taller blond, blue-eyed one had sort of a rangy build, and the look was good on him. The shorter, dark-haired, dark-eyed boy looked like he could be a runner or a bicyclist. They held hands fiercely and looked at the camera with what amounted to shyness.

"So," said the camera man, "this is Chance and Tango, and fans here at Johnnies *have seen them shoot scenes with everyone except each other, is that right?"*

The blue-eyed boy nodded and smiled. There was nothing cocky about him, just a steady sort of sincerity and a sort of deference for the guy behind the camera. "Yeah, Tango and I never got busy on camera. I don't know why." Chance looked at Tango and they both shrugged.

"Maybe we didn't look good together?" Chance asked, looking a little worried, and Tango rolled his eyes.

"Maybe we were both hung like gods and they were afraid it would break the camera."

Chance burst into raucous laughter, and Tango did too. Tango leaned over Chance's shoulder and gave him a quick kiss on the cheek. Chance blushed and looked away.

"Very cute," the cameraman said dryly. "So I understand nobody's going to get busy today—and believe me, hearts are breaking all over the place—but we wanted to do an interview with you two because you're sort of a fairy-tale romance here at the Johnnies *set, and we wanted to hear from you personally."*

"Fairy tale?" Chance echoed blankly, and Tango started laughing so hard he had to let go of Chance's hand and fall back onto the couch. "Fairy tale?"

"Oh my God!" Tango hooted. "God, like one of those old ones, where the grandmother gets eaten and they have to hack her out of the wolf's belly?"

Chance looked at Tango in disgust. "Really? Ew. Just ew, Tango. Fuckin' ew."

Tango raised his eyebrows in a rare moment of seriousness. "Think about it, Chance," and Chance blushed.

"Yeah, yeah... so one of the old-fashioned kind—you know, where the stepsisters cut their toes off to fit into the shoes and bleed to death. Yeah. That kind of fairy tale."

The voice behind the camera was amused. "So, no happy ever after for you?" and both boys grew suddenly sober.

"No," Chance contradicted immediately. "Definitely happy ever after. It's just that shit don't come easy. You don't just meet, fuck, see the future. It's harder than that."

"But worth it," Tango said softly, and Chance smiled at him, a private smile, old beyond his apparent years.

"Yeah. Worth it."

DONNIE'S parents took a cruise on Thanksgiving, so they had Thanksgiving at Tommy's house. It was going to be at Donnie and Alejandro's, because Donnie's sister was 'Yandro's roommate and that made sense. But Dex and Kane and Ethan were all without family in the area, and Donnie sort of pleaded with his lover and his sister, and in the end, it was potluck at Tommy's.

Kevin ditched his own parents around four o'clock and showed up for pie.

Considering how shitty the day had started out, it ended damned near perfect.

Chase had just gotten up to put the turkey in the oven (and thank God he'd paid attention when Mercy had done this for Christmas the year before, or they all would have been eating Chinese takeout or meat loaf) when his cell phone buzzed on the table and Mercy's face popped up.

The text said,

> *Your dad just called. I gave him your forwarding address so he didn't show up at my folks'. I'm so sorry.*

Chase blinked, and then texted back.

As long as you don't have to deal with him, it's all good. Don't worry. It'll be fine.

Then he started the coffee, went to put a hooded sweatshirt on, and waited.

It didn't take long. The pounding on the door startled him, even though he'd been expecting it, but Chase managed not to spill his coffee all over his front. He stood up and answered the door, hoping the cats had the sense to stay back in the room and sleep in with Tommy and the turtle.

He opened the door, but he didn't let Victor in.

"What the fuck are you doing here?" Victor snapped, no preamble, no nothing. He looked like hell, his gray hair lank at his shoulders, his features prematurely leathered by too much drink and too much smoke. Chase saw him detachedly, with as much emotional distance as he could manage. "You had a woman, and a life and a fucking future, and you're shacked up with some *guy*? Get your ass back to that girl and apologize!"

Chase managed to keep his tone even. "Victor, I don't love Mercy, not the way she deserves. I know that was a pretty picture last year, but it wasn't real."

"What the fuck does *real* have to do with it? That girl made you a man! I knew you was nothing but a pansy-assed little faggot, but for a little while you got to be a real man. How the hell am I supposed to be proud of you, living here with some other faggot? What am I supposed to *tell* people?"

Chase blinked. "Do you know people?"

"What the hell is that supposed to mean?"

Chase thought about it, thought about his childhood and holidays spent with Victor, thought about running away as soon as he could so he could spend the rest of them with Donnie's family. He tried to remember his dad going out to drink with friends—he could remember him coming home late from drinking, but not going out to drink. He remembered his high school graduation, because he came home from the ceremony and packed his stuff. He'd been working a part-time job and he'd gotten paid the day before, and Mrs. Donnie's Mom had given him money and his state aid for college had come in. He'd packed his clothes up in garbage bags, grabbed an old sleeping bag from the shelf, and signed up for a crappy apartment, no deposit, about four blocks away. Chase had managed construction jobs for the next six months, and by the end of the year, he'd been living with Mercy.

Had Chase ever seen his father with another adult?

"I don't care what you tell people," Chase said in the here and now. "I don't care."

"But—how am I supposed to see you? How am I supposed to have a son if you're doing this shit?"

Chase swallowed, and about fifty hours of therapy came flooding back. "It's okay if you never really have a son," Chase said quietly. "I've never really had a father. You have a kid, you have to love them. Really love them. Tell them it's going to be okay even if you think it's a lie. You don't tell them it's their fault 'cause their mother's dead. You don't call them names that're gonna make them feel like shit. You don't hinge whether or not you can love them or not on whether or not they can make a pretty picture for you. Mercy and me are never going to work. I hurt her too much pretending we could. If you want to be a part of my life, you're welcome to. But I warn you: you say one shitty word about Tommy, one shitty word about my friends, and I'll call the fucking cops and have them escort you home." It was a little less violent than the threat the year before, but that was okay. Chase didn't feel the violence, and that was sort of a relief.

Victor turned his head and spat. "Don't want a fucking thing to do with you and your 'friends'," he sneered. "You can't be a fucking man, don't want a fucking thing to do with you."

Chase grunted. Hurt. Yes, yes it did. "If you think you made my life any more perfect, old man, you are remembering the wrong kid."

Victor's face wrinkled and hardened, disgust in every bitter line. "You fuckin' killed her. You'd been a better kid, she would have stuck around, and we would have had a family."

"All we needed to be a family was love," Chase said, and a little part of him was raising a meaningful eyebrow, but Chase ignored that part for a minute. "Didn't you ever love me, old man? It feels like... God, I almost fucked up my entire life, trying to prove I was worth you loving me. Didn't you ever, even once, love somebody?"

Victor looked stunned for a minute. For a minute, he was sorrowful. "Loved her," he said, his voice lost. "I loved her so much. But she never got over being sad, son. I wasn't enough to make her better. I wasn't enough to make you happy. And now you're gonna go fuck up, and I'm not enough to fix it."

Oh damn him. Just damn him. Why couldn't he have fur and fangs and claws? Why couldn't he have beaten Chase on a regular basis? Why couldn't he have been a sexual predator? Why did he have to just be bitter and angry and sad?

"Why can't you just come in and have turkey?" Chase asked, hoping Tommy would forgive him. "Why does it have to be perfect? Why do you have to fix anything?"

Victor grunted. "Can't hang around with no faggots," he said, his bitterness back in place. "Would rather drink all day."

"Yeah, you have fun with that," Chase snapped, sad to his bones. "I've actually got people who give a shit. Let me know if you ever want to meet them." He couldn't have said which happened first—Victor turning away or Chase slamming the door—but it didn't matter. He was standing there, his hand on the doorknob, when Tommy came and draped himself over Chase's shoulders, taking a whole lot of Chase's weight and nuzzling the back of his neck as a bonus.

"He didn't even meet you," Chase muttered. "Why couldn't he even meet you?"

Tommy grunted. "Because I would have kicked his fucking teeth in. Do you have slippers on? Let's go put some slippers on, baby. Your feet are colder than a brass monkey's balls."

Chase looked at him through iffy vision. "Do brass monkeys even have balls?" he asked bemusedly, and Tommy's wicked smile should have warned him of the unexpected.

"A brass monkey is actually a little stand on a ship's deck, designed to hold those little pyramids of cannon shot you see in all the movies. The deck gets too cold, the brass monkey snaps off...."

Chase grinned in spite of himself. "You got a brass monkey's balls all over hell and fucking creation, don't you?"

Tommy nodded vigorously. "See. You don't have to go to college to learn shit; you just gotta have the right app on your phone!"

Chase turned around completely and fell into Tommy's strong hug without reservations. "I love you." He'd been saying it a lot lately. It was so sweet when it didn't come with a corset of guilt to choke it up.

"Love you too. Let's go shower—we've got shit to do."

SO THEY cooked. They cooked, they cooked, and then they cooked some more. There was turkey and stuffing and gravy and mashed potatoes and salad and green bean casserole and sweet potato pie and chocolate-covered peanut butter balls and shortbread cookies and steamed spinach and everything but waffles and fried chicken. There was so much stuff it didn't fit on the table and people had to take their plates to the counters and then eat in the living room, but it was okay. Tommy had been looking at recipes for the entire week Chase had been home, and when he wasn't at the PetSmart (which he'd turned into a real job, managing now), he was asking Chase what he thought of things like tarragon and anise. Chase had needed to go out and buy some of that shit just to see what he *did* think about it, since some of it he'd never heard about in his life.

And it was wonderful. Maybe not the stuffing so much (too much tarragon), but the people, coming in and giving each other shit and talking excitedly. At first Chase was going to be afraid things would be awkward—he was back from a month and a half in a mental institution, and he'd sort of bugged out of his own welcome-home party—but they were lucky. Kane and Dex got there first. Things could never be stiff and awkward with Kane there.

"We brought pie!" Kane said without preamble, pushing his way in from the front porch without waiting for an invitation. "And don't worry, Chase. No bugs in the fucking pie, because they're just too cool to eat."

Chase took the *pies*, plural, and looked at Dex, who was grimacing in embarrassment and mouthing "Needs. A. Keeper!" where Kane couldn't see him.

"You brought pie early," he said in some bemusement. "We haven't vacuumed yet!"

"Awesome!" Kane bounced. "Where's the kitten! C'mere, ya little fuzzball! Unka Kane's got a new toy for you!"

"Jesus, you psycho!" Tommy hollered, coming out of the bedroom from his second shower wearing only a pair of jeans. "Don't chase my cat!" (He'd spilled broth all over himself when they'd been making stuffing. Chase had finished up while he'd showered and done laundry.)

"Go get dressed, Tango—this ain't the set! I don't want to see your shit flapping around unless you got tits!"

"You say that, Kane, but I see you check out my package!" Tommy returned, and Kane chortled.

"Just making sure mine's bigger!"

Chase caught his breath then, because he thought Kane sounded way too defensive. Was it possible he wasn't as straight as he claimed?

But Dex grimaced and pinched the bridge of his nose. "Straight men," he sighed. "Whattya gonna do?"

Chase laughed, and Kane went chasing after Paulie the kitten, who ended up climbing the drapes and jumping on his head. Kane was still nursing a scratch on his temple (and cooing at the now-purring kitten) when Donnie and his people got there, with Ethan at their heels. 'Chelle spent five minutes patching him up with ointment and a Snoopy Band-Aid while Kane ogled her breasts and made cute innuendos about the cat. For a second Chase was in fear for Kane's life, and then he looked at the kitten with genuine love, and then the fear was all for 'Chelle's heart, and he had no business interfering there.

They never did get the floor vacuumed, and there were dust bunnies in the corners when they sat down to eat, but that was okay. Paulie the kitten chased the dust bunnies and Donnie's sister cooed over him and over Kane and everybody was entertained.

"So, Kane?" 'Chelle asked Chase after dinner when they were putting away leftovers and making care packages for all of the single people to take home.

"Yeah?" Chase grinned at her. 'Chelle had been a good big sister to Donnie: she was kind and nice to his friends, and she only teased him when she thought he could take it.

"He works with you?"

"Yeah," Chase said, stringing her along. "When I worked there, yeah. We worked together."

"So, he, uhm, all ac/ac, or a little ac/dc?" she asked, blushing, and Chase's grin about swallowed his face.

"He claims to be ac/dc," he said, watching her face light up completely. Then he brought in the kicker. "But he's only nineteen."

"Ugghhh!" For a moment, Donnie's older sister looked truly chagrined. Then she started a slow, evil grin. "On the other hand, bringing home a barely legal, sort of straight, gay porn star may be the last act of rebellion my parents have left open to me. I may have to take it!" And Chase was not offended when she disappeared into the living room to coo over the kitten and flirt with Kane some more.

Tommy watched them from the doorway to the living room and came over to him as 'Chelle disappeared.

"That wasn't nice," he murmured, wrapping his arms securely around Chase's waist as Chase put together a care package for Dex. Dex and Ethan were currently playing something violent and bloody on the Xbox, and Donnie, Kevin, and Kane were rooting them on. 'Chelle came up behind Kane and murmured something quiet into his ear, and Chase wished he had a closer view, because it looked like everybody's favorite extrovert blushed.

"What—siccing 'Chelle on Kane or Kane on 'Chelle?"

Tommy laughed. "Either. They're gonna make each other miserable and then they're gonna make us miserable and then—"

"And then they're either gonna break up and survive, or get married and make *really* pretty babies," Chase said with some satisfaction. "Because it doesn't all have to be about the drama, right?"

Tommy's bright-black eyes were suddenly softer on his face. "Well said, oh mighty kitchen god. When did you get so wise?"

Chase rolled his eyes and surveyed the damage. A sink full of dishes ready to go, check! Lots of little packages ready to roll when people walked out, check! Pies ready to go when dinner had settled, check! Leftovers neatly put away in the fridge and ready to be pillaged whenever, check!

"It must be the tryptophan," Chase mumbled, making sure he had everything as it should be.

"Tryptophan my ass!" Tommy grabbed his hand and hauled him into the living room. "Get your ass in here and celebrate, oh suicide king—you've got next!"

"But I'm not sure if it's all set—I had this plan, so everyone had enough—"

"Revise your plan!" Tommy snapped, still playful. "You get your best results when you change shit in midstream."

Chase did a double take at that and saw Tommy raising his eyebrows meaningfully, and he spent the next several hours playing video games and *Trivial Pursuit* and *Scene It?* with his friends.

There was no alcohol—two recovering mental patients really didn't need anything else to worry about—but that didn't mean there weren't lots of sloppy hugs at the end.

Ethan was one of the last people to leave. Unlike Kane and Dex, he'd arrived alone, and he looked rather wistfully at Tommy's trashed, warm little house as he left. He was a tactile man; Dex had remarked once that the reason he did so good in porn was that he just *adored* being touched. Any touch, any touch at all, made him happy, and one of the things Chase had learned as they'd worked together was to be careful what kind of touches you gave him. It was like being that sensitive gave the person touching him too much power for the average person. It had to be someone who would treat it with reverence.

When Chase went in for the hug, Ethan clung to him, almost shivering in his hug. "Thanks so much," he murmured. "My folks... they found out what I was doing and told me not to come home. When Dex told me I could tag along...." He shook his head and gave Chase a big kiss on the cheek, Italian style, and then turned around and did the same thing to Tommy. He pulled away and wiped his eyes. "You guys," he said, shaking his head. "You guys, I know the last few months have been rough on you, and, you know, the whole studio knows the gossip. But your house here, your home. It's a good place. You guys believe that. Believe that it's a good place, okay? And...." He swallowed. "Invite me back, okay? Christmas, Easter, Friday nights? I just really loved being here tonight."

They both went in for another hug, and he finally had to turn around and trot out of the house like he was catching a bus.

When he was gone, Chase met Tommy's eyes, and Tommy was looking at him meaningfully. Chase sighed and shook his head.

"I'm thinking about it!" he said, and Tommy grinned.

"We're gonna be daddies!"

"I said I'm thinking about it!"

"Stop wasting my time with useless protests and come fuck me stupid."

"Too late!"

"Damned straight! Get in here or I'm gonna lube myself!"

"Promises, promises—you'll just lie there and groan while I do it."

Tommy burst into cackles. "Well, if I knew that other thing was your perv...."

"Try me." Chase could hardly talk, he was laughing so hard.

Tommy suddenly got serious. "This ain't no trial run," he said soberly. "This is us, and this is real life, and tonight was about one of the best times I've ever had. I'm serious, man. I didn't think I'd ever have a good holiday again after my mother died. You just gave me something true. It was beautiful."

Chase blushed. "How am I supposed to find words for that?"

"You don't." Tommy captured his mouth then, hard and hot and furious, and 'Chelle and Kane had done the regular dishes when Chase hadn't been looking, but the dessert dishes were still there. It didn't matter. They left them to do in the morning. Chase opened his mouth to Tommy and took over, walking Tommy backward and turning lights off as they went. Tommy got to the bed and shoved the covers down while Chase stripped out of his jeans and baseball shirt as quick as he could. By the time Chase was naked, down to his bare feet and long toes, Tommy was too, and lying there, his knees spread, his crease and asshole shiny with lube. He was thrusting a fingertip inside himself, and then the whole finger down to the first knuckle, even as Chase watched.

Tommy's breathing was already quick and thready, and his hips were thrashing around, and Chase was as hard as he'd ever been in his life.

"Stop," he commanded roughly. "Use two fingers."

Tommy did, letting out a high, breathy whine, and Chase rubbed his thumb across the top of his own cock, then leaned over Tommy's bucking body and thrust his sticky thumb into Tommy's mouth so Tommy could taste his pre-come. Tommy sucked it deep inside a hot mouth and moaned around it.

"Hot and fast, Chase. Need it. Please."

Chase thrust inside him, grunting because he was so tight. God... every touch on his skin was magic, as though here, in the privacy of their bedroom, he got to be Ethan and every brush on his skin allowed him to fly. Tommy's clench around his cock was almost painfully tight, but Tommy was begging him with every breath, "Deeper... deeper... oh Christ, *fuck me deeper, dammit!*" and Chase had to, had to sink into him as deep as he possibly could.

He thrust down to the hilt and Tommy screamed, Loki the lunatic sex god alive in Chase's arms, raising his hips, fucking Chase with his slippery tight body, and Chase clenched his hips, braced his arms, and fucked right back.

"Pushy fucking bottom," Chase hissed, and Tommy's fierce sex-grin was as challenging as they got.

"You want to top, earn it!"

And Chase did, thrusting furiously, all of his joy in the moment, his joy at being *alive* and strong and happy charging through every stroke.

"Grab it!" he commanded, wanting to feel Tommy come all over them both. He wanted it, hot and vital, on his skin; wanted to touch it, taste it, wanted to lick it from Tommy's stomach and remember that life was sweet and bitter. "Grab it," he growled again, when Tommy clenched the covers next to him instead. "Grab your cock, stroke it... stroke it hard... I need your come, Tommy, need it on me, need to feel it...."

"Oh fuck!" Tommy came explosively and Chase howled, bucking without control. His arms gave out, and he thrust maniacally for a minute, finally biting Tommy's shoulder in frantic need as he came and came and came.

His hips finally stopped pumping and he collapsed, sobbing for breath, against Tommy, feeling the hot stickiness of Tommy's spend between their stomachs. He didn't give Tommy a chance to even move, just kissed and licked down his body, stopping for a moment at Tommy's nipples and then suckling on the tenderness of his stomach, the sharpness of his hipbones, the furriness of his thighs. Tommy groaned a little, his cock, flaccid and spent, stirring reluctantly, but even when Chase sucked it into his mouth and slurped, feeling it harden wasn't his ultimate goal.

Tommy's taste, tangy and real, not even pleasant, but visceral and alive, like blood but better because it was all about life and not about death or hiding or fear—that's what Chase wanted. Tommy groaned and spread his thighs and Chase continued to lick the crease of his thighs, the crease of his backside, his taint, and below. It was his own taste now and he didn't care, didn't care what it was or where it had been, it was *them*, and they were *alive*, and they were in *love*, and there was nothing dirty about that, nothing that could shame him, nothing that could repel him about this act of remembering the taste of being alive.

Tommy groaned and started to beg some more, and Chase answered by moving up, taking Tommy's now-hard cock into his mouth, and sucking hard and without mercy until Tommy cried out and came again, just a little, into the back of his mouth.

Tommy had to reach down and haul him up, and he left a trail as he went because he'd come again too. When he got there, his head on Tommy's shoulder, Tommy kissed him just like Chase had tasted Tommy's body: without reservation, without shame, everything in the thrust of his tongue about tasting love and flesh and life.

They had to stop eventually, and Tommy wiped them down, but they didn't get dressed immediately and they hardly had words until they were almost asleep.

"I'm so glad," Chase said when they were almost asleep.

"So glad what?"

"So glad I stopped. So glad I'm here. So glad… just everything."

Tommy nodded, and then passed his hand under his cheek, and then again, and then again. Chase wasn't sure how it happened—was *never* sure how it happened—but suddenly Tommy was the one in tears, Tommy was the one sobbing until his body couldn't hold out, Tommy was the one lost in Chase's arms, saying "Me too… oh God… me too… I'm so glad…." until they fell asleep, sticky, sated, warm, and tangled together in happiness and exhaustion.

TOMMY had been right—Chase missed school. While Tommy was working, Chase spent some of his time going to his classes and talking to his professors, explaining things and generally trying to clean up his mess. The school actually had a policy for Chase's situation, which was good news, because it made it possible to sign up for all of the classes he'd gotten an incomplete in and have them guaranteed upon his return. He was given a stern talking-to, however, and told that this exception could only be claimed once.

Chase looked at the rather self-important man in the suit who was signing his paperwork and said, "Of course. If I'm ever going to commit suicide again, I'll make sure I follow through." He held out his wrist for emphasis and sort of enjoyed watching the guy squirm. It was petty of him, but then, the idea that he'd just randomly bleed out in search of attention seemed awfully damned petty too.

So when that was accomplished, he had little in the way of things to do. He worked out with the guys from *Johnnies*, and that felt damned good. His little welcome-home party, Thanksgiving—those could have been flukes, but apparently porn friends were real friends, and without the constant friction of who was shooting a scene with whom, they were actually even a little more fun to hang out with. Dex and Kane especially were there for him; Ethan too, but when Chase's hour and a half was up, he needed that other thing, that drive. As tempting as it was, he refused to work out more than an hour and a half—being fit was one thing, but Tommy was right. It got boring after a while.

It occurred to him that wanting to be an engineer, wanting to finish school—those were the good parts of his vision for a perfect life, a perfect family. Improving himself, using his natural gifts at math, at planning—that was positive.

It occurred to him that not everything in his life before Tommy had been painful, or a lie. Not all of his actions were misguided. He'd had a good plan; it just needed revising.

A few days after he reregistered for school, he went out and bought a couple of things for Christmas.

Tommy already had decorations, but Chase took a look at the box and decided they needed to go bigger this year. He grabbed Dex, Kane,

Donnie, and Kevin (because they were more impressive when they hunted in a pack), and together they hit the sports stores, the mall, and (much to Kane and Kevin's intense chagrin) a couple of craft fairs.

Tommy came home later that day and found that the house had been decorated, from bottom to top, and that the house was full of people.

Tommy loved it, went with it, and forgave Chase for doing most of it himself when he saw that Chase had left the tree.

They listened to old Christmas songs (Donnie's boyfriend knew where to find them on satellite radio, and he seemed pleased to have something to contribute) and sang them, feeling silly, and Tommy decorated the tree. At the top was a brand-new silver star with a picture of Tommy and his mother in the center, and Tommy's glare promised dire things coming Chase's way, just for making him delve into such sentimental places.

It was fun—it was joyous—but it wasn't the best part.

The day after they decorated the house, Chase went and had a long talk with Doc. He'd been attending his mandated therapy regularly, but this was special. He'd talked about his father, he'd talked about Tommy, he'd talked about dreams for the future, but he hadn't talked about this.

"What do you think made her do it?" he asked without preamble. His knees weren't clutched to his chest this time. They were splayed out, and his forearms were resting on them assertively. He wanted to tackle this one head-on.

Doc didn't bat an eyelash or drop a stitch. "Your mother? Hard to say. She was probably depressed as it was. Your father—not an easy man to live with."

"Was it me? Was it because I was gay?"

Doc shook his head definitively. "Had nothing to do with you, Chase. Even if she put it on you, it wasn't your fault. You may not think so—you may never truly believe it—but I do."

Chase nodded his head. "See, the thing is... I'm thinking about it."

"Thinking about what?"

"Being a father."

"Yeah?"

"Yeah. I just… I don't ever want to do to my kid what my people did to me."

Doc put down his knitting and smiled.

And all of the hard work he'd done, all of the pain and the stupidity and the bullshit in the past, and all of the scary stuff in the future, it all suddenly seemed worthwhile. And all of the hard work to come had a purpose.

CHASE came home that day feeling exhausted but pleased, and Tommy (who'd had the day off and was sitting in front of the Christmas tree, shaking a stuffed ornament at Paulie the kitten) looked up and smiled.

"Good day?"

Chase nodded and came and sat down next to him. "Yeah. Good day. Tommy, you want to open a present early this year?"

Tommy turned to him, surprised, and watched as Chase pulled out his cell phone and pulled up Mercy's number. Very deliberately, Chase showed it to Tommy, and watched as a slow smile of recognition and understanding bloomed across that long-jawed, sharp-toothed, impossibly beautiful face.

"We're gonna do it?" he demanded. "We are?"

Chase bit his lip, smiled, and hoped for the best—which was really the most colossal gift he could ever give, even if Tommy didn't know it.

"Yeah."

"Woo-hoo!" Tommy lunged at him, knocking him to the floor on his back, and Chase only managed to keep hold of the phone with an act of will. "We're gonna be daddies!"

"Yeah, Tommy. You think?"

"Shut up, sit up, and call the mother of your child, dammit. I want details. Due dates, genders, what color to paint the walls—c'mon, Chase, you've 'bout killed me with this!"

Chase stopped and looked him in the eyes. "This is the easy part," he cautioned, and Tommy rolled his eyes.

"You think I don't know? Now c'mon, dammit! It's like the Best. Gift. Ever!"

Chase laughed and looked at the phone again. In Dex's garage were two bicycles—a matched set, one for him and one for Tommy. Tommy's had the baby stroller attachment (Dex called it a booger— Chase had no idea why) and Chase figured he'd hold up the rear. That was supposed to be Tommy's actual Christmas present, the thing waiting under the tree.

But this here—this call he was making? This was the bike, the action figure, the expectation and the joy. This was the everything he'd ever wanted, and he thought that giving it to Tommy was about six thousand times better than getting it himself. Giving it to the both of them? It was amazing.

His hands didn't even shake as he hit Mercy's number and brought the phone up to his ear. Mercy answered on the first ring, and he was grateful.

"Mercy? Yeah. You still want me to be the daddy?"

His planning brain started making whole new pictures. They were glorious.

"So," JOHN was saying behind the camera, "what do you two have planned for life after Johnnies?"

Chance looked at Tango and smiled. Tango leaned forward and nuzzled him a little, their lips parting as they met. They pulled back from the half kiss and faced the camera again.

"The world," Chance said, and Tango grinned that terrific, manic grin.

"The world," he repeated. This time, their mouths opened for the kiss, and the picture faded to black.

AMY LANE is a mother of four and a compulsive knitter who writes because she can't silence the voices in her head. She adores cats, knitting socks, and hawt menz, and she dislikes moths, cat boxes, and knuckle-headed macspazzmatrons. She is rarely found cooking, cleaning, or doing domestic chores, but she has been known to knit up an emergency hat/blanket/pair of socks for any occasion whatsoever or sometimes for no reason at all. She writes in the shower, while commuting, while taxiing children to soccer/dance/karate/oh my! and has learned from necessity to type like the wind. She lives in a spider-infested, crumbling house in a shoddy suburb and counts on her beloved Mate, Mack, to keep her tethered to reality—which he does while keeping her cell phone charged as a bonus. She's been married for twenty-plus years and still believes in Twu Wuv, with a capital Twu and a capital Wuv, and she doesn't see any reason at all for that to change.

Visit Amy's web site at http://www.greenshill.com. You can e-mail her at amylane@greenshill.com.

Also by AMY LANE

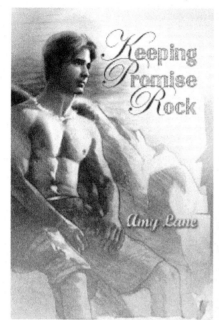

http://www.dreamspinnerpress.com

Romance from AMY LANE

http://www.dreamspinnerpress.com